I0732763

SAINT GEORGE AND THE DRAGON

King Arthur's Sister:
The
Once and Future
Queen.

by Kim Iverson Headlee

as driven by Mark Twain.

Illustrated by Sophia Kelly Shultz

and Anna Winebarger.

PENDRAGON COVE PRESS

Pendragon Cove Press editions:
Paperback, 2025; ISBN: 978-1-949997-37-8
Case Laminate Hardcover, 2025; ISBN: 978-1-949997-23-1
Hardcover with Dust Jacket, 2026; ISBN: 978-1-949997-48-4
E-book, 2025; ISBN : 978-1-949997-25-5
Pendragon Cove Media editions:
Retail Audioibook, 2026; ISBN: 978-1-949997-20-0
Library Audiobook, 2026; ISBN: 978-1-949997-31-6

Kim Headlee
Pendragon Cove Press
PO Box 1264
Wytheville, VA 24382

CONTENTS.

Contents.

Chapter XXV.

LIST OF ILLUSTRATIONS.

List of Illustrations.

PREFACE.

EING DEAD has its advantages. Chief among them is that the passage of time cannot be felt by the non-corporeal. Imagine my surprise to learn that a decade and a half had passed on earth since I was tasked to introduce *King Arthur's Sister in Washington's Court*.

It took me the best part of a decade to write *A Connecticut Yankee*, so I reckon you could say that Madame Headlee and I make quite the pair in that regard. As novelists, neither of us bother to fire up our word-factories till we have something worthwhile to show our readers.

Everything else is a waste of ink and trees.

Another advantage to being dead is that non-corporeal authors cannot be blamed for what proceeds from the pen of their ghost-writer. It's great fun to implant the very balderdashiest of ideas into Madame Headlee's brain and sit back to see what she does with them, secure in the knowledge that I remain beyond reach of all literary critics…except, perhaps, for the Critic's Critic, but I possess every confidence that she can handle him quite nicely on my behalf.

Mark Twain

MARK TWAIN
upon the occasion of my 190ᵗʰ birthday
WYTHEVILLE, VA, November 30, 2025

P.S. by K.I.H. This novel is the third in a series that begins with Mark Twain's *A Connecticut Yankee in King Arthur's Court* and continues with the sequel I wrote, *King Arthur's Sister in Washington's Court* (KASIWC). If you're not familiar with my Twainian fiction, then I suggest that you read *Connecticut Yankee* and KASIWC first. And if you have chosen this book because you read KASIWC and craved more, welcome back; I wrote it especially for you.

King Arthur's Sister:
The Once and Future Queen

A WORD OF EXPLANATION.

DREAMED that I—

There it is. I can see your eyeballs glazing already. You, like every other member of the human race, don't give a flying fig about anyone's dreams except maybe your own, when you can remember them. Even then, it's a matter of but mild curiosity, mulled for a moment and forgotten as the cares of the day rise up, yawn, stretch a bit, scratch, swill a mug of coffee, and commence badgering you for attention.

I'm here to warn you that you should care about this dream. This dream is impossible, many people claim. This dream you can't wake up from. This dream, you should pray till you sweat blood that it never happens to you.

I dreamed that I died.

Not that I was looking down upon a corpse that my dream-self somehow knew had to be me. There were plenty of corpses and almost-corpses in that cave. I, however, was not one of them. Nor was I the only living—that is to say, not in the immediate process of dying—soul present. I watched my enemy stoop to snatch up the dropped revolver, cock it, steady his trembling hand with its twin, and squeeze the trigger. My enemy was a priest. I lunged to stop him.

I felt the bullet rip through my gut.

The blow forced me into the man I'd striven to protect. We stumbled backward and crashed into the cave wall. I felt his whoosh of air as my back collided with his chest. I heard the sickening crack of bone on rock and his sharp yelp. Then he went silent and very still. I bled out against him, my life ebbing and vision dimming even as heaven's sweet hum swelled to fill my ears. As if from very far away, I heard a female voice: pleasantly modulated, resonant, and articulate, but taut with worry. My dream-self seemed to know her, though for the life of me, I can't tell you one other thing about her. We conversed a little as I died. What we said I cannot recall.

Vast darkness spread in all directions and for a span of time that I had no means—no timepiece, no breath, no heartbeats—to measure. Across that void drifted the speaker's final words:

"My dear child, I am so, so sorry!"

Child?

I lay in bed for a long time, struggling with that question rather than with the arresting fact that I had dreamed my death, I think perhaps because it was the easier struggle, the warmup to tackling the terrifying philosophical implications. My mother has been dead for twenty-five years.

Dreams are weird.

Okay, fine. That's no news flash.

Curiosity propelled me out of bed and across the flat to my desk. While the tabletop monitor shook off its own e-fevered dreams and blinked awake, I brewed a cup of coffee. Midway through, another issue from the dream hit me:

I hadn't been able to afford the Church's services since before my mother died. I couldn't name a single Church employee, ordained or otherwise; could not for the life of me fathom why one of them might hate me enough to shoot me dead.

WTH?

I put on the whole bloody pot to brew.

G— had festooned its home page with fluttering confetti and wandering balloons, antics already a week into the celebration of its centennial as a search engine. BFD. I had bigger effing deals to investigate.

Click-click-click. (Yes, I touch the virtual keyboard rather than accessing the thought receptors, and I use a sound emulator for good measure. Call me old-fashioned.) *Click-clack-click-clickety-clack.* "Dream interpreter… local." (Yes, I talk to myself as I type. Call me human.) And an extra-loud *cli-cluck* for punching "submit." For the record, adding the "local" keyword worked about as well as thrusting a section of chain-link fence through Victoria Falls. Call me not the most adept at net navigation. Whatever.

As anticipated, the first several screen loads were sponsored results. I could not have cared less. How good could those businesses be if they had to pay to get noticed? In the deluge I almost missed the unassuming article titled "Your Dreams Are Her Reality."

A strangled train whistle made me flinch. Right. The coffee was done brewing. I refilled my cup, sent a mental command to the pot to keep its contents warm, returned to my desk, and clicked on the article.

Your Dreams Are Her Reality

Posted by Marco Markson, Jr. 21 April 2093[†]

There exists a shop in a back alley of what until last year was SDO London, a modest hike from New Wembley ballpark. Named "Curiosities," its proprietor sells what the shop's name implies, everything from aardvark skulls to zombie toenails. The shop's contents do not constitute

---

[†] The article was posted five years after the death of the journalist's father, Marco Markson, Sr., which was described in *King Arthur's Sister in Washington's Court.* —*kih*

the most curious thing about it, however, and its address won't help a visitor find it.

To the casual passerby, Curiosities appears to be a fitness centre[†] for women, complete with noisy machines operated by appropriately attired, chatty, sweaty clientele.

The proprietor of Curiosities permits entry only to those guests driven to seek her out because of unsettling death dreams they have experienced. This I know for a personal fact. For months, I had been tormented by dreams of the accidental death of my father, experiencing the lethal blow of the hurtling shuttle bus as if his body had been my own...

The coffee sloshed as I thunked the cup onto the table. An entrance gate to what used to be the Sanctuary District of (SDO) London, now a rusting monument to the human cost of ignoring social ills, stood but a brace of Tube stops from my flat; New Wembley ballpark, derelict of better days and thus another cautionary monument, but one stop beyond.

The fact that Markson's post was twenty years old didn't dent my hope that the shop named Curiosities still existed. It had to exist. I craved answers. And its proprietor had to let me in for a consultation.

On my cell—yes, I own a legacy handheld communication device that doubles as a wrinkle remover; don't judge—I fired up the G– Maps app. For the hell of it, and possessing subterranean expectations, I typed the shop's name into the "search nearby" box. I may live alone, but I never cultivated the habit of talking to my wrinkle remover. I'm not so desperate for companionship that I need an AI to supply it. The pin for Curiosities appeared, a cheerful red poppy in a field of green (eateries), blue (shopping), and brown (entertainment) markers for other sites of potential interest,

† For consistency with Twain's choice in *A Connecticut Yankee in King Arthur's Court,* I elected to retain the British spelling of "center," with the exception of the baseball term "center-fielder."
—*kih*

though most of those lay many streets removed from the poppy. The real estate comprising SDO London may have been reclaimed, but its stigma will never fade.

Hovering my pointer over the poppy caused the caption to appear: "You have never visited Curiosities…but soon shall."

I swear G– gets creepier with every bloody update. What's next? Forecasting the careers of our unborn descendants?

After physically switching off my coffee pot—that function I stopped trusting to the thought receptors after a rogue AI pot converted a block of flats in Covent Garden to cinders—I grabbed my hoodie, a fan, and an umbrella, secured my flat, and set off.

True to the junior Marco Markson's word, the only people peopling the alley in question appeared to be women sporting workout gear and toting duffels, entering or exiting the same door in ones, braces, and flocks. As I approached, the flow thinned to the barest trickle and then stopped altogether. I could have traversed the final twoscore paces naked. Not that I did. You may vacate the sewer, thank you.

Tendrils of evening mist twined round my legs like feline spirits as I stared at the door. It looked as if it had survived centuries in that spot, with its age-darkened oak panels, worn brass knob and hinges, and soot-etched side windows, which obscured what lay within. From the lack of muffled sounds, I judged the place to be deserted. The whitewashed sign nailed to the lintel read "Curiosities" in an uneven medieval Gothic script that lent the impression that it had been hand lettered, and not within living memory, owing to a network of hairline cracks marring the paint.

Fine; yes, I stood there a good long time. Guilty as charged.

I suppose some part of me expected the door to creak open of its own accord, relieving me of the decision of whether to take the initiative.

What happened next I shall never forget.

As I mounted the stoop and stretched for the handle, gold lettering shimmered into view on the door's face, not Gothic as upon the sign, but in a handsome, flowing, self-assured script:

Do come in, dear child. I have been expecting you.

In my head, competing with the abrupt thrashing of my heart, I heard that same female voice from the dream repeating the words displayed on the door. The sensation felt reassuring, yet not enough so to conquer my fear. I turned to depart.

Please, the head-voice murmured, but in a firm rather than a pathetic way. *I mean you no harm, and I do indeed possess the answers you seek.*

Sincere, trustworthy.

Compelling.

When I faced the door, those words had replaced the first message. Below it appeared a curt injunction to enter. The command gave me the impression that any further delay might anger whoever—whatever?—was crafting these messages, which of a sudden seemed like the grandmama of all terrible ideas.

I sucked in a breath, grasped the handle, and obeyed.

Past the door lay a great room filled not with exercise machinery but tables and cases and shelving stuffed with, well, everything from aardvark skulls to zombie toenails. Quarter-scale replicas of old flying contraptions hung from chains bolted to the high ceiling, amid representations of birds and bats and winged reptiles that looked real enough to make me consider deploying my umbrella. Tapestries, woodcuts, and paintings competed for wall space amid swords, axes, pikes, halberds, tridents, bidents, knives, dirks, daggers, flails, maces, morning stars, longbows, crossbows, compound bows, and more types of firearms than my feeble wits could comprehend. Complete suits of armor stood at attention at odd intervals upon the floor. One of them featured a small, smooth, round hole in the breastplate where the wearer's heart would have been.

I wondered if that knight had been able to afford last rites.

Everywhere I looked—on shelves, tabletops, and sometimes just stacked to man-height upon the floor—sat books, books, more books, and even more books. Up till that moment, I had never seen one of that species up close. I knew of the existence of printed media by what scant posts G– had deigned to feed me. It surprised me how much room they required. Some of those books, I learned upon opening a few of them, had been printed more than two centuries ago.

EVERYTHING FROM AARDVARK SKULLS
TO ZOMBIE TOENAILS

As I stood, overwhelmed by the marvels and pondering what to do next, one of the books waved at me.

That is to say, its cover flipped to the vertical and began wiggling forth and back.

G— never claimed books could do that.

Instinct insisted that I quit this place at a dead run, forget that goddamned dream, and never return.

I'm not famous for heeding my instincts. Don't look shocked; I own a vintage communication-device-slash-wrinkle-remover, forgodsake.

The beckoning book seemed newer than most of its brethren. Its boards were a shiny black metal, not wrapped in cloth, leather, or vinyl. Repeating bands of color, like the aura in an oil slick, writhed across its face. As I stepped to within arm's reach, the cover stopped midwiggle to let me read it. I clapped a hand to my mouth. The cover bore my full legal name in the same self-assured script that had appeared on the shop's door, followed by a short, simple, unignorable command:

Read this.

One of the ancient texts I had perused scant minutes before had mentioned something about a young girl tumbling into a rabbit hole that transported her, quite against her will, to a turvy world. I was beginning to understand how that unfortunate lass must have felt.

I carried the book to a nearby antique wing chair, made myself comfortable with feet propped on its matching hassock, pried open my personal rabbit hole, stuck my nose full in, and began to read:

QUEEN MORGAN'S FURTHER HISTORY.

Further *history?*

"Wait," I said. "Don't I get to read what came before?"

Silly me, thinking this book-thing could hear me. I may as well start conversing with my devices' AI.

The cover wrenched itself free of my fingers and shut with such force, I could feel the waft of expelled air. My name and "read this" disappeared in uneven swaths, as if the responsible party was in a huff, leaving me the impression that I had strayed into grandmama-of-all-terrible-ideas territory. The replacement words confirmed it:

Do not be rude, child. If I deem you to need that information, then I shall give it to you.

"Rude!" I yelled. "You seem to know who I am, and yet I know nothing about you. I do know you're not my mother, but you keep calling me 'child!' Who's the rude one here?"

I eyed the cover for heaven knows how long; I quit counting after the first dozen, furious breaths. As the fury leeched from my lungs, the words shimmered out of existence. The cover remained blank for another dozen, calmer breaths until a familiar word reappeared: *Read.* Three breaths later, that word was joined by *Please.*

I opened the book and read.

CHAPTER I.
Avalon.

I HIGHT Morgan.

Please forgive me; habits bred and fed fifteen centuries ago do indeed die hard. My name is Morgan. I was a daughter, a sister, a wife, and a mother. Note well the word *was*. I was a healer and a queen. Queen of the ancient realm of Gore, and queen—"owner" was my official title—of the London Knights champion World Baseball Federation franchise. Of all those things, the only two that remain in force to-day are sister and healer. Mother and wife too, if you want me to get technical, but I stay up nights struggling not to think of my deceased son or my once and future love. I know not how many centuries separate me from my soulmate at this moment.

Ah, yes. I ought not omit the most important bit. Although I strive to be ever a faithful daughter of the Church, I am an abomination in the sight of God.

I am a sorceress.

My ladies, bless their dear, well-meaning hearts, never cease to remind me that my art is His gift, for how could it be the devil's work to heal the

CHAPTER I.

mortal wound of my brother and sovereign liege, King Arthur? How could the devil possess the power to assist me in hieing Arthur to this blessed place, an isle sheltered from the fallen one's favorite tools: the judgmental eyes of men, the meddling of their machines, and the ravages of time? How could the Author of All Things not have crafted this wellspring of magical power and permitted me to partake for the benefit of England, yea, mayhap even His entire world?

Whenever Niniane, Vivien, and Galfrieda wax philosophical in that vein, I smile and let them talk as I muddle about my work. They do not need to know that my motivation lies not with God's world, England, or even my lowly demesne of Gore.

Oh, England will one day need Arthur; I have seen it. That prophecy is not some wistful lie born of the craving to be free of an oppressor's cruel yoke, though such cravings have existed for millennia. Whether the entire world will need him remains to be seen.

What spurs me to keep helping Arthur past all rational limits is that I need him far more than anyone else does.

"Your Majesty, 'tis time!"

That was Niniane, the youngest of my ladies and therefore the one most often dispatched to fetch me whenever Arthur shows the least twitch of distress. Each time she visits these chambers where I retreat to reflect and recharge my magical reserves—and the good Lord alone knows how often that has been, for I lost count eons ago—her words vary by not one syllable. Her gift from God is eternal optimism. Either that, or the memory of a goldfish.

Most days I feel like a goldfish too, swimming and swimming in the same bloody circles, believing that I might discover something new round the next turn, whilst in reality the landscape never changes. Arthur's skull remains grotesquely dented, and he lies trapped within this tranquil limbo, unable to die or even to age, just like the rest of us.

I smiled at Niniane, rose, draped my cloak over my shoulders with a flourish (though 'twas the comfort of habit that compelled me; Avalon's weather is far more stable and mild than Camelot's ever was), and followed my little golden-haired fish in the commencement of this latest lap as she swished toward Arthur's pavilion.

In fine fishbowl fashion, the pavilion had not changed. It remained nestled amongst the fragrant profusion of lilacs and gardenias and lavender and sundry other plants whose flowers never faded. The silks comprising the pavilion's canopy and my brother's coverlet and pillows shone as brightly as they did the day our party had carried him from his sickroom, a week or an age ago, whenever that had been. The same was true for the gold-embroidered scarlet tunic and leather breeches I had conjured for Arthur to wear instead of his ruined, bloodstained armor. Said armor I had repaired after making its owner as comfortable as possible. The armor, complete with the crown-embraced helmet that was no longer hewn in twain, glistened blood-free upon its stand. A no-longer-shattered scabbard hung from the baldric looped across the breastplate. The scabbard was empty. Excalibur remained where Sir Bedivere had cast it, trapped in its own limbo of water and lake silt.

The lone man worthy to wield that magnificent blade thrashed upon his sickbed like a drowning soul.

Galfrieda sat stationed at his head, her hands flexed round him without touching him. A commendable array of sparks arced from her fingertips to his head. Golden-brown locks not pinned by his bandages stood at attention; even his thicker beard and eyebrow hairs struggled to obey the electricity's command. Agony contorted his handsome visage. Powerful muscles in his chest and limbs writhed in a relentless rhythm.

As I watched, Arthur's thrashing lessened but did not stop.

I gave Niniane a nod. "You may be right this time, my dear." I pursed my lips to fight the hope rising in my breast; I had lost count of the number of dashings too.

How she reacted to the praise I know not, for I already had stepped beyond her and also past Vivien, who was holding a tray of salves and

CHAPTER I.

bandage rolls, to take Galfrieda's place. She surrendered the post to me with neither hesitation nor comment, and rose to join the other two ladies.

Arthur's bandage, which Vivien reported having applied earlier this morning, showed red evidence that his wound was oozing again. I took the fact in stride. At first it had been a constant source of alarm for all four of us till I realized that this periodic leakage must be his body's way of repairing itself, perhaps relieving pressure built up by the accumulation of too much fluid. Why it never killed him I learnt to ascribe to the inherent magic of this place, not to our mean efforts, though my long-ago inspiration to use our hands to focus energy onto the wound did seem to mitigate the condition.

I settled onto the cushioned seat Galfrieda had vacated, positioned my hands much as she had done, and started to hum. My ladies added their throaty notes to mine.

Said humming was another divine inspiration, based upon the dim recollection of an article I had read during my second lifetime about the medicinal value of a cat's purr. Avalon has no cats, nay, nor any other creatures save for us and the holy women and men who serve us, but we perform as best as we might. Unlike cats, we invent tunes or sing remembered snatches to keep the repetition from driving us mad. My ladies would never know that some of those snatches could claim origins in the virtual reality television advertisements for fast food, fast cures, and fast cash.

That we have not gone mad already remains a matter of debate.

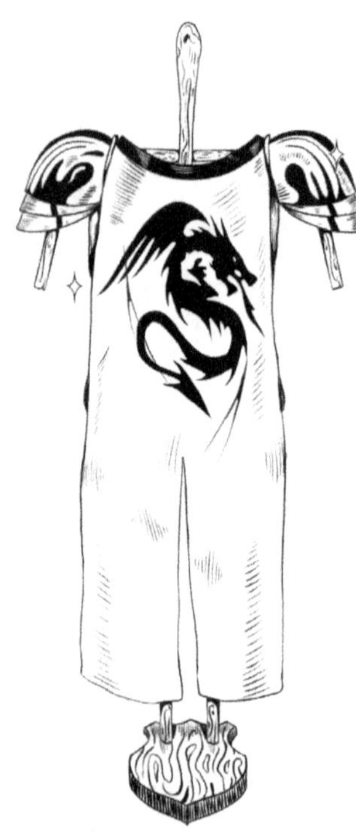

28

You, canny reader, might presume that I would think about my brother and rehash the events of our lives, his and mine, that had brought us unto the shores of this wretched, blessed place. That might have been true the first thousand times I had sat humming and conjuring over his riven head. You might be surprised to learn that even the most deservedly guilt-riddled mind ceases to blame itself in due course. I was. If the cessation ever gives me a mote of pleasure, you shall be the first to know.

I did, however, derive some comfort from visiting the treasure vault of memories of my beloved Sandy: our soul-satisfying intimate moments, naturally, but even our stormiest silences I relished reliving time and time again. The make-up sex was…well. Its details are no one's concern save my own.

Fine; I shall toss you a bone. Think of your own make-up sex sessions, and then multiply those feelings a hundredfold.

Lord God in heaven, I miss my husband.

Arthur's thrashing began anew, yanking me from my reverie. I grasped his head to steady it, knowing what would transpire and making the choice anyway.

Images slammed into my mind. I had seen them before and more besides, images of men fighting, maiming, and killing one another, over and over like some endless, hideous dance. Worse were the glimpses of horses and war hounds whose faithful service had ended upon the point of a sword, arrow, or spear. Worse still were the dying men screaming for help that would never come. The images' familiarity made them not one whit less ghastly.

"Be at ease, dear brother," I murmured. "Your battles are at an end." Not that those words ever helped, but like a memory-challenged goldfish, I remained hopeful that on the next lap, the landscape would change.

Wonder of wonders, this time it did.

CHAPTER II.
The King Awakens.

RTHUR STOPPED struggling, though anguish contorted his face, and his eyelids jerked to the rhythm of his nightmares.

I released his head and pressed two fingers to his temple. His anguish begin to lessen.

"Lady Niniane," I said, exerting effort to banish excitement from my tone, "please fetch the device from my chambers."

She dipped a curtsy and rose to depart, but Galfrieda caught her arm. "Your Majesty, you know you cannot—"

Of course I knew, but I could not have cared less. In retrospect, and with deep regret, I confess that I should have cared…but enough of that pity party. I must not get ahead of myself.

I pumped disapproval into my glare. Galfrieda desisted with a murmured plea for forgiveness and freed Niniane to complete my request.

I withdrew my fingers from Arthur's temple. To Vivien I said, "Please remove the bandage so Lady Galfrieda may examine the king." I wanted to be sure that Galfrieda got as good a look as she needed to settle her doubts.

The scalp wound looked stickier than I would have liked, but Galfrieda's fingers did not get excessively bloody as she probed it.

CHAPTER II.

(No, she was not wearing gloves. Avalon's creature ban extended to the microscopic world, as evidenced by the fact that the breath exuding from our mouths remained ever sweet without the intervention of fluid, paste, powder, or brush.)

Galfrieda's expression was even sweeter. "His Majesty's skull is whole!"

To Vivien's relieved "Thank God!" I replied, "Amen."

By this time, Niniane had returned. I directed her to set the dormant device on a side table and join us at Arthur's head. "I believe he is ready, but I shall need your help. All of you."

We had rehearsed this moment, the ladies and I, more often than any of us could recall. This time I laid both palms, one atop the other, lightly upon his wound site. At my nod, the ladies stepped in to lay their hands upon me: Galfrieda grasping my right arm and shoulder, Niniane my left, and Vivien with both hands flat upon my back. Their humming began in concert with mine, the deeper tones tapping stronger magic, and I reveled to feel my power strengthen with the addition of theirs. I curbed my revelry lest it wreak harm upon my brother.

I had wrought enough wreaking to destroy three lifetimes.

Sparks arced and flashed round the wounded crown. Arthur gasped and groaned through clenched teeth. I redoubled the intensity of my healing magic and the fervency of my humble prayers. I sensed moreso than heard the others making similar efforts.

The lifting of my hands signaled my ladies to break contact. I opened my eyes, scarcely daring…

Of Arthur's dreadful wound, naught but a faint scar remained.

He opened his steel-gray eyes.

A supreme act of will kept me from swooning in sheer relief. I have no idea whether any of the others swooned or not; I was consumed with drinking in every restorative drop of my dear brother's compassionate—if more than a mite confused—gaze.

"Morgan, what are you doing here? You are in grave danger!" He pushed himself up on one arm; with the other hand, he patted the velvet swathing his chest. That prompted him to look about, though slowly. His brow furrowed with every new incomprehensible sight his brain reported. "What is this place? Where is the battlefield?" He stared longest at his flawless armor and scabbard. "I died!" That last bit was more gasp than words. Frankness invaded his gaze when he turned it upon me. "Did I not? Is this heaven? Are you dead too?"

Heaven, hell…for half an eternity I had been wondering whether Avalon constituted both sides of that particular coin. I stood no closer to an answer now. However, we could engage in that pleasant debate another time. I kept my tone brisk. "We are in Avalon." His lips pursed and his chest swelled. Raising a hand to forestall his outburst, I gentled my voice. "Peace, Arthur. Whole though your skull may be, your brain yet recovers from the blow it took. If not for my enchantment upon the counterfeit scabbard, Mordred would have—"

"Hold." His scowl descended into execute-the-prisoner territory. "*Counterfeit* scabbard?"

My heart kicked into a canter. "'Twas after Sir Accolon's—" Mindful of the need to tread carefully, I drew a thought-collecting breath. "In seeking vengeance for his death, I stole and destroyed Excalibur's scabbard. What you carried to the Camlann battlefield on the Salisbury Plain was a nonmagical copy." Closing my eyes and pressing my hands together as if in prayer, I suppressed a fresh surge of guilt. "My most excellent liege, I regret that action and humbly crave your pardon. I strove to reverse my grievous error in the parlay tent, but if you cannot forgive my treason…" I let myself inhale a mote of hope. "My life is yours to do with as you will."

His hands curled round mine lightly, soothingly. "My sins against you are no less grievous, Morgan, and I pray for your forgiveness."

We shared a long embrace. Upon parting, we both felt obliged to swipe tears from our cheeks.

Steering us back to the business of the moment, I said, "I shall endeavor to impart the other information you require in easy stages."

His body needed to adjust to being alive by easy stages, too. I asked Niniane to bring biscuits and an Omega-3 laden tisane replete with a generous dollop of honey to mitigate the fishy taste.

By the cant of his head, I could tell Arthur was attempting to make sense of his cleaned and repaired armor. "How long have I lain senseless?"

"I do not know. A tome in my Castle Gore library described the flow of time as being different here. It also gave this place a name with which you might be familiar: the Isle of the Blest."

"Ah." He gave a cautious nod. "Different—how?"

"The author reported making multiple sojourns of varying lengths. Upon his return, sometimes days or weeks had passed in his rightful world, sometimes decades." Centuries too, though I dared not utter it. I drew a breath to gauge Arthur's reaction, but he seemed to be taking the information in stride. "Sometimes he discovered that no time had passed at all." The fact that the author's final visit had resulted in him going backward in time—and hence why his book had been available for me to acquire—I also kept to myself.

"This place lies nowhere in Camelot, of that I am certain." The circling of my brother's hand indicated the pavilion and its lush setting. "And it is not some secret garden in Castle Gore?"

I shook my head.

"Why?" The vehemence of his question startled me, focused as I was upon maintaining a healing aura upon his brain. He must have interpreted my hesitation as confusion, for he forged on with, "Why bring me to this fey realm to heal me? My death at Camlann must have been foreordained by God. Why did you defy His will?" And the most direct hit of the lot: "You despised me, sister. Why did you not let me die and claim my throne for yourself?"

Fair questions for a concussed patient. I provided the easiest answer: "You lay upon death's brink, and I needed Avalon's magic to augment my healing skills. As for your other questions, I pray you let me ask one of my own." He gave a single, sharp nod. "What of the ill-fated parlay do you remember?"

"I remember…" Intense concentration creased his countenance. Galfrieda and I supported his back so he could sit all the way up. He turned and swung his legs over the bed. With his leave, I sat beside him. Niniane delivered the light repast. Arthur thanked her and downed three biscuits, followed by a long pull of the tisane. After taking a breath, he finished it. His visage lightened. "I remember you! You were inside the parlay tent. A strangely garbed wizard stood beside you. He was full of bluster and bombast and—and he intended to kill you! So I—I…oh, merciful God."

He buried his face in his hands. I hugged him to me. The contact made those damned battle images burn my brain as surely as they must have been tormenting his. Through that horrificness wafted strains of our mother's favorite cradle song. I dredged the rest of the tune from the bosom of my memory and hummed it.

His words tumbled out in an anguished rush: "In saving you, I doomed the realm. Thousands upon thousands of good men, their wives, their children, my knights, my nephews…" Gazing at me, he sucked in a deep breath and blew it out with puffed cheeks. "Uwaine fell protecting me, Morgan. I am sorry I could not prevent his death."

I knew it was not for want of trying; I had watched the scene play out in Arthur's mind countless times, including the necessarily brief but tearful last-rites prayer he had intoned over my son's lifeless form. I blinked hard to stem the tears. "Thank you for being with him," I whispered.

He nodded and captured my hands between his much larger ones. His gaze became unfocused for a few moments, and he winced. "Oh, God. Guenever, Launcelot…I am so, so sorry."

"They loved you, Arthur," I assured him, "even if they could not avoid loving each other." That last bit I could have kicked myself for uttering.

"They shall never know"—he clenched his jaw but failed to still the trembling of his chin—"that I forgive them."

A thousand comforting lies sprang to mind, but prevarication was one vice I had never cultivated. The best I could offer without straying too far from the truth was, "I believe, somehow, they knew."

Tears winning free of his brave eyes, he wrapped his arms round me and sobbed his grief against my chest. I stroked his short-cropped hair, his broad shoulders and back, all the while humming as loudly as I could manage. Tears summoned by the reminder of my son's death clouded my vision and clogged my throat. I am not certain when my ladies joined in, but at some point I felt their comforting hands and heard their healing notes.

After a time—how many eons passed, I know not—I sensed the easing of Arthur's tension. I shifted, and the ladies withdrew to a respectful distance.

"Arthur," I said, applying gentle pressure to his shoulder. My implicit command engendered the opposite effect: he clung to me tighter. "Your England shall endure."

He straightened at that, dried his eyes, and lowered his eyebrows, which I read as disbelief—though they had not descended low enough to eclipse the ray of hope lightening his countenance. "How can you know this?"

I smiled. "I have seen it. So shall you."

Arthur did not share the smile. His gaze returned to his armor and empty scabbard. Puzzlement furrowed his brow. "As I lay in the blood-churned mud with no hope of surviving my wounds, I entrusted Excalibur to Bedivere. To be purified in the lake. And to await the hand of a king who would not stain it with the blood of his people." I thought he might begin to weep again, but he set his jaw. "My people…Ah! Most holy, merciful God, my *people*…"

I took his hand into both of mine. "The past is past. The game goes on."

His eyes widened like twin shield bosses. "You said that to me before! When you…no. No, no, no. It—it cannot be." The astonishment yielded to quizzical. "In the parlay tent, Mordred stood poised to attack me, and our men had drawn swords to charge one another. No, they *had* started charging. And then you…you stepped into the midst of that madness to swear fealty to me?"

I did not kneel before him as I had done that day, but I did clasp my hands like a supplicant. "Arthur Pendragon, High King of England: I, Morgan, Queen of Gore, do humbly acknowledge you as my rightful lord, liege and master…"

"Your very words! And I uttered my acceptance of your vow, but"—his brow's furrow spawned furrows of its own—"how could that be? No one else was moving, not even to take a single breath. It must have been a dream."

By that I knew his memory was intact; he was as ready as he was ever going to be. I asked Galfrieda to give me the time-folding device. To her credit, she did not question my order in front of our liege.

"That fey scrap of metal—it lay upon your hand in the parlay tent," Arthur said.

I affirmed his statement but did not enlighten him regarding how very long it had taken me, amidst the numberless hours spent healing his head, to learn how to bend this bauble to my will. If he had asked me, I would have told him, of course. Swearing fealty to one's God-ordained liege entails serving him in all matters, minuscule as well as great. I meant my fealty oath more seriously than any other vow I had made in my entire sixteen hundred years of existence, save one. And that one I stood so close to fulfilling that I could scarcely contain myself, the Royal Rules Committee's insistence on stoicism be damned.

Rising, I clapped my hands thrice. "Ladies, the armor! We do not have much time."

I slapped the time-folding device to the back of my hand. It bonded at once and grew warm.

Arthur rose too. Heedless of the ladies strapping on the myriad pieces of his armor, he eyed the time-folding device with a mixture of awe and distrust, as if it were a claw shed by the legendary Black Beast of Aargh. After Vivien worked his dragon-emblazoned surcoat over his head, he went right back to staring at my hand and the device's blinking green light, his expression conveying equal measures of wishing for a magnifying lens or a dagger. When Niniane presented him with the scabbard and its baldric, that seemed to break the spell. "What good is this without my—its sword?" Sorrow and frustration escaped on his sigh. He never had been one to pay the Royal Rules Committee any mind.

"Take it. The scabbard's physical repair is augmented by a stronger spell to guard your life. The journey we are about to undertake shall feel like…" What to say to a man whose skull had been cracked like a coconut, a seasoned warrior for whom physical pain was but one inevitable facet of the job? Then an irreverent thought sprang from my days of binge-watching vintage fictional time-travel stories. I had no time to explain the Marvel *Loki* television series reference—much less its World

Tree rooted technology—but the description was too apt to resist: "Like dying and being born all at once."

"Brilliant." Grimacing, Arthur lowered the baldric over his head. The scabbard settled into its familiar place against his hip. He stared at it as he said, "We walk into another battle?"

"I hope not." I twined my device-free arm with his and drew him close. "But my intuition warns me to be prepared."

Galfrieda passed her lord his helmet, which he tucked under the arm I was not clutching as if both of our lives depended upon it. In point of fact, our lives did depend upon my not letting Arthur go. As if reading my mind, I felt him grasp my hand.

Avalon disappeared in a blinding flash.

The gut-wrenching agony began.

I knew what to expect; I had traversed the span of centuries twice before, and yet the knowledge did not help. I could not hear Arthur's screams above my own.

CHAPTER III.
The Return of the Queen.

SPARKS AND little lightning bolts flickered across my vision. A million spots winked in and out, in and out, like fireflies seeking mates at an extra-innings night game. My every nerve felt as if it had its own acupuncturist in attendance. Lucky them.

God, how I hate time travel.

So did Arthur, to judge by the fact that I felt obliged to cast a triple-strength warding spell to prevent my hand from being crushed to goo in his metal-clad grip. I willed upon him a calming spell for good measure. Relaxing his fingers, he gave me an apologetic almost-smile.

Then it occurred to me that our journey must be done, for I could see his face.

Why, yes, intuitive reader, time folding *is* faster than a speeding neuron. Thank you for noticing.

The details of our destination wavered into focus.

We were standing inside an office, a vast one belonging to a high-ranking executive, to judge by the dark mahogany paneling; solid gold fixtures and plush carpets; top-shelf scotch, vodka, and other bottles of spirits clustered round the sundry-shaped crystal drinking vessels upon the Egyptian

CHAPTER III.

granite bar; overstuffed leather couch and chairs; and the separate meeting table in addition to the executive's desk, which was flanked by shelves laden with trophies, rare collectible merchandise, stacks of media cases, and other curios. The desk itself stood nigh clear of detritus: a few papers here, a tablet device there, a writing instrument or two in between. The desk's embedded horizontal monitor, half eclipsed by a chronicle and its carved, gilt oaken case, displayed a logo that I, during the latter days of my second lifetime, had helped to design. It remained stationary beside a rotating series of images that warmed me from crown to toes: Sandy and me on our wedding day.

I forgave him for the redecorating he had done to my office…and for succumbing to the belief that he might not see me again. For sooth, I had not been certain of my return either.

Whatever content was being broadcast upon the full-wall projection screen to our left I could not discern from my angle. By its muted sound, I judged that the program must be in a commercial break.

Championship pennants and banners competed with framed,

ALEXANDER "SANDY" LEROY CARTER

autographed jerseys for every available handspan of wall space. A floor-to-ceiling window overlooked the stadium. The field, fences, railings, and unprotected bleacher seats sported a dusting of snow.

The right corner of my mouth tugged upward, and not because of the season's charm or the room's decor. The chronicle that lay upon the desk before me I had not seen since departing with Arthur for Avalon.

With a touch of magical help, I discerned the text displayed in the lower right corner of the desk monitor: *Friday, 11/29/2092.*

'Twas well that I looked when I did. In the next breath, the comely young woman dressed in a sumptuous, shrimp-colored gown standing betwixt me and the office owner's desk began hopping about as if she were a Highland games sword-dance competitor, obscuring my view.

The dance stopped. "Either I'm about to disappear again," she said with astonishing calm, "or—"

My mouth's left corner lifted. So did my heart.

The comeliest of men and manliest of lovers, who had shot up from his swivel seat behind the desk, broke into the biggest, dearest grin I had ever been privileged to see him make. The grin was not directed at his shrimp-gowned companion.

Beside me, I felt Arthur tense as if preparing to pull away, like the determined toddler who does not know that the pretty tiger plans to eat its "guest." Feeling my motherly instincts activate (I was yet too new to the job of being his sister, in spite of the untold Avalonian eons I had spent toiling over the comatose him), I applied gentle pressure to his forearm, willing him to desist till I could ascertain that it was safe for us to move.

"Arthur," I murmured, "I have ever so much to explain to thee." Mindful that he was my king, I hastened on with, "I pray you grant me leave to be the first to converse with these good folk. The lady Clarice is my apprentice and dearest friend. And the gentleman"—hoping Arthur would not overreact in his capacity either as my brother or king, I drew a swift, soft breath—"is Sandy—Alexander Leroy Carter,—my husband."

CHAPTER III.

Arthur disengaged his arm from mine. He swayed a bit, and I reached for his arm, but he steadied himself and broke into an indulgent smile. I took that for affirmation and all but flew into Sandy's arms.

I heard Clarice squeak, "Your Majesty!" Her words escaped in a breathy rush, as if a gas pipe were relieving an abrupt indigestive onslaught. Whether she intended her greeting for myself or my brother was of no importance to me. The sound of rustling fabric suggested that she might be introducing herself to Arthur—I had dispensed with the curtsying requirement for my Apprentice Number One years ago, and I did not expect her to have forgotten that mote of kindness; by the monitor's reported date, I had been gone about thirteen months—but my time-stressed neurons lacked the wherewith to expend any more thought upon the matter. By the woody, metallic *clunk*, I inferred that Arthur had deposited his helmet on the conference table.

I am reasonably certain, fair reader, that you have never sojourned across fifteen centuries once, to say naught of thrice, or spent God alone knows how long being suspended out of time, whatever in heaven's name that meant in scientific terms. Thus I do understand that you might not be equipped to grasp how joyous I felt in that moment. I doubt whether Sandy fathomed the depth of my joy either, but that mattered not one whit to me.

After the initial collision of our lips, whereby we each assured the other that we were in fact real—and really *here*—upon tacit agreement we pulled back to gape wonderingly, reverently at one another. With the speed of a frame-by-frame video review, Sandy lifted his hand to caress my cheek, my jaw, my chin. His other hand joined the first. The butterfly lightness of his touch set my facial nerves afire and sent their acupuncturists dashing for the nearest lake for to submerge themselves till the blaze could whoosh past. I mimicked that move upon his face, delighting in the nubby roughness, the *here*-ness of his stubble.

I pulled off my crown and conjured myself into my favorite game-day attire: a black suit and red silk blouse, a solid gold London Knights logo

"WE EACH ASSURED THE OTHER
THAT WE WERE IN FACT REAL."

pin gleaming upon the jacket's lapel. Sandy chuckled as he adjusted the line of his adoring gaze to accommodate the lift supplied by my Pradas.

"My God, Morgan. I thought I'd never see you again."

My God, how I had missed hearing those deep, dulcet tones.

"Have I been gone so long that you have forgotten what I dubbed you at our last meeting?"

"Was it something like"—his smile broadened—"once and future love?"

"Precisely like." I felt my smile shade to sultry. "I did mean it quite literally. One of these days, dearest Sandy, you shall learn to believe me."

His hand coaxed the circlet from my grasp. "My sweet, precious soul-mate, you shall always be my once and future queen." He settled it firmly atop my head. His hands cupped my face.

He is—was—such a daisy.

Stepping closer, pressing the full length of my body to his such that not even Excalibur, were it here, could have parted us, I glided my fingers through his hair, reveling in the rediscovery of its silken, curly wisps. He released my face to complete the embrace, sliding his hands down my back. They ignited a delicious trail of tingles all the way down.

The second meeting of our lips was as slow and deliberate as the first had been reckless and wild. Our tongues caressed one another in blessed reunion. Our throaty gasps and murmured nothings proceeded as if from a single mind. The level of soul-satiating bliss Sandy engendered within me leapt leagues beyond anything I had ever experienced, before or since. To say that I did not want the moment to end would be the greatest grandsire of all understatements.

I wish to God, to the core of my soul, that I had possessed the foresight to cast a time-freezing spell.

Sandy's mouth hardened. His fingers convulsed, digging into my waist.

My body's tingling ceased as if it had never been.

The fuster-clucking confusion my eyes reported can best be described as what happened to billions of people and creatures when Marvel megavillain Thanos snapped his fingers to create his idea of a perfect universe—said billions crumbling to ash and blowing into nothingness—followed close on by their reconstitution into solid matter…if twentieth-century Spanish surrealist painter Salvador Dalí had performed the reconstituting.

I had never suffered so complete a loss to explain what had happened in my entire life.

CHAPTER IV.
What the H—?

EMEMBER THOSE fireflies? They swarmed about my face with a bloody vengeance, and each one had dragged its mate and in-laws to the party. The acupuncturists resumed their torture. I fancied that I could hear their gleeful cackling as they jammed in their microscopic needles and twisted.

I tried to step back, scrub my eyes, and retreat from that hard mouth and those cruel fingers, but he gripped my arms so tightly that I could not wrench myself free. Worse, disorientation had destroyed my focus for casting magic.

A woman—presumably Clarice; I did not think it was me, but my optic nerves and their sensory brethren remained yet too shot by whatever had just occurred for me to be certain—gasped.

The screech of metal on metal made me flinch. In the next breath, I forced myself to stay calm; Arthur must have reached for the sword he had forgotten was no longer there. "What the devil?" he rumbled.

CHAPTER IV.

I blinked hard, fast, and often, but those buggish spots refused to vacate my vision. One fact, however, was clear. The man gripping me whilst baring more teeth than a dragon that had doubled its hoard could not be my husband.

"Well, well, lass. I donna know where ye came from, but I'm right glad you're here."

I would have recognized that dour Scottish growl anywhere. It belonged to a man I had killed under circumstances disturbingly similar to this.

We must have somehow slipped backward to the time when Sandy and I were estranged, when this man, Ewan McBain, was employed as the Knights' general manager. My brain raced to recollect the timeline. This had to be before that fateful night when I had been compelled to use lethal force to defend myself from his vengeful attack. But how had the time slip occurred? Why?

He yanked me closer, those ugly lips squeezing into an uglier pucker. The stench of alcohol oozed from between them. Behind me, Arthur's challenging growl had begun to swell. That he could—and would—kill McBain with his bare hands, I did not doubt. I could not afford to risk losing any answers McBain might provide.

"*Cadail!*"[†] I commanded.

Of the languages I could have chosen to focus the energies of this spell, there is none quite as satisfying to utter as Scottish Gaelic. Plus I reckoned it could not hurt to communicate directly with McBain's wild Celtic blood.

Obediently he went limp in my arms and began to snore. My knees sagged under the abrupt, fifteen-stone deadweight. Mindful of the second rule of queenship, I resisted the impulse to groan. Arthur, growl abandoned, took McBain from me and half carried, half dragged him to the overstuffed couch.

Except the couch was not overstuffed. Its frame was a wretched monstrosity of scratched, chipped pine wood whose varnish was peeling. Of

---

† *Cadail*, pronounced *kuh-TEEdl*, is the Scottish Gaelic imperative for "Fall asleep!"—*kih*

the scant few cushions it possessed, to claim they were stuffed would be a kindness. Stuffed with what, I dared not contemplate.

Whilst Arthur got the man settled, with Clarice watching them, twisting and untwisting a shrimp-colored fold of her skirts between her hands, I turned a slow circle of my office.

Correction: the sad, looted remains of my office.

The projection screen, trophies, pennants, banners, jerseys, balls, and stacks of game programs, highlight reels, season recap books, and other media were gone. The basic furnishings—desk, table, bookcases, chairs— were sub-basic; they were cheap, plain, and Godawful drab, just like the couch, the paneling, and the light fixtures. A bookcase filled the spot where the bar had been. Its shelves, and those of its sundry utilitarian siblings, sagged beneath the weight of rank upon rank of fat, black binders distinguishable by naught save the degree of fading evident upon the plastic, suggesting a progression of age.

Arthur's crowned helmet was the only item of quality to occupy the transformed room, ruling the inanimate peasantry from its tabletop perch like any feudal overlord.

The desk had a computer, I think, but not of any type I recognized. It squatted in a large, bulky, inelegant beige lump upon the desk; two lumps, counting the primitive input device attached to it by a cord that had been taped in several places, with a stretch or two showing the need for a sticky black bandage. The computer and its keyboard looked as Godawful as everything else in this (pray, forgive me for being inaccurate, but words fail here) office.

A logo featuring a mounted knight did adorn the monitor's screen. The knight and his destrier struck the same pose as the figure rearing and slashing upon my lapel, but the "London Knights" lettering had been replaced by "Persimmon's Soap" arching over the horse's head and the point of the knight's upraised sword. The brag "All the Prime-Donne Use It" splashed across a rippling ribbon underneath.

My chronicle was gone. Not this one, but the edition I had left in the care of my scribe in Gore, which I presumed Clarice had retrieved during a recent sojourn to the past, owing to her being clad in the shrimp-colored gown with another time-folding device bonded to her hand.

What the h—?

I strode to the window. I felt more than saw Clarice join me. Snow still dusted everything, which struck me as odd (as if the missing chronicle, memorabilia, luxury furnishings, top-shelf liquor, and bleeding-edge electronics was not odd enough).

She mumbled a question about the stadium. I dismissed it as nonsense and continued trying to make sense of the impossibilities laid out before my eyes.

The falling-out with McBain and its tragic result had occurred in high summer. I recalled how pale gray the sky had been so very close to midnight that terrible night. McBain had not served as GM for much more than three months before that. Then there was the matter of—

"Ms. Hanks!" She had refrained from jostling my arm, but her pitch and volume, along with the choice to resort to my twenty-first-century alias as standard protocol whenever we stood amongst those who did not know the ancient me, did the trick. I met her gaze with a level of firmness that I hoped would stop her from sliding into outright panic. "Where. Is. The. *Stadium?*"

"My dear, whatever do y—"

She pointed. With a mounting sense of dread, I looked out the window.

The ball field lay where it had always been, if the noble term "ball field" could in fact apply to the weedy, seedy expanse that seemed more slushy dirt than field. A few men wearing shabby winter coats were tossing worn baseballs to each other. One had an honest-to-God glove, though its cracked leather and occasional laces relegated it to the category of museum reject. His fellows were obliged to make do with their mittened hands. Nobody could manage to catch a ball without juggling it, even the man with the glove, and there was not one halfway decent throwing arm amongst the lot. Even so, I got the distinct impression that I knew these men from…somewhere.

In place of the audience seating loomed factory buildings. On closer examination, the crumbling brickwork, dry-rotted doors and window casings, rusted hinges and fittings, and soot-smudged windows made me doubt whether the stadium's seating had ever existed. A four-storey-tall representation of Sir Persimmon sprawled across one of the buildings, sooty windows notwithstanding, in the precise location whence the ballpark's scoreboard had reported innings and the teams' runs, outs, hits, and errors; the soaring joys and the crushing defeats.

I began to form a theory, and I prayed to God Almighty, His Son, and all His saints that I was in error.

Repeated punching of the button on my time-folding device yielded no change in our environs. I asked Clarice to try activating hers.

After several tries, she shook her head. "Their zero-point charges must be spent."

Arthur, who had been alternately watching McBain and me, said, "Zero—? What the devil has happened? Where is your husband? Who is this varlet on the couch?"

Anyone else would have had to endure being ignored, and like it or die. "I shall explain when I can, my liege. For now, my instinct warns me that we must needs hurry."

My apologetic smile proved no match for the impatient storm eclipsing the confusion upon his face. Clarice chimed in with, "His name is Ewan McBain, Your Majesty. She killed him seven years ago."

Right. Like that was going to help.

"Morgan? The first man you were with looked like Sir Accolon, whom *I* killed."

I did not appreciate the reminder of that most gut-wrenching of days, which had turned my soul septic with the craving to murder my brother and liege, thus ultimately banishing me—and now Arthur and Clarice with me—into this future purgatory, but I had to like it. Or die.

"What the bloody, fonging hell is going on?" Arthur glared at me as if this—all of it, down to the frayed wires, gouged wood, and chipped paint—was my fault.

I feared he might be right.

"Arthur, I wish to God I knew." The impulse to sigh had never loomed stronger, but I resisted it. "Can you please bear with me and Clarice whilst we investigate?" He folded his arms. The glare dimmed by not one watt. I took that for grudging acceptance and addressed Clarice. "Do you think you can operate that"—I jerked a nod at the desk's electronic tumor—"thing and learn more about our situation? It shan't give you any trouble." By that last bit I meant that I had sent it a magical mental command to release its security lockout. My apprentice might have been able to accomplish this task, but I was unwilling to expend the time to find out.

"Yes, ma'am." Clarice peeled off her defunct time-folding device, stowed it in a side-seam pocket, sat in front of the computer, and started pressing keys in rapid succession. I removed and pocketed my device too.

Eyeing the snoring McBain, Arthur drew me aside. "That man dared to threaten you?" To his credit, he kept his voice low but not one jot less menacing. "He shan't get another chance." He lunged for McBain's throat.

I stepped between them. "This Ewan McBain did not seem to know me. We must have somehow sojourned to a different time. Or mayhap a different place."

"Neither, Ms. Hanks."

No messenger in the history of the world with a countenance as ashen as Clarice's has ever reported good news. My stomach suffered a most unqueenly lurch.

CHAPTER V.
More Questions Than Answers.

"WHAT DO you mean, this is *still* November the 29th, 2092?" If the shrillness of my tone could have cut like a literal knife, it pains me to admit that I would have killed everyone within earshot, myself included.

The Royal Rules Committee would have had a field day sitting in judgment upon my myriad decorum breaches.

I drew a calming breath.

"Twenty ninety-two! How the bloody hell is that even possible?" Arthur demanded, that rage-storm threatening to break. "What have you done to me, Morgan?"

"Peace, Arthur. Try to have some patience. I am as confused as you are, but I—"

"I am the king! Others must have patience."

And there it was, that rage-storm from my brother, the King of Predictable. I pursed my lips to curb my grin. "You said the same thing to

Merlin minutes before laying eyes upon your bride-to-be, and look how that turned out for all involved."

Aye, that was cruel of me, but his sail luffed on cue. With a muttered injunction to carry on, he removed his baldric and laid it and the scabbard upon the meeting table beside his helmet so he could lower his armored bulk into a chair near McBain's couch, glaring at me moreso than at his charge. I could live with that glare. The screeching and scraping made my once-and-present nemesis stir a bit, but he did not wake. As a precaution, I bolstered the sleeping spell.

Leaning past Clarice's shoulder, I peered at the monitor. The location's reported street address matched that of New Wembley Baseball Stadium. "So this must be my office."

"Not exactly, ma'am." She twisted her neck to slide me a sympathetic glance, faced forward, and tapped a key to display the next page.

Its text made me blink thrice. "Persimmon's Soap Factory…in continuous operation here since…1859? Present factory manager: Ewan McBain." Another page showed the company's history, detailed in reverse chronological order beginning with McBain's tenure. It scrolled past my eyes, but I could not bear to read it.

The 1859 founding would go far to explain the shabby feel to this place, but what had become of the stadium? Had my Knights organized in another city? Was Sandy with them?

Reining in my pulse's jolting canter, I instructed Clarice to search for the World Baseball Federation to retrieve a list of current teams and host cities.

Zero records found.

Even Arthur, who had been Camelot's best shortstop, looked crestfallen at that.

A general search on "baseball" yielded a lone paragraph about the children's game of "base ball." A statement in another article admitted that some adults indulged in the recreational pastime for exercise and stress relief, but there seemed to be no organized leagues at any level of expertise. My brother perked up—evidenced by more clanking as he sat forward, gauntleted hands to plated thighs—when Clarice found an announcement, dated within the past week, advertising open tryouts for an adult team in London. However, its FMI link, along with any potential information about other teams, failed to deliver on its promise, yielding instead the annoying "Page Not Found" announcement.

"Wait, Ms. Hanks, I—"

Arthur's abrupt, cacophonous rise from the chair halted Clarice. "Why the bloody hell does that woman keep calling you 'Miz Hanks'?"

It is not a sound policy to enchant one's sovereign liege lord without permission, but I needed no prophetic vision to know that, unchecked, his armor-amplified ranting would knell the death of us all. Boosting my charm to its fullest, and with a calming spell prepped for deployment, I glided to him and, with his leave, laid my hand upon his chest.

"'Ms.' is an honorific for ladies," I said.

By the gentleness with which he disengaged my hand, I judged that I would not need the calming spell. "I understand that much, Morgan. But the other bit? 'Hanks'?"

"'Morganna Hanks' is an alias Clarice invented for me during my previous sojourn to this century when I needed a means of masking my identity. It pleased her to invert Sir Boss's name in the alias's formation."

"Ah. Hank Morgan…Morganna Hanks." Arthur's grin surprised but heartened me, for it signaled another step along his healing journey. "You could not have been pleased by the association with your magical nemesis, dear sister." The grin widened.

Long had I suspected that he had planted spies in my court at Castle Gore, as I had done in Camelot, to stymie each other's war efforts; his grin confirmed it. "You know me well, dear brother." A glance at Clarice showed an embarrassed flush coloring her cheeks. I forestalled the bloom with a smile. "I have embraced the alias for quite some time," I assured her. "What name would you suggest for my brother?"

CHAPTER V.

Whilst my apprentice pondered the question, Arthur asked, "Are you certain I will need an alias, Morgan?"

I felt certain of nothing, but, "'Tis always best to be prepared, is it not?"

Arthur grunted affirmation.

"How about 'Arthur Richards'?" Clarice offered. "'Richards' is an inversion of—"

"*Àrd-righ*, meaning 'high king,'" Arthur said with a commendable Scottish Gaelic accent. He tossed me another grin. "What? Did you fancy yourself the only royal to study the tongue of the people hailing from the Northern Marches?" I chuckled my approval, and he said to Clarice, "Well done, my dear. Arthur Richards I shall henceforth be. As to a title…what is the masculine equivalent of Ms.?"

"Mister," she said. From her intake of breath, I surmised that she had planned to launch the gender-neutral Mx. into the honorific mix, but I stopped her with the barest shake of my head. I could foresee her remarking upon the Superman adversary Mister Mxyzptlk too, and the nomenclature detour already had stretched longer than I would have liked.

The new-minted Mr. Arthur Richards, oblivious to my silent exchange with Clarice, said, "A corruption of 'master;' I should have guessed as much. Mistress Clarice, have you aught else to report from your studies of"—he pointed at the monitor—"that?"

"Oh! Yes, sir." She adopted her reading voice: "London's Lord Mayor invites all interested parties to try out for several open positions upon the roster of the Knights base ball team. Drafted players shall be required to commit to a winter training regimen and a twenty-game schedule versus sanctuary district teams across the European Confederacy beginning in Spring 2093. Room, board, uniforms, equipment, transportation, and a modest stipend shall—"

"Sanctuary districts?" said Arthur and I together. His tone, of course, conveyed ignorance; mine, incredulity.

I explained to him what a sanctuary district was and that the twenty-first-century London of my acquaintance had never possessed one.

None of the grand old European cities did; that particular, depressing phenomenon wherein society's human detritus was sequestered out of sight and out of mind had been confined to America, to that great nation's everlasting shame. Then, of course, I had to give him the thirty-second "rebellious colony of religious and criminal misfits, but we got past that and are now fast friends" explanation of what America was and why its people had evolved into self-righteous do-gooders that *could* feel shame over the implementation of what had seemed like a fine idea at the time. I concluded with a ninety-second rundown of my pre-Avalon misadventures across time.

ZERO RECORDS FOUND.

My international experiences, first as American president Malory Hinton's campaign boss and later as owner of the London Knights WBF franchise, had not exposed me to any governing body dubbed the "European Confederacy." Given the earlier educational delays, I felt beyond thankful that Arthur did not ask.

The ever-blooming, never-aging boredom of Avalon—preferably without anyone to heal, kin or otherwise—was looking better by the moment.

None of that lessened my craving for answers regarding our present predicament. Or the world's predicament; apparently, for some unfathomable reason, sanctuary districts now existed nigh everywhere. According to Clarice's research, most had been established in the nineteenth century.

CHAPTER V.

When keyword searches of "America," "London Knights," "World Tournament," and "Morganna Hanks" yielded zero results, on a whim I suggested that Clarice try a search on Malory Beckham Hinton. That retrieved one article naming her as the "Presider" of the "Mid-Atlantic Confederacy." Clicking the hyperlink revealed that confederacy as consisting of the sanctuary districts of Baltimore, Columbia, Fairfax, Philadelphia, Richmond, Roanoke…

"Stop," I said to Clarice, who had continued reading aloud, but I hoped God would heed my plea and deliver me—all of us—from whatever madness into which we had stumbled.

Clarice obeyed.

God snorted.

Typing the name Sandy Carter into the search box displayed an ominous "Access Restricted." The same result appeared when Clarice supplied his legal name, Alexander Leroy Carter.

"Sandy, my dearest love, where are you?" I whispered.

As the silence persisted, I realized that I could no longer sense his presence anywhere upon this earth. Our link had been as tenuous as spider silk during my tenure in Avalon, but strong enough to maintain a tether to my sanity. Now the tether was gone. I clenched my jaw to battle my trembling chin.

Arthur's expression grew sympathetic and then determined. "What does it say about me?"

The last question I ever expected to hear from my brother snapped my spiral. He was legendary for placing others' needs above his own, even whilst pumping his last pints of lifeblood into the mud. His decision to surrender Excalibur to the Lady of the Lake for to await the next worthy wielder was a prime example. I never would have pegged him for an ego surfer.

And yet his request made sense. Since the present and near-past appeared radically different from what I had known, a query about Arthur and his reign might provide a stable foundation from which to research where history had begun to warp, and why.

"Do it," I said to Clarice.

She typed "King Arthur" into the search box and submitted the request.

Klaxons blared. And then, to borrow one of Sandy's quaint vulgarities, all hell broke loose.

CHAPTER VI.
Familiar Minions.

CCESS PROHIBITED by Papal Authority."

I had never read anything so ludicrous in my life. Either of my lives.

The office's door banged into the wall. The hallway klaxons blared louder. Three uniformed security guards rushed in. Their faces seemed familiar…and at odds with the weapons in their fists, which resembled the nineteenth-century projectile-launching firearms preferred by the Connecticut Yankee, not the beam-emitting pistols native to the twenty-first century of my acquaintance.

Arthur stood.

"Peace," I whispered to him, leaning close. "Recall how…" On the cusp of mentioning what might be another forbidden topic, I kept my words vague. "Recall how a brash friend of yours dealt with some of your… companions."

The hand that had begun groping for the absent sword knotted into a fist. I laid a calming spell upon the guards, lest they perceive Arthur's movement as a threat.

CHAPTER VI.

I straightened, remembering—as I hoped Arthur did—how quickly death could fly from those muzzles. During my first lifetime, I had sat beside Arthur and Guenever in the royal box as we and the rest of the kingdom watched Sir Boss, the baseborn ass Hank Morgan, employ such a weapon to kill the noble and mighty Sir Sagramor with but a single shot to his steel-plated chest.

Then it occurred to me that men resembling these security guards, alongside their Connecticut teammates, had battled my Knights in the World Tournament of 2088. The box-score data of those seven epic games, especially the four that the Knights had won, glimmered in my mind's eye. Memories clamored for attention: the blowouts (theirs); the come-from-behind wins (ours, all save one); the thrill of each Knight hit, stolen base, putout, and strikeout; the rookie's walk-off homer to win us all the coveted marbles…

In the midst of this mental reveling, the greater implication hit me.

Why were American Yankees—elite baseball athletes, no less—employed as minions at a decrepit old factory in London that stood on the site of its vanished baseball stadium?

Before I could voice my question, Stan Boleyn, whom I had known as a marvelous third-baseman, started with, "Who are you? How did you get in here?" He speared Arthur with a glare. "And you, factory mascot guy. Shouldn't you be out pounding pavement somewhere?"

My brother sucked in a short, angry breath, but I mouthed a plea for him to stand down, and his face relaxed a fraction with the exhale. "This good gentleman and his lady companion here seek to be hired for a special advertising campaign." 'Twas as good an excuse as any, and I wagered upon the fact that these castle guards would not know their liege's business. "I represent them." I felt relieved to note that Arthur possessed wit enough to refrain from gainsaying me. Clarice had worked with me long enough that I trusted her discretion, and she did not disappoint.

Howie Elton, a world-class catcher of my former acquaintance, walked to the couch and shook his employer's shoulder. When that failed to wake him, Elton rounded on us, his scowl-sneer a gash marring his otherwise handsome face. "What's the matter with Master McBain?"

Master?

Whatever. My brain felt taxed enough without inviting unwanted implications to muddle everything.

I pointed a nod at McBain, releasing the spell. In due course, he began to rouse.

"He swooned." To my former nemesis I said, "You shall be fine."

"I donna feel so fine." McBain, with Elton's help, sat up, rubbing his head. "Percival, kill that damned alarm."

The man I had known as the left-fielder Ector Percival holstered his weapon, approached the desk, and politely but firmly asked Clarice to move. She surrendered her seat and hastened to join Arthur and me. My brother paid her no heed, engrossed as he was in studying the man who shared the name—but not the countenance—of one of his best knights. Concerned that he might be overloading his brain for a fruitless endeavor, I caught his attention and shook my head. He sighed but continued watching the computer's new operator, though with reduced intensity.

After Percival made a few strategic taps, the klaxons fell silent. I should have foreseen the trap and acted to avoid this spot of trouble, but my time-boggled wits had yet to make sense of our situation.

Seeking another avenue to diffuse tempers, I sashayed to McBain, stretching forth my hand. "May I, Ewan?"

"How in hell do ye know me name?"

"She knows a great many things," Clarice bragged. I tried to silence her with a thought, but her mental shields remained firm. She chugged on with, "And she has healing ma—"

"A healing gift." I chided her lapse with a stern glance. Frowning an apology, she averted her gaze. I returned my attention to McBain, who was massaging his temple. His loud, uneven breathing betrayed his struggle not to wince. "Your head hurts, Ewan. I can see it. Please let me help you."

"Go ahead," he grumbled. I replaced his fingers with mine. A few moments later, he removed my hand. "It's better now, thanks." He said to Elton and Boleyn, "Restrain them."

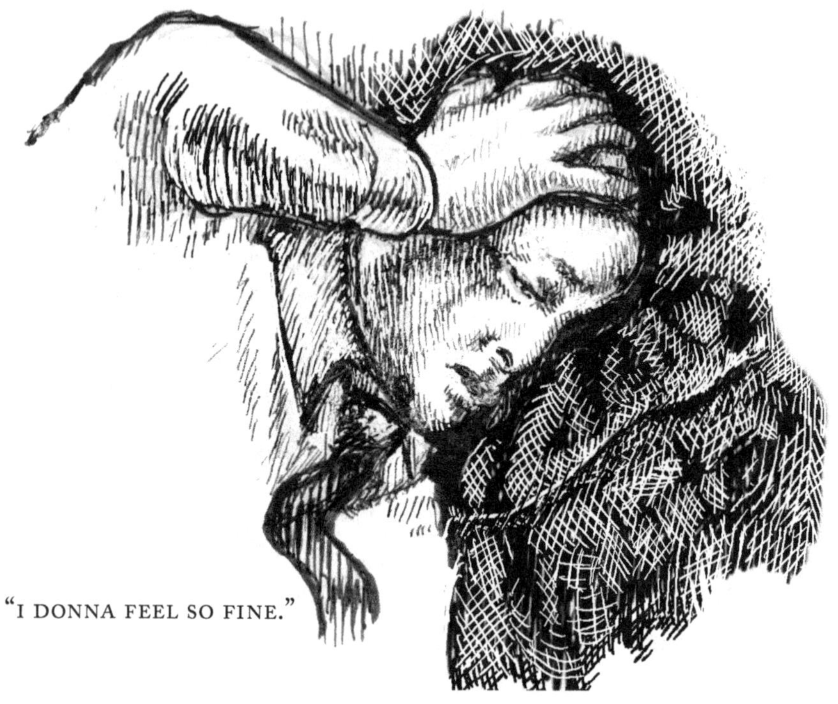

"I DONNA FEEL SO FINE."

I wiggled my fingers in the semblance of a nervous twitch. The guards stayed in place. "That shan't be necessary, Ewan. We are no threat to you. We only seek information."

"Yeah," Percival chimed in, making me wish the immobility spell I had placed upon McBain's minions had included a silencing component. "Information about a Church-restricted topic."

"Which one?" McBain asked with a level of moroseness to suggest that thousands of topics had fallen under papal bans.

My curiosity overcame the instinct to impose silence. I lifted my spell on Percival.

He hit several keys and shook his head. "No idea, Boss. Search history has been wiped."

Clarice flashed me a triumphant little grin; my apprentice had not veered off her game. I let her bask in my silent approval but regretted the loss of focus when Percival's peers won free of my restraining spell. They stepped to within grasping distance of Arthur and me whilst Percival rose from the desk to approach Clarice.

Arthur gestured at his empty scabbard and then raised both hands, fingers splayed. "Upon our honor, good sir," he said to McBain, "we carry no weapons."

That, of course, was the royal *we*; he knew my habit of carrying a dirk concealed upon my person. Arthur had been the one—during a brief period as youths when we had stood upon amicable terms, before he had betrothed me to King Uriens in what later proved to be a failed attempt to stave off rebellion—to suggest the practice to me. He had gifted me the best dirk of his collection at the time and taught me how to wield it with lethal precision, as the other McBain had discovered moments before his bloody demise. When I had conjured myself into my game-day attire for Sandy, the sheathed dirk had become attached to my belt, beneath my jacket.

I banked upon the male propensity to underestimate women and kept my expression benign.

Elton took Arthur's measure. "That's debatable, Tin Man."

Whilst my brother cocked an eyebrow, mouthing the words "Tin Man" with a face more angry than confused, Clarice blurted, "He has more honor in one tin pinkie than all of you put together!"

McBain expelled a noisy sigh. "Fine. No restraints." He leveled his glare upon his men before directing it at Arthur, Clarice, and me. "But if any of them makes so much as a suspicious twitch, shoot them."

I waved a calming gesture and with it, cast a calming spell, directing a double dose upon Arthur, whose posture had stiffened—that is to say, more than his steel union suit was already doing for him. The last thing any of us needed was for him to go all heroic and reckless. I felt disinclined to haul his self-sacrificing derriere back to Avalon, even if I believed I could attempt the journey from here.

"Gentlemen—Ector Percival, Howie Elton, Stan Boleyn—yes, I know your names." With an unspoken apology to my absent husband, I added a dash of flirt to my smile. "I also know you all to be excellent baseball players, though you played for the Connecticut Yankees."

Percival said: "Connect-cut?"

Boleyn said: "What the hell is a Yankee?"

Elton said: "You mean *yang qi*…'oxygen?' Lady, do we look Chinese to you?"

I sidled closer to the guards, grin heating and hips swaying.

McBain said: "Donna let her bewitch ye, men."

His obedient minions sharpened their stances and their glares.

If I had permitted men to stand firm in their resolve to resist my charms, I never would have notched three of the four bedposts in my castle's chambers to the very tip, to say naught of beginning work on the fourth before said work had been terminated by my first sojourn through time…and the subsequent introduction to my soulmate, Sandy.

I shifted my attention to McBain and picked up his hand, caressing it in a slow, soft, suggestive manner. "A terrible mishap brought us here"—wherever *here* was—"and we seek a means of reversing it."

If Ewan McBain had been my first attempted conquest, all of my bedposts would have remained as pristine as on the day of their creation.

"Right. Tell it to the Lord Mayor." He yanked his hand free of mine, scrubbed it against his thigh, and strode for the doorway, ordering his men to usher us out. "Dealing with you lunatics is above my pay grade."

In the glare he leveled upon me, I caught a glimpse of the McBain who had tried to strangle me at midnight in a London park seven years—and another lifetime—ago. I willed my heart and my breathing to remain as steady as my gaze and my stride.

Clarice followed close on my heels and Arthur guarded our backs as we stepped out of the factory manager's office and further into the unknown.

CHAPTER VII.
SDO London.

UTSIDE THE soap factory, we found ourselves marching the streets of a twenty-first-century London that appeared every inch as dismal as Persimmon's establishment. Pitted brick, cracked concrete, tarnished brass, sooty glass, rusted iron, and dry-rotted timber greeted our gazes at every turn. Now and then, some intrepid soul had tossed up a bucket of paint or planted a tree, but those efforts were too few to effect much impact upon the whole. The snow, which had looked charming from McBain's window, was busy devolving into a pervasive black slush that served to deepen the city's overwhelming sense of doom.

I had to exert a fair effort to keep hidden my shattering heart.

By this time, Clarice was walking beside me. To judge by the periodic trembling of her chin, she seemed to be fighting a similar battle, and losing whenever a gaggle of ragged street urchins swept by us, or we trudged past a homeless family eking an existence in the doorway of an abandoned building. When I glanced back at Arthur, he did not meet my gaze. Immersed in his role as our protector, he was doing his utmost to take in all the sights, swiveling his head this way and that, expression intent. I dropped back a pace to watch him pay especial attention to the odd mix of motorized and horse-drawn conveyances.

CHAPTER VII.

Perhaps he was noting the fact that armed guards rode in the automobiles and trucks, whereas civilians were constrained to either walking or employing four-legged modes of transportation.

The urchins, though displaying no compunction about pestering other pedestrians, gave our party a wide berth. The adult civilians seemed too engrossed in their drab lives to pay us any heed. They moved much as my peasants of Gore did, with heads bowed and feet shuffling ever onward, glancing up and dodging to avoid being mown down by one of the mobile patrols. Most carried a beaded necklace in one fist, and their lips twitched in what I presumed to be constant, silent prayer.[†] The twitching and shuffling got faster whenever one of them chanced to notice us.

Every street guard at every checkpoint eyed us with suspicion. That is, they eyed Arthur, Clarice, and me. When McBain and his men flashed their IDs without being asked, and McBain reported their mission, all of us were waved onward without incident. Each time I walked away, I could feel hot stares impaling me between the shoulder blades and at other strategic points along the backside of my anatomy. I imagined my brother and my apprentice felt the same way. I cast bolstering spells upon all of us; such scrutiny can be debilitating if left unparried.

The checkpoints occurred with greater frequency as we hove closer to our destination, a massive, ornate building that towered over the squalor like, well, like every castle in every feudal realm was designed to do, including mine and Arthur's. Not one chipped brick or hunk of rotting wood dared to show itself here. This temple to God alone knew what sported an impressive collection of marble steps, columns, and sills; alabaster siding; ebony doors with gold hinges, knobs, and kick plates; and cut-crystal panes that admitted light but stymied the inquisitive.

Waiting for us at the final checkpoint was none other than my former Knights first-baseman starter, Burnham "Rocky" Thorpe.

---

† The term "rosary" dates to 1547 and was therefore unknown to Queen Morgan, though beaded strings were employed in her day as a focus for prayers by hermits, monks, nuns, and other clerics. —*kih*

Pray, forgive me the conceit that this Rocky Thorpe was "mine." I knew he was not, but even as the brain seeks to identify faces in an abstract wallpaper pattern, I hungered to find a friendly face in this leagues-from-friendly situation.

This Thorpe was a teammate of Boleyn, Percival, and Elton, and they greeted each other warmly. With McBain, however, he was all business: glaring and intractable.

"Let us pass," McBain growled. "I have important—"

"Sorry, sir. Closed judicial session today by order of the Lord Mayor," Thorpe said. "Come back next week."

"What are you talking about, Rocky?" asked Boleyn.

Percival elbowed him. "Ain't it obvious? Our Lord High ex-teammate ain't seeing street rabble." To Thorpe he said, "Join us for a pickup game after your shift?"

Thorpe displayed the first genuine grin I had seen since that awful moment when McBain replaced Sandy in my arms. "Sure! The lads inside may be up for it too. I'll ask on me break."

"I know his Lordship will want to speak to me about these prisoners," McBain insisted. "May we use a holding cell whilst I sort things with him?"

Thorpe gave a bored nod at the adjacent jail building, which was as squat and squalid as the courthouse was majestic and imposing. "Sort away, sir."

McBain thanked Thorpe. Next he barked orders to his men to escort us to the jail and then meet him inside the courthouse. As they led us away, I caught a glimpse of my once-and-should-be dead nemesis mounting the steps to enter the temple of justice.

Inside the jail's admittance area, Elton, Boleyn, and Percival signed us—that is to say, Clarice Centralia, "Morganna Hanks," and "Arthur Richards"—into the care of one of the jailers, who conducted us to a cell that featured three cement walls, bars across the front, a barred slit of a window high upon the rear wall, a narrow bed bolted to an adjacent wall, and a sink and open toilet in the opposite corner. Arthur yielded the bed

"COME BACK NEXT WEEK."

to Clarice and me whilst he claimed a spot near the window, back turned
to the wall of bars and looking outside as best he could, given the window's
angle. Then he flattened himself against the barred wall and craned his
neck for to see as far up and down the hallway as he could. Upon finding
no enlightenment there, he returned to the window to repeat the cycle.

That was my brother, always assessing the situation. He had given
plenty of attention to the jail's corridors and our jailer on our way to the cell.

Perhaps at this point, fair reader, you might be wondering how a
sixth-century king could acclimate to fifteen centuries of time travel and its
sundry differences with relative ease. My answer is simple: the technology
Sir Boss had introduced to our era—the telegraph, electricity, bicycles,
steam locomotives, mass-printed newspapers, projectile-firing weapons,

and so forth—was not far removed from what we were observing in this altered twenty-first century. Arthur had not been exposed to the same advancements I had, such as flying limos and hovering office buildings.

Clarice leaned her head close to mine. "When will you get us out of here?" she whispered.

"Are you daft, child?" Her hope crumpled to hurt. Grimacing, I gentled my voice. "Forgive me; I must confess this situation is…unsettling. I cannot manipulate a timeline about which I know nothing." Tears had begun to dot her lashes, wringing my heart. "Some of the people do seem familiar, though. I am unsure how this fact can help us, but do not lose hope." She gave me a brave nod. For all of our sakes, including Arthur's, I refrained from adding "yet."

Although I too had been whispering, Arthur turned and eased onto a knee beside where we sat upon the cot. "You can manipulate time?" The incredulity broke through the murmur's mask.

I bent close to him, dropping my voice lower still. "It is the means by which I came unto the twenty-first century from the sixth. My magic collided with the actions of another man—the man who tried to kill me in the parlay tent."

Arthur stood faster than any plated knight I had ever seen. "That warlock caused the battle!" He pivoted, took three paces to the wall, and smashed a metal-clad fist into it. Cement dust and shards littered the floor. "He caused me to draw Excalibur upon my own people." Arthur bowed his head until it touched the wall, his breathing loud and ragged. His fist began smacking his thigh, hard. "*I* started that Godforsaken battle. I started it…"

His gaze seemed to focus inward; his countenance, haunted. I could well imagine what he was seeing, for I had seen it many a time inside his mind during the eons I labored over his healing: the horizon-to-horizon carnage, the River Cam running red, the skies blackened by a legion of ravens, the cackling corpse robbers, the wailing wives and children…the latter two being an amalgam of scenes from previous wars, since he had lain too close to death to witness his final battle's aftermath. It made me wonder to what extent he was blaming himself for all of them. I said:

"Arthur, stop. Please." I rose, approached him, and touched his arm. His motion stilled, but he would not look at me. "I could have prevented Mordred from turning against you. That battle was as much my fault as his, Ambrose Hinton's, yours, or anyone's."

"You forget Launcelot and Guenever." Misery weighted his tone, the misery of love that knows it can never express itself to its beloved again. Misery I recognized well.

Though Launcelot had been but a fortnight's pleasant diversion, and Guenever meant even less to me, that did not prevent my heart from breaking for Arthur.

I tightened my grip upon his forearm. "Who knows what good I could have—should have wrought? If we debate these points for a year and a day, we shall stand no closer to an answer. Or a solution."

He sighed and put his back to the wall. "Regardless of how that day started or ended—or why—I would do it again to save your life, Morgan."

His admission humbled me beyond the ability to verbalize my thanks, and I bowed my head. In spite of my best efforts, tears slipped free. He tugged off a gauntlet to catch them upon my cheek with warm, gentle fingers. I marveled that so simple a touch could be so comforting. That was the nature of Arthur's magic, the ability to make the most unworthy of varlets feel valued.

Even me.

He lowered his hand, replaced the gauntlet, and said, "It saddens me that the battle seems to have obliterated all record of my reign."

I was about to question him about the uncharacteristic nature of his self-focused statement when Clarice perked her head. "Maybe not, sir. My search got an 'access restricted' message, not a 'no record found' one."

I added, "Access restricted by the pope, no less. I wonder…"

"Bishop Gildas?" Arthur asked.

"*I* STARTED THAT BATTLE."

CHAPTER VII.

"I did instruct him to write that an adder had triggered the battle, and I suggested that he did not see which knight had drawn first. I deemed the ambiguity might better serve your history." [†]

"I appreciate that, Morgan," Arthur said, "and if the Church's mediator had been anyone other than Gildas, your plan should have worked. Still…" He stroked his beard, his gaze intense but unfocused for a moment. "Bishop Gildas bore me no love for the deaths of his rebellious father and brothers, but he was not well connected. I cannot imagine how he could have grown powerful enough to have influenced Pope John II to suppress my chronicles."

"Some English bishop imposed an interdict," Clarice supplied, "but I didn't think to inquire who it was when I journeyed there in person, and Hank Morgan didn't name the man in his account of the events either. Could he have been your Gildas? Perhaps someone helped him grow his power base?"

I gave a long blink. "Almighty God, I hope not. Else I might not ever repair this timeline."

My prayer was interrupted by the sound of an object rapping our cell's bars. I looked up to see Percival, Elton, and Boleyn standing beside the jailer, who had tucked his baton under an armpit and was unlocking the door.

"Time to see what His Majesty wants to do with you lot," Elton said.

"His Majesty?" Arthur asked.

"Yeah, you're in luck." Boleyn waved us through the open cell door. "The court is in closed session for King Richard to pass judgment on some high-value prisoners. Seems you're to be lumped in with them."

"Some luck." Clarice glanced at me. "I don't suppose you have an eclipse spell prepared?"

An eclipse would never fool these people. I said: "Pray that I possess something better."

[†] Queen Morgan's description of her influencing Bishop Gildas regarding what to write about how the battle started comes from my screenplay adaptation of *King Arthur's Sister in Washington's Court*. —*kih*

CHAPTER VIII.
Holding Court.

MAZE of twisty passages, leading past cells too numerous to count, connected the jail facility to the courthouse. Here existed all manner of human detritus, from the mutely despondent to the robustly aggressive. In some instances, entire families had been incarcerated. Each inmate, regardless of age, looked overtired, underfed, and utterly devoid of hope.

Observing their conditions forced to mind the wretches I had consigned to oblivion in Castle Gore, and I fought down shudder after shudder. I could not help but wonder how many of these unfortunate souls had been imprisoned for no worse crime than calling some noble's glorious auburn hair "red."

The jailer cautioned us to keep to the centre of the corridor as he led us in single file, shepherded by McBain's guardsmen. Within moments, many inmates rushed to the bars, rattling them and shouting for food, drink, or clemency. The dispirited ones remained hunkered at the backs of their cells, hugging knees to chest and howling, moaning, weeping, or staring dumbstruck at the meaninglessness that had come to define their lives.

When Arthur strayed too close to one of the cells, its occupant tried to snag his armor. I could not fathom why. If the wretch had hoped to retain any piece he might have broken off, the guards would take it from him in a trice and slug him senseless for their trouble. Arthur sent me a beseeching gaze, in which I read his wish not to harm the prisoner and his hope that I could employ magic to diffuse the situation.

I twitched my head no. Our plight was precarious enough without the risk of being labeled religious abominations, if I was correct in my supposition about the extent of Church domination.

Magical intervention proved unnecessary. Percival shoved Arthur clear, smacked the inmate's knuckles with his baton, tucked it back underneath his arm, and shooed us on our way without sparing the instigator a second glance.

I did. The expression in the prisoner's eyes triggered a double-take. Belligerence yet resided there in abundance, but I saw something else: a strand of hope.

The question of why the prisoner's hope had arisen consumed my thoughts for the remainder of our journey through the dungeon maze. Was it something in Arthur's expression? His mode of dress? The fact that he had refrained from rebuffing the offender himself? Clarice had done naught but utter a gasp before Elton had hustled her to safety; had her sympathy influenced the prisoner? Or—unlikely as it seemed—had I somehow inspired the hopeful spark? By the time we were escorted into a vast, round, vaulted expanse identified as our destination, the judicial chambers, I stood no closer to an answer. I set aside the puzzle of the prisoner to concentrate upon our new environs.

The chamber, all marble and granite and gleaming brass and glossy mahogany wood, reminded me of the rotunda Arthur had built to house the Round Table. He might have been thinking the same thing, the way he craned his head about, slowly, as if ingesting the sheer opulence of it all. The wooden gallery of benches was similar to the one in Arthur's hall, encircling three-quarters of the building's perimeter save for wide aisles occurring at thirty-degree increments to allow visitors to find seats without being obliged to climb past too many of their peers. There the similarities ended, for it had been one of Arthur's greatest joys to sit amongst his knights. Inside this rotunda, a dais rising at least eight feet from the chamber's floor filled the perimeter's remaining quarter-arc. A carved, gilt throne, elevated several more feet, occupied the centre of the dais. The carving on its kick panel resembled the twenty-first century Great Seal of Britain, though the lettering of its motto seemed wrong. I risked a vision-enhancing spell that lasted just long enough to discover the wrongness's depth: Rather than *Dieu et Mon Droit*—French for "God and My Right"—the sentiment proclaimed *Son Droit*, "His Right." As I pondered whether "His" referred to God, the pope, or the king, the latter appeared via an upper-storey entrance concealed by the throne and claimed his place upon it with the efficiency and grace of long practice.

Lesser, though still imposing, chairs arced away from the throne's base. Armed guards stood at attention upon the steps leading up both sides of the dais and the throne's platform. The dais chairs and most of the gallery's benches were populated by men in black robes and white wigs. Closer scrutiny revealed a number of women amidst the robe-and-wig troupe. Even the throne's occupant sported similar regalia, though his robe was trimmed in gold. A smattering of attendees wore black cassocks, some featuring red trim, buttons, and sashes. Their skullcaps covered short-cropped, unbewigged hair; priests, I presumed. None of them were women.

The centre of the chamber, large enough to have fit the Round Table and a full complement of worthies and their retainers with space to spare, lay empty of furnishings, though one section of marble was marred by four triplets of holes drilled in a square configuration. Here two dozen prisoners, surrounded by three times as many guards, stood facing the throne. Even subdued by chains as thick as my arm, the prisoners exuded menace. Convicted murderers, perhaps.

Arthur, Clarice, and I were herded into the line. The prisoners regarded Arthur with undisguised rage (heaven alone knew why), and they leered at

CHAPTER VIII.

Clarice and me (everyone knew why). Our guards, snickering, withdrew to stand with their peers.

I cast a calming spell upon the convicts and hoped for the best.

If by now, astute reader, you might be thinking that I had perforce to cast a great many calming spells, you have indeed grasped the right of it.

One by one, the king passed sentence upon each prisoner. His voice sounded familiar, but standing at the back of the line put me at a disadvantage that my vision-enhancing spell remained powerless to reverse. No charges were read and no quarter was given; whatever these men had done had earned them death by electrocution, to occur on the morrow. After the sentence was pronounced and recorded, three guards stepped forward to escort each convict to await his doom.

Clarice was the only one of us who seemed appalled by the way these men's fates were being decided. For Arthur and myself, this style of judicial proceeding was nigh identical to the means by which we had upheld the rule of law in our respective kingdoms, although Arthur had been experimenting with jury trials during the latter days of his reign in the vain hope of keeping his adulterous wife clear of the executioner's pyre. Since I had suffered direct experience with the judicial system of the original twenty-first-century timeline, I wondered whether the papal ban on the details of Arthur's reign had aught to do with the lack of evolution in this timeline's application of justice.

When it became our turn, I thought that perhaps for the first time this day we had drawn a fortunate break. The Lord Mayor of London proved to be my former starting shortstop, Mark Sonoma, and the reigning monarch of England was the man who had recorded three saves for the Knights in the 2088 World Tournament, Rick "Bonny Baron" Boniface. A quick survey of the gallery, now that I was not distracted by ravening prisoners or the chamber's architecture, revealed many other men and women I could name—players, coaches, team office workers, groundskeepers, maintenance crew. McBain was sitting in the gallery too. Recalling yet again that these were not "my" people, I forced myself to make the mental shift, beginning with elevating Rick from Bonny Baron to King Richard.

Sonoma—sorry; *Lord Mayor* Sonoma—rose from his chair at the base of the throne's platform.

"What are you pulling, McBain? Some kind of publicity stunt with this knight, damsel, and, what, a PR woman? Solicitor? I told you our contract is firm. We shall not order one more bar of soap," Sonoma declared.

McBain, clad in a creased gallery robe and a wig that appeared as if a blind man had done him the favor of slinging it onto his head, stood and raised his right hand, palm outward and fingers rigid. "No stunt, Lord Mayor, I swear. One moment I was alone in me office. The next moment, I was kissing *her*, with these other two looking on." With his raised hand, he pointed first to me, and then to Arthur and Clarice, as if there might be another knight, damsel, and PR-woman-or-solicitor present. I knew I never should have hired that wattless bulb as GM.

Laughter rippled throughout the chamber. McBain blushed.

Sonoma grasped an ornate cane from beside his chair that I had not noticed earlier. To my surprise and growing concern, he used it to help him navigate the steps down from the dais. What weight he put on his left leg made him grit his teeth. The more steps he took, the angrier he appeared. By the time he reached us, I fancied that I could see steam billowing from his robe's neckline.

"His Majesty is not interested in your fantasies, McBain. Guards!"

McBain's guards joined the chamber guards hemming us. Deeming it less risky to explain what had actually transpired than attempting to fashion a falsehood, I raised a hand and said:

"Lord Mayor, Master McBain speaks the truth. Our truth is stranger still. One moment I was kissing my husband inside my office as owner of the London Knights baseball team. The next moment, the office, stadium, and grounds had transformed into Persimmon's Soap Factory."

Sonoma reared back, grinning. "McBain, you old dog! You never said anything about having a wife. A right dishy one too."

Whilst McBain spluttered an impotent denial, I said, "Ewan McBain was not—is not—never shall be my husband. I am married to Sandy Carter."

This round of laughter boomed loud and derisive.

King Richard said, "The late mayor of SDO Boston? Lady, that's the best jest I've heard in weeks!"

"Late—?" I felt my knees weaken and the blood drain from my face. Clarice slipped a hand beneath one of my elbows, and Arthur supported the other.

"Executed, three weeks ago," said the king. "If you were his wife, as you claim, you'd know that. And you'd know why."

I wanted to ask him but could not force out the words.

"Our queries got us 'access restricted' messages, Your Majesty," Clarice said.

"Alexander Leroy Carter murdered Ira Desmorel, the mayor of SDO Baltimore, over a gambling dispute." The king's tone was not unkind, but I derived no comfort from it.

"Oh-h-h-h, Sandy…" Yes, my whisper required every hyphen and ellipsis. Thank you for noticing.

The news confirmed what my heart had been bleating at me since the first moment this weird time slippage had occurred. Before, whenever Sandy and I had endured estrangement, I could sense his presence wherever in the world he had gone. It had gifted me with the assurance that he would always return to me, even when our separation stretched into weeks and months.

Now I felt numb, hollow, forlorn; as if the greatest love of my life—all of my lives—had never existed.

"I am so sorry, Morgan," Arthur murmured, his fingers contracting upon my arm in a sympathetic echo. His gauntlet pinched my skin a bit. No sensation registered beyond the agony of my shattered heart.

The queenship rules have never needed to address bad posture, it being job number one of every royal's nanny and tutor to pummel those habits out of their charges; but at that moment, I would not have cared if the Royal Rules Committee had classified it a capital offense. As I slumped against my brother, Clarice stepped forward and curtsied. "Your Majesty, have I leave to state our case?"

"I FELT NUMB, HOLLOW, FORLORN."

"Please." King Richard gave an inviting wave at odds with his tone. "I could not have commanded better entertainment than this."

"We come from a different timeline, Your Majesty, one in which Queen—"

"Morganna Hanks," I said.

Clarice nodded her apology at me and regarded the king. "—Morganna Hanks knew many of you as world-class baseball players. Some of you played for her team. Others played for opposing teams. I am her friend. Our companion is Ar—"

I straightened, flicked my fingers to halt Clarice's word-mill and to banish all trace of my distress, stepped away from Arthur, and craned my neck up at King Richard. The moniker "Arthur Richards" of a sudden seemed an unfortunate choice, so instead I said, "This man is our bodyguard. He is of no consequence. If you consent to release us, upon my honor we shall not trouble you again."

"No trouble at all. I look forward to seeing you again, tomorrow." The king grinned. "Prior to your execution."

Small metallic creaks heralded the commencement of Arthur's bristling. I flashed him a "stand down" hand signal without looking at him and said to King Richard, "On what charge, Your Majesty?"

"I don't like you three. That's all the charge I need." King Richard's grin soured to a sneer. "Sonoma, lock them up with that other lunatic McBain found at his factory last week." He pointed at Arthur. "And have someone pry that one out of his tin can before he hurts somebody."

"As you will, my liege," Sonoma said. He beckoned to the guards and then went back to leaning upon his cane, trying hard to look imposing in spite of the pain.

I gave Arthur a short shoulder rub that, in spite of the armor and padding layers, I hoped would reassure him. Whether it did or not, he allowed the men to strip him down to his quilted undertunic and leather breeches.

Sonoma's misery spawned an idea. I tried to sidle closer to him, but one of the guards, a man I had known in my second lifetime as one of my starting pitchers, blocked the way. Rather than address Cody "Codfish" Haddock, however, I said to the Lord Mayor, "The Mark Sonoma of my acquaintance was a world-class shortstop who injured his knee making a play in a post-season game last year. He underwent surgery to correct the damage, and he returned to the field. I infer that you have not."

The Lord Mayor's gaze filled with memories. A magical nudge revealed in my mind the game he was recalling. "I dived for a screaming grounder, made the play to win the game…" He glared at me as if his injury was my fault. Perhaps, in some weird way, it was. "Every physician I've seen insists that my base ball days are done." I saw snatches of those memories too.

"If you disagree with them, visit my cell to-night," I said.

His critical glare became tempered by a spark of hope. "Lady, what can you possibly accomplish—"

"She brought me back from the dead," Arthur stated.

I have never wanted to kill him more so than in that moment. I flashed him a murderous smile. "He exaggerates, of course," I said. "Besides, ligaments are not as difficult to repair as skull bones and brain tissue."

"Brain tissue!" The Lord Mayor's hope spark died. "McBain was right. You are a flock of raving lunatics."

Sonoma ordered his guards to escort us back to the jail. My hope spark died too.

CHAPTER IX.
OLD BRAD.

RESSED IN naught but woven plant fibers and tanned animal hides as we quick-marched amongst our guards back into the jail's maze, Arthur looked far less comfortable than I had ever seen him, even when he had sprawled, dying, in the dirt. A proud burden, he had called armor in those days, and it was an apt label. Stripped of that aspect of his identity, the slope of his shoulders and creases on his brow proclaimed his anguish and confusion about how to fight this new battle—or even whether he *could* fight it. He never had been one to collapse into a dithering puddle upon encountering a monumental setback, but I would not have thought less of him had he chosen this moment to make an exception.

It had felt thus for me during the early days of my second lifetime. The royal circlet I had been wearing during my first bout with time travel—not my sumptuous crown of state, which had been locked in Castle Gore's treasure vault—had proven an invaluable lifeline to my identity and my sanity. Arthur, sans Excalibur and now sans armor, including his crown-encircled helmet, did not even possess that much. I yearned to conjure a circlet for him but dared not do so until I could learn more about this Godforsaken world.

I could not speak for Clarice, who seemed honor-bound to keep pace with the guards in spite of her gown's swishy, bulky limitations, but I must confess that I stood upon the brink of collapsing into a dithering puddle myself…had already done so, counting that display in King Richard's courtroom.

I twined my arm with Arthur's. His startled look melted into an appreciative smile. He patted my hand, gave a brisk nod, and tugged me along.

We reached the appointed cell without incident, and all but one of the guards withdrew. The remaining guard found the correct key, played out the retractable line attached to his belt so he could reach the lock without being obliged to hump it, and opened the door.

An ancient, red-robed lump was sitting hunched over, his silvered, red-capped head cradled in gnarled, liver-spotted hands, upon the cell's bench.

"Here's your new cellmate," Haddock announced to us. "Calls himself Ratcliffe. Cardinal Ratcliffe, if you can believe it. There's no Vatican record of him."

The name mocked my memory's fringes, but I failed to dredge a reference. The bench's occupant refused to acknowledge anyone's existence.

Haddock ordered Arthur, Clarice, and me into the cell and locked the door behind us. I left Clarice to approach the lump, cautiously, as if she were stalking a unicorn, and I turned my attention upon the guard.

"Enjoy your pickup game, Codfish," I said with a wink.

Haddock seemed on the verge of thanking me until my knowledge of his nickname made him stare agape. He clopped his mouth shut, shook his head, gave us a dismissive wave, turned, and departed.

By this time, Clarice was standing so close to the lump on the bench that it could have fondled her had it been of such a mind. "Ratcliffe," she said. The lump did not move. "Brad Ratcliffe?"

He raised his head, and his chapped lips twisted into a grin. "None other," he said.

His eyes were red-rimmed and bleary, his hair was gray (upon second evaluation, I deemed "silver" too generous a label) and all but gone, his flesh sagged in copious folds as if it were trying to escape his bones, and his teeth were long and yellow,—but an unpleasant memory revived. It had been years since I had thought of the odious toad, to say naught of associating with him. The man leering up at me seemed far closer to the age of his father, but there could be no mistaking the arrogance of his petty little tin-plated countenance.

Clarice said, "But you're so—so—"

Had the grin widened any further, his skull would have split. "What, distinguished? Spiritual?"

"Ancient!" she squeaked, and slapped a hand over her mouth.

Her rudeness did not appear to faze him, though I gave her a silent reprimand.

"How observant, Clarice Centralia. And Morganna Hanks, a pleasure to renew your acquaintance as well." He regarded Arthur for a long moment. "That would make you, sir, the great—"

"Be silent," I snapped. The toad had no choice but to obey the magical injunction. I surveyed the ceiling, located the security camera, and disabled it with a thought. Upon reconsidering, I modified the spell, and not for Ratcliffe's benefit. He knew the nature if perhaps not the extent of my powers.

"That will bring attention faster than opening the ballpark gates on Free Beer Friday," Clarice cautioned.

I appreciated her reference to one of the more pleasant memories of our previous life, but I judged it safer not to acknowledge it. "They can see us," I said, "but they shall believe we are speaking Russian. With luck, there shall be no one to translate."

Clarice grimaced. "Are you certain you want to trust to luck? That hasn't been in great supply for us."

Fair point.

Arthur gave me his harry-till-the-prisoner-cracks stare. "Why did you conceal my identity just now and earlier, from that king?"

"Your identity tripped an alarm at the factory," I reminded him. "We cannot proceed till we know why."

"I can tell you why," Ratcliffe said, "if you promise to deliver me from this hellhole."

My apprentice scoffed. "Your Majesty, you cannot consider—"

I silenced her with an eyebrow set to stun. To old Brad I said, "You have yourself a deal. What did you do to our timeline?" I needed answers before attempting to enlist his support to undo the damage.

"Very good, Ms. Hanks." His chuckle was a raspy whine with all the pleasantness of nails on a chalkboard. "But of course Ms. Centralia helped me."

"What? No! I couldn't possibly have!" From the panic in her eyes, I deduced that she feared I might choose to increase my eyebrow's potency and fry her dead on the spot.

I patted her shoulder. "I believe he means that impressive curse you laid upon him, dear, the day Ambrose fired him and I took over as President Malory's campaign boss." Clarice's panic subsided. I returned my attention to old Brad. "A curse you deserved, as terribly as you treated the men and women serving under you. You still deserve it, by the look of things. Pray, continue."

"It started the night of game seven of the 2088 World Tournament," Ratcliffe said.

Game seven! In a blink, I relived the night in all its terrifying, exhilarating detail: the Knights' initial lead of four runs, Connecticut delivering seven unanswered runs to threaten a third blowout, their starting shortstop suffering a critical injury and my freezing time so I could heal him without the world being any the wiser, the Knights making up the run deficit and pulling ahead but Connecticut answering to tie the game, followed by the walk-off homer delivered by my second-baseman to end the game and the tournament. And then the very private and oh so very satisfying after-party Sandy and I enjoyed…

I gave Ratcliffe a quizzical look. "London won, we celebrated, and Connecticut went home." Camelot's shortstop crossed his arms, his expression crosser still. I promised to tell Arthur about those games another time, play by play, and he brightened.

"Right," Ratcliffe said, "but it wasn't supposed to end that way. Ambrose had planned to confront you that night, but your security detail was too efficient. They wouldn't let him through." Of course, they had not; I had trained them well. The old toad puffed his chest. "When he finally got the opportunity to see you three years later, he brought me to London with him. During your meeting, I was waiting outside your office with his spare time-folding device and orders to go after him if he didn't return at the expected time."

"Ambrose?" Arthur asked.

"The 'wizard' you killed," I said.

Ratcliffe nodded as if the news had come as no surprise. "That confirms my hunch. The only thing I learned about his fate was how tricky time-folding that far into the past can be. By the time I arrived, everyone of importance was dead or missing"—he pointed a nod first at Arthur and then at me—"and nobody could claim to have seen a man matching Ambrose's description."

"Excalibur still bears the stench of his entrails," Arthur informed him.

I coughed to mask the laugh; buried in fifteen centuries of lake silt, Excalibur would be smelling more like fish dung.

Ratcliffe bowed his head. "I suspected that too, sir," he murmured. His gaze rebounded and hardened, glaring at no one but Arthur. "I found Bishop Gildas and helped him win the Battle of the Sand Belt. That victory was the key to getting him and his Church cronies to trust me."

Arthur's eyes narrowed. "Battle of the Sand Belt?"

CHAPTER IX.

"A battle fought after your"—saying "death" would have felt too unsettling for me, never mind how it would have been perceived by Arthur—"disappearance that the Yankee should have won."

"The reversal ensconced the Church as you see it today," bragged old Brad. "From my research, I knew that I could avenge Ambrose if I convinced Gildas to keep your legend from being born by suppressing the memory of your reign,—though a lone copy of the stories exists in the Papal Secret Book."

"What, like the Presidential Secret Book in the *National Treasure* sequel?" Clarice asked. Old Brad grinned.

"The convincing would not have been difficult," Arthur conceded, "but I cannot imagine how Gildas could have gained the pope's ear. He was a low-ranking bishop serving in a backwater kingdom, as far as Rome was concerned." Bitterness invaded my brother's tone; his run-in with Rome over the Launcelot-Guenever debacle had to be feeling as if it had occurred just the other day. I stroked his shoulder. He shrugged my hand off.

"That's where I came in," said old Brad. "I parlayed my twenty-first-century knowledge into becoming a nobleman of note without falling into the same trap as my nineteenth-century counterpart, Hank Morgan, did. I had no interest in governing, just in helping Gildas rise to prominence within the Church. From Bishop of Camelot to Archbishop of Canterbury, to cardinal, thence to Rome and the Throne of Peter. It took decades." Ratcliffe pulled at his cassock. "But it was not without its benefits."

"Popemaker." I did not bother to bleed the disgust from my tone.

"His Holiness was so grateful, he ordained me, made me a cardinal, and kept me as his special assistant for another twenty years. I have to say, I found the papal intrigue quite fascinating."

Clarice, who had been watching Ratcliffe with emotions oscillating between curiosity and contempt, said, "Why wait so long to return? For that matter, if you liked your job so much, why return at all?"

"Because, dear girl, when kingmaking and assassinations and land acquisitions become old hat, it's time to move on."

"Horse dung," I said. "You wanted to see how you had affected the timeline."

"Guilty, Mother Confessor."

"Not what you'd bargained for, was it?" Clarice said.

Ratcliffe rasped a laugh. "You'd be astounded at how much morality and law had hung upon Arthur's 'might for right' ideal. Without it, societies across the globe never progressed out of the feudal, every-lord-for-himself mindset, which evolved into this 'sanctuary district' governing structure. Joffrey Baratheon's exploits were child's play in comparison."

"Joffrey—?" Arthur began.

I said, "No one you would have ever wanted at the Round Table." Clarice added a vigorous nod. I returned my attention to old Brad. "The Church's teachings—love, forgiveness, obedience—surely that had to hold some sway."

"You would have thought," Ratcliffe said, "but Church corruption progressed at lightning speed. Men like Martin Luther were born, sure, but they were eliminated before their ideas could take root in peoples' hearts and minds. The faithful pay for indulgences; all sacraments, including communion and last rites; and to bribe the clergy to pray their dearly departed into heaven. The Magna Carta never was drafted. The United Kingdom doesn't exist. And America—ha, well, at best it's a conglomerate of mutually distrustful sanctuary districts that unite when needed to combat a common threat. Communications and transportation are locked down tight by Presiders, so that level of threat doesn't occur often."

Clarice voiced the thought that had blared in my mind: "You sound proud of it all!"

"And why not? You have to admit it was a pretty impressive accomp—"

I had heard all the self-satisfied croaking I could stomach. Any hope I might have held of Ratcliffe helping us restore the timeline evaporated. I hit him with a suffocating spell without bothering to employ the Darth Vader finger-squeeze schtick. Ratcliffe clawed at his throat. I debated how long to let him gasp before ending him. I said:

"You accomplished the murther of my husband, the one man I ever loved in my entire life—all sixteen-hundred-plus years of it! And God knows whatever millions of atrocities besides. The deaths of innocents, and the good people who were never born as a result. The suppression of intellectual, spiritual, and economic advancement." I wanted to go on, but rage constricted my throat even as I was constricting Ratcliffe's.

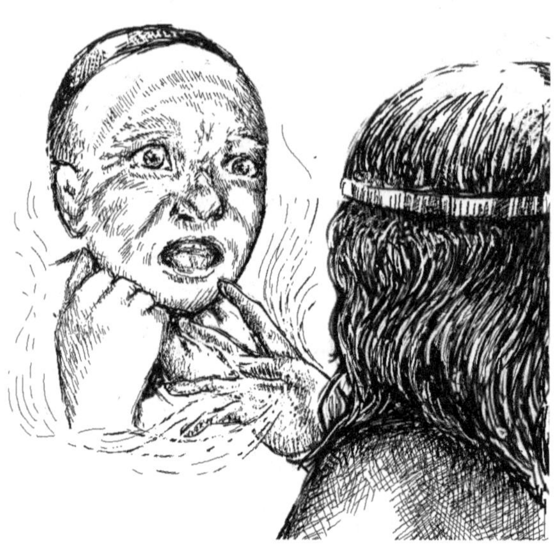

"I DEBATED HOW LONG TO LET HIM GASP."

Clarice gripped my forearm and gazed into my eyes. "Your Majesty, killing Ratcliffe won't bring your husband back."

Of course, I knew that. But someone had to pay. Absent Gildas, Ratcliffe was the next logical target.

I raised my right hand. Sparks arced between my splayed fingertips. Still gasping and clutching his throat, Ratcliffe shrank back, encountered the cell's wall, and looked so very pathetic as he flattened himself against the cement, as if attempting to ooze into its pocks and cracks.

"I shall avenge Sandy. Our captors shall be next. And then everyone who had a hand in Sandy's death." Never had I felt my resolve run so cold, so certain. So dangerous.

A gentle hand came to rest upon my shoulder.

Arthur's.

As his energy flowed into me, I felt my rage ebb. I clung to the rage, feeding it, willing it to grow again.

"Morgan…"

I glared at Ratcliffe as I addressed Arthur: "Here is where you are going to command me to let this odious toad live."

"In the parlay tent I believed you were a changed woman." His tone sounded sad but kind. "I still believe it."

I closed my eyes to trap the welling tears, lowered my hand, and released the spell.

Ratcliffe gasped awhile longer before he recovered breath enough to blurt, "You Goddamned bitch! We had a deal!"

Folding my arms, I clucked my tongue. "Such language from a man of the cloth. I shall indeed honor our deal. But not on your account." I glanced at Arthur, who withdrew his hand from my shoulder. In Scottish Gaelic I commanded Ratcliffe to sleep…forever.

Old Brad yawned, stretched, and pivoted to lie upon the bench. He was snoring within moments. The drooling commenced not long after that.

"We needed more information from him, did we not?" Arthur said.

"What we need is locked in the Vatican," I declared.

"That secret book he mentioned?"

"La, heavens, no. We know our stories, dear brother. What we do not know is how the Church mucked with our era to cause them to be forgotten."

Clarice gave Ratcliffe a worried look. "Won't someone be able to rouse him?"

"Not with this spell in force," I said. "And trust me, there is no enjoyment in executing a sleeping prisoner." I did not bother to state the obvious: he would perish from lack of food and drink. Clarice was smart enough to solve that equation herself. By the sympathetic cast to her features, it appeared that she had.

"Morgan…" So had Arthur.

"Yes, my liege." Suppressing a sigh, I waved a hand over the drooling, snoring lump, modulating the spell. "His bodily needs will wake him when necessary."

Arthur rolled his eyes. He could get away with it. In the next breath, his expression sobered. "What happens to him if we repair the damage he has wrought?"

I did not chide him for the *if* either; I harbored similar doubts myself.

"Let us call it a creative way of delivering upon my promise."

The sound of a cane accompanying a limping tread, alongside a set of footsteps that sounded far more purposeful, attracted my attention. I sent Clarice to the bars to confirm my guess. She looked back at me and nodded.

Within moments, Mark Sonoma hove into view, led by the guard Shane Edgars, a relief pitcher and my first acquisition as Knights owner following the shameful four-straight-game loss to Connecticut in the 2080 World Tournament. Edgars unlocked the cell for Sonoma to enter, locked him in with us, and remained on duty in the corridor.

Supported by his cane, Sonoma faced me. In spite of his infirmity, his pose reeked of arrogance. "You claimed you could heal me, woman. So, get to it."

Arthur knotted his fists. "This *lady* is a queen…ly model to all ladies of every station." Silently I applauded his recovery from what could have been a most awkward gaffe. "I suggest you treat her with more deference."

Edgars drew his pistol. Arthur began to advance.

I raised a hand and impaled Arthur with my glare. "Hold, Wart." My use of his childhood nickname, from a time when I had outranked him by being older, produced the desired effect. He desisted in midsurge.

Edgars kept his weapon trained upon my brother, though more for intimidation than in the hope that he could hit his mark through the cell's bars without hitting any of the rest of us.

"Please forgive my bodyguard's zeal, Lord Mayor." I gave Sonoma a shrewd appraisal. "But without the patient's faith, I can do nothing."

Sonoma signaled Edgars to holster his weapon. Arthur returned to my side. Sonoma's arrogance dissipated with his sigh. I heard Clarice release a relieved sigh too. I checked my sigh; Arthur had come within a gnat's eyelash of identifying me as a queen, a fact which could further complicate our lives.

To stave off that nagging concern, I approached within touching distance of Sonoma and, with his consent, I began massaging his neck and shoulders.

"I'm sorry, Madame Hanks. I've spent thousands, and nothing has worked."

"Tell me," I said, less for the information itself than to distract him from what I was doing.

A picture emerged of his past eighteen months, a nightmare of surgeries, follow-up examinations, physical therapy, and drugs, punctuated by brief attempts to return to the playing field only to have the knee buckle and hurt worse than before. I let Clarice prompt him whenever his story faltered; I kept circling round him, humming softly, always touching some part of him, focusing my energies, my thoughts, and my prayers till at last I came to be kneeling beside him, both hands covering the injured knee.

The energy flow surged. He jerked back with a gasp.

I gazed up at him. "Trust me, Mark."

"I do want to play again," he said, "more than you know!"

I smiled; he was ever so much like the Mark Sonoma of my acquaintance. "I have an inkling."

He stepped to within reach. I bowed my head, flexed my fingers against his knee, and intensified my song.

He gave an agonized groan. "What are you doing?!"

Edgars hovered his hand over his pistol's grip.

I sent the ligaments one final energy burst, released Sonoma's knee, and rose. Whilst he gasped through the pain, I snatched his cane and retreated to the back of the cell.

"Hey! I need that!"

"Come get it, then." I gave the prop an inviting wiggle.

CHAPTER IX.

Determination creased his features, and he took a tentative step. The knee held, of course, but his stride faltered as he closed upon me. He lunged for the cane. I relinquished it and helped him to right his stance.

"It didn't work." He turned away with an abrupt, angry movement and ordered Edgars to unlock the cell. "As I expected."

Edgars obeyed. Before Sonoma could step through, I asked him how much pain he was experiencing.

He stopped but did not face me. "Actually…" His head cocked a bit, first to one side then the other. "There isn't any. First time since the incident."

"I repaired the ligaments, but strengthening the muscles is your task," I informed him. "Or you may choose to rely upon your crutch till the end of your days."

The Lord Mayor of London and former star shortstop flinched his shoulders and departed without looking back. The sound of two sets of footfalls, and the clack of the cane, faded down the corridor into nothingness.

CHAPTER X.
Young Sarah.

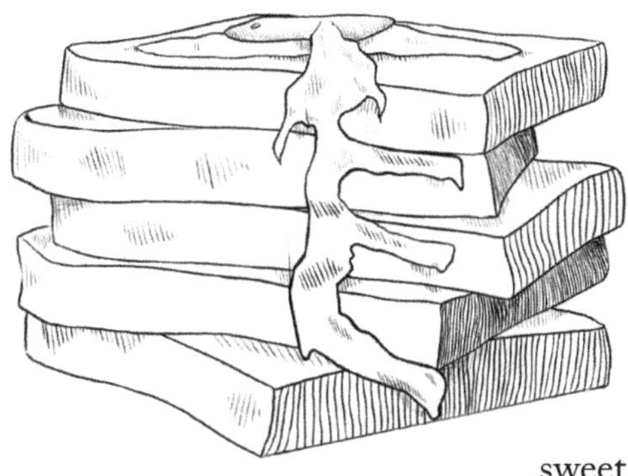

ARLY THE next morning, after we had choked down a meal of crunchy eggs atop runny toast (do smooth that scrunch in your face, sweet reader; I am not exaggerating, and no magic of mine could have made that food the slightest degree palatable), Edgars ushered us into the judicial chamber. Its gallery was packed to nigh bursting. The lone empty seat upon the lower dais, the Lord Mayor's, I expected to become filled soon enough. Edgars parked us in the centre of the floor's expanse, facing the throne.

Two major details struck me as being different.

A second chair, every handspan as ornate as the throne, had been placed on the upper dais. The man occupying this seat, whose mode of dress prompted my mental shift from his familiar nickname of "Deacon" to cardinal, I had known as one of my best starting pitchers. He also had served as the team's unofficial chaplain; hence the nickname, which his teammates always had uttered with highest reverence. Given Ratcliffe's description of present-day America, I presumed that this Vermont Lawson bore a different Christian name, but my chances to verify this theory fell upon the spectrum in that vast expanse between slim and none.

CHAPTER X.

That the king was obliged to share centre stage with a ranking member of the Church for executions came as no surprise; it had been a requirement when Arthur and I had ruled too.

"Remind me to stop wondering what it would be like to reinstate public executions," muttered Clarice beside me, tossing a nervous glance past her right shoulder.

She was referring to the second major change that had been wrought overnight within this chamber. The collection of holes I had noticed the day before had been eclipsed by a massive metal chair. Wire ropes as thick as Arthur's biceps snaked from the chair, across the floor, up and across the dais, and on up some more to the control box bolted to the armrest of King Richard's throne.

A pair of white-uniformed men were wheeling away a gurney bearing the shrouded remains of the chair's latest occupant. The men's panting suggested this was not their first trip of the day. A veritable Siege Perilous, indeed. I clenched my fists to still the shudder that threatened to sweep through me. Clarice and Arthur appeared to be waging similar battles.

The fingers of King Richard's closest hand drummed in a steady, deliberate, nonstop rhythm.

"Silence, prisoner," ordered King Richard. Clarice had stopped talking several seconds ago, but whatever. She bowed her head. "Guards, strap in her companion, Master Tin Man."

As Edgars and several other men-who-were-not-my-Knights rushed to grasp Arthur's arms, drag him to the chair, and force him to sit, I reached a decision and strode forward. "Is Your Majesty so eager to commit regicide, then?"

"Him?" King Richard barked a laugh. "You're better than a truckload of jesters, woman. We know you and your associates are spies from SDO Moscow."

"Ah. You translated the tape of the security footage from our cell," I said.

"The Lord Mayor is handling that detail." The king's fingers drummed faster and louder. "He'd better get here soon."

My thought too, although I suspected that voicing it would buy us more trouble than any of us could afford.

Whilst I formulated an appropriate retort, the far doors banged open. Mark Sonoma stood framed upon the threshold, again dressed in his ceremonial regalia but this time without his cane.

"Your Majesty," Sonoma said, pitching his voice to carry across the chamber, "I suggest that you review this report before you act."

"Approach." King Richard twitched his shoulders like a grumpy peacock in molt. "But I don't have all day to waste." Sonoma bowed, stampeded across the distance as if attempting to catch a departing commuter train, and took the dais stairs in leaping bounds all the way to the top, prompting gasps and murmurs to sweep through the gallery. Even Clarice uttered a pleased grunt. "Well, well," said the king. "Does this miracle mean I have my prized shortstop back?"

"I hope so, my liege. And it was indeed a miracle"—he favored me with a stately nod—"that Morganna Hanks wrought."

I returned the gesture. "I am honored to be of service, Lord Mayor."

"Silence, woman." If the king confused my having nothing further to say with obedience, that was his problem. To Sonoma he said, "Why would a Muscovite spy bother to help you? The better question is…how?"

"How, I don't know. But they're not foreign spies. Security found a device inside the camera that caused the audio to translate into Russian."

At that moment, something transpired that I had experienced just once before, in my original life. The ancient me had received a vision of Arthur's fatal battle, goading me to seek him out, for in those days I had been, quite literally, hell-bent to exact my revenge upon him for our decades of unresolved strife. That waking vision, my gut informed me with a painful twist, had been the catalyst for my misadventures through time.

As I descended into the vision-induced trance, the pain receded.

The trance gave Sonoma's voice a distant, artificial quality. "Lip-reading confirmed that they were speaking English…about changes to a timeline that, perhaps, had been better than ours."

"Balderdash!" thundered the king. "They bamboozled you into believing their nonsense. Now, if you will excuse me, Lord Mayor, I have today's final batch of prisoners to dispose of."

I broke the trance with a shake of my head.

"Your Majesty, wait. Please." My use of that magic word commanded King Richard's full attention. Whilst the vision's myriad details yet swirled in my mind's eye, the single most important fact was, "Your daughter is dying." And the fact most important to this timeline's three unwitting visitors: "I can save her."

He pounded his fist on the armrest. "I'm sure you can. Just as I'm sure this is another load of balderdash."

Sonoma said, "Your Majesty, you saw me move. My healed knee is not 'balderdash.'"

King Richard gave him a dismissive wave. As his hand descended upon the controls, I contemplated my options. None seemed promising.

The royal bodyguard posted upon the top step snapped hand to ear. After a few heartbeats, he hastened forward to whisper something into the royal ear. King Richard reared back, stood, and pointed at me. "Bring Hanks. Her companions stay put. If she fails—or if this proves to be some sick ruse—she can watch them both fry." He yanked off his wig, shied it into a corner (prompting a guard to hustle after it), and disappeared through the upper door.

The scant moment I was given to make eye contact with Arthur and Clarice was nowhere near enough time to ascertain whether they had been comforted by my assuring nod.

If I had thought to become better acquainted with the affluent stratum of this version of London, those hopes proved futile as I was hustled with King Richard amidst a dense knot of guards from the judicial chamber to a private parking facility for his black-windowed ground crawler. Two guards climbed in with the king and me whilst another pair piled into the driving compartment and the rest of their peers mounted a fleet of what could best be described as motorcycles, though far less elegant than those I had seen in the other timeline, rather like the sleek vehicles' poor country cousins.

The poor country cousins, however, managed to keep pace with our automobile; I could tell by the engine noises and fossil fuel fumes, the latter prompting me to invoke an air purification spell. I could have seen outside with the aid of magic, of course, but I forced my curiosity into the backseat behind trying to establish a rapport with the man who looked more like every other frightened parent to walk this earth than the sovereign of a major realm.

My attempts to draw him out of his worried state, either by gentle words or by the discreet application of magic, failed. For the entire journey to the palace, he sat saying nothing, staring at nothing, wrapped in his gold-embroidered black velvet cloak as if it could shield him from the horror of losing his precious baby girl. In spite of the fact that Arthur's, Clarice's and my fates hinged upon my performance, my heart went out to him. I have endured my fair share of cloak-huddling too, with a view no less terrifying than his must have been.

In due course we arrived at the palace's private car park, disembarked, and hurried past legions of guards and servants so fast that I had no time to note the details of our surroundings or its populace beyond the single unifying fact that everyone, to the last greasy garage varlet and overburdened chamber maid, exhibited more worry lines across their foreheads and around their mouths than I had believed humanly possible.

I had a better opportunity to inventory the royal nursery's gilt furniture, plush carpets, pillows, and quilts, and the plentiful array of toys as the resident's father approached what appeared to be the lead physician. The girl, no more than five, lay pallid and unmoving upon the large, canopied bed whilst a servant finished mopping a section of floor near the princess's head and another servant placed an empty bucket upon the spot.

The acrid scent of disinfectant failed to mask the vomit's stench.

"Where is Queen Catherine?" demanded the king.

CHAPTER X.

The physician, a small but vigorous, silver-haired man with an intelligent glint and a brisk manner, rose from his seat beside the bed and bowed to his liege. "Her Majesty collapsed from distress. Doctor Sykora attends her in her chambers." His accent bore a pleasing Spanish lilt.

"Thank you, Doctor Jusay." King Richard gave a thoughtful nod, as if his wife collapsed every day. Given their daughter's plight, I would have been more surprised if she did not. "And Princess Sarah's condition?"

Bowing his head, Doctor Jusay puffed out a sigh. "I have done all I can, Your Majesty."

No doubt. Princess Sarah would need a miracle, and those of his profession did not trade in supernatural currency.

I swept past the physician without so much as a by-thy-leave and knelt beside the girl. Doctor Jusay spluttered a protest, but the king commanded him to desist. 'Twas no endorsement, but I possessed neither the time nor the desire to coddle my vanity. I grasped Sarah's hand and began to sing softly, soothingly. Contact with the princess confirmed what I had suspected: legions of cancerous cells had invaded her bloodstream. I imbued my spell-song with the ability to locate and reverse the rogue cells' mutations, and I sang it as if to-morrow would never come.

I tried not to dwell upon the disturbing fact that if I failed here, to-morrow would not come for this poor wee waif, Clarice, Arthur, or me.

"Somehow, she managed to get Sonoma capering like a gazelle," King Richard murmured to the physician. I could not afford the risk of breaking contact with the princess to gauge Doctor Jusay's reaction, though I heard it in his surprised grunt. "I'm hoping she can do the same for my Sarah."

To state that I was, too, would be like stating that cancer was a disease.

Her hand began warming within mine, and I willed as much energy into her failing little body as I believed it could handle. Sensing a mote of progress, and deciding that the risk of failure trumped the risk of overload, I redoubled my efforts.

"Princess Sarah's blood disorder has reached the critical stage," whispered Doctor Jusay. "All we can do now is ease her suffering."

"Is there no hope?" the king whispered back.

I interrupted my concentration long enough to look up, catch the royal gaze, and say, "There is always hope."

"Madame," began the physician, his tone ramping to severe, "you cannot just march in here and—"

The princess, though still unconscious, gripped my hand. I smiled, rose, delivered a final surge of energy with my return squeeze, and turned so the men could see what I already knew. Her father gasped, no doubt realizing that she looked far less pale than before. I lifted the little hand and beckoned the physician closer.

"Have you a device that reveals the mysteries hidden in the blood?" I asked.

"Of course," he said, his tone thawing a mite in spite of itself.

"THERE IS ALWAYS HOPE."

CHAPTER X.

In fact, I had noticed—and identified—the medical equipment upon entering the chamber, but I let the good doctor direct my attention with a sweep of his arm at a table laden with a microscope, centrifuge, slides, tubes, and a desktop computer that appeared to be at least three generations younger than its ancestor serving the soap factory. Magic may be my favorite area of expertise, but spending nigh onto a decade inhabiting the other twenty-first century had gifted me with a passing fair knowledge of the scientific arts, with a particular interest in the sciences related to healing.

"You may take me at my word that the princess's blood flows hale once again," I said, "but please do test it yourself."

Whereupon Doctor Jusay commanded a nurse to bring him a needle, slide, and specimen cover. When he pricked Sarah's finger to collect a sample, she woke with a whimper. I bent down, smiling, to stroke the girl's hair.

She smiled back at me, turned her head to gaze across the nursery, and uttered the single most blessed word any father ever wants to hear: "Daddy?"

The king rushed to gather her into his arms. I gladly moved aside and used the distraction to blink back my relieved tears. "I'm here, darling!" He did not leave a single spot upon her face or head unkissed. Her giggles sounded weak yet, but I would have wagered my crown of state that it had been many a day since the last time she had uttered such an endearing sound.

"Where's Mommy?" she said between her father's kisses.

The king glanced up and nodded at a servant, who returned his nod with a fist-to-chest salute and dashed from the nursery. "She will be here soon, sweetkins, I promise."

At the lab table, the physician spun upon his stool to regard us. "The woman's assessment is correct, Your Majesty. I do not know how she did it, but I see no evidence whatsoever of Princess Sarah's cancer." The nurse attracted his attention by presenting a fistful of papers the printer had finished disgorging. He perused the documents, his eyes widening by the second. "Praise God, Jesus, Mary, and all the saints! Even the cancer blood markers are gone." Doctor Jusay fixed his gaze upon me. I had not seen such reverence in any person's eyes since the day my first husband, King Uriens, presented me to the people of Gore as his bride…before I unleashed my powers upon them for to establish my control, thereby warping their reverential awe into dread, and thence, upon repeated cruel demonstrations, into outright fear.

Those choices number high upon my list of regrets.

This day, the doctor's reverence humbled me to the point where I could do naught but give him the briefest smile and nod.

Amidst the expressions of relief and gratitude made by King Richard and the attending servants, Sarah looked up at me and beamed. "Daddy, who is this nice lady?"

The king gave me a frank look. "Someone who has earned any reward within my power to bestow."

I might have begun enumerating my requests, but the queen entered just then, gave a joyous squeal, and beelined for her daughter to begin the hugging and kissing routine all over again, which the dear little girl did not seem to mind in the least.

Close upon Her Majesty's heels rushed a handsome, dark-haired man in a lab coat whom I presumed to be her attending physician, Dr. Sykora. He beelined for his colleague, who updated him on the princess's condition with far more excitement than I believed that breed could ever possess. Dr. Sykora refrained from sharing Dr. Jusay's elation until he had scrutinized the test results for himself…and after his skepticism transformed into unabashed wonder. I had not blushed in God knows how many centuries, but there could be no mistaking the heat rising in my cheeks.

My unexpected rescuer, the king, excused himself from his family and drew me aside. The doctors stopped mutely worshiping me to attend to their young charge, making it far easier to govern my vascular responses.

"Freedom for myself and my companions, of course," I said in response to King Richard's query. "And safe-conduct transport to the Vatican, an audience with the pope, and access to the Vatican archives."

"You didn't ask for sainthood." His grin revealed the mild tease.

"I do not have time to pose for an icon portrait." My deadpan delivery prompted the king's chuckle.

"Freedom for you lot is a given; you may set your mind to rest upon that point, Madame Hanks. Transport and safe conduct, I can arrange. Consider it done. An audience with His Holiness I can request on your behalf…but cannot guarantee. I'll ask Cardinal Lawson to look into it." He stroked his clean-shaven chin. "As for accessing the Vatican archives, that's for Pope Gildas to decide."

I felt as if I had been standing atop a table whilst a third-rate magician assayed, with middling results, his jerk-the-tablecloth trick. "Pope—Gildas?"

"The thirteenth. Do you know him?" asked King Richard.

"No, Your Majesty." I drew a breath, sent up a silent prayer on the exhale, and hoped for the best. "But I am certain His Holiness is as benevolent as he is merciful."

"You're right on that score."

The king's sarcasm torpedoed my hope and sent it crashing at my feet.

CHAPTER XI.
CONFESSIONS AND REVELATIONS.

ING RICHARD called a special practice session of the SDO London baseball team later that afternoon, and he allowed Arthur, Clarice, and myself—now well fed, showered, and clad in attire more befitting our "station," whatever on God's earth that could be—to watch. For Clarice and me, it meant soft woolen dresses with modest necklines and hemlines, low-heeled shoes, and no circlet for me, the surrendering of which left me more than a shade uneasy, and not on account of the Crown-sanctioned theft.

Said theft also included the confiscation of our defunct time-folding devices. When Clarice would have objected, I telegraphed her the idea that repairing the timeline ought to address her concern.

Arthur, whose battle crown already had fallen into King Richard's possession, was obliged to don the unfrilled shirt-and-trousers ensemble favored by men for the past two-hundred-plus years, including Sir Boss upon his arrival in Camelot. The mandated mode of dress seemed to be of no concern to him as he canted forward upon his seat, palms rubbing his thighs except to applaud a worthy hit, catch, or throw. His unconscious—oh, dear Lord, please forgive me that unintentional pun—behavior suggested to me that he would have been happier had he been invited to try his mettle with bat and glove against these men. I had watched him play during the Boss's sixth-century tenure. This day, Arthur would have acquitted himself with great honor, regardless of whatever position he might have been assigned.

These London Knights possessed nigh the same raw talent as my team, but they had not received the benefit of world-caliber coaching.

They did not have my Sandy to lead them.

Stifling a sigh, I pressed fingers to temple. Clarice laid a hand upon my arm. I patted her hand, and she withdrew it. Oblivious as any male sports enthusiast, Arthur praised another of Sonoma's line-drive catches. One quick, graceful pivot later, and the hapless base runner went slumping into the dugout as the double-play's second victim. 'Twas a superb move, worthy of any world-championship highlight reel; and if someone had told me that Sonoma's knee had been crippled beyond hope the day before, I never would have believed them had I not performed the healing myself.

Under more pleasant circumstances, I would have been clapping too.

We—Arthur, Clarice, and me, of course, but also King Richard and his entire team—departed for Rome the next day. The pope owned a team too and had invited SDO London to compete in an exhibition series versus the Vatican City Cardinals. Overheard snippets of player talk during the flight suggested that their star pitcher, Cardinal Vern (my earlier hypothesis about his given name proved correct; since America did not exist, neither did the state of Vermont) Lawson, had offered to excuse himself from the roster, but the pope would have none of it.

"If my Cardinals can't handle your heat," Lawson said to his grinning teammates in an aged voice I presumed was an imitation of the pope's, "then perhaps they shouldn't be in the kitchen."

Clarice, from her position near the players, chuckled; once Arthur worked out the metaphor, a few beats later, he barked a laugh too. The uninjured him had been, without fail, much faster on the uptake. However, that his brain had exhibited yet more evidence of his grandsire-of-all-concussions was of less concern to me than wondering what Cardinal Lawson might have told the pope about me or my companions, or the conclusions His Holiness might draw from said information. I could not share in Cardinal Lawson's jest.

I had expected weeks of being stalled whilst Pope Gildas mulled his options. Outright refusal had been a distinct possibility for which I had formulated a counterplan, though its implementation proved unnecessary. The alacrity with which he had acceded to my request troubled me more deeply than any dealings I had conducted with other heads of Church or state, my brother during the decades of our estrangement included.

I feared that this twelfth namesake of Arthur's ancient enemy knew who Arthur and I were, and that we represented a threat he intended to eliminate.

During a private moment upon the plane, after most of the players had fallen asleep, Clarice and the remaining players had donned headsets and activated the gaming systems embedded in the seat in front of them, and Arthur seemed to have acclimated to life inside this flying steel beast's belly as evidenced by the fact that he no longer felt obliged to death-grip his armrests, I confessed my concerns to him.

He agreed with me. "But you decided to undertake this journey anyway, despite your misgivings?" I gave an affirmative nod. "What do you hope to accomplish at the Vatican, Morgan, if knowledge of my reign has been suppressed this long?"

I wondered the same thing myself. For his benefit as much as mine, I said, "I hope to find clues to help me travel back far enough to at least save Sandy." It sounded less lame in my head, I swear.

Clarice paused her game, removed the headset, and regarded me. "Why not go back to the point where Ratcliffe's manipulation started?" Of course she had been monitoring our conversation whilst immersed in playing a game; I had expected nothing less.

Brilliant though my Apprentice Number One might be, there had been times when she failed, in the most spectacular fashion, to think through a situation. This was one of those times. I chalked it to the distraction presented by the videogame. "Would you have me try a spell, spun from speculation and good intentions, and kill us all?" Harsh, mayhap, but accurate.

She bowed her head. "Of course not, Your Majesty."

I gazed out the window at the billowing clouds, which now and again parted to reveal glimpses of the land below, and stroked my wedding ring. "In attempting to save Sandy, I may kill us anyway. If I jump alone, you two would become lost in time." I twisted to regard Clarice and Arthur. "And yet I cannot ask either of you to take such a great risk in coming with me."

Clarice said, "You never have to ask."

Arthur said, "My oath to defend you, Morgan, knows no boundaries of time or place,—or person. Though Sandy bears the countenance of my avowed enemy, if he is this important to you, then he too falls under my protection."

I laid my palm to his cheek and smiled. "My husband is—was—a good man. I think you would have liked him, Arthur. But…" I removed my hand as a disturbing thought occurred. "Oh, dear God, no…no!" I shut my eyes and thumped the window with my fist.

Arthur gripped my shoulder. "Morgan?"

I forced the words out like retching poisoned food: "I never existed in this timeline. The Sandy Carter who was executed three weeks ago was not *my* Sandy." Arthur wrapped his arms round me as best he could within the confines of our seats, and I collapsed, sobbing, against his chest. As raw bacon draws forth a splinter, his compassion drew forth a festering splinter of an altogether different sort: "Please forgive me for all those years of strife and malice, Arthur! Such a stupid, bloody waste…"

He hugged me fiercely, protectively. "Forgiven, dear sister. And"—his hesitation prompted me to look at him, and he grinned—"forgotten."

A genuine laugh welled from the pit of my stomach and burst forth like a bubbling fountain. My tears evaporated. With a flick of my hand, their evidence disappeared from his clothing too. I gave his chest a playful slap. "Who knew my brother was the King of Understatements?"

"Thanks to the first Pope Gildas," Clarice said, "no one but us."

"Hah!" That burst of Arthur's was loud enough to have drawn unwanted attention if not for the audio-muffling spell I had applied to our row of seats prior to takeoff. "Brilliant, Mistress Clarice."

I might have found her statement funny had it not been the literal truth. She must have sensed my thought, for she flashed me an apologetic grimace. "It was indeed a brilliant observation, my dear." Her visage brightened, as I had hoped it would; there lay no wisdom in giving our hosts the impression that aught was amiss.

Our windows' views tilted, indicating descent. The sun had set during our flight. Floodlit, towering spires swung into view, interspersed with buildings bedecked with garish, flashing, multicolored lights that seemed more at home in Las Vegas than the Eternal City. Dark swaths marked whatever squalor might be lurking in those shadows.

Given His Holiness's decisions regarding our party, I surmised that we would discover what Gildas's twelfth namesake knew sooner rather than later.

My suspicions proved true when our plane was met on the tarmac by a vehicular entourage—a bus, an automobile resembling a hearse, and a fleet of motorcycles far more sleek than their sad London counterparts—each bearing the Vatican City coat of arms. The lead motorcycle rider, a respectful but taciturn man I had seen in the other timeline in the Connecticut Yankees bullpen, though his name escaped me, ordered the baseball team onto the bus and Clarice, Arthur, and myself into the hearse.

Can you spell "foreboding," my intelligent reader? Good; I knew you could.

Cardinal Lawson excused himself from the team bus to join us. I did not for one second believe he made that choice for our benefit, if he had even possessed a choice, which I doubted, given his religious allegiance. Though he chatted with us, interjecting mild jokes when appropriate and pointing out city landmarks as we rolled past them, I reminded myself that this man was not the Deacon Lawson of whom I had been fond but a minion of Pope Gildas XIII. To any questions he posed, I kept my answers short and vague and, I hoped, not incriminating. Arthur upheld his role as my bodyguard and politely redirected Lawson's questions to me. Clarice did not interest Lawson in the least. This freed her to maintain a warding spell over us all without distraction.

She and I had taken turns keeping protection spells in place for the flight from London, and we worked in concert during the takeoff and landing, the most vulnerable phases for any flight and therefore the easiest to sabotage.

Why, yes, I could not trust the as-yet unseen pope as far as I believed I could heave him. Very perceptive of you.

Our hearse—excuse me, limo let us off in front of a rather unassuming building, as expectations went, though its insides defied the impression lent by its outside, appearing to have been crafted entirely of black, white, and gray marble. The roof over its central walkway was supported by ornate columns as thick as hundred-year-old oaks. Between each column stood an alabaster statue of a previous pope, all holding a fist-thick book (presumably the Bible, but in this cockeyed version of the world, it could have been a vintage Sears & Roebuck† catalog for all I knew) and striking similar, beneficent poses with the other hand like a collection of holy Kewpie‡ dolls.

At frequent intervals along our route stood members of the pontifical guard in their distinctive uniforms. I never would have imposed that puffy, gold-and-blue-striped livery upon my security forces of any era. They saluted as we strode past them. The first time I caught Arthur squaring his

---

† Sears, Roebuck and Co., commonly known as Sears, is an American chain of department stores and online retailer founded in 1892 by Richard Warren Sears and Alvah Curtis Roebuck. The company began publishing its paper catalog in 1893, and it boasted such a wide and varied array of products that it soon thereafter became known as a "wishbook."

‡ Kewpie is a brand of dolls and figurines that were conceived as comic strip characters by American cartoonist Rose O'Neill. The illustrated cartoons, appearing as baby cupid characters, began to gain popularity after the publication of O'Neill's comic strips in 1909.

—kih

shoulders in response, I whispered a caution that they might be saluting their commander, who was leading our party. Though Arthur conceded my speculation's validity, he continued to incline his head a fraction at each subsequent salute, proving that some habits are indeed impossible to break.

My gaze was drawn, as if by design, to the far end of the hall. It featured a high, black marble edifice, not unlike the throne dais inside the judicial chamber of SDO London. The main difference: a circular tube light embedded in the wall behind the papal throne, centered upon its occupant's head.

Good God, the lengths to which some men would go to achieve an effect.

The commander stopped us at a point designed to force us to nigh break our necks to regard the pope. I laid a hand upon my chest. If anyone mistook the gesture as a sign of respect, I would not disabuse the notion. In truth it was a spell to keep myself from retching at the holy audacity.

"Ah, Cardinal Lawson." By the profusion of wrinkles, I judged Gildas XIII to be closer to his eighth decade than his seventh, though the wispy orange hair visible past the skullcap belied the notion. "A pleasure to meet you in person, my son." The crackling of his voice cast its vote for decade eight.

Cardinal Lawson gave a deep bow, held it thrice longer than I would have, and straightened. "The pleasure and honor are mine, of course, Your Holiness." He beckoned us to step forward, forcing yet more strain upon our necks; with the merest hand twitch, I bolstered us with the magical equivalent of arnica. "May I present to Your Holiness the visitors from the court of King Richard of England?" The holy nod prompted him to continue. "Morganna Hanks, Clarice Centralia, and their bodyguard."

The pope deployed a smile I did not trust. "Thank you for your assistance in this matter, my son. You may join King Richard and the rest of your team now. Soldier Ludwig shall guide you."

The appointed guard saluted. Cardinal Lawson bowed again, and both men quit our company.

The papal smile shaded to predatory. "Your bodyguard's name, Madame Hanks?" His tone set every nerve in my body on high alert.

"My name is—"

"YOU'RE FIRED."

I brushed Arthur's arm and gave him a slight shake of my head. My lips nigh touching his ear, I reined my voice to a whisper. "Volunteering information is never a wise policy."

Arthur glared at me but remained silent.

"We have become lost upon our journey, Your Holiness," I said. "We seek information that will help us return to our rightful place."

"Your rightful time, you mean." Pope Gildas raised a hand, and not to deliver a benediction. "You, Queen Morgan le Fay, and your royal brother hail from an altogether different timeline and seek to restore it." That hand curled into a fist and thumped the armrest.

I stilled the urge to grind my teeth. The papal secret book old Brad had mentioned must not have recorded pronunciations of our names, though how Pope Gildas could have used it to identify Arthur and me, to say naught of our mission, remained beyond my ken. 'Twas a rare happenstance for me, and most unwelcome. My heart jolted into a canter. I willed it—and my voice—to remain serene. "I crave your pardon. I know naught of what you speak."

"Please spare me the innocent act," said the pope. "Lying is a sin."

I opened my mouth, but Arthur was faster. "Then I presume this audience is concluded. Your Holiness has no reason to help us and every reason to hinder us."

"And with a single raised finger," said Gildas, demonstrating, "my guards shall gut you all." The guards' postures and grips upon their weapons tensed—all save one, whose reaction time was a few beats slower than that of his fellows. "You're fired," said His Holiness. Whilst that man, his halberd resting upon one shoulder, quit the audience hall, the pope made a circling motion with his finger. The remaining guards surrounded us with lowered weapons.

There could be but one reason why we were not street meat already.

"We possess something you want," I surmised.

"Or need," added Clarice, "like tech knowledge."

CHAPTER XI.

"Correct, my daughter," said the pope. "Vehicles, computers, communication equipment. Defensive equipment. Weapons."

The pope flicked his hand as though shooing a fly, and the guards returned to their posts.

"Not all sanctuary districts are loyal to the Vatican." The thoughtfulness of Arthur's tone revealed genuine interest in the pope's situation. Even when we were children, my brother was a quick study; small wonder I had never defeated him in open conflict.

In the sigh Gildas heaved I could smell the garlic that had seasoned his supper; given the distance separating us, that was saying a lot. "The Eastern Caliphates are on the rise again. No pope has ever done more for the faithful, and I need superior defenses to preserve my…children."

Balderdash, I thought. This humbug was more interested in preserving his own image. I could work with that. Vain men were ever so much easier to manipulate than most.

"Clarice possesses such knowledge, Your Holiness." Although American football was not my sport of preference, I did know what a Hail Mary pass was…and when to lob it.

"Ms. Hanks!"

I excused myself and drew her aside. "You worked with the people in Ambrose's lab, did you not?" She nodded, but her open mouth heralded her intent to protest. I refused her the opportunity. "And his"—I hit upon an appropriate euphemism for the time-folding device—"temporal toy was not the lab's only project, yes?"

She confirmed my assumption, though by the pursing of her lips she looked less than pleased to do so. I returned my attention to the pope. "Clarice, with my brother's help, will trade that knowledge for the privilege of my unrestricted access to the Vatican archives."

"A fair proposal, Queen Morgan, with one exception. Your brother shall serve the Church by putting his weaponry knowledge to a…more demonstrative use."

In Libro Veritas

To paraphrase every important *Star Wars* nonvillain in the history of the franchise, I had a bad feeling about that. But I had to accede and like it. Or die.

"Your Holiness?" asked Arthur.

"Patience, my son. God's blessings upon you all."

The pope sketched the sign of the Cross. If only I believed in the sincerity of his benediction.

"See to it that my guests are settled in their quarters, Commander Reinhold," said Pope Gildas.

The commander's name awakened an unexpectedly pleasant memory: Yankee relief pitcher Dorn Reinhold had subbed in during the latter innings of 2088 World Tournament games one and five. Both games had resulted in London wins. With effort, I flattened my smile.

His Holiness flashed the most genuine smile he had displayed during the entire audience. "After discharging that duty, my son, you may prepare your team for the game."

"Yes, Your Holiness!" Commander Reinhold executed a smart salute, a smarter about-face, and set a brisk pace for us and the rest of the guards in our escort detail.

"That was easy," observed Clarice, a tad breathless as we strode within the knot of guards. "Sort of."

"That was a formality," I said.

"His Holiness does not believe we shall succeed," Arthur said.

"His Holiness may be correct," I said.

Clarice gave me a panicked look. "Intuition? A vision?"

Mindful that anything we uttered in front of the guards would find its way to the holy ears, I modulated the telepathic reassurance I gave her into the vocalized "Cautious concern, my dear."

CHAPTER XII.
The Holy Rollers Casino, Fight Club & Nunnery.

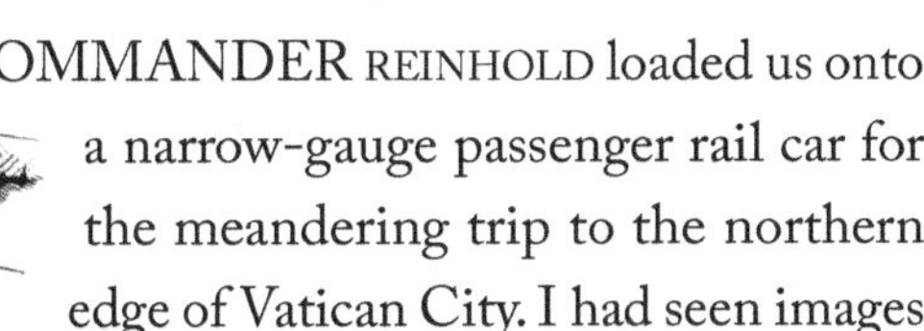

OMMANDER REINHOLD loaded us onto a narrow-gauge passenger rail car for the meandering trip to the northern edge of Vatican City. I had seen images of such conveyances in the original timeline but had never occasioned to ride in one, having been far too busy with political, personal, and team concerns to visit any of the self-proclaimed happiest places on earth.

Give me a flying limo or the Transatlantic Bullet Train any day.

Please do not misunderstand; I appreciated the commander's lecture describing the histories of the landmarks that we passed—churches, museums, libraries, residences, administrative buildings, squares, fountains, and the countless markets, restaurants, and gardens, the aromas proceeding from which swirled throughout our rail car in a delicious kaleidoscope of competing fragrances,—and I appreciated sparing my feet. I am certain Arthur and Clarice did as well. But by the time we arrived at our destination, I felt as if my head was going to explode.

We rolled to a stop in the station servicing the most garish of the establishments visible during our aerial approach. Proud, flashing orange neon lettering announced its name: "Holy Rollers Casino, Fight Club & Nunnery."

The "Fight Club" had to refer to the ancient stone amphitheater whose station was but a short hop from the one where we disembarked. Although smaller than the Nîmes amphitheater, this one displayed no lack of lighting or patronage. Our open-air trolley had allowed us to hear the crowd noise, though at the time I had associated the lauds with nonlethal athletic competition rather than blood sports.

The casino, lodged within the Holy Rollers Hotel, bustled with patrons, many of whom sported clerical garb representing various orders. The nunnery, occupying the adjacent building, appeared to be hosting a steady stream of visitors too, clerical and otherwise; mostly men.

Said Clarice in a low whisper, "Somebody has a sick sense of humor if 'Nunnery'[†] means what I think it does."

I pointed a nod at my brother, who was busy with his own evaluation of our surrounds. "His father consigned me to such a place in my youth. Those women taught me many arts beyond that of prayer."[†]

"Church-sponsored gambling and prostitution…we are *not* in Kansas anymore." A tendril of fear invaded Clarice's tone.

Arthur gave her an abrupt, confused look. "Can sass—what?"

"Sorry, sir," she said. "I keep forgetting that your experiences are different."

He forgave her with a smile.

By this time, Commander Reinhold and his men had led us to the hotel's steps, where we paused. "You shall be staying elsewhere," the officer said to Arthur. He nodded at a nearby cracker box structure bearing the name "Fight Club Barracks."

---

† The term "nunnery" had, by Shakespeare's day, devolved into a euphemism for "whorehouse," which was the inference Clarice made. Queen Morgan's response hints at the fact that the devolution was already well underway by the closing years of the fifth century, prior to her political marriage to King Uriens, and a millennium before Shakespeare's birth. —*kih*

My stomach dropped. I surged for my brother but was hauled back by two guards.

"Unhand the lady," Arthur growled.

"A moment, please, Commander." I flashed a beguiling look.

At Reinhold's nod, the guards released me.

"Do not try to elude us, Morganna Hanks," he warned.

A young nun walking in our vicinity paused to give our party a curious stare. That in itself I would not have found strange, as well accustomed as I was to notoriety, but none of Vatican City's other denizens had troubled to pay us the slightest heed. She and I locked gazes for a moment before she lowered her head and hurried to the nunnery.

I returned my attention to the papal guard commander. "Escape is not my intention, good sir."

Reinhold's low "humph" I took for mollification.

As I faced Arthur, I tugged a ring off my right index finger and palmed it. I refused to part with the wedding ring that had bound me to Sandy even to save my soul, were that an option; this other ring had been a gift from my mother and Arthur's, Queen Igraine, which I had selected for its emotional connection to Arthur as well as to me. I imbued it with a healing spell, much as I had done with Excalibur's scabbard, and passed it to him in the act of grasping his hand. His surprise lasted but a moment. Discreetly, he worked the ring onto his left pinkie. I covered that hand with both of mine, continuing to bolster the spell.

"For safekeeping?" Arthur asked.

"Precisely." My smile felt immeasurably sad. "God be with you, my dearest brother and liege, even as I cannot be." I prayed as hard as I could that the spell would prove strong enough.

Arthur only had time to kiss my fingers before his guards pried us apart. Commander Reinhold and his remaining underling would not let me watch my brother leave but ushered Clarice and me up the hotel's steps without further delay.

"I've heard that his first match will be tomorrow," Reinhold volunteered.

Ever so many retorts begged for release; I had trouble deciding upon the most benign: "His Holiness does like to move fast."

The commander gave a noncommittal grunt and signaled his subordinate to open the hotel's door.

We stepped into a drug dream of strobing lights, dinging bells, and drunken whooping,—and that was just emanating from the hotel's bar, the monitors of which were displaying video feeds from the Fight Club arena to a standing-room-only house. The casino's entrance, dozens of yards from the hotel lobby, was disgorging yet more head-splitting noise and distractions.

"This way, madame," Reinhold was saying as he angled for the reception desk.

All call me Queen.

I halted, confused. That bit had flashed across my mind not as my own thought but as if somebody else had uttered it.

Somebody not inhabiting my immediate vicinity.

Somebody powerful enough to pierce the psychic ward I maintained for the express purpose of preventing unsolicited intrusions.

Somebody who had just vaulted atop my list of people I possessed no wish to meet.

"Ms. Hanks, are you all right?" Clarice asked.

For my unparalleled skills in leechcraft, most call me "The Wise."

I recognized the tone as belonging to the version of me that had not been long removed from my ancient, arrogant, and altogether unpleasant self.

The guards' furrowed brows proclaimed mounting suspicion. I raised the shield projected by my disarming smile.

No man dares call me "le Fay," lest he die.

"Of course I am all right, my dear. Just a mite…fatigued." I gave my head a swift shake and completed the march to the reception desk. That headshake was no act.

The fact that I was sensing the invocation of my first chronicle, which I had enchanted to project a holographic homuncula[†] of myself reading it aloud, I had no doubt. What I had difficulty believing was that someone in this butchered timeline—a millennium and a half[‡] of someones, in sooth—had troubled to preserve the book. The better question: lacking my guidance, how could anyone have learnt how to cancel its magical lock and operate it?

"Name, please," stated the desk clerk in a flat tone.

I hight Morgan.

An energy discharge engulfed my body, as if the Unknown Somebody was using magic in my vicinity. Clarice's magical signature bore a subtle feel; this Somebody's magic felt…strident? Urgent? The polar opposite of warm and fuzzy? Pray, forgive me, patient reader; I have never before occasioned to compare the invisible qualities of practitioners' magical discharges. In any event, I was certain Clarice was not responsible. She remained occupied answering the clerk's questions, oblivious to the sensations that, apparently, targeted me alone. I gazed into the closest security camera, reaching out with my mind. My mental probe hit a well-crafted wall. I inclined my head a fraction in approval; to survive in this hostile social climate, the wall's builder would have to possess master-level skills.

If the practitioner interpreted the gesture as my acceptance of their challenge, well, then so be it.

"Madame Hanks?" prompted Reinhold.

"Is something wrong?" asked the clerk.

Blinking, I broke contact with the person watching the camera feed and regarded the clerk. "I am sure your accommodations shall be acceptable."

---

† "Homuncula" is derived from the Latin *homunculus*, meaning "little man," to serve as the invented female version of the noun.

‡ Timeline clarity: The Yankee Hank Morgan arrived in A.D. 528 and spent approximately 10 years in that era, and 537 is the date commonly ascribed to King Arthur's final battle at Camlann. Therefore, 537 to 2092 constitutes roughly a millennium and a half.

—kih

CHAPTER XII.

The clerk scrawled the room number on the key folder. Reinhold snatched it and stared at it long enough to commit the number to memory before passing the folder to me. Rude, but not surprising. "Matins[†] is at oh-three-hundred. Follow everyone to the hotel's chapel." He swung about and pointed to a doorway opposite the casino entrance, near the lift bay. "My men will meet you there to escort you to breakfast and then to your appointed tasks."

Clarice's jaw dropped open. "Oh-three—three o'clock in the morning? He can't be serious!" she said to me.

"His Holiness requires us to observe all canonical hours,[‡] every day, as good sons and daughters of the Church ought," Reinhold recited with the hollowness of a schoolboy.

"Clarice and I are nothing if not good daughters of the Church," I replied, stripping all trace of mockery from my tone. "It is our honor to comply."

The answer did not buy us the privilege to locate our room without an escort; not that I had held much hope of that outcome, though it had been worth a go.

At our room's door, when Reinhold and his underling seemed hesitant to leave, Clarice's patience shattered. "Have you been ordered to tuck us into bed too? Maybe sing a lullaby as you f—?"

"Clarice Centralia!" I thundered. "Govern your tongue."

---

† Matins (derived from the Latin *matutina,* meaning "in the morning") is the first canonical hour of the Divine Office. Originally occurring at midnight, over time it became combined with the office of lauds (from the Latin *laudibus,* meaning "praise") by most religious orders to afford adherents a longer sleeping period. Queen Morgan would have wagered her crown that the first to have instituted this mote of sensibility would have been an order of nuns.

‡ A canonical hour is one of the daily offices of devotion that compose the Divine Office. While the schedule can vary by religious order, it commonly combines matins with lauds at 3 a.m., and continues at three-hour intervals with prime, terce, sext, nones, vespers, and compline (9 p.m.). The strictest orders observe matins at midnight and lauds at 3 a.m.

—*kih*

Reinhold gave her a cool look. I pressed the key card to the lock, opened the door, and all but shoved her inside.

"She and I have no intention of going anywhere without my—our companion." I caught myself before revealing Arthur's sibling status. By now, that status had to be an open secret, but I refused to lend aid to the rumor mongers. "Upon my honor, we shall cause you no trouble."

That seemed to satisfy him. Both guards saluted me with brisk nods, spun, and quit our company.

Once I had entered the room and shut the door, Clarice started blurting an apology.

Eyes closed, I held up a hand, and she fell silent; she knew from our days of campaigning for President Malory that I was invoking a spell to disable all video and listening devices. My sweep verified that our chambers were camera free, but microphones had been concealed behind the bathroom mirror, underneath the desk, inside one of the floor lamps, and

HANDWRITTEN NOTE ON REVERSE:
"WE'RE **NOT** IN KANSAS ANYMORE."

129

embedded in the frame of the Pope Gildas XIII portrait hanging on the wall between the beds. The pope's minions had missed attaching one behind the crucifix adorning the wall above the television monitor, opposite the pope's portrait; that is what I would have done, blasphemy or no. I took extra care to ensure that the monitor could transmit in but one direction.

I opened my eyes and lowered my hand. "That should buy us some privacy." I was tempted to cover the papal portrait but discarded the idea as one that could buy us no end of trouble.

"They were watching?"

"Watching, no. Listening, no longer. As to your question about the canonical day, we must attend chapel every three hours for communal prayer except at midnight." I was surprised to learn that this draconian version of the Church had conflated matins with lauds—to wring more productive work out of its less sleep-deprived minions, no doubt—but I kept the comment to myself in the off chance that I had missed a bug.

She made a distasteful grimace, but it was not my place to pass judgment upon it. The subject of her religious convictions had never surfaced before to-day; the pronouncement I had made to the guard commander upon her behalf was solely for her physical protection. As with anyone who walked this earth, the condition of her soul lay betwixt her and God.

After a moment, her expression turned earnest. "God! I just hope the archives are nearby, or you'll never get anything done."

"I surmise that is Pope Gildas's general intention."

Panic flashed in her eyes. "What information could I possibly give his scientists?" She pressed a hand to her chest as her breath started escaping in short pants.

I grasped her hand, willing her anxiety to ebb, and guided her to sit in the comfortable-looking lounge chair positioned between the window and one of the beds. "Anything you can dream up should suffice, my child."

Her breathing lengthened and quietened, and her gaze became unfocused. A blink later, she regarded me and grinned. "If I get stuck, I could quote old *Star Trek* episodes!"

I returned the smile. "As long as it sounds plausible."

"Fair point," she said. "*Babylon 5* it is, then. Ah!" She snapped her fingers. Between them appeared a laser pointer, which she proceeded to turn on and squiggle its dot in a random pattern upon the carpet. "I'll focus light through a ruby and see how long it takes them to scramble about like cats!"

As she stowed the device in her purse, we shared the first unrestrained laugh since this wretched temporal calamity had occurred.

My mirth faded when I noticed the room's vista. Our—what, hosts? wardens?—had given us an unobstructed view looking down into the Fight Club arena. I enchanted the window's glass to magnify the gladiator combat just ending with the removal of the loser's body, a wide, bloody streak marring the sand the entire way to a set of solid black double doors opposite the papal box. The doors' framing had been crafted to suggest a cave's mouth.[†]

After the survivor departed through a different exit, this one decorated along the supports and lintel with a profusion of painted laurel leaves, the announcer began. I nudged his volume: "…special match commanded by His Holiness between Vatican City's favorite, Saint George…"

A giant warrior clad in scanty armor rose through a trap door in the arena floor, stepped forward, doffed his helmet, and turned a slow circle, waving his sword with no more trouble than if his fist had been empty. The rippling muscles, gleaming teeth, and glistening sweat broadcast in closeup on the stadium's Jumbotron screen lent mute testimony to the fact that his weapon had been crafted for lethal combat, rather than as a movie prop.

The crowd's appreciative roars seeped through our window without enhancement, electronic or magical.

After the roars dwindled, the announcer continued: "… and a newcomer to the Holy Rollers Fight Club: the Red Dragon."

---

† Most world mythologies associate caves with passages to the Underworld, Otherworld, Hades, Abaddon, Hell, and other names for the realm of death. —*kih*

In the rightful timeline, the WBF baseball team from Kraków, Poland competed as the Red Dragons. The color of the fiery reptile on Arthur's heraldry was scarlet, which birthed in me an irreverent wish to rack the pope for labeling my peerless warrior-king "red." I could not see Arthur's expression behind his visor's dense mesh, but the rigidity of his stance suggested his anger level. I rather doubted that the pedantic color name had aught to do with his emotional state, however.

Arthur's equally scanty armor had been smeared with red paint, the first detail I noticed upon his entry via an adjacent trap door. This lift featured a turntable that modeled his rig as he emerged from the arena's underbelly without his being obliged to move. A dragon's head and neck crested his helmet. As he advanced onto the arena floor, a supple red metallic tail attached to his belted loincloth, bearing ridges that suggested a dragon's dorsal plates, sketched a trail in the sand behind him. Like his opponent, Arthur was barefoot; for better traction upon the sand, I surmised, though I fought the instinct to entrap my armrests in a death-grip. Foot injuries ranked high upon the list of nonlethal wounds that could lead to the death of a warrior in any era. I sent to heaven a mental prayer for the warding of Arthur's feet even as I projected more healing energy into the ring I had given him…which I could naught but presume he was wearing beneath the red leather glove covering that hand. He carried no shield but wielded two swords of medium length and breadth. The crowd greeted Arthur with some claps and cheers; boos constituted the overwhelming majority of his welcome.

As the spectators watched him comport himself with regal dignity in spite of the comical armor, cheers swelled to drown the boos.

No amount of dignity could overcome God knows how long he had lain comatose in Avalon. In theory, my healing spells had preserved the robustness of his muscles, and he had not been winded by any of the walking thus far, either here or in London, but this combat would be the first real test of how far his body had recovered. I pressed my forehead to the glass atop his image, my eyes moistening, and I prayed for all I was worth, for his head as well as his feet, and every body part in between.

Clarice joined me at the window and gripped my shoulder. "Commander Reinhold lied to us!"

I had sensed no guile in the officer, and I told her so. "He was misinformed, no doubt," I said, "so that we would enter meekly into this confinement."

"His Majesty will be all right." Her hand conveyed equal measures of concern and comfort in its gentle contraction. "Won't he?"

Betrayed, killed, brought back to life, brought forward in time, betrayed again into a fractured time, captured, forced to fight for the pleasure of others…

What in heaven's name had I done? How in the name of everything holy could I even hope to correct my heinous mistakes?

My gut's knot pronounced its dire prophecy.

The gladiator dubbed Saint George saluted Arthur with his sword and then faced the pope, who was sitting in his luxurious box, surrounded by cardinals and guards, his right hand raised as if in benediction. Arthur followed his opponent's example.

"I have done what I can, Clarice." I covered her hand with mine for a moment before lifting it off my shoulder. "The rest is up to him."

Pope Gildas waved the sign of the Cross and dropped his hand in a chopping motion.

The warriors rushed together, shouting and swinging their swords. Arthur, swifter and more agile, scored quick hits. Saint George possessed superior strength. Whenever his blows connected, they drove Arthur back. Both combatants tried a variety of athletic techniques to gain the advantage: tripping, rolling, leaping, spraying sand. Arthur mastered the art of weaponizing his dragonesque tail. Cuts appeared on both men.

"Should we not help him?" Clarice asked.

Of course we should, but doing so would jeopardize my chances of righting this timeline. "I learnt with my baseball players that enhancing their prowess could unleash undesirable consequences," I said. "If Pope Gildas suspects me of using magic in defiance of Church strictures, he will withdraw what little support he has given us…or worse."

She shivered and chafed her arms.

"I am the notorious sorceress," I reminded her. "Belike His Holiness is unaware of your gifts, and I shall guard that secret with my life, if need be."

Her grateful look warmed my soul, and we continued watching the contest.

The ring I had given Arthur carried risks aplenty. I confirmed that he was wearing it the first time Saint George wounded him, and a subtle glow appeared through the glove, indicating the ring's healing effect. To everyone else, the glow should have appeared as but a natural flash of light hitting the sword's hilt. Saint George, however, appeared to reach his own conclusions and redoubled the fury of his attack. My brother, likely seething over his treatment at the hands of the pope, demonstrated no trouble returning the rage.

After an intense exchange, Arthur bore Saint George to the ground and held him there, swords crossed at the man's neck like scissor blades. I released a relieved breath. Panting, Arthur looked toward the papal box.

Pope Gildas jabbed his thumb at his own neck. From the public seating came isolated shouts of *"Iugula!"*

The vast bulk of the crowd uttered a collective gasp. So did Clarice. Arthur, scowling as fiercely as any live dragon, lifted his swords, swung them to the vertical, and drove them into the sand on either side of Saint George's head. During his youthful studies of Roman combat, he had to have learnt that *iugula*—the Latin word for "throat" and, in medical texts, the jugular vein—had morphed into vernacular usage as the gladiatorial command for executing the opponent. He tore off his helmet, flung it down with a sandy clatter, and turned the full force of his draconic glare upon the pope.

"Finish him, Red Dragon." The holy words ran as cold as the metal forming the heavy gold crucifix plating his holy heart.

"I have no quarrel with this man, Your Holiness." Ever the diplomat, Arthur kept his tone pleasant and respectful, if winded by his bout and by the struggle to cage his rage. "He fought well and deserves clemency."

I, of course, had expected nothing less, but Arthur's decision seemed to surprise the crowd. After a few heartbeats of stunned silence, filled by another shout or two of *"Iugula!"* the arena erupted into thunderous cheers.

Movement in the papal box attracted my attention, and I magnified the view. The cardinal seated at the pope's left hand, Dillon Charles, a man I had known a lifetime ago as the manager of the Connecticut Yankees, leaned to whisper into the holy ear.

I boosted Cardinal Charles's volume: "Blessed are the merciful, Your Holiness."

Pope Gildas flashed his subordinate a severe look before facing forward, nodding and smiling with radiance (however insincere) to rival the very sun itself. He reversed his signal.

The cheers escalated as Arthur helped Saint George rise. Both men waved. When the pope again raised his hand, silence descended upon the stadium.

"Until tomorrow, then, Red Dragon," said Pope Gildas. "I shall find a more worthy opponent for you."

This, to the man who had defeated the cruel oppressor of Saint Michael's Mount in single combat, a giant with twice the height, four times the girth, and eight times the prowess of the gladiator Saint George? Perhaps this thirteenth Pope Gildas stood as ignorant of Arthur's ancient exploits as his predecessors had caused their people to be.

In spite of instincts to the contrary, I let a little flame of hope warm me.

The pope rose, and so did the stadium's occupants. He delivered a blessing over the immense ring of bowed heads, Arthur's and his opponent's included. After the pope finished and departed his box, the arena began to empty, though many spectators, their postures conveying wonder and approval, had paused to watch Arthur wedge a shoulder under Saint George's armpit and help him begin the trek to the victors' exit. The gladiator's leg wound, though not life threatening, would have forced him to crawl if not for Arthur's assistance. Effecting a cure was limited by the distance, but I pressed my fingers to the glass and did what I could. The tension creasing Saint George's face lessened, and his injured leg started bearing more weight.

"His Holiness won't forget this," murmured the defeated warrior.

"I would defy the devil himself on behalf of one of my knights." That was vintage Arthur. I smiled in spite of the fact that I had come within a hair's breadth of watching him be killed again.

Saint George halted midlimp and gave Arthur a quizzical stare. "One of your—what?"

"Someone like yourself: a man of arms, and a man of faith. My knights believe"—I saw Arthur's sigh in his shoulders' slump—"believed in using force only for what was good, right, and honorable."

"Those virtues are in short supply here," Saint George said.

My brother's shoulders slumped a bit more. "So I have seen."

As I disenchanted the window and turned away whilst Clarice closed its blinds and curtains, I did not trouble to stifle my sigh either.

CHAPTER XIII.
Level S24.

OT BEING privy to the mind of God, I could not be certain why it had pleased Him to cause my assigned guards to be Connecticut baseball players of my former acquaintance: to whit, switch-hitting slugger and center-fielder Billy Montel, and the decade older but still solid catcher and left-handed batter, Christian Berea. They met Clarice and me, as Commander Reinhold had promised, at the hotel's restaurant after we had finished breaking fast. To state that our meal was worlds better than the torture served on a plate in London's jail would be like stating the pope was Catholic. Upon further reflection, let us, sweet reader, table the debate regarding whether the pope presiding over this darkest of timelines could, in fact, be called "Catholic."

His Holiness might want to kill us—Arthur and me in particular, and Clarice if she failed to prove useful—but evidently not by starvation. I presumed that Arthur was being fed as well as we were. Every potentate knows that starving minions deliver poor entertainment value.

My wariness ignited when Montel and Berea escorted us on foot from the hotel. Taking the light rail would have been faster, I later learned, proving my suspicion that the pope intended to help me only to a degree. I took it all in stride, literally as well as figuratively. I had no other choice.

Pedestrian travel yielded a happenstance that perhaps His Holiness did not intend, else I am certain he never would have permitted it.

The squalor that I had surmised to be present but hidden under cover of darkness during our nighttime descent into SDO Vatican City revealed itself in the strengthening light of day. Homeless people of all stripes crammed themselves into every available alley. My best guess was that because these alleys were not serviced by rail, over time they had fallen into neglect, as had the denizens.

The cheerful red cobblestones that paved our route were such murder on my and Clarice's heels that I gave serious thought to hanging propriety and transforming our shoes into sneakers. We hobbled within scant yards of the alleys. Upon one pause, as I propped myself on an abandoned building so that I could adjust my shoe, I chanced to peer round the corner and into the bleary eyes of a moaning woman. Every inch of her exposed flesh—what little of it I could see beneath the ragged woolen shawl she had pulled over her head—was covered with festering pustules.

Compassion welling, I reached for her. Berea hauled me back.

"That woman has smallpox," he said. "It's not safe for you here."

Who knew the disease better than I, who had shepherded President Malory through such a hazardous environment? In the next breath, I realized that no one in this timeline would have known of my expertise.

Another thought struck me. If the pope had planned for me to suffer an accidental death, why order his men to keep me clear of diseased people? Why not allow me to come into contact with the contagion (presuming, incorrectly, that I would not be able to protect myself) and hope nature would take its course?

The guard's actions could be a ruse. If I had to work hard to convince him to let me through, he could then lodge blame for my consequences upon my shoulders. This theory required testing. To say naught of my genuine desire to help the diseased woman.

"I know, Chris. Please unhand me," I said.

Berea released my arm, but Montel stepped between me and my access to the alley. "It's a big problem among the city's poor, Madame Hanks," he said. "You'd only be endangering yourself." The concern in his tone took me by surprise, and I gave him a measuring look.

"I can help her, Billy," I insisted.

"Ms. Hanks, you're not equipped," Clarice said.

Of course that was not an issue for someone of my means, and I knew my apprentice understood it. I lifted an eyebrow. She pointed to a figure toting a pack of supplies and swathed crown to sole in a protective suit, complete with a bulky filtration mask. The figure was identifiable as a nun only by the crosses stitched at strategic points upon her gear and by the feminine hitch to her gait as she closed the distance to our position.

The mask hid the nun's face, but she seemed to stare at me a goodly while before giving us all a polite nod and a murmured blessing. She stepped past us without further comment and entered the alley. If her behavior seemed odd to our guards, they voiced no comment, except:

"It's the sacred calling of the Sisters of Faith, Hope, and Charity to minister to the sick and destitute," Montel said.

Berea grinned. "Yeah, and by night they minister to those with… other needs."

He and Montel shared a chuckle.

Right: the Holy Rollers Nunnery. I was not amused.

Neither, apparently, was Clarice. She whispered to me with no small measure of asperity, "It's *our* calling to finish before your brother gets paired with a warrior he can't defeat."

"True, my dear," I said.

The small motion of my hand I designed to look like acquiescence; in reality, I cast a healing spell. As we resumed our course, I heard the woman's moans stop—and not, I knew without needing to look, because her heart and breathing had.

I gifted myself the luxury of reveling in a dollop of satisfaction.

CHAPTER XIII.

At length, we stopped in front of a tiny, plain, single-storey building, one of dozens fronting St. Peter's Square. Here the guards forced Clarice and me to part company. My hug masked the application of a warding spell, imbued with a heaping side dose of inspiration. Berea cleared his throat, she broke the embrace, and he escorted her in the direction of a modern-looking office complex that had to house the science academy.

The pope's left-hand man, Cardinal Charles, approached Montel and me from the direction of the basilica's impressive colonnade. He inclined his head and invited me, trailed by Montel, to follow him into the head-quarters of the Vatican archives.

I glanced about, confused. The building appeared too small to hold two millennia of records, even if they had been digitized. Based upon the level of technology I had observed in London, thorough digitization seemed unlikely. And the existence of offsite storage seemed equally unlikely, given this timeline's pervasive climate of suspicion and fear. I did not trouble to hide my disappointment. "It appears I shall complete my search before nones† to-day."

The cardinal's weathered lips cracked a smile. "It's bigger on the inside."

My eyebrows shot up; I had trouble believing that this timeline, forged when the memory of the best crusader for All Things Good had been sup-pressed by papal authority, would have birthed its own version of *Doctor Who*, but the association was too fat a pitch to miss.

"*Allons y*,"‡ I said. Whether Cardinal Charles recognized the catch-phrase of my favorite Doctor, I could not ascertain, but his smile broadened.

---

† Nones (derived from the Latin *nonus*, meaning "ninth") is the fifth canonical hour of the Divine Office. It occurs at 3 p.m., the ninth hour following the office of prime, and it is the root of the word "afternoon." Though in present-day usage it's spelled without the *s*, I have retained the archaic spelling to avoid confusion with the synonym for zero, "none."

‡ *Allons y* is French for "let's go there" and was scripted for David Tennant in his portrayal of Doctor Who's 10th incarnation. Fannish wisdom states that your first Doctor is your favorite, and this proved true for my late daughter—though, alas, she never got to see Tennant reprise the role in the 14th incarnation. My favorite is also my first: Tom Baker, the 4th Doctor. *—kih*

I returned it with a slim one and followed him into the building. Montel, of course, ensured that I strayed not one step from the cardinal's course.

The doors opened onto a cavernous lobby that featured a security checkpoint manned by Swiss guards, a guarded booth for stowing umbrellas and outer gear, and precious little else. Upon the walls hung painted portraits of the sitting and—I surmised—most recent popes. My smile turned more genuine when I beheld who was waiting at the checkpoint, chatting with the guards. The priest faced us, mirroring my smile for a moment before his expression collapsed into confusion. Cardinal Charles introduced him as Cardinal Canoli, archives director. This cardinal was a robust and comely man half Charles's age.

"Madame Hanks, have we met before?" asked Cardinal Canoli.

"I crave your pardon for my rudeness, Cardinal," I said. "You remind me of a fine left-fielder I once knew."

The brightness of his countenance could have lit the room. "Really? I play left field for SDO Vatican City! Coach Charles must have told you."

"Coach?"

The older man confirmed it with a brisk nod. "You're a base ball fan, Madame Hanks?" Cardinal—Coach—Charles asked.

I deepened my smile and added a splash of playful sultry. "And now my darkest secret is out." A suggestive shoulder-twitch completed the effect.

The men grinned nigh unto the leering point. Cardinal—Left-fielder—Canoli waved me past security and ordered Montel to await my return in the lobby.

"Canoli!" called Cardinal Charles as his colleague ushered me into the lift bay. "Make sure Madame Hanks gets to chapel at the appointed hour."

"Of course, Coach. I'll see you at practice after sext."[†]

The old coach-cardinal departed with a wave, and Montel settled in with his counterparts manning the lobby checkpoint.

[†] Sext (the shortening of the Latin *sextus*, meaning "sixth") is the third canonical hour in the Divine Office. It occurs at noon, the sixth hour after the office of prime. —*kih*

"IT'S BIGGER ON THE INSIDE."

The lift bay contained four doors, each with its own key-controlled call button. The signage identified the lifts as serving different areas of the archives: the chapel ("Level S1"), the cafeteria and administrative floors ("Levels S2–S5"), and two lifts for the record storage vaults.

Cardinal Charles's bigger-on-the-inside claim catapulted into spectacular-understatement territory.

Canoli stood before the lift marked "Levels S16–S25," swiped his card, and pressed the call button.

Whilst we awaited the lift, I said, "I would love to hear more about your team, Cardinal Canoli."

"We're solid, except at shortstop," he confessed. "You wouldn't happen to know any?"

"Perhaps," I said. "If His Holiness will consent to release him from his current service." I did not harbor much hope of that happening, but one lesson I have learnt in sixteen centuries is that people can be surprising if given the chance.

"He might. We're slated to play SDO London tonight, tomorrow night, and then an after-nones game on Saturday."

I surmised that getting Arthur excused to play for the Vatican team to-night would be out of the question, and to-morrow did not seem likely either. To-day being Wednesday, and operating on the assumption that Arthur would compete every day against opponents of increasing prowess, I calculated his odds of surviving till Saturday.

I would not have taken that wager.

To mask my plummeting spirits, I asked, "Is London not a bit far afield for your usual opponents?"

"Oh, yeah." He bobbed an enthusiastic nod. "A real treat for all of us!"

By this time the lift had arrived. We stepped through the parted doors, Cardinal Canoli pushed the button labeled "S24," and the car started down.

"Twenty-four floors down?" I asked. "When it is far less expensive to build up?"

"You'd think, right? But the most recent attack of the Eastern Caliphates, three popes ago, taught us that lesson. Pope Benedict was stoned for betraying us to them." The left-fielder cardinal closed his eyes and bowed his head. "Thank God those infidels didn't have an accurate targeting system, or we'd have lost everything."

"Amen," I murmured, and I meant it.

"These days, however…" Cardinal Canoli regarded me. "Can your companion really help us?"

Both of them could, but I did not believe he was referring to my brother.

"Clarice is the ablest assistant I have ever had, save one. And him I married, once upon a time."

I blinked hard, twice.

The most elusive myth known to womankind is that of the "happily ever after," but the knowledge has never stopped anyone from wishing for it with all her soul.

At level S24, the lift doors opened onto a small foyer where another security checkpoint stood between us and a single pair of solid steel doors. Covering an adjacent wall from floor to ceiling hung a floorplan titled in medieval Gothic script "St. Innocent I (401–417) through Gildas II (676–687)." I left the cardinal conversing with the guard to approach the floorplan for a closer look. Each major section was labeled by pope, forty in total, and subsectioned by year whenever a pope's reign spanned such calendar divisions.

To say that my task would not be completed by nones to-day would be like saying…well, you know. (And we shall not entertain that discussion now, either, persistent reader, but I commend your memory.)

After signing in both of us with the guard, Cardinal Canoli pulled a pair of document gloves from a pocket of his cassock, gave them to me, and I donned them. He pointed on the map at the section titled "St. Gildas I."

Saint Gildas?

God help me. I had never sent forth such a simple prayer in such reverent earnest.

Cardinal Canoli, perhaps mistaking my hesitation for confusion, said, "Three aisles to your left and all the way back. Each pope's section has its own terminal, though on this level the computer records are incomplete. The guard, Manny Martino—our starting second baseman, by the way—will come for you when it's time for prayer. This building has its own chapel."

The latter fact I had already noted, but I let the well-intentioned remark pass. "Thank you, Cardinal Canoli. You have been most kind." I meant that in reverent earnest too.

"From a base ball fan, 'Father Bambino' is all the formality I need." He flashed me a smile and then addressed the guard. "Manny, you take good care of her, got it? Moving bins, answering questions, or whatever else she needs."

"Got it, Father," said Martino. "We still on for practice after sext?"

"That's the schedule." The cardinal reached for my gloved hands, appeared to realize that he might compromise the documents' protection, and sketched the sign of the Cross instead. "Godspeed, Madame Hanks. See you in chapel."

"Until then," I said. "Father Bambino."

The left-fielder cardinal beamed.

Martino unlocked the doors and opened them onto a long, dim, narrow aisle, the end of which became swallowed in the gloom. I could see enough, anyway: stacks upon stacks, row after row of metal bins, each containing God alone knew what manner of papal minutiae, forty popes' worth. I glanced back at Father Bambino, and he encouraged me with a smile and shooing motion. I squared my shoulders, faced the doorway, repeated my silent plea for divine assistance, and strode through.

CHAPTER XIV.
LESSONS IN THE PSALMS.

AYS PASSED in a blur of grinding tedium for us. The routine never varied by one jot: rise at oh-two-thirty, dress, pray, confer with Clarice regarding our previous day's accomplishments and brainstorm new ideas, pray, eat, and begin our respective tasks, which were segmented in three-hour intervals to accommodate the other mandatory chapel (coupled with eating and WC) breaks. She, at least, was making headway: the scientists had, as anticipated, demonstrated great interest in her laser experiments. Their introduction to the red light beam had drawn polite commentary along the lines of "Ooh, how pretty,"—until Clarice ignited the lead scientist's paper notepad. (That she had employed magic to enhance the effect was a secret she confessed to me inside our hotel room's closet in the softest of whispers; I assigned as "penance" the injunction to keep up the good work.) After his colleagues had extinguished their boss, and his screaming had ebbed below an ear-shattering decibel level, the science team recognized the weaponry applications, and the real work began.

BLESSED RELIEF

My progress, by comparison, was not worthy of mention. Fine; if you insist. The lighting was poor, the Latin was poorer still, and most of the sixth-century parchments had suffered from exposure to air and time, suggesting that their transfer to the low-humidity archive vault had not occurred soon enough. The first bin I had selected showed evidence of having been dropped at least once during its internment: the brittle parchment had shattered and become jumbled. I spent my entire first day piecing fragments together to make linguistic sense of the mess only to learn that it was a collection of financial records from the latter years of Pope—excuse me, *Saint* Gildas's reign.

Though God in His mercy grant me another sixteen centuries, I shall never become accustomed to calling that adder in clerical robes a saint.

Each day that week, Clarice and I worked till vespers[1] unless a ballgame was scheduled, in which case we stopped three hours earlier, at nones, to pray, change, eat, and attend the game…or as much of it as could be played between vespers and the final canonical observance of the day, compline.[2] A defense-favoring rule mandating that the batter strike out on a foul ball kept the games moving apace. Fatigue barred me from enjoying the games as much as I could have, though I must admit to feeling relieved not to own either team. And 'twas a most blessed relief to give my eyes distant targets upon which to focus. Even though Clarice and I attended as the pope's guests, I felt no compunction to cheer solely for the home team. My first expression of appreciation over a London play—an unassisted out short-stop Mark Sonoma made at second base that became a double play when he gunned down the batter at first—drew judgmental stares from some of the pope's high-ranking minions, but I smiled at them and carried on.

I did, for the record, retain the good sense to refrain from criticizing any of the Cardinals, on the field or off.

Clarice spent much of her time at ballgames studying piles of notes she had brought along, planning for her next session with the pope's scientists. With the laser-pistol project idea turned over to the papal weapons development group, her think-tank associates had begun to pressure her for the next big idea. A bottomless repository of comic-book lore, in addition to her command of science fiction trivia, proved to be quite the asset. Pope Gildas was excited to inform me that a team of his explorers was preparing for an excursion into the Dark Continent to seek the rare and valuable vibranium, a (fictional; *shhh*, do not tell) metal of alien origin possessing tremendous defensive properties.

With luck, Clarice, Arthur, and I would be long gone before the explorers returned with empty hands and emptier pockets.

On evenings when there was no baseball game, Clarice and I holed up in our Holy Rollers Hotel room to watch Arthur fight. The pope always invited me to the papal box, but I had declined each time, pleading fatigue.

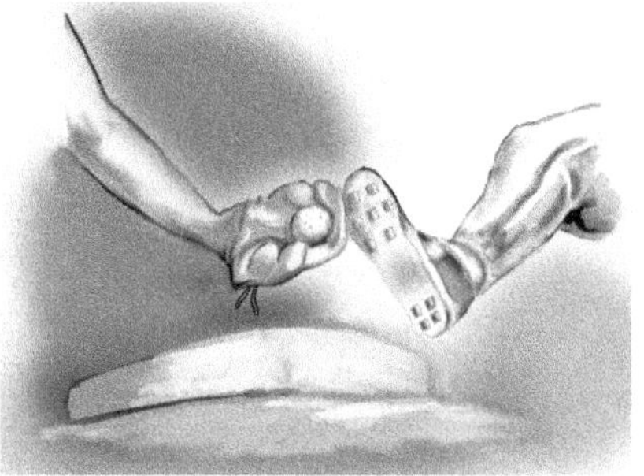

OUT AT SECOND

CHAPTER XIV.

Though my excuse was no lie, the complete truth was that I craved the freedom to give my brother unrestricted help. Thus far, thanks to more than three decades of armored combat training, he had remained undefeated without any magical assistance beyond his health-restoring ring, but his wins were taking longer to accomplish with each new opponent.

I had never considered myself to be an empath, but the physical toll upon his body I had begun feeling upon mine as though I were absorbing his opponents' blows.

By Saturday at sext—that is to say, noon—I, Morgan the Wise, stood in the archives' chapel no wiser with regard to evidence by which Ratcliffe had warped the timeline. Between the strain upon my eyes, neck, and back, compounded by the emotional strain of watching Arthur's peril and the mounting pressures due to my lack of a breakthrough, I felt my battle to keep a positive outlook seeping away like blood oozing from a thousand cuts.

I had not realized till that moment how much I had come to depend upon the chapel prayer services to bolster my morale.

The Saturday sext prayer service began much as every other, with Father Bambino watching his acolytes light the altar candles, douse the lighters, and then take their assigned seats beside the choir.

The choristers rose, opened their folders, and began a lilting rendition of the one hundredth Psalm: "All people that on earth do dwell, sing to the Lord with cheerful voice. Him serve with fear, His praise forth tell; come ye before Him and rejoice…" [3]

I had little to rejoice over, except perhaps the fact that Arthur, Clarice, and I remained alive, but I hoped the Lord would grant me points for making an effort, however feeble.

Greetings, Queen Morgan, daughter of Duke Gorlois and Duchess Igraine, half sister of King Arthur, mother of Sir Uwaine, widow of King Uriens…and wife of Alexander Leroy Carter.

What the h—?

I clamped off the blasphemous thought and opened my eyes but kept my gaze trained forward. A different sounding Somebody had invaded my head—in spite of the redoubled wards I had raised after the hotel episode—and this time I would find them. Or die.

The choir was still singing Psalm 100. Since I was standing midway back from the altar—in fine medieval tradition, this chapel contained neither pews nor kneelers—I could see perhaps half the congregation, which consisted of guards (some of whom I recognized), administrative staff, restoration specialists, building custodians, food service personnel, and other archive employees. The mental dialogue left me with the impression that the person stood close by, but no one in my field of view betrayed any indication of having greeted me thus. In my mind I said:

Who are you? How do you know these things about my life?

The choir finished and sat.

Father Bambino, carrying his Bible, mounted the pulpit. "Hear the words of Psalm 119," he said, flipping to the marked page. "Blessed are the undefiled who walk in the law of the Lord."

Please don't be alarmed, Your Majesty. I am a friend to you, your royal brother, and your companion.

I should hope so. I let a generous dose of ire color those words. *Explain.* The thought-invader had forfeited the courtesy of a *please.*

The cardinal continued, "Blessed are they that keep His testimonies, and that seek Him with the whole heart."

The Sisters of Faith, Hope, and Charity have been guarding your secret for a millennium and a half, awaiting your return.

I felt my eyebrows quirk upward and scratched my forehead to mask the movement. Such a religious order had not existed during my first lifetime, and I had not heard tell of them during my second either.

"They also do no iniquity: they walk in His ways. Thou hast commanded us to keep Thy precepts diligently."

Thumbing his Bible, Father Bambino announced a switch to Psalm 13. Worshipers holding Bibles thumbed along with him.

CHAPTER XIV.

We can help you, Queen Morgan.

How?

I hoped this Sister of Faith, Hope, and Charity could sense my towering skepticism.

The archive records are fragmented, mayhap beyond recovery. They contain naught but hints of the information I seek. And not one single syllable about Arthur. The latter fact was too discouraging to mention to a stranger who had invaded my head without my leave and who had yet to prove that she was not an enemy, to say naught of her claim of being helpful.

"How long wilt Thou forget me, O Lord? Forever?" quoted the cardinal. "How long wilt Thou hide Thy face from me?"

Gildas the First, aided by Cardinal Ratcliffe, was very efficient with his documentation purge.

Wishing my unknown companion would tell me something I had not already learnt, I clenched my jaw.

Continued Father Bambino, "How long shall mine enemy be exalted over me? Hear me, O Lord my God: lest mine enemy say, 'I have prevailed against him;' and those that trouble me rejoice."

The verse calmed me enough to ask, *What do you suggest?*

"I have trusted in Thy mercy; my heart shall rejoice in Thy salvation."

I conceded the psalmist's point about trust, though I felt less certain that the concept of divine salvation applied to me.

We need to meet, you and I. After the prayer service, look for the nun you see in the quarantined alley each morning.

Though unsure that I could identify her sans the mountain of protective gear, this conversation had gifted me the desire to try. *She is you?*

"Our final reading is from Psalm 139." The cardinal turned to the spot. "If I climb up into heaven, Thou art there; if I go down to hell, Thou art there also. If I take the wings of the morning and remain in the uttermost parts of the sea; even there also shall Thy hand lead me and Thy right hand shall hold me."

One of my Sisters. I am their Mother Superior.

"Yea, the darkness is no darkness with Thee, but the night is as clear as the day." Father Bambino concluded with the benediction and dismissed his flock with God's peace.

I could not feel that peace.

I need a plan to shake my escort.

God shall provide, my daughter.

1. Vespers (derived from the Latin *vespera*, meaning "evening") is the fifth canonical hour of the Divine Office and occurs at 6 p.m. Synonyms include "evening song" and the millennium older version, "evensong."

2. Compline (derived from the Latin *complere*, meaning "to complete") is the sixth canonical hour of the Divine Office, so named to convey the sense of completion to the day's secular as well as spiritual activities.

3. The traditional musical setting for Psalm 100, now known as "Old Hundredth" (or "Old Hundred"), was composed by Louis Bourgeois in 1551 and is used in many Christian churches to accompany the lyrics to the Common Doxology. In *The Adventures of Tom Sawyer* by Mark Twain, the congregation sings "Old Hundred" to celebrate the reappearance of Tom Sawyer, Huck Finn, and Joe Harper at the funeral service being held for them after they had gone missing and were presumed dead. —*kih*

CHAPTER XV.
PROVIDENCE.

OD *SHALL provide.*

Of course, I knew that; being an abomination did not blind me to spiritual precepts.

God had provided plenty in my past two lives: wealth, status, fame, a fine son, a peerless liege lord and brother, an adoring soulmate.

Most important, He had provided the chance to shed the hatred, anger, resentment, and bitterness that had blackened my soul through no one else's choices but my own…or so I had believed.

For God had un-provided most of those blessed provisions in an eye-blink, leaving me, my brother, and my closest friend friendless and adrift in this fresh hellscape of religion gone berserk in a planet-wide asylum governed by its inmates.

Small wonder my research had hit a wall, and its name was the blackness present yet in my soul. I realized with no small jolt of despair that its spiritual focus had swelled, threatening to smother the infant light I had begun, through the course of my first time sojourn, to nurture.

By this time, the other worshipers were departing the chapel, but I could not will my feet to move. Self-loathing drove me to my knees. I felt neither the slate floor's hardness nor the cold. I presumed that my escort, Billy Montel, had remained with me, but that fact remained unverified. I had bowed my head till my chin rested upon my breast. My hands clenched one to the other like two lovers drowning in a storm-ravaged sea. Squeezing my eyes shut failed to counter the sting of my tears. No prayer would heed my summons except:

Bless me, heavenly Father, for I have sinned.

A slow-treading set of footfalls approached my position but then processed past me. The sound stopped. I forged on with my prayer.

You alone know how long it has been since my last confession; I do not, and I am sorry. Please forgive me for that lapse.

The whispered voices that had proliferated in the silence I could have boosted with a magical nudge, but I lacked the volition to try.

I have sinned against Arthur, Clarice, my good people of Gore. My husband Uriens and our son, Uwaine. My beloved husband Sandy. Most especially Sandy…

A sob welled from the depths of my soul, goaded by the cruelty I had inflicted upon him during the earliest years of our association,—and the fact that he had grown to love me anyway. A shuddering breath kept the sob imprisoned.

I heard more whispering and more footfalls, this time sounding as if made by many pairs of feet, heading to the exit. I did not ascertain whether that left me alone; I lacked the volition for that too.

This time the whispering—soft, halting, and broken—was mine:

"My Lord…and my God. My worst sins are"—I drew another breath and sighed it out—"against You. Please forgive me for doubting You, for viewing Your bounty in my life as the product of my hands alone. For my selfishness. My arrogance. My pride. I implore You to purge me of everything that hinders me in being a better servant for You."

The searing pain that lanced my gut brought to mind Sir Launcelot and how he had wounded himself with his own sword in an attempt to purge himself of his illicit love for Guenever. I had chanced upon him bleeding in the forest, bound his wound, took him back to my castle, and commenced the process of helping him forget her. I convinced myself that my charms and sexual favors had succeeded,—not for the good of Arthur or his realm, mind you, but to score a victory against Guenever by possessing that which she never could.

Some months after Launcelot had departed Castle Gore, Lady Niniane showed me the chalk sketch he had drawn upon a wall of the chamber he had occupied. The sketch depicted a knight kneeling, head bowed, at a crowned woman's feet. Niniane fancied the queen was me. Such was my fancy too. I commissioned the court artist to preserve it with all manner of pigments, and I commanded him to take special care in painting my features upon the queen's face.

The pair of gray mourning doves, winging above the queen's right shoulder as if intending to alight there, proclaimed the artist-knight's truth as clearly as if he had inscribed her name. My symbol is a trio of ravens. After languishing a fortnight in my castle, Launcelot knew this as well as anyone did.

Merciful God, how blind, how ignorant, how unforgivably cruel I had been.

Still am.

This soul-rending sob refused to be denied. I would not have been surprised to learn that every resident of Vatican City had heard it.

A hand came to rest—gently, tentatively—upon my head.

"You are not unforgivable, my daughter."

Fist to lips to mute my gasp, I straightened, heart thrashing. How much had I uttered aloud? I had no idea.

CHAPTER XV.

Father Bambino was kneeling beside me. The hand he had placed upon my head shifted to reach for my fist and draw it away from my mouth. With the kerchief he held in his other hand, and with my leave, he dried my tears.

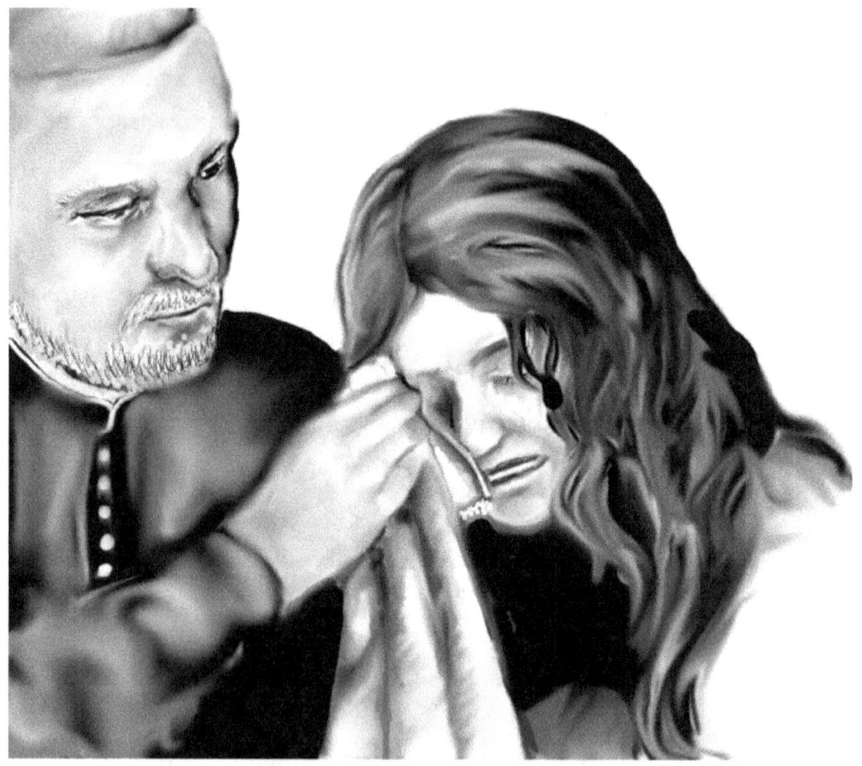

"YOU ARE NOT UNFORGIVABLE."

"Fear not, my daughter. No one else heard your confession."

"You will not—?" I hated to entertain the idea that any man of the cloth would betray a penitent's confidence, but in this weird version of the world into which I had been thrust, who could say what were the religious norms? Especially when the supreme defender of said norms stood as close to being a proven enemy as anyone could be without my possessing ironclad proof.

"I won't. You have my word." The cardinal's smile, as gentle as his hand had been, sealed the promise and inspired me to reach a decision.

"Father Bambino, do your duties permit you time to take a short walk with me?" The cant of his eyebrows invited me to explain. "I would like to continue my confession, but not inside the confines of a box, or even this lovely chapel."

"What of your work inside the archives?"

"I could use a spot of fresh air." The admission was no lie. If the act of chafing my arms lent the impression that I had become a mite claustrophobic, I did not disabuse the good father of the notion.

Fingering his chin, he seemed to ponder this for a while. At length, he said, "Are you not concerned about being overheard?"

Oh, aye, plenty concerned, truth be told. For my own benefit as well as the cardinal's, however, I said with as much assurance as I could muster, "God shall provide."

Provide He did, and moreso than I felt I deserved.

Without further questioning, Father Bambino summoned the lift to take us topside. In the lift lobby at ground level waited the faithful Billy Montel. The barest crease of his brow provided the only measurement of his impatience level; he stood as rod-straight and immobile as the papal portraits flanking him. The cardinal dismissed Montel to change clothing for the pregame baseball practice. "I shall assume full responsibility for Ms. Hanks's person and behavior," he added. "Enjoy your well-deserved respite, Billy."

Montel was too professional to gush his thanks, but I read it in the sharpness of his salute, the speed with which he faced about, and the spring in his step. Through the frosted glass of the building's outer doors I saw his shadowy form head in the direction opposite to that which I intended to take.

I set a comfortable pace that the cardinal seemed content to match; not so purposeful as to raise his suspicions, but not dawdling either. I respected the fact that he must be a busy man, and thus I did not wish to commandeer any more of his time than necessary.

After we had progressed several streets from the archives, sharing no more momentous conversation than the delicious coolness of the weather, the delightful misty spray of this fountain, or the soothing scent of the flowers festooning that bush, Father Bambino said:

"Please forgive my rudeness, Madame Hanks, but you seemed genuinely distressed in the chapel, and I do wish to help you." The abrupt knotting of my eyebrows must have convinced him to suck in a breath. He puffed it out. "Why do you believe yourself to be unforgivably blind, ignorant, and cruel?"

Oh, dear God. I *had* uttered all of that aloud.

I paused beside the closest fountain, mindful to stay upwind of its spray to preclude the need for invoking a drying spell. The statue of a robed man clutching a club in his left hand, a book in his right, and live flames shooting from his head stood smiling beneficently within the circle of water jets. Apparently, Jude served as the patron saint of desperate causes in this version of reality too. Hammered silvery bits and bobs lay shimmering in the fountain's shallows, shaped like crutches, limbs, eyes, ears, hearts, animals, now and then an entire person; each trinket no larger or more detailed than a board-game token, in all likelihood fashioned of tin rather than silver, and yet left here in gratitude for some event demonstrating God's mercy in the donor's life.

The sheer volume of these offerings, contained in but one fountain, amounted to a great deal of mercy by anyone's reckoning, but I could draw no comfort from them. Lost in this Godawful version of time, with dwindling hope of finding the first clue to becoming un-lost, compounded by the sin of having dragged Arthur and Clarice into lostness with me…I embodied the biggest lost cause ever to have existed.

How could I confess that my blindness, ignorance, and cruelty traced their roots back fifteen centuries in the history of a world so alien to the good cardinal's knowledge and experiences? What in heaven's name had I been thinking to state that I had wanted him to hear my confession? How much of this world's madness had infected me?

Quite a lot, it seemed.

Father Bambino, perhaps sensing my inner battle, rescued me from the lame excuse I had been a breath away from uttering. "I realize that you have no cause to trust me," he said. "I also realize that some confessions are too private to share with another soul. Whether you unburden yourself with me or not, I respect your decision." He laid his right hand flat over his heart, the solemnity of his expression softened by compassion. "I vow never to betray any choice you make." That hand contracted into a fist but remained atop his heart. His expression shaded to purposeful, complementing his brisk nod. "My lady."

The only way the cardinal could have surprised me more would have been to call me his queen. The ancient knightliness of his salute implied it beyond all doubt.

With effort, I constrained the widening of my eyes to the barest allowable twitch. The Royal Rules Committee did concede that queens and kings were in fact human, not automatons. And yet inside I felt boundless gratitude for the kind ally God in His mercy had seen fit to provide me.

My sole regret: not possessing a tiny silver effigy of myself to cast into St. Jude's fountain.

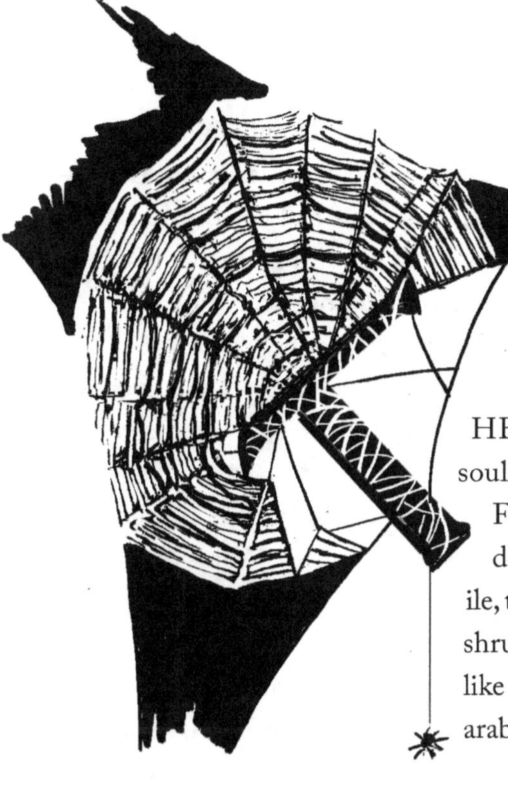

CHAPTER XVI.
MASKS.

HE UNANSWERED question of my soul's blighted state hung between Father Bambino and me like a dew-spattered spiderweb. So fragile, the slightest puff might drench the shrubbery below. The wrong answer, like a careless hand, could wreak irreparable damage.

Failing to say anything of a sudden seemed just as wrong.

"I have committed atrocities," I whispered, eyes downcast, "of the commandment-shattering sort." Once that admission had won free of my lips, the rest followed like battle-mad troops. It was all I could do to prevent them from turning into a pack of berserkers to wreak havoc wherever they might. "I coveted my brother's…status." (The many times I had attacked Camelot from within as well as without churned in my mind.) "I bore false witness against his wife." (The enchanted drinking horn incident might be stretching that point, since the vessel never came into Guenever's hands, but my intent to expose her—when in fact she and Launcelot had at that time shared no greater treason than wistful looks—had been clear.) "I am

163

a thief." (I have stolen lands, treasure, livelihoods, loyalties, you name it.) "I am an adulteress." (My bedposts bore witness to that fact, and oak does not lie.) "I am a murderer." (Twice by my own hand, dozens by my legal right; and God alone knows how many men, women, and children died in my ancient, unrighteous causes.)

As I sucked in a breath to confess the most damning point, Father Bambino captured my hands. He did so without my leave, but the tingling warmth dispelled my desire to pull away. I had heard priests utter assurances of divine forgiveness often enough, but this was the first time in my sixteen-hundred-year existence that I *felt* forgiven.

It emboldened me to raise my chin and gaze at my confessor.

"The past is past," said the cardinal, one corner of his mouth quirking upward. "The game goes on." His grin now in full force, he complemented it with a wink.

My very words! Words I spoke to my team, to President Malory, to Arthur; yea, even to myself as the occasion warranted. Words of encouragement, of comfort, of assurance. Of forgiveness.

How could he possibly—?

Nay. My amok-running self might have existed at the dawn of this turvy world, but that particular collection of words would have been as alien to her as floating glass castles and smoke-flatulating steel dragons. Father Bambino's choice to utter them must have been a coincidence.

I smiled my appreciation none the less.

He pressed my hands before letting go.

"I believe your destination is in sight, Ms. Hanks," he said with a nod in the direction we had been walking. Whilst not prohibited in the Royal Rules, I would have had to squint hard to make out the neon lettering of the Holy Rollers Hotel and Casino sign, obscured as it was by lesser buildings and their garish signage. At least, that was the destination to which I presumed he was referring. "And now I must beg your pardon; I have much to accomplish before nones worship."

"Many, many thanks, Father." I meant it more earnestly than he could know. However, "Did you not promise my guard that you would escort me?"

"I accepted responsibility for your behavior and safety, and I entrust your safety to God." Again he favored me with a grin. "I trust it's safe to entrust your behavior to you."

I inclined my head. "You have my word."

Father Bambino drew the sign of the Cross in the air before me, bade me a pleasant day, and headed for the archives.

Had Castle Gore been populated with but one cleric of Father Bambino's nature, my first life might have been quite different indeed. Strike that; it *would* have been different.

On the other hand, I never would have met Sandy, or lost him…

I banished the speculation before it could drive me any madder than I had already become.

Your Majesty?

Case in point: that head-voice from the chapel had returned. I asked—

Are you here?

A discreet glance round located no more candidates than a young man walking a brace of spaniels, a woman pushing a pram whilst her toddler "helped," an elderly couple tottering up to St. Jude's fountain with as much purposefulness as their frailties would permit, and a squad of Vatican guards marching past all of us, firearms shouldered and eyes front.

In the alley.

Right. The alley, half a block from my present position, the mouth of which also had lain within Father Bambino's line of sight when he had spoken of my intended destination; the alley I had purposed to stop well shy of, for his protection as much as for my own.

I invoked a disease-warding spell and set course for Smallpox Central.

In addition to the homeless pox victims, the alley was occupied by three nuns garbed crown to sole in identical protective gear. One of them noticed my approach, gestured to her sisters, mayhap along the lines of continuing their ministrations, which they did after casting glances in my direction, and hurried to intercept me before I could enter the infected zone.

"Morgan—Morganna Hanks?" she asked, the pause between both forms of my Christian name short enough to convince anyone who might have overheard that she had committed a slip of the tongue. I could not see her face through the filtration mask without magical assistance, and I did not deem the assaying of such a spell to be a necessary risk in this instance, but the deep, pleasant modulation of her voice suggested that she might be past childbearing years.

I inclined my head. "And you, good sister, are—?" *The one who conversed with me in the chapel?*

Indeed I am. "Mother Mary Galfrieda," she said, mirroring my head dip, "at your service."

I willed my eyebrows to stay level. Galfrieda was the name of my oldest lady-in-waiting, first in Castle Gore, and then in Avalon. The name was too unusual—sans the customary addition of "Mary" to honor the mother of Our Lord—to be coincidental.

"Are you at my service?" I narrowed my eyes. "Or do you intend for me to be at your service?"

She stammered a plea that she did not understand my meaning.

I tightened my jaw to curb my welling impatience. "This meeting place has but one purpose, Mother Superior." I surged past her into the alley, chose a position behind a tower of boxes to prevent my being seen from the main street, mustered my healing energy, and channeled the power into every pox-riddled alley denizen.

Within moments, the cries and sighs stopped; within minutes, not one pustule, festered or otherwise, remained in the lot. This fact the other two sisters confirmed by performing thorough examinations of each person. My senses could discern it by the clearer look and cleaner scent of the air.

The mother superior bowed her head and held the pose. "Please forgive me for doubting you." *Your Majesty.*

Of course that last bit she had to keep between the two of us; she had no way of knowing that I had magically located and disabled the area's surveillance devices prior to unleashing my spell.

I found her chin beneath the filtration mask and lifted her head. "It is my honor to ease their suffering." As I withdrew my hand, guilt forced my head and my voice to droop. "I hope it counts in some small measure as atonement for the suffering I inflicted upon my own people," I said. Then a thought occurred:

You seemed confident of my identity whilst I was in chapel. What happened to change that?

"Again, please forgive me, but I needed to be certain beyond all room for doubt."

By this time, the other two nuns had finished their duties and joined us. Mother Mary Galfrieda promised the alley dwellers that they would continue receiving food, drink, medicines, and other supplies, as well as assistance to assume new lives as productive citizens, and she concluded her speech with a blessing punctuated by the sign of the Cross. We exited the alley, and all three nuns doffed their masks. As I had surmised, the mother superior appeared to be the oldest, with crow's feet and frown line wrinkles complementing the graying wisps of hair that had won free of her wimple. The youngest she introduced to me as Sister Mary Niniane, a golden-haired beauty whom I could well imagine to be a favorite amongst Holy Rollers patrons; the third, a brunette, was attractive in an older, more settled way. Perhaps you, my intelligent reader, have discerned the pattern, but for completeness of the record I shall state her name: Sister Mary Vivien.

"Come, my daughter." The mother superior crooked a finger. "We must repair to my office to continue our conversation in private."

I eyed her as if she had suggested that I commit a grand felony. "You know I am being watched, right?" Not at this moment, perhaps, but, "Cardinal Canoli will grow suspicious if I don't return to the archives for nones worship, will he not?"

Mother Mary Galfrieda's lips twitched. "Father Bambino supports our cause." Those words were so low, I was tempted to invoke a boosting spell.

"Ah. Fellow baseball fans, I see." And it explained how the left-fielder cardinal knew my "past is past" catchphrase. "Very well; please give me a few moments to prepare."

That neither the mother superior nor her sisters pressed me for an explanation attested to the fact that they understood as well as I did that "Morganna Hanks" could not risk being seen entering the nunnery. I retreated to a secluded spot and transformed my visage into that of an elderly woman. Inspired by the venerable lady I had seen approaching the fountain, I conjured clothing similar to hers, complete with orthopedic flats, a clutch purse and matching pillbox hat. I tugged the hat's netting to obscure as much of my now wrinkled and liver-spotted face as I could, stooped to emulate the woman's posture, summoned a plain wooden cane, and returned—at a much slower pace—to the nuns.

I could see clouds of protest gathering on the mother superior's face. Suspecting that she might balk at the likelihood of our walk taking longer, I said, "Any younger, and I might be recognized. I shall resort to this gait only whilst in the presence of other people. The surveillance cameras along the way I can disable as we approach them."

Her nod I took for acceptance. I invoked my device-detection spell, and we set off.

The advantage of appearing old is that honest folk pay you no mind, except mayhap to tip their caps as a show of respect; the advantage of being in the company of nuns belonging to a God-honoring, pope-fearing society is that even the dishonest people harboring thoughts of preying upon the weak dare not do so. Whenever we chanced to encounter someone whose countenance blared danger, I pumped stern disapproval into my glare. If they perceived my expression as that of the hag that haunted their most terrifying nightmares, so much the better. No one had any business preying upon the weak; I never needed Arthur to teach me that. (Let us avoid exploring the idea that the ancient me may have indulged in more than her fair share of preying, shall we?) The potential assailants looked away with satisfying alacrity and went on with their lives with one less crime to be obliged to confess.

In due course, we closed the distance on the Holy Rollers Casino, Fight Club & Nunnery. The club marquee's lights had been switched off. One young man was steadying the ladder whilst his companion ascended to the sign, which read, "POST-SEASON EXHIBITION BASE BALL GAME VERSUS SDO LONDON: SOLD OUT."

"No surprise there," Sister Mary Vivien said to Sister Mary Nininane as they strolled in front of the mother superior and me. "I'm glad we bought our tickets early."

Sister Mary Nininane bobbed an enthusiastic nod and squeaked in agreement; apparently this incarnation of the Lady Nininane of my acquaintance was a bit of a goldfish too. "I can't wait to see the London Knights in their sexy uniforms!"

"I can't wait to see them out of uniform," retorted Sister Mary Vivien. The two nuns shared a giggle.

By this time, the lettering announcing the "base ball" game's sellout status had yielded to the words "MAIN EVENT TONIGHT."

Curiosity flaring, I asked the nuns to pause well shy of the workers' hearing. As the man on the ground passed up a second bucket of letters, I murmured to the mother superior, "I presume by your names that you are descendants of my original ladies-in-waiting, in spirit if not by blood."

We three are the latest links in an unbroken chain dating back a millennium and a half, to the year after the great battle that ended your brother's reign. Every one of us down the centuries has labored in secret to preserve the ancient knowledge—your knowledge.

My chronicle. The mother superior hid a nod in the scratching of her chin. *How ever did your order come by it? For that matter, why was your order founded? Surely that had to fly in the face of the religious landscape of the day.*

"Not in public, please," she whispered.

The venerable woman was quite right, of course. I returned my attention to the marquee…and had to fight the impulse to drop open my jaw.

"BEHEADING GAME" had been added to the sign.

"That's a new one for a main event," said Sister Mary Vivien.

The event's title triggered a raft of memories, none of them pleasant. I pressed a hand to my temple.

"THAT'S A NEW ONE."

"Morganna?" The mother superior touched my forearm, concern and compassion radiating from her that I welcomed despite the unsolicited contact. "Are you unwell?"

I did not shrug her off right away.

"I engineered such an event hoping my brother would accept the challenge. Our brash young nephew intervened and could have been killed. Sir

Bertilak gave Gawaine a year and a day to prepare, and it took me every last moment to craft a strong enough defensive spell."

During my explanation, the final statement had been added to the marquee: "IRADIVUS VS. RED DRAGON."

"Iradivus† is one of my favorite gladiators, but who in heaven's name is the Red Dragon?" asked Sister Mary Niniane. She glanced at me, and her eyes widened. "Oh-h-h!"

If despair was showing but half as evident on my face as I was feeling in the pit of my gut, the dear goldfish-child possessed every reason to be concerned.

---

† "Iradivus" is a Latin mashup I invented from *ira* ("wrath") and *divus* ("a god"), to mean "wrath of god" but in a more masculine way than the correct phrase, *ira dei*. The name was first used for a popular gladiator in an early chapter of my novel *Liberty* (HQN Books, 2006). This Iradivus incarnation enjoys a kinder fate… unlike most other residents of the darkest timeline. —*kih*

CHAPTER XVII.
Lessons From the Past.

OR THE life of me, I cannot recall the remaining journey to Mother Mary Galfrieda's office. I surmise that I was dumbfounded by shock from the moment I saw the "IRADIVUS VS. RED DRAGON" announcement till I fetched up in her visitor's chair, the mother superior herself kneeling at my side, chafing my wrist.

"Your Majesty, please."

The vocalization of my title brought me to my senses. A swift magical sweep ascertained the absence of surveillance devices, audio as well as video. The room was a modest but comfortable size, furnished with bookcases, side tables, a desk, and cushioned chairs crafted from aging but well dusted and lovingly oiled oak. Electric bulbs encased in frosted glass emitted a cozy glow. An arm-long brass crucifix adorned one wall. Upon a pedestal beneath the lone window sat an enormous Bible, open to catch the afternoon sunlight, which shimmered off the gold-leaf lettering of the right-hand exposed page. A framed picture on the opposite wall, presumably of Pope Gildas XIII, had been turned to face inward. Under other circumstances, I might have smiled at that spot of rebellion.

None of the other Sisters of Faith, Hope, and Charity attended us.

I bade her rise. She did, and claimed her seat behind the desk.

"Thank you, Mother Superior. I am quite all right now." More or less. In truth, more less than more: Arthur was doomed, and 'twas I—yet again—who had accomplished his dooming. I made this confession to my kind hostess.

The penance she assigned me? "Use your magic to save the king." When I opened my mouth, she lowered her eyebrows. "You claimed it had worked for your nephew."

Her statement made me wonder whether I had nicknamed the wrong nun "goldfish."

"God knows how I wish it were that simple," I replied. "Back then, I had three hundred and sixty-six days to develop a strong enough enchantment. It would need to be a hundredfold stronger than the warding spell I placed upon the ring I gave my brother at the commencement of our time in this city. I cannot marshal that much power—to say naught of bending it to my will—in less than three hundred and sixty-six minutes."

"You are that certain?" In the quiet question rang the damning indictment.

I gazed at the box sitting atop the mother superior's desk, an artifact I knew well, for I had crafted it myself. In the first timeline, Clarice had retrieved it from my scribe in Castle Gore and brought it forward in time to Sandy's office, but the book had been sitting atop his desk, untouched by any of us, during the temporal shift. My best explanation for the chronicle's presence here: the shift must have instigated the return to its last stable location, in Castle Gore, thence to be recovered by my original attendants, who must have managed to magick themselves out of Avalon whilst my seneschal still held the castle. In Gore, the horrors of Ratcliffe's meddling belike convinced them to establish the Sisters of Faith, Hope, and Charity for to preserve my lore till their successors could reunite me with my tome. The irony that the order had enjoyed centuries of Church-sanctioned protection whilst Papa Church remained ignorant that it had been guarding that which it had sought to obliterate was too fat a pitch to let streak past me, but I did.

The throes of my despair had robbed me of the inclination to posit my theory to the mother superior.

I expressed my anguish in a long sigh and enjoined the Royal Rules Committee to go eff themselves. "I am powerless to save him this time."

"I don't think so."

No discourtesy marred her tone, but I took umbrage none the less.

"You understand nothing of magic." Since she had demonstrated kindness to me, I refrained from adding, "you fool."

Mother Mary Galfrieda steepled her hands as if in prayer. After a few moments, she turned them horizontal. Upon each palm flickered a blue flame.

"Morgan the Fool" catapulted to frontrunner as a new label for myself. I could envision some drunken French troubadour mutating it into the gender-incorrect "Morgan le Fou."[†]

"Your ladies learned from you," the mother superior reminded me. "Their successors not only taught their apprentices but conducted research and experiments to expand upon that knowledge." She clapped her hands, and the twin flames melded into a tiny tornado. A blink later, the tornado erupted into a basketball-size blizzard. Snowflakes no bigger than the business end of a pin swirled between her hands before disappearing into a burst of sparkles that shimmered into nothingness.

Weather magic practiced upon entire countrysides is difficult enough, but the precise control required to manipulate the elements between one's hands stood far beyond any climate spell I had ever dreamt of attempting.

I allowed my appreciation for her demonstration to emanate from my gaze. However, one crucial point remained inescapable:

---

† The gender-correct French in this instance would be "Morgan la Folle." *Folle* is the origin of the word "folly"…and it being based upon a female noun is more than a trifle insulting since the biggest follies—wars, for example—are, in the main, instigated by men. —*kih*

"Only our Lord Jesu possessed the power to breathe life into a corpse. With the Green Knight, I made Gawaine and Arthur's court believe they were conversing with a severed head. That sorcery also took weeks to prepare."

"Your Majesty, the Bible teaches us that anything Jesus did, we can do if we believe."

"That is far easier to recite than to practice." Why, yes, that was grouchy of me. Thank you for noticing.

The mother superior canted closer to me. "Why should it be? When you invoke a spell, you do so with the belief that it will work as you intend it to. Protecting your brother and Iradivus from harm is no different."

"Yes, it is, dash it!" Lacking armrests, I pounded my thigh. I hoped that the Royal Rules Committee, wherever in heaven (doubtful) or hell (if there was any justice) they might be, was enjoying the grandest of times effing themselves. "Their lives, their very souls stand at risk! The tiniest mistake in the spell, and—"

"And, what? They end up somewhere far different than expected, with no way to return to their rightful life…or time?"

As assessments went, that one was a broken-bat homer, I concede the woman that. It made me wonder whether her teacup weather magic had ensorcelled me too.

"What! No! I—" Reining in my runaway emotions became job one, or that damned committee really would start haunting me. "My spell was correct. Ambrose interfered with his thrice-cursed time-folding technology."

"The only thing Ambrose Hinton did was destroy your self-confidence, Your Majesty."

The cheek!

"Preposterous. I have worked plenty of magic since then. Much of it is recorded here." I rapped upon the box encasing my chronicle. "You and your Sisters witnessed my healing and disguising spells."

The mother superior blew a soft riff. "According to your own words, you manipulated time on two separate occasions. Was that a lie?"

"Three, counting my failed attempt to travel to 1879 Connecticut that landed me in Maryland of 2079 instead. On those other occasions, I stopped time for a few minutes. That is the extent of what I can accomplish without technology. I used a time-folding device to bring Arthur from Avalon to England of 2092." Never mind the physical and metaphysical implications of a realm that existed outside of time. Seeing no need to explore these speculations, I concluded with, "Since I was obligated to enchant its power source to life, whether that act counts as time-manipulation magic is a matter of debate." I directed a glare at the hidden face on the portrait. A shade more intense, and it would have burst into flames. "Here, technology serves the pope alone."

Mother Mary Galfrieda cracked off another homer:

"Are you so eager to watch your brother die?"

I uttered a low, rueful laugh. My ancient self, of course, would have been leagues beyond eager. "Not to-day." Blinking did naught to block the tears. I swiped them off my cheeks.

"Arthur is a nexus, like Jesus half a millennium before him," said the mother superior. "If Jesus had died in the wilderness, we wouldn't have a savior. If Arthur dies here…"

If Arthur were to die here, I did not believe that I could carry on. The wave of my emotions crested, forcing me to invoke a calming spell. The spell steadied me enough to say: "God help me. First Sandy, and now…I cannot lose Arthur too. I—I just cannot." My voice dropped to a raw whisper. "I have no idea how to save him this time."

The mother superior opened the case, withdrew my chronicle, fanned to one of the final pages, and activated the projector. My one-tenth-life-size hologram appeared on the desk, gowned and crowned, sitting hunkered beneath a cloak. The image raised its hooded head and said:

"Time! Time to rise up, shake loose the webs of despair binding my brow and blinding my eyes, and strive to resurrect a ray of hope from this dark disaster!"

The hologram stood and threw off the cloak, jutting her chin.

CHAPTER XVII.

I stood too, fists clenched, welcoming the confidence projected by the hologram into my own being. Together, the mini me and I said:

"Fortune's fool I may be, but none may deny that I am King Arthur's sister and Queen of Gore: healer, sorceress, and a force with which Fortuna must reckon."

The blessed reminder flowed through every corridor of my mind, body, and soul, stronger than the strongest healing magic imaginable, purging my doubts and conquering my fears.

After a few... what? Moments? Eons? I felt a gentle hand rest upon my shoulder. Mother Mary Galfrieda had risen from behind her desk to join me.

"Those words are no less true in this era. You must return to the source of their inspiration, Your Majesty."

"TIME TO RISE UP!"

Doubts and fears, it pains me to admit, ofttimes do not remain conquered. I shrugged away from her and closed the book. The hologram disappeared, and I picked up my chronicle. "I have more to learn in the archives," I said, looking at the office's door.

"Like hell you do."

I slammed the book onto the desk and glared at the woman. "How dare you!"

She twitched an unruffled shrug. "You know every detail of the parlay tent, from the length of the quills to the moment the adder appears. That's all you need for your magic to transport you there."

Fair point. However, "You forget Ratcliffe. How can I envision such a world if I do not know how he affected it?"

She had the stones to laugh. "Seriously? You're going to let that stop you when you were hell-bent to travel blind to Hank Morgan's century to exact your revenge?"

Her observation sucked the wind from my sails. "Rage clouded my judgment that day, I confess. But if my spell succeeds, you and everyone else born into this timeline shall cease to exist."

She crossed her arms. "You don't know that. We could be born into a better world. I, for one, would welcome it. So would my Sisters." Her expression became firm but not unkind. "Would you prefer things to go on as they are?"

Had I been Arthur, I might have ventured a most unroyal snort. "With every monarch distrustful of each other, and the Church maintaining an iron grip over them all? That *was* my world, once. And, once, I did not imagine that it could—or should—change."

Smiling, I patted the book, returned it to its case, secured the lid, and set upon it a spell to return to Castle Gore in the event of another temporal shift. "I thank you for the reminder." Regarding the mother superior, I added, "Both of you."

Forming the sign of the Cross, she wished me Godspeed. I thanked her for that too.

CHAPTER XVIII.
Return!

A S IF perched upon my throne, I sat rod-straight on a chair in our hotel room, hands clutching the armrests. The fates of Arthur, Clarice, myself, and indeed the entire world depended upon my success. As the defiant thunder rumbled closer, my knuckles whitened to the point that my hands could cramp, and I cast a swift bolstering spell. I harbored no desire to impose a weather delay upon the ballgame scheduled to begin at the top of the hour.

Recalling Mother Mary Galfrieda's demonstration of control, I constrained the lightning to flashing cloud to cloud; never cloud to ground. A delay might have aided my cause, but my nerves already felt afire from the strain of waiting. I doubted whether Arthur's nerves could bear an extended wait either.

During a private break on my first day in the archives, I had tried to observe, via the ring I had given Arthur, what he was experiencing. The images were foggy and useless, so I had abandoned further attempts. This evening, I resolved to apply a remote-viewing spell at the earliest opportunity. I dared not caveat the vow with my success in casting the most important enchantment of my magical career.

I clamped off the thought before it could destroy my focus.

Can you spell "no pressure?" Excellent; I knew you could.

The door opened. I paused my meditation and glanced up to see Clarice bustling in, carrying an envelope bearing the papal seal.

"The desk clerk gave me this." Midway through extending the envelope, she seemed to realize the purpose of my posture and pulled her hand back. "I'm sorry. I'll come back later."

She turned to depart, but I raised a hand. "Please wait, my dear. I need your assistance. Doubtless you hold His Holiness's invitation to join him for the Fight Club's main event."

At my bidding, Clarice opened the envelope, pulled out the invitation card, and grimaced. "Yep." She tossed card and envelope onto a nearby side table and plopped, deflated, onto a chair in front of the blank TV. "I'll bet you won't be going to the baseball game, then."

"Later. I hope."

She cast me a forlorn look in direct proportion to how much the pressures she had endured for the past week had mounted upon her. "How can I help?"

"Do you remember how we influenced the vote in President Malory's election?"

"Oh, yeah. That was an all-hands-on-deck situation, twenty-four-seven." She released a long sigh, and her gaze became disturbingly distant, as if she were staring into a bottomless abyss. "Seems like a lifetime ago…"

I arched an eyebrow, sharpening my tone to match. "It was. To-night you are the only deckhand available to me, so buck up, please, and get to swabbing."

She grinned, closed her eyes, and commenced the summoning of her magical energy.

Once the forces within me pulsated like the wattage of every Vatican City public building on every night of the week, I felt as ready as I was ever going to be. I hoped Clarice felt ready too. I called a halt and asked her to switch on the game.

"I do miss watching my Knights." Of course, these men were not "my" Knights, but they stood as worthy successors. My sole wish: that Arthur had been tagged to play in this game rather than as this night's Main Event headliner. An intended headless headliner too. I might have shared the pun with Clarice if it had not been so Godawful close to the truth.

The broadcast showed both teams—the Vatican players garbed in red and the Knights in black—lined up along the base paths, caps doffed and held over their hearts. The familiar music blaring from the loudspeakers accompanied the crowd's unfamiliar refrain "God save our pope." I cocked my head, stood, and approached the TV.

"God save our king," Clarice murmured.

"God save us all," I said.

As Clarice and I were preparing to be seen in public, which meant deciding whether a dress of battleship gray or gunmetal gray was more appropriate for the papal box, a messenger delivered surprising gifts for both of us.

"From His Holiness," the messenger announced with the swelled chest of someone to whom such high honors do not often fall. He set the boxes upon the table. I gave him every last mite of the pope's stipend, and I directed Clarice to do the same.

God willing, we would not need SDO Vatican City currency after to-night.

"Thank you, madame!" The messenger rendered as sharp a salute as any of my knights, steel-plated or otherwise, and quit our presence.

Each box contained a custom-tailored skirt suit, blouse, belt, low-heeled shoes, hose, and handbag. I should not have been surprised to find everything was solid black, down to the last swath and stitch.

"Funeral garb," Clarice grumbled.

Mayhap, but I chose an interpretation that made her smile: "London Knights colors, of course." I damned the risks to hell and back and conjured solid gold logo lapel pins for myself and my apprentice, and we transferred our ID cards and makeup into our new handbags. I stowed my dagger beneath my jacket, and we departed for the stadium.

The pristine white pontifical regalia sported by Pope Gildas XIII gleamed in stark contrast to our black suits. He and I could have sung the 1980s duet "Ebony and Ivory," if the tune existed in this version of the world; true to the song, "perfect harmony" was the last term I would apply to His Holiness and me. No doubt mindful of the TV cameras trained upon us during my and Clarice's arrival, he greeted us warmly and insisted that I sit at his right hand. This would complicate my efforts to maintain magical concentration throughout the game, and perhaps that was the pope's intention, but I saw no way to refuse without raising his suspicions, or those of his guards. I was thankful that His Holiness left Clarice to sit where she pleased. I resolved to make the best of our situation.

What choice had I else?

'Twas a great game, even by the baseball standards to which I had grown accustomed, the lead see-sawing as the innings progressed. Please forgive my lack of details, kind reader; I remained too busy balancing my magical focus against the necessity of making polite conversation with the pope to take note of very many plays. I do recall applauding worthy hits, steals, and outs for both teams, which I did frequently enough for His Holiness to commend my diplomacy. I assured him that I appreciated the athleticism, regardless of uniform color. Ever have I enjoyed watching the male form in action—in uniform as well as out—and this night delivered enjoyment aplenty. I wished that I *could* enjoy this spectacle without dreading the one to come.

The game's ending, however, stands crystal clear in my memory.

The scoreboard at the bottom of the ninth showed London leading 4–3, no outs, with runners on first and second. London's left-handed reliever, Cardinal Lawson, was facing the Vatican's cleanup man, the switch-hitting, home-run-threatening Monty Montigliano.

If my plan succeeded, the outcome of this game would not matter one fig in the Grand Design (okay, fine; arguably, the game would not matter either way), but old habits do die hard, and I could not resist the urge to send a mental suggestion to the London coaching staff to put in the right-handed Boniface.

A coach in the visiting dugout called time, the umpire acquiesced, a phone call was made, and in trotted Boniface from the bullpen. He and Lawson shared an arm grip, and then Lawson passed Boniface the ball and jogged off the field. Montigliano stepped out of the right-hand batter's box. After a few warmup pitches, the umpire thundered the order to play ball. As expected, Montigliano assumed his stance in the left-hand box for facing the right-handed reliever, which yielded the bonus of being a few steps closer to first base.

"Get him with your forkball,[†] Baron!" I yelled. Why, yes, my magicking had taken a toll on my memory. Thank you for noticing.

"*King Richard*, Ms. Hanks," whispered Clarice.

Montigliano fouled off the first pitch, took a strike, and watched a forkball miss half a hair to the inside. As in the series' earlier games, the batter could strike out on another foul ball.

"'Bonny Baron' is a fine nickname for His Majesty, would you not agree, Your Holiness?" I said.

His Holiness did little more than utter a holy grunt.

The vaunted Montigliano went down swinging.

Two to go.

I smiled to see the next Vatican batter, and not because I believed that he would hurt his team's chances: Cardinal Bambino Canoli. Whilst many of the guards had been courteous and even friendly after learning how much

---

† A forkball is a baseball pitch in which the ball is jammed between the forked index and middle fingers. Its flight path resembles a cross between a knuckle ball and a fastball. This pitch was used to great effect by Pittsburgh relief pitcher Elroy "Roy" Leon Face, nicknamed "the Baron of the Bullpen" and other baronial permutations throughout his 16-year major league career. The character of Richard "Bonny Baron" Boniface employs Roy Face's pitching style and (in KASIWC) mirrors his contributions to the Pirates' 1960 World Series win over the New York Yankees. —*kih*

CHAPTER XVIII.

I knew about baseball, Father Bambino was the lone man hailing from this sanctuary district—indeed, this entire corkscrewed timeline—that I could consider a true ally.

"I must say, Madame Hanks," began the pope, "you seem remarkably serene considering what's to transpire next." He had been peppering me with little barbs like that throughout the game; small wonder that I chose not to retain his blather for preservation herein.

I responded to this barb as I had done to all the others: with as much sweetness as I could muster. "Can any one of you, by worrying, add a single hour to your life?"

Below us, Canoli whiffed a curveball. The second pitch was a fastball, low.

"Good eye, Father Bambino!" called Pope Gildas, and the batter waved back before crouching for the next pitch. To me the pope said, "Our Lord Jesus never resurrected a beheaded man."

"That we know of. Your Holiness." In sweetness, Clarice scored a ten out of ten, but I resolved to chide her later for hesitating on the title.

Canoli ripped a screaming grounder up the middle, a stride to the left of second base. Both Vatican base runners took off. London's shortstop lunged to scoop up the ball, beat the Vatican runner to second, turned, and fired to the first baseman to put out Canoli at first.

The announcer concluded his commentary with, "An excellent double-play by SDO London's Lord Mayor Sonoma ends the ball game. Knights win 4–3. Godspeed to His Holiness, and to all the players, stadium workers, and fans!"

His Holiness looked none too thrilled, but he stood and applauded. A few beats later, so did the rest of the crowd, though I felt in no rush to regain my footing just because someone laying official claim to the virtue of holiness had done so. Many of the London players looked to the papal box. Some, including Sonoma, waved. Now, I stood, and I blew them a kiss. Had it been possible, I would have gifted Father Bambino with a farewell kiss too. I whispered to His Holiness my first barb of the game:

"Perhaps Our Lord is not pleased with those who contemplate breaking the sixth commandment—'Thou shalt not commit murder'," I supplied, in the off chance that the book with which he had posed for his statue indeed had been the Sears & Roebuck catalog.

'Twas a pleasant conceit that the pope might have been mulling my suggestion whilst he smiled at the players and dismissed the teams with the sign of the Cross. The field emptied of players, coaches, umpires, and other baseball personnel, and those of us occupying the papal box returned to our seats. Before facing the field, I gave Clarice a discreet nod.

"King David in the fifth Psalm assures us that if a man takes refuge in God, He will protect him," the pope said.

Not one item had been rearranged on the field; even the bases, home plate, and the pitching rubber remained in place. From opposite team entrances, my brother and the other gladiator strode onto the field. Both were clad in full medieval-style plate armor but carried no helmets, shields, or weapons. As they approached the pitcher's mound, the referee joined them from the home-team dugout, an axe balanced upon his shoulder.

You are a force with which Fortuna must reckon.

"Dear Lord, I do hope so," I said, as much in answer to Mother Mary Galfrieda's mental comment as to Pope Gildas's verbal one.

I cupped my hands upon the armrests, concealing the tiny lightnings I summoned upon my palms, and I closed my eyes. I trusted Clarice to be doing the same.

The announcer said, "And now, the main event! Something never before exhibited at the Holy Rollers Fight Club! Hold onto your seats, folks; you're in for the treat of a lifetime!"

The insides of my eyelids turned orange from the lightning flash, followed a heartbeat later by the boom.

"That one was real close, folks!" observed the announcer, whose super-hero name had to be Exclamation Pointman. "Thank God it didn't delay the ball game! We'll keep a close eye on the radar, but in the meantime, Your Holiness, ladies, and gentlemen, we are honored to present to you… Iradivus and the Red Dragon…in…the Beheading Game!"

Showtime.

Lightning flashed again, but its thunder proved no match for the crowd's cheers.

I am a force with which Fortuna must reckon.

The announcer, in surprisingly exclamation-point-free fashion, explained the rules: "Each man may assay one blow upon the other…if he is able. Lots were drawn moments ago, and the warrior who has won the privilege of striking first … is…Iradivus!"

Clarice whispered, "Naturally."

I speared her with a glare, and she returned her focus to the magic.

The pope rose and made the sign of the Cross. The referee passed the axe to Iradivus. Arthur knelt, head bowed and neck bared.

I am a force.

Iradivus hefted the axe and swung it to the ready.

FORTUNA'S RECKONING

I am **the** *force.*

If anyone's attention had been directed at me instead of being riveted to the axe blade, they would have seen balls of energy whirling upon both of my upturned palms. Clarice's too, I hoped.

I **am** *the force.*

The axe began its descent. Clarice and I smote our hands together.

I. Am. The FORCE!

"Ath-thill!" I shouted, the Scottish Gaelic for "Return!"

As the axe made contact with Arthur's neck, the spell unleashed a concussive blast that nullified the crowd's roar. Light exploded round us like a thousand thousand flashing cameras. That agonizing sensation of my every molecule being ripped asunder returned with a vengeance.

God, *God*, *GOD!* How I despise time travel.

CHAPTER XIX.
YOUNGER BRAD.

OTHER MARY Galfrieda's suggestion of returning to the parlay tent was not an option. I could not risk repeating those events and bollixing them. Instead, I chose what I believed to be the optimal location, surmised how it must have looked in the days following the inevitable, horrible battle, and hoped for the best.

My supposition, alas, proved correct.

Arthur—quite intact, to my boundless relief—Clarice, and I found ourselves standing alone on the elevated gallery overlooking the Round Table. Aside from the handful of pigeons whirring amongst the rafters, we were the gallery's lone occupants. Rather, Clarice and I occupied the gallery. My brother had materialized downstairs and was approaching the table at a hunter's pace, as if not wishing to spook it into taking flight.

Truth be told, with a black shroud draping every chair, and the fabric swathing Arthur's chair trimmed in gold, the massive old refugee from a giant's dining hall was doing a fair job of spooking me.

Arthur knelt beside his chair for no short span of time, expression somber but head unbowed. At length, he rose and fingered his shroud's gilt trim. He did not need to shudder; I was doing plenty of that for him. Geese had to be trampling both of our graves.

Clarice, perhaps sensing my distress, touched my arm, and I patted her hand. "I shall be fine, my dear," I insisted.

"What happened?" she asked, *sotto voce*. "I thought we—"

"Where we are is obvious. Whether we have preceded Ratcliffe's arrival is another question altogether," I said. "But first, let us see to my brother."

As a precaution, I cast aging spells upon Arthur as well as myself, and I clothed us all in peasant garb. My instincts served me well; whilst Clarice and I hastened down the gallery steps, the hall's main doors burst open, and a trio of armored guards stampeded in, brandishing spears. Their livery answered the temporal question: each tabard featured a stylized representation of the time-folding device, rendered in gold on a black field, where Arthur's gold-fielded scarlet dragon should have been.

Arthur glanced at his magically withered hands and arms jutting from drab, shabby clothing, and he stooped his posture, allowing his hands to tremble as he raised them at the guards' approach. The Yankee had subjected Arthur to a similar—though physical rather than magical—transformation. That my brother seemed to have recalled Sir Boss's lessons came as welcome proof that he had shed time travel's mind-numbing effects.

The oldest guard, in his sixth decade to judge from the visible wrinkles, poked Arthur's chest with the spear. To the guard's credit, his hands did not tremble to hold the pose. "What evils are you making here, old man?" he demanded of Arthur. After assessing that Clarice and I posed no threat, he paid us no further mind.

"Evils?" Arthur asked in an admirable old-man voice. "Fair sir, I ken not your meaning."

"There was a great light and sound like unto thunder." A touch of awe muted his tone. The narrowing of his eyes marked the awe's abolishment. "You must be a sorcerer!"

Not to be outdone by my brother, I summoned my best crone voice. "Prithee forgive three humble starvelings, kind sir. We were searching for food and got lost. We know naught of great lights and thunderings. Mayhap such doings have disrupted someone else's quest?" My stomach, through no prompting of my own, chose that moment to rumble long and loud. I played the effect to the hilt: "Oh! Dearest sir, prithee show us to the kitchens afore I expire at thy feet!" That last bit I uttered to support my disguise, of course. I knew my way round this vast stone heap as well as its rats did.

The old guard pivoted and pointed with his spear. "Out the big doors, turn left, and follow your nose." He signaled his fellows to raise their spears and let us pass.

Arthur took a few shuffling steps, paused, and addressed the guard. "How long has the king been dead?"

A brilliant question, and I wished I had thought of it. I snuffed the emotion before it could touch my face.

"A fortnight, God rest his soul, and Sir Mordred and Sir Launcelot and all the Round Table knights with him. Thousands more besides."

"Thousands…" I heard the crack in Arthur's whisper, and not, I surmised, because of feigning old age. He reassembled his composure to ask another brilliant question: "Who holds Camelot now?"

Suspicion returned to the guard's face. "Why should you care, old man?"

A new form darkened the doorway behind the guards, dressed somberly but sumptuously. A large pendant gleamed upon his corpulent breast. The guards stepped aside to let him through. To the lead guard he said, "Why shouldn't he care?"

Beside me, Clarice blurted a whispered, "Brad!" She slapped a hand over her mouth and lowered her head.

I prayed that Ratcliffe had not heard her, but 'twas not to be. He approached close enough for me to identify the object bouncing against his chest as his time-folding device. Recognition lit Clarice's eyes too, until she must have recalled that she should not know what the object was, and

THE GOVERNOR OF CAMELOT

she averted her gaze. Ratcliffe scrutinized Clarice long enough to make me thankful for my foresight. Rather than aging her, which she might not have been able to sell without coaching, I had added generous swaths of peasant filth to her exposed skin.

"Have we met?" asked the decades younger version of the lump we had encountered in the SDO London jail.

"Nay, me lord!" she squeaked in a passable British accent, and dropped a deep curtsy, keeping her head bowed.

Ratcliffe returned his attention to Arthur. Without bidding Clarice to rise, I might add, the ignorant ass. I dropped a hand onto Clarice's head in a signal to hold the pose till the ass left our presence, to save her from making an ass of herself too.

"Camelot belongs to the Church," Ratcliffe told Arthur, his tone conveying so much triumph that I worried Arthur might break character. "Its governance falls upon me by order of Gildas, the Archbishop of Canterbury." He jabbed his thumb at his own breast, above the time-folding device, and bared his teeth in an unflattering grin.

Archbishop?

The promotion must have been granted within the past fortnight; as but a mere bishop Gildas had served as mediator of the ruined parlay. Denizens of my preferred version of the twenty-first century had coined/ will coin/whatever a term for such a promotion: "failing upward."

Arthur, mayhap experiencing similar thoughts, shot me a glance before saying to Ratcliffe, "And a passing fair job of it ye be doing, no doubt… m'lord." If Ratcliffe noticed Arthur's hesitation with the title, he let it pass without comment. I resolved to invite my brother to attend my chat with Clarice regarding the finer points of maintaining a subordinate's disguise.

That chat needed to come before our heads became spear finials, but I had another task to accomplish first. Whilst Ratcliffe had been conversing with Arthur, I had inched for the toad. Now I stood close enough to pet his time-folding device. "Ah! Such a pretty bauble, me lord."

Ratcliffe slapped my hand away. "Beat it, crone! Begone." The pose he struck, hands on hips, exuded menace. "Don't let me find any of you here again, or it'll be the dungeons for you."

"Thank'ee, me lord! So sorry, me lord!" I was going to have to scrub my teeth till my gums bled; I had no idea how serfs could carry on entire lifetimes of this balderdash.

The three of us hurried out as fast as our supposed infirmities would permit.

When we were out of earshot, Arthur called a halt to address me: "Honor forbids me from attacking an unarmed man, but you muffed your opportunity to dispatch Ratcliffe." He was referring to the dagger that remained concealed upon my person, which now bore elevated risk by cause of the station projected by my disguise. Peasants were pilloried for possessing weapons of any stripe.

Dispatching the toad had not been my intent—even had I believed I could have dodged the law's standard punishment of death for any peasant daring to attack a noble—but I did not get a chance to explain before my ever-helpful apprentice chimed in with, "Our very presence here could be altering the timeline in ways we cannot predict."

"Just so," I said. "If there are witnesses to Ratcliffe's demise, God alone knows what disasters may result."

Arthur stroked his white-whiskered chin. "Then we need a way to draw him out. I must think on this." He strode forth a couple of brisk paces before remembering to age his gait.

"Good job," I whispered to him. "Though please do try not to choke on the toad's honorific next time. Resurrecting you is ever so much trouble."

Admonishing a king is tricky business, but I find humor to be a useful companion in most instances, including this one. Arthur returned my smile with a murmured, "Point taken, dear sister."

"You shall do well to remember this point too," I said to Clarice.

The peasant filth eclipsed her blush, but I could sense it in her lowered gaze. "I'll try to do better…" I lifted her chin with a finger and then shook it at her. "That is to say, I crave thy pardon for my slow wits…mum?"

Mum…The music of that lone word thrilled my soul as no other word, in any lifetime or timeline, ever did before, or since. I cracked a grin with my magically tooth-deprived mouth. "Mum, indeed. Prithee forget it not, daughter."

I practiced a soft version of my crone chuckle as I resumed my doddering pace, leaving Arthur and Clarice to follow as they might.

In every each of Camelot's halls, colonnades, and courtyards, we saw Ratcliffe's men dismantling evidence of Hank Morgan's nineteenth-century improvements: electric lighting, telegraph wires, advertising posters, printing presses and other machinery; not even the tiniest scrap of newsprint had escaped their attention. Castle residents not bedecked in Ratcliffe's uniform were shuffling about their appointed tasks—bearing food or drink, toting laundry baskets, delivering tools, and so forth—with heads hung low as if to raise them would bring certain death. Given what I knew of Ratcliffe's motivational style, I would not have been surprised to find death for disobedience on his judicial menu.

Although I supposed that gawking might have been expected from the country folk we presented ourselves to be, I refrained…until we got to the open door of the Yankee's laboratory. Inside, Merlin was leaping and capering about like a man half his seven-decade age, cackling nonstop as he wrought magical havoc upon test tubes, beakers, metal supports, titration devices, Bunsen burners, Petri dishes[†], notebooks, and whatever other scientific apparatus Hank Morgan had left behind. The chamber's owner must yet be sojourning with his wife and daughter in France, I reasoned, else he would have acted to thwart Gildas, Merlin, and Ratcliffe.

The wizard, happy as any dozen slop-bound hogs combined, paid us no mind as we paused for a few moments to witness the carnage. Even Arthur shuddered as we moved on.

A score of paces later, Clarice said, "I'd hate to be stuck here too long."

I gave her a sympathetic smile and crafted my response to imply my acceptance of the fact that she had risked breaking character: "That shall depend upon our outcome with Ratcliffe."

---

† The Bunsen burner was named for Robert Bunsen, the German chemist who introduced the apparatus in 1855. The Petri dish was named for German bacteriologist Julius Richard Petri, who introduced this object in the 1880s. Twain, a great lover of science and technology, would have been familiar with both items. *–kih*

CHAPTER XIX.

Another shudder rippled through me, longer and more disturbing than my reaction to the destruction of the Yankee's equipment,—which at the time I attributed to the tragedies Ratcliffe and Merlin had inflicted, though now I know better. Please forgive me, dear reader; I shan't digress any further.

I asked my brother if he had developed any ideas.

"Whatever happens must be an external threat to the castle. All my knights are gone"—he kept his tone level, but I heard the sorrowful note in his emphasis of the word *all*—"and I have yet to see evidence of the standing army being rebuilt, so the threat's magnitude should be beyond what a troop of guards can handle. Something magical, mayhap summoning an eldritch creature?"

Sound military thinking, as expected from the vaunted warrior-king; however, "Magic use may put us at risk of discovery. Keep thinking, please," I said.

After a few more paces, Clarice brought up a fair point: "We'll need a means of support. We don't have a pope to pay our bills."

We had paused at the intersection of two corridors. I peered round the corner for a few moments before straightening to regard my companions. "We cannot risk entering the royal chambers; besides, I expect Ratcliffe will have looted them already. I shall see to our monetary needs." To Arthur, I said, "Thank you for allowing me to maintain a private set of chambers here. I never appreciated your generosity till now."

"You are most welcome," he said. "A tad late, but welcome."

I gave him an apologetic grin. To both, I said, "Please meet me in the town. 'Twill be wisest for me to assay my chambers alone."

Arthur grasped Clarice's shoulder and hunched over. In his old-man voice, he said, "Thank God Hank taught me how to be someone I am not."

Amen, I thought, and then received a divine reminder and asked them to wait. I grasped Arthur's hand, the one bearing the defensive ring, which I proceeded to imbue with a remote-viewing capability strong enough to function across time as well as space, I hoped. Not that I feared we would become separated in time, but given all the other ludicrous events that had transpired, I could not be too careful. "I have added an extra layer of magical protection," was the only splinter of truth he needed to know.

CHAPTER XX.
STRANGERS IN A
STRANGER LAND.

THE MAGIC ward I had set upon my chambers in the wing dedicated to Camelot's regular royal guests, the most notable (aside from myself) being King Pellinore, remained in force. It suggested to me the hypothesis that magic must exist apart from space and time, since enchantments perforce dissolve upon the practitioner's death, a fate I have yet to suffer despite my sundry traverses across a certain set of fifteen centuries. Proving the hypothesis might illuminate the metaphysics of Avalon…were I to possess time to investigate the matter. The explanation of how I now, in fact, strive to achieve said objective lies beyond the scope of my promise to abstain from further digressions.

From behind Pelli's door, the suite before arriving at mine, rumbled the baying of "a thirty couple hounds," as my Camelot neighbor-friend would say, trusting his audience to know he meant sixty hounds. So, the canny and tenacious, if a tad muddle-minded, king had caught the Questing Beast at long last. No doubt she proved as effective a deterrent as any ward of my devising, though I pitied the servants assigned to feed and clean up after her. That dear old King Pellinore might have become a casualty of the Battle on the Salisbury Plain, I had no wish to contemplate.

CHAPTER XX.

Fear of reprisal from Morgan le Fay must have operated as a deterrent too; not one guard stood watch along this corridor. Either that, or the guard captain had wearied of his men being the featured attraction of the Questing Beast's high teatime. The snake-leopard-lion-hart creature could have been vegan, for all I knew, but the image of her swallowing a guard whole and spitting out the sword, for to pick her teeth, lifted my spirits a mite.

Heaven knew how many mites it would take to lift my spirits a measurable amount, even with the assurance that Arthur and Clarice would look after one another quite well as the champion heroes I knew them both to be.

I disabled my ward, unlocked the door, and stepped inside.

Never underestimate the value of familiar environs, beloved reader. The ability to find every coin, every jewel, every scrap of silk, every comb and brush and button and ribbon exactly as I had left it soothed me far more than I could have imagined possible. I had to remind myself of the need for haste, else I might be drinking in the comfort yet still. That said, in some perverse way I felt as if I were a stranger in my own chambers, mayhap owing to the utter strangeness of the world I was attempting to repair.

The silks, hair implements, buttons, ribbons, and such I left where they lay. Though tempted to bring as many of the jewels as I could carry, I doubted whether the Church-controlled postwar economy could support my selling them for anything within a baseball's throw of their value, never mind the inevitable, unavoidable question of how a "peasant" woman could have come by them other than theft. The jewels would remain safe behind my reestablished magical ward, should the need arise for their liquidation.

I conjured three plain leather pouches of modest size and sturdy construction (my own pouches were anything but plain and therefore unsuitable to accessorize our disguises), stuffed them to nigh bursting with coins of various sizes and metals, reset all my locks and the ward, and departed the chambers, bidding the Questing Beast a mental farewell as I passed Pelli's door. The rumbling seemed to change in quality, as though she were wishing me good fortune. I thanked her and hurried on.

"SHE COULD HAVE BEEN VEGAN, FOR ALL I KNEW."

Arthur and Clarice I found on the steps of Camelot's town chapel. The belfry's bell was shrouded in a looser (and therefore cheaper) weave of the black fabric swathing the Round Table's chairs, and its clapper was tied back. Wooden planks barred the building's windows and doors. Stuck by an arrow to the door's eye-level horizontal plank was a parchment sheet that read:

Closed By Order of His Grace, The Archbishop of Canterbury

It was signed "Bradley Ratcliffe, Governor of Camelot." The arrowhead had obliterated the date.

I resisted the urge to rip down the accursed thing.

As I dispensed the pouches to my companions, who knotted them to their belts, the sounds of wailing and crying arose in the distance and grew louder: a funeral procession sans priest, prayers, and candles. The coffin was sized for a child.

My heart seized; a parent never forgets. I remain forever grateful that I had set aside our differences enough to dispense an extra hug to my son, Uwaine, prior to his departure for what would be his final battle. My lone regret remains that I failed to banish my anger regarding his choice to fight for Arthur; had I possessed that capacity, perhaps I could have protected him.

Had I possessed that capacity, it stands to reason that my life, Uwaine's life, Arthur's life, yea, perhaps even the entire world's fate would have taken a very different turn.

The procession passed the church and its yard, the gate of which also had been planked shut. The pallbearers kept their eyes fixed forward as if to deny a child burial in sanctified ground were the norm. My heart broke for all of them.

After the procession had moved well beyond the ability of any in its train to overhear us, Clarice whispered, "A funeral without a priest? A church with barred doors and a gagged bell? In this era?"

"This era," I said, allowing disgust to color my tone, "is the Interdict."

Though Arthur's posture remained that of an old man's, his whisper reverted to its natural state: "My wife, my friends, my knights…all gone… would God I had not lived to see this day."

I gave him a curious look. "Would you have rather died on the Salisbury Plain?"

"I should have."

Panic stabbed my chest. I drew a deep breath. "You cannot mean that. Without you, the world has no hope."

The funeral procession disappeared through the castle's gates, and Arthur gave me his full attention. Frankness invaded his gaze. "Without my *legend*, the world has no hope. There is a difference."

Clarice piped in with, "Even Jesus had to die to achieve His full power and glory."

"Just so," Arthur said. "Explain it to Her Majesty, Clarice, as she seems to be having difficulty grasping the concept."

"I grasp the concept with perfect clarity. I simply do not—"

Clarice raised both hands and lowered her voice. "Please forgive me, Your Majesties, but I suggest we table this discussion for a safer location." Her nod pointed us to a small armed patrol rounding the corner of a nearby building.

I turned to Arthur, but he was already making his old-man way for the nearby White Horse Inn. I would have preferred the privacy of a friend's house, but by his admission all his friends were gone, and three "peasants" caught trespassing in a dead noble's abode would fast-track us to the dungeons. Clarice and I caught up with him before he reached the weathered doors.

Inside, the inn's atmosphere was as somber as any ten Interdict-era funeral services combined, with no music and naught but a smattering of morose laughter amongst the handful of patrons. Even the sputtering fire's glow seemed bereft of cheer. An ample array of seating choices greeted us. The proprietor did not; his countenance hosted a battle between wariness of the "strangers," relief that we had chosen to drop coin at his establishment, and dubiousness that buying anything was our actual intent. We commandeered a table in a dim, smoky corner that looked too clean to have been occupied at any time during the Interdict, laid down a handful of coins that thawed the innkeeper's disposition nigh to gushing, and commenced with drowning our sorrows,—which proved far easier than crafting viable solutions.

Four pints later and retaining admirable control of his old-man voice, Arthur declared, "For a corpse, this is the thirstiest I have ever been." He drained his tankard and raised it to signal delivery of another.

"Be thankful you are not my jester," I said.

He gave a dry chuckle, mayhap recalling how many unfunny jesters the ancient me had executed.

The serving maid brought his replacement, collected a farthing and the empty vessel, and bustled away. Since the room's noise level remained low, we resumed sitting hunkered over the table, heads close together and voices softer than church whispers. We held no fear of fostering suspicions; the other patrons were conducting their business in likewise fashion.

Clarice said to Arthur, "There has to be a way to get your throne back. Then you could do whatever you liked to Ratcliffe."

"Without my knights and my army, or even Excalibur, I cannot see how."

"I can locate and retrieve your sword without difficulty," I said. To state that Arthur brightened at this prospect would be to state that Excalibur was sharp. "Manpower remains the key issue to resolve." The royal brightness dimmed.

"What about the vassals of Gore?" asked my apprentice.

"This is the Interdict, Clarice," I reminded her. "Even were we to make it to Gore,—no certain wager, that—I would first have to deal with the ancient me, but our paltry force of five hundred men would prove no match for the thousands the Church now commands." I felt no compulsion to torpedo morale yet further by stating my concern regarding how many of that five hundred might have defected to the Church…or had been killed by their vengeful mistress in the attempt.

Arthur nodded bleak agreement, but then a thought seemed to cheer him. "Sir Boss would not have sat idle whilst the Church had its way with his wondrous devices and our people. He must yet be in France."

The reverence with which he pronounced the Yankee's devices as "wondrous" convinced me to keep my misgivings about the interloper to myself. That, and the "enemy of my enemy" precept, which could in fact transform the Boss into the most valuable ally we could enlist.

"From what I recall of the Yankee's chronicle, he didn't stay idle in exile," Clarice confirmed. "But he also…"

She trailed off when four youths, cloaked and hooded, with foaming pints in their fists, claimed the table adjacent to ours. Arthur's grin displayed a set of teeth enchanted to appear broken or missing. "If one man knows where Sir Boss is, that would be Clarence." He tossed a nod over his shoulder at the youths.

As he pushed back his chair, I laid a hand upon his arm. "Speaking to them is too risky."

He pulled free. "Acting without gathering information is riskier yet. Your spell upon my person holds, aye?" I gave a reluctant nod, and he straightened. "Then fear not."

My fear refused to be quelled on the mere grounds of his say-so. The smallest thing any of us said or did could engender disastrous consequences. I activated a volume-enhancement spell that allowed Clarice and me to hear the proceedings, and I resolved to act should the need arise.

By this time, the youths had finished their pints. Arthur intercepted the serving maid and paid for their second round.

The young man possessing the greatest air of authority—which was not saying much, given how they were hunkering down like the rest of us—said to Arthur, "Thank you kindly, venerable friend. Please join us." Arthur snatched his tankard off our table and dragged his chair to theirs. The serving maid delivered the drinks, and the youths saluted my brother with tankards aloft. "To what do we owe this boon?"

"I wish to learn of Sir Boss," Arthur said.

I wished my brother had learnt the art of small talk.

The lead youth exchanged nervous glances with his lieutenants. To Arthur, he said, "Why would you believe we know anything about His Lordship?"

"I have seen ye in his company, good youth," Arthur replied. "It pleases him to call ye Clarence, though your Christian name is Amyas."

This led to more nervous glances that tried extra hard not to look nervous, the result yielding the opposite effect.

One of the lieutenants said, "How would you know—"

"Never mind that, Ælferd," said Clarence. He regarded Arthur, narrowing his eyes. "Who are you? Why are you here?"

CHAPTER XX.

Arthur raised both mock-wrinkled hands and waved them in a calming gesture. "I be loyal to the Crown, same as Sir Boss, and I wish to help his cause. It dismays me to see the Church's doings to my ki—kin and home."

That Arthur had almost said "kingdom," I had no doubt. It took me seven swallows of ale to drown the urge to expel a relieved sigh. Clarice finished her tankard, too, and procured refills for us both.

Clarence shook his head. "Sorry, friend. Unless you can change yourself into a bird and fly across the Channel, there's not much else you can do for us."

"He lives in France yet still, then," Arthur said.

"With the Lady Alisande, aye," Clarence replied. "One of her men got a copy of the last issue of the Camelot *Weekly Hosannah and Literary Volcano!* before Archbishop Gildas destroyed our operation. The Boss may have read about the king's death by now."

To Arthur's credit, he did not flinch at the mention of his death, though I confess I was smitten with the irreverent urge to bleat that the report was greatly exaggerated.[†] Such indiscretion would have landed us dungeon accommodations faster than if we had voided ourselves on Ratcliffe's boots.

The lieutenant named Ælferd[‡] said, "That was more than a week ago. We don't know why the Boss hasn't returned already."

Arthur pondered the liquid in his tankard before taking a pull. He swiped foam from his lips with the back of a hand and said, "Did he leave any instructions, should things go amiss in his absence, and the king's?"

[†] In June 1897, *The New York Herald* reported that "(Twain's) indomitable energy has at last left him…" The *New York Journal* published a story the next day that included Twain's rebuttal: "The report of my death was an exaggeration." Queen Morgan's version is based upon the article printed in *The Evening Star* of Washington, DC, two days after the *Herald*'s account: "Mark Twain says that his reported death has been greatly exaggerated." The version of the quote that may be most familiar to readers comes from a November 1897 issue of *The Commercial Appeal* of Tennessee: "Some time ago a report of Mark Twain's death was sent to England, and one of his English friends cabled to Hartford to ascertain if it were true. Mark at once cabled back: 'Reports of my death are greatly exaggerated.'"
There is no accounting for journalists.

[‡] Ælferd is the name of one of the enemies Gyan (my Guinevere character that I daresay Twain would have liked) kills in battle in my Arthurian historical-fantasy novel *Morning's Journey*, setting up Ælferd's fiancée, Camilla, as an enemy in a later book. **Spoiler Alert:** One Ælferd manages to get buried with his head. —*kih*

"Nay. Methinks he never expected to be gone this long. We've been operating from the contingency list I worked up," Clarence said. "But there's so much yet to do, and so few of us."

Arthur's circling finger indicated all the youths seated at the table. "Just you lads?"

"Fifty-two, including the four of us," Clarence said. "The best defensible position close to the castle is Merlin's Cave, and we've started laying the groundwork, but we have the sorcerer himself to contend with."

"There I may be of some use. Just to-day I watched Merlin pillage Sir Boss's chambers in the castle." I questioned Arthur's wisdom for volunteering that bit, which could have spawned an awkward conversation about how an "old peasant" had gained access.

The fact that the cadets flinched not a single eyelash testified to their desperation for assistance.

"Yeah," said Ælferd, "the humbug had it in for the Boss; that's old news."

I marveled at Hank Morgan's influence, never imagining that young men bred in this era could have adopted his nineteenth-century speech patterns in but a handful of years. In the next breath, I decided that I should not have been surprised. The twenty-first century in general, and Sandy in particular, had done much to influence me in perspectives as well as in speech.

"Can you keep Merlin busy?" Clarence asked my brother.

Arthur nodded. "I might also know of a way to summon Sir Boss, but I must verify this with someone else and can make no promises." He refrained from glancing at me, which I appreciated. I began pondering how I could accomplish such a summons, sans telegraph or any other technological means.

"Keeping Merlin out of our hair for a week or two will be good enough, friend!" After the cadets' chuckles played themselves out, Clarence continued, "Say, what do we call you, aside from 'friend'?"

"You lads may call me…" Arthur's grin shaded to mischievous. "Wart."

CHAPTER XXI.
To You We Hail!

HE SMALL, rough round table in our shared chambers at the White Horse Inn proved steady enough to support the water-filled basin whilst I awaited the moon's pleasure. Clarice sat in silence beside me, poised to assist. Arthur reclined on his bed, though not asleep, to judge by the absence of snoring.

I could not fault him; had our roles been reversed, I would not have been sleeping either.

I dissolved the enchantment supporting our peasant garb, filth, and aging without fear of discovery, for the night had progressed well past the last hour for expecting company, and I had ordered the room to remain dark. The basin's contents required moonlight for the spell to achieve full potency. I conjured hunting leathers to replace Arthur's Vatican armor, for to minimize any noise his movements might make. Since Clarice suggested that we exchange the pope's gifts for our favorite period-appropriate gowns, I had her cast that spell for the practice.

For the umpteenth time, I glanced out the unshuttered window. The clouds' glow betrayed the lunar power they were conspiring to obscure. Curbing my impatience with a long blink, I sent a mental suggestion to the offenders. They took the hint and scuttled on their way, warning their misty fellows against assuming their places.

Light from the full moon flooded the chamber and struck the water. That was my cue.

I revived memories of Hank Morgan and Lady Alisande on the day they had visited Castle Gore, superimposing their visages upon a supposition of what their French manor house—specifically, their bedchamber—might look like without straying into inappropriate territory by imagining how the chamber's occupants might be passing the time if they were not asleep.

Gripping the basin, I stared at the water, into the water, and past it as an image of the Yankee's actual French bedchamber appeared. Clarice uttered a soft gasp; I surmised that she could see it too. I heard a bed's ropes creak; that had to have been Arthur sitting up. The scrying spell was limited to transmitting visuals. I read the Yankee's lips as he muttered in his sleep:

"Mrs. le Fay…great ambiance…smoke?"

I indulged in a satisfied smile, gave Clarice a nod, and projected my consciousness into Hank Morgan's dream.

I found myself in full command of my hearing as well as sight, seated upon the dais in Castle Gore's banquet hall beside my husband of that era, King Uriens. Our son sat upon his father's right. Hank and Alisande occupied the seats beside Uwaine, and my favorite lover of the period, Sir Accolon, sat upon my left. The rest of Gore's worthies and their ladies occupied tables below the dais. Servants circulated, dispensing food and drink; mostly drink. The hounds were entertaining us with squabbles over dropped bits. Their howling sounded more musical than the noise emanating from the court musicians' gallery. The revelers' laughter was too frequent and too loud to suggest anything within a bone's throw of sobriety.

The atmosphere looked garish and distorted by a gray haze that nobody else seemed to notice.

Hank brandished his pipe. "King Uriens, may I smoke?"

"Go right ahead, my boy," replied the king. "I am dead!"

"What—?" Hank again. Though his responses remained his own, I was manipulating everyone else's.

I took advantage of his surprise to say, "As a door-nail. Both armies and all the Round Table knights too."

"And King Arthur?" Hank asked.

Having anticipated that the Yankee might inquire after his friend, and having no desire to either lie to the man or reveal our secret quite yet, I created a familiar distraction.

King Uriens said, "I am ever so parched. Page!"

The king's catamite scurried to the dais, bumped my knee, and sloshed wine from the pitcher he was carrying. On the day I had evoked, the boy had been presenting a golden salver of sweetmeats; for the dream, I pulled an entry from the Yankee's playbook and selected a substance possessing more inherent flair. The wine spattered my gown and puddled at my feet. I drew my dirk and stabbed the page. Blood gushed out, which the not-quite-dead page caught in the pitcher and poured into the king's goblet. Uriens finished it in four gulps.

Of course the page had dropped door-nail dead in reality; I had to make the Yankee believe he was dreaming, or I would have run the risk of him waking before I could finish my mission.

Uwaine lifted his goblet overhead. "Drinks all round the vale!"

Accolon said, "Three hails for the dead door-nail!" He raised his goblet level with Uwaine's and extended it toward King Uriens. "To you!"

Everyone shouted, "We hail!"

As the bleeding-but-not-dead page kept catching his blood to refill the goblets, the revelers—even Alisande—clanked and drank. Hank was the lone exception, and "horrified" did not come halfway to describing his expression. No one paid me any mind as I rose and stepped closer to him. Suppressing the impulse to hug Uwaine, I reached behind him to grasp the Yankee's shoulder. Hank seemed thankful to look at me rather than his blood-guzzling wife.

"Sir Boss, you must return to Camelot at once," I said.

"Fly, fly! Ere you all die!" added my son.

"To you!" Accolon gestured with his goblet and favored me with his most intimate, sultry smile. 'Twas in truth my Sandy's smile, down to the

THE PAGE'S LIBATION

last delectable nuance, and it nigh destroyed my focus. With all the madness that had transpired, I had quite forgotten that, barring the millennium and a half separating their births, each could have been the other's identical twin.

"We hail!" The revelers' booming refrain wrenched me back to the task at hand. Had I succumbed to the towering temptation of kissing "Sandolon" (you invented that mashup too, clever reader; I know you did) in that dream-moment, I might be a contented prisoner of the Yankee's mind yet still.

"I have to muck about as a knight-errant." Why Hank's brain conjured that excuse I shall never know.

A loving smile bent Alisande's bloodied lips. "There is where you err, my dear."

"Disguise yourself," I advised. "The Church controls England now. Her knights will kill you on sight."

"Church is master; travel faster!" Accolon pointed his goblet at Hank. "To you!"

For the third and final time, the revelers chimed, "We hail!"

Panic leapt to life on the Yankee's face. "The Church? What do you mean, Mrs. le Fay? Mrs. le Fay!"

I withdrew from Hank's mind and resumed my study of his sleeping face, which looked as far from peaceful as the sun from the earth. He thrashed his limbs, waking Alisande, and I sharpened my concentration for lip-reading.

Perhaps still bound by the dream, Hank said, "Mrs. le Fay!"

"Hank?" Alisande prodded him. "Hank!" No response. She cocked her arm and punched his shoulder harder than I would have expected from that slip of a girl. "Wake up, my love!"

He opened his eyes, confusion clouding his features as he rubbed the shoulder. "Hey, that hurt! What? Where—?" Glancing round, he grasped Alisande's moonlit hands and whooshed out a long breath. "That was one right humdinger[†] of a dream."

---

† "Humdinger," of unknown etymology but most likely a variant of "hummer," dates its first use to 1896. Since Twain demonstrated a fondness for applying the derisive adjective "humbug" to some of his characters—notably, Merlin—I can envision him selecting "humdinger" to suggest the quality of being the polar opposite of a humbug. —*kih*

"Prithee tell me about it," she said, her fingers contracting round his.

"Well, for starters, Queen Morgan le Fay told me everyone at Camelot was dead, the Church was in charge, and I should return post haste." His shudder conveyed his decision to keep the dream's gory details to himself. "Weird!"

Alisande disengaged one of her hands to clap it to her bosom. "Everyone—dead? Oh, Hank!"

He drew her into an embrace. "Don't you fret, Sandy. It was just a silly dream. Although I get the strangest feeling…"

You had better be getting more than a feeling, I thought, but I held my peace and kept watching.

Alisande rose, lit a taper on the bedside table, crossed the room to a chest, and lifted its lid. "This should put your mind at ease. I would have given it to you sooner, but you have been ever so busy working on your chronicle." She withdrew a sheet of newsprint, set the taper back on the little table, and returned to the bed.

Unbridled joy lit Hank's features. "The Camelot *Weekly Hosannah and Literary Volcano!,* as I live and breathe! How in heaven's name did you come by this? Better yet, when?"

"I dispatched a man last week, thinking the news of home might cheer you," Alisande said. "He returned with this the day before yesterday."

"Bless your bones, Sandy!" I clenched my shoulders; I knew the fate of her blessed bones. "Let's see what you've got."

Hank's elation dissolved into slack-jawed horror as he angled the paper to catch the candlelight.

In two-hundred-point lettering blared the headline:

Alisande's eyes showed not the faintest glimmer of understanding. "What is wrong, my Hank?"

Lowering the paper, he gave her a sad smile. "If we get through this, I'm going to have to teach you to read. But for now, dream or not, the old girl is right: I must go home at once."

Just when I was beginning to believe that I might like the Yankee, he up and called me "old." The statement's apropos did not erase its cheekiness.

"I shall speak to the servants about minding our daughter in our absence, and then I shall start packing for us both," Alisande said.

"But, Sandy, it will be dangerous! And Hello-Central needs you."

"Hello-Central shall have a grand time with her 'aunties' and 'uncles.' You know she loves them all with abandon, and how they dote upon her." Her sweet smile stiffened into determination. "But me no buts, Hank. 'Ever and always' was my wedding vow to you, and I should be a poor wife to break it now."

I hoped the ass appreciated the great treasure that was his wife.

Blinking, I gave my head a slight shake and looked up, flexing fingers grown stiff from clutching the basin for God knew how long. The moonlight had surrendered to the first rays of dawn.

"Success?" asked my brother.

"Did you ever doubt, Your Majesty?" I teased.

I took Arthur's diplomatic silence for yes but forgave him anyway. The faux Arthur in a twentieth-century whimsical and musical but overall wrong rendition of our lives—the primary insult being that its author portrayed me as the queen of chocoholics and then deemed my scene to be optional; fie on all the companies who choose not to pay the extra license fee to include it in their productions—did offer one dollop of wisdom:

Only fools never doubt.

"I'M GOING TO HAVE TO
TEACH YOU TO READ."

CHAPTER XXII.
WIZARD WRANGLING AND OTHER CHORES.

ATER THAT day, following a brief trip to London to inspect some magical handiwork that I had initiated remotely after completing my dream session with the Yankee, Clarice and I visited the Camelot market seeking supplies. The White Horse Inn's meals were a rotation of beef, pork, venison, and chicken, each trencher accompanied by a loaf of black bread. The proprietor kept a tidy establishment, but on the second day of our stay it became apparent that the word "vegetable" owned no place in his vocabulary.

I had expected goods to be scarce and prices high, but that did not prevent me from being appalled. The low quality of the meager offerings tracked in direct proportion to the lack of customers.

To stave off a dungeon detour as we flashed our cash, I dressed us to project the images of modestly prosperous crofters rather than dirt-grubbing peasants, and we both were content to pose as mother and daughter. I maintained my crone persona, and Clarice wore a light veil, rather than soot, to obscure her face.

After purchasing the best of the greens, carrots, radishes, cucumbers, peas, leeks, and onions, I gave the parcels to Clarice and doddered to the apothecary shop, site of our true mission. This was the only vendor in town enjoying brisk business; the doors stood wide open as if proud to reveal how well stocked was the shop they warded.

I paused on the threshold.

That was an act for the benefit of the shop's most notorious customer. As I had hoped, the old humbug noticed my hesitation.

"G'wan in, mum." Clarice gave me a little, scripted nudge. "Be not afeared."

Merlin did his best not to grin as he resumed the process of examining the herbs. Hank had been quite right to dub him a humbug.

I buried that opinion under a cartload of old-woman trepidation.

To make it seem as if she were attempting to put me at ease as I inched into the shop, she began rattling on with, "Mum, 'twas the strangest thing! All those poles and wires and fiddly bits, gone one day by the Archbishop's command, and back whole and hale again the next!"

I added a slight tremor to my hand as I crossed myself. "The work of sorcery, and no mistake. A sorcerer who has no love for—or fear of—the Church. Ye were wise to hie yourself away from that wretched place." In the Yankee's chronicle, he had in fact confessed to fearing the Church but had always taken especial care to project absolute fearlessness of everything.

Merlin, who by this time was haggling with the apothecary, glanced our way again. The shop keeper cleared his throat, and the wizard resumed the task at hand.

Clarice dropped into a tone engineered to make Merlin work harder to overhear. "Do ye think—?"

I modulated my volume to match. "Sir Boss's work, aye, beyond doubt. And where Sir Boss be, trouble follows."

Purchases tucked under one arm, Merlin looked out the window. The stumpy remains of a felled telegraph pole lay in his line of sight. With an exaggerated swirl of his midnight-dark robes, he pivoted and oozed closer to Clarice and me. His thin grin did naught to improve his visage. "Pray, forgive me, good women. Of what do you speak?"

Uttering an alarmed squeak, I flung up my hands for good measure. "The mighty sorcerer Merlin! Let us flee, daughter! Flee, I say!"

I reached for Clarice's hand, but Merlin caught me by the arm. I had no idea the old humbug could move so fast. His grip, however, would not have detained a butterfly. I chose to stay caught.

"Good mother," he crooned, "prithee fear me not. If there be trouble brewing, I must quench it ere it spreads."

"And how may we be assured that we shall not be caught up in your net?" The question begged to be punctuated by the crossing of arms, but that would have broken his grasp, so I kept my arms uncrossed.

Merlin released me, rubbed his thumb against two fingers, and produced a bright red copper coin between them. Clarice surged for it, but Merlin snatched his hand back. "Take me for a fool?" he thundered.

Clarice shrank from him. "Nay, kind sorcerer!"

"LET US FLEE, DAUGHTER!"

221

"Answers before reward, woman." The thunder in his tone subsided a few decibels.

My "daughter" tossed me a "nervous" glance. "G'wan, lambkin," I said. "Tell His Wizardship where you saw this spot of sorcery."

Clarice dropped His Humbugship a deep curtsy.

"Outside London, if it please Your Wizardship. Day afore yesterday. Affrighted me to the bone, it did! Straightway I hied here to me mum."

"London! I saw to that work myself just last week." He unlimbered his tongue and cursed like a bishop, concluding with, "I must needs return." After signaling Clarice to rise, Merlin cast his gaze heavenward, but I had no idea what he might be seeking; no Power greater than himself, I would wager. "Be there no end to Sir Boss's sedition?"

Clarice and I regarded him with the expected level of confusion.

"Ah, what do you simple women know of loftier matters?" he nattered on. "You have done well, and I thank you most kindly for the report." He gave Clarice the copper and produced a second one for me. I bit mine, and Merlin laughed. "'Tis as real as thee or me, good mother."

I came within a nose hair's breadth of snorting at that but curtsied to him instead. Clarice followed my example. Though she rebounded right away, I held the pose till after Merlin had departed, to bridle the impulse to show that pompous old humbuggy ass just how simple I was.

With the wizard out of the way, seeking to dismantle yet again the telegraph lines that I had magically reassembled in London, the work to fortify Merlin's Hill began in earnest. Arthur's involvement kept him away from the town from dawn till dusk. The remote-viewing function of his ring proved useful for monitoring his progress in helping Hank Morgan's cadets build fences to protect a score of Gatling gun[†] emplacements, as well as concentric electric fences ringing the hill at sundry elevations. Pole- and

---

† An early type of machine gun, the Gatling gun is a rapid-firing, multiple-barrel firearm invented in 1861 by Richard Jordan Gatling of North Carolina. Powered by a hand crank, it's a precursor of the present-day electric-motor driven rotary cannon. —*kih*

tree-mounted floodlights dotted the hillside. Arm-thick wires that snaked beyond the brow of the hill serviced the fences and lights, but I could not fathom how that much electricity was being produced. Arthur's duties never took him near the power source, and he (rightly, I had to concede one evening whilst he and I discussed the day's accomplishments) refused to disrupt his work to indulge me.

He did frequent the cave, showing me a large bank of switches and unlit tell-tales connected to wires winding deeper inside. With each visit, he added a crate, barrel, box, or armload of foodstuffs, water, blankets, clothing, tools, or armaments to the growing store of siege supplies, taking care to leave each container grouped with its fellows and far enough away from the cave's mouth to escape the reach of any rain that might chance to slant in. A ditch carved into the rock ensured that rainwater and other liquids (let us not dwell too much upon that, shall we?) would flow away from the supplies.

The mystery power source made me all the more curious, so I extended my senses to the local raven population and found one willing to fly over the site whilst I observed through her eyes. The brave creature had been misused by Merlin in a similar way, years ago, so the convincing took no small effort on my part. 'Twas only after I promised a lifetime supply of corn for her and her mate that she gave her consent. I am certain that the first double handful of kernels I magicked into place at her feet as we conducted our mental negotiations convinced her of my sincerity. Delivering upon the "lifetime" clause of our contract would be a matter of planting a suggestion in the mind of a local farmer that it would be fine Christian stewardship to share a bit of his harvest with his raven neighbors. I selected the third most prosperous farmer in Camelot's jurisdiction; the first and second, I surmised, would be too busy trying to out-prosper the other to want to feed freeloading birds. For good measure, I dropped the suggestion into the mind of the farmer's wife too.

CHAPTER XXIII.
The Experiment.

VER THE course of the next several days, Lady Raven showed me plenty, slaking my curiosity by a hundredfold.

A river approached the back side of Merlin's Hill, its natural course flowing to the left as viewed from the castle. (Prithee do not enquire about the compass directions, merciful reader; no one of consequence in my native era ever bothered with them, and I had discovered no need for the knowledge as either campaign boss or baseball franchise owner either.) A contingent of Hank's cadets, overseen by Ælferd, had dug a channel from the river in front of the hill and were now damming it with sandbags. Upstream turned a twenty-foot waterwheel connected to a commercial-grade Gramme's Dynamo. This detail Clarice filled in for me based upon my sketch, adding that it appeared to be the dynamo model destined to be invented in 1878. God alone knows how she happened to possess this mote of engineering trivia; I did not trouble to ask her.

The propulsion axle connected to the waterwheel extended through the dynamo to the jump-start mechanism, a stationary bicycle. A lever controlled a series of gears to power the dynamo via bicycle, waterwheel, or neither; which is to say, the neutral state. Each time the raven flew by, regardless of the hour, the lever stood locked in neutral, which explained why the lights stayed dark and the fences could be touched without shocking the toucher. The barrel-thick wire bundle connected to the dynamo led up and round the hill to the control panel mounted inside the cave, the raven confirmed for me. She was such a daisy. Be assured that she received an extra corn ration for her initiative.

My feathered friend's final pass across the base of the hill revealed cadets burying bundles of dynamite sticks encased in glass cylinders—called "torpedoes" in the parlance of the Yankee's native era—in a wide verge composed of sand at least four feet deep. Where that much sand had been procured, how, and when, I attributed to work the cadets must have performed prior to Arthur's involvement. Lady Raven flew on along the road serving Merlin's Hill, where Arthur was laboring with another cadet, overseen by Clarence, to bury more of these dynamite torpedoes in the roadbed.

The corvid, intelligent though she might be, owned no ear for human language. I dismissed her with profuse thanks and activated the remote-viewing function of Arthur's ring. The ring would oblige me to read lips, as with the scrying bowl, but that carried the virtue of my not having to unscramble sounds jumbled inside the raven's brain.

Arthur and the cadet were digging and filling at a fast clip, racing the thunderhead that had begun clogging the sky during Lady Raven's passes. They had no sooner buried the last torpedo when a troop of Church knights came clopping up the road, backlit by a lightning fork. Clarence signaled retreat, and the trio dived for cover behind a nearby rock outcropping. I sent Arthur a mental suggestion to grip the rock so I could continue watching the patrol.

My dear obliging brother deserved an extra corn ration too.

The troop commander wheeled his horse to face them. "Ho, varlets! Stay and make answer to the Ch—"

I imagined the "-urch" must have ended as a gurgle when he and his knights rode over the torpedoes. As the lightning's thunder enhanced the manmade concussion, men and horses exploded into a shower of flesh, blood, bone, hide, and scrap metal. Dislodged vegetation, stones, and dirt complemented the devastation. Amongst the patrol there were no survivors, neither man nor beast.

Clarence and the other youth popped out from behind the rock sporting ecstatic grins. They seemed heedless of the plummeting rain that made short work of flattening the dust cloud. By Arthur's slowness to stand, I surmised that he was horrified. The abrupt movement as he must have clapped hand to chest confirmed it.

He stepped through the slaughter field, turning this way and that, giving me as full a view as he could. The rain was busy transforming the area into a muddy, bloody swamp.

I shared Arthur's horror.

TESTING THE HYPOTHESIS

"Why the face, Wart?" asked Clarence. "The test was a resounding success! With any luck, we'll get Ratcliffe the same way."

Arthur again faced the detritus-strewn road, some of it starting to float off. "They were men…" As with every other time I had monitored him via the ring, he sent me mental renditions of his speeches so that I could reconstruct them here as if I had heard him speak them aloud.

"They were our enemies," Clarence reminded him. "They would have done the same to us."

The lad had a fair point. Rule Number One in wartime: "Do unto others before they do unto you." Otherwise known as the Crimson Rule.

I was about to give my brother a mental chiding to this effect when he said, "They had no warning. Even the vilest enemy deserves the choice to prepare his soul for death."

Another fair point.

Clarence glared at Arthur for several moments before his gaze collapsed into acquiescence, no doubt by cause of my brother's harry-till-the-prisoner-cracks stare. "Fine. Harold, get warning signs made and posted."

Arthur's cadet-companion, the one Clarence had called Harold, saluted his superior and hurried for the castle. By this time the other cadets, sweaty and filthy from burying their torpedoes (though the rain had begun making inroads to dilute the sweat and filth), a holstered six-shooter bouncing at each youth's hip, had arrived to cluster round Arthur and Clarence. I recalled that Harold had been thus armed, as was Clarence, leaving Arthur the sole man not packing heat.

No surprise. In his view, a pistol was no more honorable than a dynamite torpedo.

My brother asked, "What of the bodies?"

Clarence glanced at the carnage. "No time now. After the battle we'll give 'em the burial they deserve."

With Clarice at the market procuring the day's vegetable rations, no mortal stood witness to my unroyal snort. Arthur, bless his too-trusting heart, did not snort.

Ælferd waded through the throng to reach Clarence. "It's all done," he reported. "The dam, dynamo, wiring, everything. Now what? Test the dynamo?"

"Pray it will work," Clarence told his second-in-command. "For now, it's one more of Sir Boss's curiosities. We can't risk revealing its purpose until absolutely necessary." He pitched his voice for the fifty-man assembly. "We return home to await Sir Boss."

"Oughtn't we guard our position?" Ælferd asked.

Clarence shook his head slowly, as if hunting for a reason not to reject the sensible idea. "We're running mighty short on excuses for our absences."

"I say deploy a small force in four-hour shifts. Ye do not want all of this"—I imagined a grimace forming in Arthur's hesitation—"hard work to become undone by enemy hands."

"True enough, Wart," Clarence said. "We'll go with six per shift: two inside the cave, two at the dynamo till we power it up and its own heat can protect it, and two watching the road. Squeeze off a round at any sign of trouble, and the other guards will help you." One of the few youths privileged to bear a brace of pistols, Clarence drew the weapons and raised them high overhead, pointing upward. "The Boss will be mighty pleased with us!" The rain had quit, and I expected him to shoot his pistols for emphasis, but I saw neither smoke nor recoil. The other lads appeared to appreciate the pose, evidenced by clapping, waving, jumping, drawing weapons, and flapping jaws in what had to be cheers.

After everyone had calmed to middle school standards, which is to say not by much, Ælferd singled out three pairs of cadets and issued their assignments. As those lads rushed to their posts, he ordered the rest to regroup at headquarters after supper to learn when their shifts would be, and he appointed someone to locate and inform Harold of the mandatory meeting.

Clarence, Ælferd, and those cadets not assigned to the first guard-duty shift headed back to town. Arthur followed them. The youths, in their excitement, soon outdistanced their "elderly" friend. He later told me that he had used the excuse of supposed infirmity to ponder the experiment, its aftermath, and its implications, physical as well as moral. During our discussion, he confessed to liking Clarence's battle plan less with each passing minute.

I did not like it either, but I reminded Arthur that it ought to allow events to play out as recorded in Hank's chronicle, with the lone exception of Ratcliffe leading the Church's knights rather than some British nobleman the Yankee had not deigned to name. Together we prayed to God, Jesu, Mary, Jude, and every other saint we could name that the battle would serve to erase Ratcliffe and the changes he had inflicted upon the rightful timeline.

CHAPTER XXIV.
TOAD GIGGING.

S ANTICIPATED, Ratcliffe had appropriated Arthur's suite for himself. This I knew by cause of the remote-viewing spell I had placed upon his time-folding device when I touched it before quitting Round Table Hall the day of our arrival. To my astonishment, he had not looted the royal chambers, as near as I could tell. The lavish furnishings, cushions, draperies, linens, even the gem-studded golden plates, goblets, and eating utensils all seemed present, down to the last bejeweled shrimp fork. It suggested Ratcliffe's inability to find a fence.

The toad had, however, helped himself to Arthur's clothing. I spared my brother that detail in my report. There exists a good reason why in the fairy tale the toad must transform into a prince. Royal raiment looks ridiculous on amphibians.

Prithee do not misunderstand me, fair reader. I did not expend copious time stalking Ratcliffe. For one thing, the spell behaved much like an organic eye, limited to gazing in whatever direction its bearer chanced to be facing. Unlike an eye, the time-folding device possessed no peripheral vision; nor could it pan of its own volition, or mine. The best I could accomplish, if I desired an altered vista, was to send Ratcliffe a mental suggestion that he should turn elsewhere. When the subject is not a cognizant partner,

231

as Arthur was, too much suggesting can cause even the dullest dullard to develop suspicions, so I schooled myself to exercise extreme caution.

For another thing, I possessed no wish to memorize the minutiae of Ratcliffe's routine. During the first three days I learnt enough to know when to tune in for his guards' reports, his conferences with advisers, and his sojourns to the town and countryside. I trusted my instincts for catching unexpected events, such as what transpired the evening of the cadets' experiment.

This remote-viewing session began with Ratcliffe seated behind Arthur's desk, his toady arms not long enough for the wrists to clear the plush purple velvet, fur-trimmed sleeves of Arthur's dressing gown, reading a parchment sheet by lamplight that, owing to its angle and the lamp's underpowered nature, I could not decipher. A supply requisition, to judge by the single-line, few-word bullet points. The remaining stripe on the hour candle, nestled in a mound of melted red and white wax, indicated the hour to be at about eleven of the clock.

"Enter," Ratcliffe said.

Please grant me a moment to clarify how I knew this, since I could not have heard the knock upon the door, and the toad's face remained hidden from my field of view once I memorized his sleeping schedule to spare me drool-distorted images whenever the device chanced to fetch up next to his toady face. The answer is a child's affair for simplicity: everyone rehearses. To snare the mental telegraphing of one word, I had to be quick, but by now I had been afforded numberless opportunities for practice.

The door opened, and a guard entered; the guard's captain, to judge by the gilt trim adorning his boiled-leather armor and scabbard. My interest piqued. No news delivered this late at night was ever good.

"Prithee forgive the interruption, my lord."

The soldier advanced into the chamber, perhaps upon Ratcliffe's wave, for the view shook a bit. "Have you the patrol's report?" he asked.

"They have not returned."

"What?" Ratcliffe stood and stalked up to the man. "They're hours overdue. You didn't see fit to dispatch another unit?"

The guard captain looked chagrined and a touch fearful, though he held his ground. "There was a storm. Did my lord not hear the mighty thunder like unto Our Lord commencing Judgment Day?"

That description matched the collision of the thunderclap and the torpedoes' detonation, pinpointing the patrol in question. At the time, I had presumed the Church's knights to be operating under Gildas's orders, but given Ratcliffe's association with the new-minted archbishop and the patrol's proximity to Camelot, Ratcliffe being their commander made more sense.

Of a sudden I realized that he must not have been afforded an opportunity to read the Yankee's chronicle prior to traveling to this era, or he would have jailed Sir Boss's cadets before they could set spade to ground. I thanked God for that monumental mercy. Otherwise, my chances of righting the timeline would have stood on par with the knights' chances of surviving the minefield.

"Thunder! You afraid of getting wet, girlie?" Well could I imagine the toad's accompanying smirk.

"Nay, my lord, but I came to report—"

"Times may change, but people sure as hell don't," Ratcliffe muttered.

"My lord?"

Ratcliffe pivoted, and the chifforobe swung into view. He opened it and pulled out Arthur's forest-colored leather hunting tunic and leggings. Ratcliffe faced the guard captain. "You're taking me on a bow hunt. Spears too. Round up five men, all dressed and armed for night hunting, and meet me in the courtyard."

"But, my lord, the Interdict's curfew—"

Again the view shook a little, and I glimpsed Ratcliffe's dismissive wave. "Interdict rules don't apply to guards checking out a possible threat." The guard bowed and would have departed, but Ratcliffe said, "Wait. You came to report something?"

"Aye, my lord. Travelers. A man and a woman, seeking shelter at the castle."

"In violation of the curfew?"

My very thought. I had not stuffed it into the toad's mouth, I swear by all that is holy.

"They looked weary and bedraggled, my lord, and mayhap ignorant of such things. I turned them away." The man's chest swelled, as though he was reveling in the rightness of his decision.

"Imbecile! You effing, rotten imbecile! Dollars to doughnuts that was Sir Boss!" Why, yes, I could "hear" those exclamation points, each one a

"HAVE A CARE, ARTHUR."

234

prick to deflate the guard captain's chest. "Dispatch a patrol to apprehend him. Send a messenger to Archbishop Gildas. He'll want to get here pronto. While you're at it, detail an escort to fetch Merlin from London too."

In spite of the dressing down, the soldier owned the stones to ask, "What of Lady Alisande?"

"Leave her be," Ratcliffe said. "It's Sir Boss I want."

I broke my trance somewhere in the middle of the guard captain's string of "Yes, my lord" and "Right away, my lord" and other solicitous noises as his stones realized that they were, in sooth, naught but pea gravel. The hairbrush I had been holding at the session's outset remained in my hand, a habit I had cultivated to project a sense of normalcy should I be disturbed by someone other than Arthur or Clarice. Those two knew better, of course, and I found them seated yet still on Arthur's bed, discussing in low tones the day's events.

Arthur stopped midword when he saw me regarding him. His cocked eyebrow invited an explanation.

"It begins." I abandoned the hairbrush next to the scrying bowl. A sick feeling began churning in my gut.

"What?" From his tone, I sensed that his frustration was a step away from embarking upon the warpath. My gut did not care.

It took me a few breaths to recall that my brother had not read the Yankee's chronicle either.

"Something you were never destined to live long enough to see, Arthur." I knew he despised ambiguity, but for the first time in my existence, the penchant for directness fled. It possessed more wisdom than the rest of us combined.

Clarice supplied the clarification, complete with a shudder as I fought to suppress my own emotions: "The Battle of the Sand Belt…"

Arthur pressed her hand between his, released it, rose, and approached me. "I take that to mean that Sir Boss has returned. I must help him."

"Have a care, Arthur," I said. "This shall be more terrible than any battle you have ever witnessed."

Perhaps recalling the cadets' experiment, he sighed. "Can you not prevent it?"

I hated to dim the hopeful spark that had kindled within his eyes, but, "Could I prevent you and Mordred from having a go?"

The truth forced him to bow his head. I stood and laid my hand upon his chest, over his heart. His hand rose to cover mine, and his head adopted a determined cant.

"Then for the sake of my knights and soldiers who perished at Camlann, for my surviving people, and for the wondrous future you have described, which sprang from the people's memories of the ideals I labored to instill, it is imperative that I help Sir Boss win this battle." Arthur's steel-gray eyes glittered with resolve. "Bradley Ratcliffe and the changes he wrought must be obliterated. No matter the cost."

A chill tormented my spine in direct proportion to how powerless I felt to dissuade my brother from his chosen course. As I gripped his hand, I bolstered his ring's protection spell with every last drop of magical force I could muster.

"Sir, please remember that meddling with the outcome could alter the future in ways we don't want," Clarice said.

Arthur grinned. "Right. Have I ever mentioned how much I love time travel?"

She and I shared his chuckle. He kissed my cheek, saluted Clarice with a brisk nod, pulled his hood up and as far forward as the fabric would permit, remembered to age his posture and voice as he bade us farewell, and was gone.

CHAPTER XXV.
Meetings and Partings.

HE NEXT several hours unfolded in a kaleidoscope of perspectives as I switched between Ratcliffe's time-folding device and Arthur's ring to monitor the concurrent events in which the opponents engaged. Rather than wasting words to announce each switch, I shall spare you that tedium and signal transitions with decorative flourishes. I trust that you, canny reader, shall endeavor to keep pace.

With Arthur having just departed my presence, I began with Ratcliffe. Recall, if you will, that the toad had donned Arthur's dark hunting leathers. His men were dressed much the same, in darkness if not in quality, and they had smeared soot on their foreheads, cheekbones, noses, and chins. Every man had ridden forth armed with a spear, hunting knife, bow, and full arrow quiver. I watched them dismount, leaving the spears with their horses, at the site where the Church knights had met God. Not a man in the lot carried a torch. They kept clear of moonlit ground to the extent that the ruined boulders and vegetation would allow.

CHAPTER XXV.

Ratcliffe moved much as Arthur had done, surveying the carnage from every angle. No scavenger creatures had ventured into the blast site, as near as I could tell; the scattered body parts and shrapnel appeared undisturbed. At one point, Ratcliffe watched a man flip over a mangled shield. A severed hand gripped its straps. The startled guard would have dropped the shield, but Ratcliffe lunged to catch it. If I did not know the odious toad better, I would have sworn that he laid the shield on the ground with reverential care. Rather, I surmised that he wished to make as little noise as possible.

Their survey of the blast site concluded, they retrieved their spears and slipped between the trees to creep round the base of the hill. On the far side, with the hill eclipsing the castle, Ratcliffe and his men halted to part the bushes.

Perhaps a score of paces beyond, two cadets were guarding the dynamo and waterwheel, marching back and forth between the machines and saluting one another as they strode past, like windup tin soldiers. The wheel was turning at a brisk pace, but the dynamo remained in its neutral state, not accepting the water's power.

Two arrows split the night.

Both cadets fell without drawing their pistols.

Whilst Ratcliffe and two of his men closed in to ensure they were dead, I prayed for the lads' souls.

Arthur descended the sleeping storey's outer staircase to the tavern's back door. He dragged it open to find his preferred table occupied by Clarence, who also was wearing a plain cloak. The lad had pulled its hood down so far, I wondered how he could see. As Arthur collected a tankard from the proprietor and paid him, he stretched a bit, showing me that the tavern stood all but devoid of patrons, as though everyone had been tipped off to the impending calamities and had fled for safer environs. Those who had not fled sat too far gone in their cups to care.

Why, you might be thinking, did I not issue Arthur a mental warning that Ratcliffe was on the move?

I have had God alone knows how much time to ponder this very issue, and I stand no closer to an answer. Part of the reason lay tied to the fear of jostling the timeline overmuch. Another fear stemmed from the fact that Arthur was never alone during any phase of the battle, and I had no wish to make him appear fey in front of witnesses, conversing with someone who was not present,—or worse, to distract him at a crucial moment. Perhaps I became so engrossed in the watching that I forgot that I *could* communicate with my brother. I should like to think that I had not lost control of my faculties to quite that extent, but the truth is, I do not know.

Arthur claimed the seat opposite Clarence. "You heard about…the arrival." In my mind, his words sounded more like a statement than a question.

"How did you?" Clarence asked.

"Fear not; my source is discreet and has the cause's best interests at heart."

"Good," said the youth. "We could use another supporter."

Clarence jerked up his head, like the deer that hears a twig snap. Arthur twisted to show me the tavern's front door, which had opened to admit a man and woman dressed in mud-spattered clothes and cloaks. The splotches looked so dark and fresh, I fancied that I could smell the dank, peaty moors they must have been obliged to traverse. Their hoods, like everyone else's, had been drawn close to shadow their faces. Clarence stood and hastened to them. The newcomers shared brief hugs with him.

The lad led the way to where Arthur was sitting, but his companions kept a cautious distance. "You can trust Wart, sir," he said. "He's been a huge help to us."

A startled look crossed Hank's face, what little of it I could glimpse under the hood. He bent to peer at Arthur. "The man I knew who answered to that nickname was my age, not my father's. What's your given name, good sir? Which of my man-factories made you?"

I was curious how my brother would answer, but he did not get the chance. Everyone at the table tensed, Alisande included. Then the sounds of hoofbeats and jingling harness registered in my trance-fogged ears, followed close on by the strident commands of a troop being ordered to dismount and tether their horses.

The soldiers had halted below my window.

Them I could do nothing about without causing an unwanted stir, so I resumed my trance.

Remembering to feign an old-man slump, Arthur stood and extended his hand. "The man in control of Camelot moves against you even now," he said.

"Ratcliffe's men!" Clarence added.

"Who the hell is Ratcliffe?" Hank demanded.

Finger to lips, Arthur began ushering Hank and Alisande to the rear door.

When Hank balked, Clarence said, "First we've got to get your lady wife to safety."

"Upon my honor, she shall be safe with my sister and niece, sir," Arthur assured Hank.

Though Clarice and I had been posing as mother and daughter all this time, never once had Arthur referenced the faux relationship. I knew she would be charmed by this change of royal policy. I was.

"You are most kind to offer, venerable friend," said Alisande. "But I shall not leave my husband."

"That defensive position is no place for a lady," Arthur insisted.

"But—"

Hank cut his wife's protest short with a kiss. "But. This'll be right nasty business, love, sure as shootin'. I'll feel heaps better knowing you're safe in the stands, not stuck smack in the middle of the rodeo arena."

She sighed and proffered a reluctant nod.

"WHICH OF MY MAN-FACTORIES MADE YOU?"

Arthur eased open the door, peered outside, and pulled back. "Leaving safely may be moot. Two guards patrol this door."

Clarence shifted closer to Alisande. "I have an idea." He grinned at her. "With my lady's permission?"

She gave it, and he leveled his arm as if inviting her into an embrace. At Hank's encouraging nod, she accepted Clarence's invitation. "Follow my lead," the youth advised her. Hank and Alisande shared a parting kiss.

Arm in arm, Clarence and Alisande staggered for the door, feigning drunkenness. The lady began a string of most unladylike hiccups for added effect.

"First room at the top of the steps," Arthur said to Clarence.

"Then assemble the rest of the lads and meet us at the hill," ordered Sir Boss.

Clarence gave a thumbs-up with his free hand, pushed open the door, and the "lovers" stumbled out.

Ratcliffe and his men inched closer to the waterwheel and dynamo. One of the cadets, not quite dead, reached for his pistol. A guard slit the youth's throat before he could squeeze the trigger.

Facing the dynamo, Ratcliffe said, "So this is what caused so much havoc the first time around. Not bad, Hank Morgan, not bad at all."

"My lord?" asked the troop's leader, the man who had delivered the report of Hank and Alisande's arrival.

I felt a similar level of confusion…until I realized that the toad could have learnt the battle's basic details by means other than by reading its instigator's chronicle.

"Wedge the spears into the waterwheel," Ratcliffe ordered. He regarded the rest of the troop. "You gang, look for more sentries and eliminate them."

As the men set about their tasks, Ratcliffe grabbed the two dead cadets' revolvers and slung their bullet-stuffed bandoleers across his chest. The bandoleers crossed each other beneath the time-folding device, leaving me an unobscured view of Ratcliffe's next act of sabotage: using his hunting knife to hack at the wires leading from the dynamo.

I presumed that Hank was standing behind Arthur. I could not see him as my brother watched Clarence and Alisande through the cracked-open door. The aforementioned brace of guards rushed at the "drunken" couple, spears leveled. Standing—swaying, rather—with their backs to Arthur eliminated any chance of discerning what Hank's lieutenant might be saying, but by Alisande's head bobbing and shoulder shaking, I surmised that she must have been continuing a nonstop stream of hiccups and giggles.

The guards argued about what to do with the presumed drunkards. At length they chose to be lenient, on the grounds that their primary order this night was to catch Sir Boss. I refrained from tapping into the Yankee's thoughts to gauge his reaction to the announcement; I had no wish to startle him and destroy his and Arthur's best chance of escape. I increased the odds by mentally suggesting to the guards that they escort Alisande and Clarence up the staircase. I adjudged that suggestion to be of low risk, since the action lay within the scope of the guards' duties. When the group had ascended midway, the fugitives slipped through the door, rounded the corner, and disappeared from sight.

My most fervent prayers went with them both.

CHAPTER XXVI.
Mrs. Hank Morgan.

CLARENCE AND Alisande arrived at our room moments later, the delay long enough for me to give Clarice naught but the swiftest of briefings. Once we had conjured ourselves into our crofter personae and clothing, she answered the soft, fervent knocking by opening the door a fraction.

"Strangers, mum!" she said over her shoulder in a mock-frightened stage whisper. "What do I do?"

"Send them away!" I whispered back.

"No! Please, I implore you!" The fear shaping Clarence's whisper sounded very real.

"Wart sent us," Alisande said.

"Me dear, daft brother did what, now?" I tottered to the door, and Clarice deferred to me. Keeping them dangling too long would attract the guards, but I had to sell the idea that Alisande and Clarence were unexpected—and therefore unwanted—guests. "Whyever for?"

Clarence drew a breath to answer, but Alisande raised a gloved hand.

"Good mother, I shall be pleased to explain if you permit me ingress." She nodded at Clarence. "My escort has business elsewhere and shall not trouble you or your fair daughter, I swear on my mother's bones." The hand she laid to her heart underscored the vow.

I grunted reluctant affirmation and beckoned her in, allowing feigned impatience to propel my wave. Clarence saluted all of us with two fingers to the temple, turned, and departed. Clarice secured the chamber's door to the sounds of his dwindling footfalls on the staircase.

Here my vaunted foresight failed me. I should have planted a remote-viewing spell upon him. Or, better yet, given the lad some enchanted token to pass to the Yankee so I could monitor his doings.

Nobody, as the saying goes, is perfect.

Least of all me.

In fine "good mother" fashion (though Alisande's sincere use of the title—in contrast to how it had sounded on Merlin's lips—forced me to resist a flinch), I began clucking and fussing over the "poor exhausted dearie" by bustling her to the seat closest to the fire, taking her cloak with the promise to get it dried and brushed of the mud and mystery bits, offering her any clothing of my "daughter's" to replace her travel-stained garb, and serving her what food and drink we had on hand. For the latter she expressed the most gratitude, confessing that her tavern repast had been aborted by the troop's arrival.

"Now, why should an innocent lamb like yourself be afeared of guards?" I wondered aloud.

"Not me," Alisande said between bites of gravy-soaked bread that had not yet cooled into a state of tasting thoroughly terrible. "My husband."

For many reasons, I did not press her to reveal his name. Chief amongst them stood the need to preserve Clarice's and my disguises. I understood the peasant class well enough to know that ignorance was the best shield they could ever hope to possess.

"The fine strapping youth who escorted you?" Clarice asked, making me wish my briefing had included the injunction to remain silent. I remedied that oversight with a mental command, and she gave me a sheepish nod.

If the question had seemed out of line for someone of our "station," Lady Alisande paid it no mind. Her gaze adopted a dreamy, faraway quality. "No…" She snapped out of it with a slight shake of her head. "My husband went with your brother. Cl—my escort has gone to join them."

This was not the same silly, smitten girl who had arrived at my castle riding pillion behind the Yankee all those eons ago. That she remained smitten by him was obvious (and more than a trifle puzzling), but now she was governed by a level head. One of the gifts bestowed by motherhood, no doubt.

I reached a decision and telegraphed it to Clarice.

"Ye have not asked aught about us, dear lamb," I said to our guest, "and I thank'ee for that kindness. But before another word is said, and to assuage any fear ye might yet harbor that ye can in sooth feel safe under our protection, ye must needs know who we really be."

An eyeblink later, the crofter disguises yielded to the shrimp-colored gown favored by Clarice and a black one for me, and my infirm posture, thinning gray hair, and abundant wrinkles vanished.

Alisande dropped an immediate, deep curtsy. "Your Majesty," she said in a whisper full to bursting with reverence and awe but, to her credit, not one jot of fear.

I raised her with a graceful, if abbreviated wave. "In the flesh, dear child," I said, "but not in the same spirit as the queen of your acquaintance. That woman never would have deigned to help any soul other than herself. Your husband's secrets and yours remain indeed safe with me."

Mrs. Hank Morgan seemed to chew on the claims for a while. A slow nod accompanied her eventual acceptance. She appeared ready to say something else when the abrupt widening of her eyes heralded a revelation. "Wart must be—"

I shushed her but tempered the admonition with a slight smile and beckoned to Clarice, who swished closer. "Please permit me to introduce you to Clarice, my apprentice…and the daughter of my heart."

Though I might perchance by the grace of God experience sixteen times sixteen more centuries, the radiance of Clarice's answering smile I shall never forget.

"My dear," I said to Alisande, "you must be truly exhausted. Clarice shall help you see to your evening needs and answer your questions. Within reason," I added, eyebrows lowered at my ofttimes too-eager apprentice.

With the young ladies thus engaged in becoming acquainted with one another in pleased if hushed tones, I grasped my hairbrush and a long auburn tress, entered a meditative state, and went back to work.

CHAPTER XXVII.
At the Crossroads.

DAWN HAD begun to streak the sky as Ratcliffe and his men crept up to the sandbag dam. Intent upon the machinery, the toad and his men missed seeing cadets Ælferd and Harold crouching nearby.

"Dismantle it, men!" ordered Ratcliffe.

As the Camelot guardsmen hefted sandbags, the cadets dived for cover behind a wall of boulders and started shooting. Two men fell, double-tapped and still. Ratcliffe and the others dropped their burdens and scattered.

Ælferd said something to Harold, who reloaded and holstered his gun. Whilst Ælferd laid down enough fire to force the saboteurs into retreat, Harold dashed for the waterwheel as if all the demons of hell were chasing him.

Arthur and Hank, now sans cloaks, had risked the road for its better footing as they ran to Merlin's Hill. If Hank thought it odd for someone of Arthur's pretended age to maintain the pace, he did not show it. Of a sudden he

251

pulled up short, cocked his head in the direction of the sandbag dam, and took off at a dead sprint, leaving the "old man" to follow as best he could.

In spite of the undulating vista as Arthur pumped his arms, I could make out several mounted figures approaching on the road. My brother must have seen them too. He caught Hank and dragged him off the road. Arthur pointed, Hank abandoned his resistance, and together they sought cover behind a massive stone crossroads marker.

As they monitored the riders, Ratcliffe and two of his men ran by Arthur's position, heading for the castle. What had become of their mounts, God alone knew; spooked by the gunfire seemed a passing fair guess. The horsemen—Gildas amidst a ten-man contingent of Church knights—spurred their mounts to catch the runners from behind. The two groups halted well beyond any prayer of my being able to read their lips, but from the gestures it became apparent that Gildas was furious with Ratcliffe.

Such a shame.

Hank broke cover to start sneaking closer, but Arthur snagged his arm.

"I've got to hear what they're saying!"

The Yankee wrenched free and resumed his foolhardy course. Ratcliffe, his hand upon the bridle of Gildas's horse, seemed to be placating the archbishop. None of the guards were looking at the crossroads marker.

Timeline be damned!

That was Arthur in my head. In a flash came the telegraphing of his equally foolhardy intention. He ignored my mental protest and drew himself up to his full height.

"Hank. You must see to your men." I did not need to hear my brother to know that he had foresworn his old-man voice.

Whilst everyone else's attention remained fixed upon the argument raging between Gildas and Ratcliffe, Hank stopped, pivoted, and returned to face Arthur.

"What did you say?"

The confusion clouding the Yankee's face heralded a battle to reconcile the familiar voice with the illusion of wrinkles, liver spots, bad teeth, rheumy eyes, and wispy gray hair.

"Ratcliffe doubtless has meddled with our defenses," Arthur said. "From that spate of gunfire we heard, I surmise that the cadets forced his retreat, but we must ascertain the damage and make any needful repairs."

Hank's face split into a huge grin, and he clapped Arthur's shoulders.

"Well, I'll be. It *is* you! But how—that is, I read—"

"I shall explain as we go."

I did not bother to caution my brother against wreaking further damage upon the timeline. He would have ignored me anyway. Again.

The view through Arthur's ring swung to show me a second wing of riders approaching from the direction opposite that from which Gildas and his escort had arrived. Hank and Arthur hurried to put the crossroads marker between them and the newcomers.

"Brer Merlin," Hank said. I recalled that Ratcliffe had dispatched men to London for to retrieve the wizard, and their arrival vector and its timing seemed right, but I could not fathom how the Yankee could have identified one hooded rider amidst the score of others until I realized that one of the head coverings was, in sooth, Merlin's signature pointed hat. "This can't be good."

Merlin split from his escort to approach the archbishop. Their conversation was brief. Gildas made the sign of the Cross, and the Church knights departed in various directions. Merlin offered his hand to help Ratcliffe mount, and two men of his escort extended the same courtesy to Ratcliffe's guards. Gildas and Merlin, with Ratcliffe behind him, spurred their horses toward the castle, surrounded by Merlin's escort.

"Come," Arthur said, tugging with his ring hand upon Hank's sleeve. "Ratcliffe does not know you have escaped his net. Let us capitalize on that advantage, however slight."

After verifying that they were not being watched, they resumed their sprint for Merlin's Hill.

"THIS CAN'T BE GOOD."

In the brightening dawn, Arthur and Hank approached the dynamo and waterwheel, through the woods, to find Ælferd and Harold pinned down by archers. Ratcliffe's men must have forced Harold to retreat, for the power plant lay dormant. Both cadets were shooting at Ratcliffe's archer-snipers without success. The infrequency of their shots suggested how low on ammunition they must be. From Arthur's stealthy reconnoitering, we both could see the archers in the tree line, spread far enough apart that Ælferd and Harold were shooting at about forty-five degrees away from each other.

Hank and Arthur's course had positioned them between and behind the archers. They must have realized it too; they shared a nod and split up, angling for different targets. As if telepathically joined themselves, each jumped his man at the same time. The cadets saw the snipers being neutralized and ran to begin wresting spears from the waterwheel.

The ring's images became a jumble of flesh, clothing, vegetation, and dirt as Arthur grappled with his opponent. He subdued the archer and finished him with a rock to the head. Upon grabbing the man's knife, bow and quiver, he looked at Hank in time to watch him be felled with a tree branch to the midsection.

As Arthur raced to assist Hank, that archer shot arrows at the cadets working exposed at the waterwheel. Harold took an arrow in the shoulder but managed to hitch his good arm and half his body onto the spear he had been wrangling. The spear broke with the lad's fall.

Miracle of miracles, that spear's removal allowed the water pressure to snap the others. Ælferd shoved the lever toward the waterwheel. The dynamo began slowly to turn.

The archer must have heard Arthur approach. He swung to face my brother, arrow drawn. After an abrupt shift of the ring's image, I glimpsed the arrow whizzing past. Arthur's arrow hit its mark but failed to inflict enough damage to neutralize the threat. Both men drew again.

By this time, Hank had sat up, shaking his head. I mentally shoved him to notice Arthur's danger, whereupon he crouched and sprang at the archer, grabbing the man's bow arm and forcing it down. With the risk of hitting Hank too great, Arthur dropped his bow, charged, collided with the enemy archer, knocked him flat, and punched him cold. Hank grabbed that man's weapons, stuffed the extra arrows into Arthur's quiver, passed him the bow, and they dashed to the dynamo, which was turning faster.

Ælferd, who had been inspecting the wire bundle, jumped up.

"Sir Boss! Wart! Well met and many thanks for the assist! But the dynamo—"

Hank traversed the wires leading away from the dynamo and discovered Ratcliffe's work. He ordered Ælferd to put the dynamo into neutral. The cadet obeyed with a two-fingered salute.

Arthur, squatting over one of the fallen cadets, pressed his fingers to the lad's neck. Finding no pulse, he closed the glazed eyes, crossed himself, and moved to the next body.

Hank and Ælferd kept watch on the dynamo as it spun to a gradual stop. Whilst Ælferd manned the lever, Hank stooped to begin splicing the wires.

After completing his prayer for the second fallen cadet, Arthur crossed himself again, rose, faced the injured Harold at the waterwheel…and saw two more archers sneaking upon them from the woods. He unslung a bow, nocked an arrow, drew, and aimed at the closest man.

The archers leapt into a sprint, and Arthur's arrow missed.

The would-be attackers' bodies jerked like puppets whose master had suffered an epileptic seizure. They fell, lifeless before they hit the ground. Arthur swung round to show me the hilltop Gatling guns, barrels smoking, their operators whooping and waving. Clarence stood chief amongst the gunners. Ælferd returned the waves; Harold, whose shoulder was a bloody mess, could not.

Arthur would not.

He gathered the wounded boy into his arms and carried him to Sir Boss. Melded by our telepathic link, I could not discern where Arthur's simmering anger ended and mine began.

Harold—youngest of the cadets I had seen via either of the ravens or Arthur—was barely conscious, his face pale as death.

Ælferd abandoned his post to grasp Harold's hand. Hank stood and stroked Harold's face. The lad offered the Yankee a weak smile, followed by an even weaker, "I freed…the waterwheel, Boss…"

"Good job, Harold," Hank said. "You saved us all."

Harold winced. His eyes closed and his head lolled. Hank felt Harold's neck. His nod to Arthur looked hopeful.

"I shall carry this brave lad to the safety of the cave and tend his wound as best I may," Arthur said. "However, in the meantime—"

"Don't you fret none. Ælferd and I will get the dynamo going post-haste."

Arthur's struggle to contain his cresting anger made all my muscles clench too.

"In the meantime, *Sir* Boss, I suggest you contemplate the cost of involving children in your war."

'Twas unfortunate that Hank's pet was standing too far away to be included in the dressing down. Per the Yankee's chronicle, Clarence—upon this day having attained the age of about five and twenty—had recruited the cadets. By the young man's own admission, he had selected "…none younger than fourteen, and none above seventeen years old." Any older, so Clarence's logic went, and the person would have lived too long steeped in the superstitions of the age to be useful to the Boss's cause.

The most profound miracle of the day: how Arthur himself had come to recognize the decision's towering wrongness. As king, he not only had inherited our forebears' superstitions and policies, but their questionable morals too. He had loved Guenever too much to ever exercise his *droit du seigneur*—the legalized privilege of the overlord to plant a bastard into the womb of every peasant bride, a "right" infamously and cheerfully exploited by every other male potentate across the globe, spiritual or civil, for a millennium to each side of our native era. However, the Yankee had witnessed Arthur render judgment in favor of a bishop-landlord in such a case, proving that Arthur's attachment to dubious morality remained intact. Another facet of that morality defined children as naught but assets to exploit…a facet not unique to our era either, alas; and as proof I cite the child labor laws enacted by America, beginning a quarter-century before Hank Morgan's birth, during the rightful timeline. I would have wagered my crown of state that no laws of the sort had been enacted in the timeline Ratcliffe had engineered,—but that is beside the point.

My point regarding Arthur is that whatever mechanism had shifted his moral perspective—whether by talking to Clarice or me, his locker-room interactions with the pope's gladiators, other influences of which I am unaware, or some combination thereof—I had never felt more proud of him for it.

CHAPTER XXVII.

Arthur turned and stalked with the unconscious Harold up the hill's path. My final view of the Yankee showed him shrugging as he resumed his wire-splicing work.

Whether the arrogant ass spared so much as one moment's consideration for my brother's advice, I shall never know. But I rather doubt it.

CHAPTER XXVIII.
ON THE BATTLEMENTS.

INUTES PAST sunup, a clamor of people shouting, animals lumbering, and wagons creaking in the street below our window swelled to shatter my concentration. A fog of dung-reeking dust, kicked up by the parade, seeped through our window's imperfect seals. Alisande, bless her exhausted heart, slept through the commotion and the strengthening stench. I sent Clarice to investigate. She reconstructed her crofter disguise and quit the chamber whilst I commenced enacting spells to seal the window and sweeten the air.

Her report confirmed my suspicion: the townsfolk were evacuating to the castle. Clarice advised that we do the same, and I concurred.

I woke Hank's wife and conjured us a hasty meal as she dressed. We downed our sops and ale in three gulps apiece, checked each other's disguises, and departed the inn to join the throng. Though not an outright stampede, the jerking and jostling and jumping about made me thankful that I was not an octogenarian, else I would have met an uncelebrated end under a carter's rig.

CHAPTER XXVIII.

The drawbridge guards—their scruffy, gray beards and craggy, scarred faces appearing a good two decades past customary retirement age—paid us no mind as they admonished everyone to hurry inside so they could raise the bridge. We, along with the rest of the refugees, complied. All the other guards we saw as we peeled away from the crowd to sneak to the battlement stairs seemed to hail from the same vintage. Furthermore, the stables, I noticed as we passed, stood empty. This convinced me that Ratcliffe had, in the words of his native era, gone all in, taking every last able man and mount to the battlefield and leaving the not-so-able to defend the castle as best as they were, well, able.

Concealed by a wall of barrels and bales, I created less heavy versions of the guards' body armor, boots, helmets, weapons, and tabards for Clarice, Alisande, and myself, foreseeing that the change would stave off attention. The ladies accepted their new disguises without comment. No one challenged us as we marched up the staircase and assumed our "posts." Even the guards up top stood transfixed by the scene unfolding beyond the castle's walls. They seemed not to care that three of their "fellows" had crowded into a single crenel.

Alisande decided it would look more natural if she moved to the adjacent crenel. Though responsible for her protection and loath to let her depart from my side, I could not fault her logic.

Clarice conjured for herself an era-appropriate spyglass formed of a pair of lenses bound by a leather cuff and commenced scanning the field. I extended my senses and located my raven friend amongst the flock already beginning to amass, her mate soaring beside her. They flew to me, agreed to assist, and I rewarded them each with a heap of cracked corn to bolster their strength; the sun would set before the killing zone became safe for them to feast upon the, shall we say, tender raw bits. In short order they finished their snacks, bobbed their little black heads at me in thanks, preened, and winged back to the battlefield.

Eye to spyglass, Clarice said, "The knights are driving a huge herd of cattle at the Sand Belt! That didn't happen before."

Alisande, who had rejoined us to marvel at the "tame" ravens, said, "Before—what?"

Clarice lowered the glass to regard her. "I crave your pardon. I meant to say that I have never seen such a thing before."

I had wondered how much of our past—future?—whatever she had shared with Alisande; now I had my answer.

"Nor shall you again," I said.

I closed my eyes, propped my spear against the wall, and flexed my fingers.

Through my connection with Lady Raven, I watched the cattle obey my prompting to veer away from the Sand Belt.

Hapless Church knights, unable to check their momentum, detonated the buried, glass-encapsulated dynamite torpedoes. Dozens of explosions sent rocks, sand, debris, metal and glass shrapnel, and flesh hundreds of feet into the air. The raven flock scattered, scolding. My feathered friends reported being unhurt though shaken. I apologized and assured them that they would experience no more "fire-storms."

Subsequent waves of knights reined their horses to dismount and regroup. The cattle herd thundered out of sight to God alone knew where.

After the smoke and dust had cleared, a vast ditch appeared in place of the minefield. Lady Raven made a pass to confirm that it encircled the hill and that it contained the sundered remains of too many knights and horses for an accurate count. Yea, for the record, corvids are brilliant with numbers, but only when the subjects exist as individuals, not—if I may borrow one of the Yankee's scientific phrases—homogeneous protoplasm.

The surviving knights, obliged to continue on foot, renewed the assault.

Cadets dismantled the temporary dam, flooding the ditch and sweeping more knights to their deaths. Once the flood had calmed, the next wave of knights waded the ditch's chest-high waters and headed to the outermost fence ring.

"At least that part of the defense worked as planned," Clarice said.

CHAPTER XXVIII.

"Thank God for small mercies!" That squeak came from Alisande, who had not yet returned to her "post" in the vacant crenel beside Clarice and me.

None of us, by the by, had troubled to disguise our voices. The helmets' visors provided distortion aplenty. Anyone chancing to overhear would believe us to be boys deemed too young to experience war's horrors

"THAT DIDN'T HAPPEN BEFORE."

firsthand, pressed into castle-guarding duty owing to the direness of the situation. The deliberate sloppiness of my tailoring—sleeves an inch or two too long, and so forth—fostered the illusion. The oddness of our speech could be dismissed as the silly fancifulness natural to all boys.

Having forded the ditch, the knights surmounted the first fence without incident and surged farther up the hill. Through Sir Raven's eyes, I watched cadets manning the hilltop Gatling guns start shooting, but they could not fell enough knights to stem the tide.

"No electricity," Clarice deduced. "Without help from electrified perimeter fences, the cadets won't stand a chance—they'll run out of bullets!"

"Not if I know my Hank. See you any sign of him, Mistress Clarice?" Alisande asked.

Clarice repositioned the spyglass. From its new angle, I surmised that she had trained it upon the summit of Merlin's Hill.

"Is that him just inside the cave's mouth?"

Clarice passed the spyglass to Alisande. Whilst she attempted to duplicate Clarice's angle, I asked Sir Raven for a closer look. The bird found Hank at the bank of switches, in the process of flipping on the main breaker.

"Aye! He works his power-magic," Alisande confirmed. "Wart and several cadets guard him."

I was about to access Arthur's ring when knights in contact with the second fence ring went rigid and halted, electrocuted. Their charred bodies started smoking. Alisande made a strangled noise. She barely got the spyglass back into Clarice's hands before she doubled over to vomit. Clarice paled a little, but she resumed watching the battle, doubtless desensitized by her decades of television viewing and video game playing. I laid a hand on Alisande's back, humming softly. The lass straightened and wiped her lips.

"Do you need some tea to purge the vileness from your mouth?" I asked her.

She grimaced. "Only if it will purge the vile sight from my mind as well."

Right.

I returned my attention to Lady Raven, who was keeping her bright black eyes on the battle. More knights, climbing farther up the hill, past the still-smoking bodies of their companions, fell to Gatling gunfire. I warned the brave bird not to swoop too close. The knights that reached the next fence got electrocuted too, but their companions kept advancing till enough of them came in contact to short it out. The surviving knights climbed higher, scrambling over the bodies of the fallen, in spite of the constant gunfire. Not even in the goriest of grand melees had I ever witnessed such gut-roiling carnage, and I had to force myself to remember that these events were unfolding as was needful for ensuring a restored timeline.

Sir Raven watched Arthur and Hank leave the cave to descend the hill where the first few knights had climbed close to their position. Hank shot and killed a knight. Arthur grabbed that knight's sword and moved off to engage another.

"How on earth did she get up there?"

Clarice gestured with the spyglass, and I asked Lady Raven to fly past the cave's mouth. A person dressed as an old peasant woman was conversing with some of the cadet sentries.

"That is no *she*," I said. "That is—"

"Trouble!" Clarice said.

"Merlin," I said. The name's utterance spawned a glimpse of a future event not recorded in the Yankee's chronicle. My heart lurched.

"Hank!" Alisande cried. The vision clouding my mind's eye blinded me to what had alarmed her. She strode to the battlement steps and started down. Clarice laid the spyglass aside and took a step in her direction, but I caught her arm, willing my panic to remain at bay.

"What did she see? Is her husband hurt?" I asked.

"I have no clue why she spooked. I don't think she could have seen anything, but Hank and Wart have started engaging the enemy at close quarters." She gazed at Merlin's Hill for a long moment. What she saw there, I shall never know…though I could guess. At length she faced me, resolve stiffening her posture. "I need to go and help."

"Clarice, please." My grip upon her arm tightened in direct proportion to my rising panic. "I implore you to stay."

Her surprise yielded to determination. "What would you have me do? Stitch shield covers? Sorry. I forgot my needle and thread…a millennium and a half from now."

My mind raced through the options. A spell could stop her, but she would never forgive me. An explicit warning could yield more harm than good. Never mind that begging held no place in my vocabulary; to do so

THE AMASSED CHIVALRY OF ENGLAND

might make Clarice suspicious, which could cause disastrous results. This left me with the hardest act I have ever performed.

I let her go.

She made for the stairs, unaware of the tears brimming in my eyes.

So much death this day…

A long blink cleared my eyesight, and I sent Arthur a mental warning about the disguised Merlin. No power in heaven or on earth could have stopped me from protecting my apprentice, my friend…and the daughter of my heart. I grasped my spear.

Midway down the battlement stairs, I paused, braced my free hand on the wall, bowed my head, and implored—nay, *begged* God to protect us all.

CHAPTER XXIX.
FOR ENGLAND.

UNSET FOUND Clarice, Alisande, and me, still disguised as castle guards, picking our way up Merlin's Hill. For a few minutes, the iron armor encasing thousands of corpses looked garishly golden. I cannot recall when I became nose blind to the stench of smoking flesh, but I was grateful for that mercy. So many ravens had descended that it was impossible to tell where their bodies ended and twilight's feathering shadows began.

Along our route, we encountered no survivors.

We stayed together but did not converse as we climbed, and we were not the only ones to remain silent. The Gatling guns sat unmanned, and the ravens felt no compulsion to fight amongst themselves for coveted morsels.

The silence was so complete, it might have become an entity unto itself.

By my reckoning, we were about one-third of the way to the summit when single-shot gunfire rang out, startling me. It seemed to have originated from farther up the hill, perhaps near the cave's mouth. Satisfied with the denseness of shrubbery giving us cover, I asked the ladies to bide whilst I accessed Arthur's ring.

I caught glimpses of my brother's peasant garb, as well as the sword he had taken from a knight who had fallen earlier this day. From the ring's height above the ground, I could tell that Arthur was no longer bothering to act like a stooped old man. He,—along with Hank, Clarence, Ælferd, and surviving cadets not manning other posts—ranged the hillside a short way down from Merlin's Cave, checking for wounded knights. Those men wanting help received it; the hostile ones were shot.

"So many thousands dead by our own hands…" Clarence said.

Arthur dropped the blood-streaked sword to stare at his hands. He lurched to the closest tree and slumped against it.

God, please forgive me!

I felt his heartache as if it were my own. An echo of his mental plea burst from my mind.

Hank stepped over to lay a hand on Arthur's shoulder. The cadets kept examining the fallen.

"You okay, Wart?"

"I daresay I shall never be 'okay' after this wretched day is done," Arthur said.

A needle of fear iced my spine.

"Bosh." The Yankee made a dismissive wave. "In one master stroke we've eliminated hidebound thinking. Now we can start afresh, build a great Republic, educate the masses. You can even lead it, if you want."

Arthur straightened and shrugged off Hank's hand. I could feel his wrath ignite.

"What I *want* is an end to the overwhelming guilt of slaying former brothers-in-arms for no other crime than following the power-mad Church. Can your 'fresh start' do that for me, Sir Boss?"

Neither man spoke for a handful of breaths. If the Yankee's glare was sharp, my brother's had to be sharper. At length, Arthur moved to another survivor and squatted to examine the knight's wounds. I presumed that Hank did the same; the ring's sole view was stained crimson.

That changed in an eyeblink. Arthur leapt up and rushed to where Hank had fallen. The Yankee's hands were fumbling to remove a dagger protruding from his own gut. Arthur completed the removal and jammed a wad of torn surcoat into the wound. He must have turned aside then, for I glimpsed Clarence dropping the culprit with a single bullet.

Arthur rallied cadets to carry their leader into the cave. As they obeyed, he knelt beside the knight who had stabbed Hank. He eased off the knight's helmet to cradle his head, and he made the sign of the Cross in front of his face. The victim, blood welling from a hole in his chest, had stretched his mouth as wide as a catfish,[†] struggling for air.

"Why, Sir Meliagraunce?" Arthur asked.

"For…England." The catfish mouth stretched wider still. Panic invaded the dying knight's gaze.

Sadness flooded our telepathic link.

"Go with God," Arthur said, gripping the knight's hand, "and please forgive me, if you can."

"Who…are…you?"

Sir Meliagraunce gasped a final time. His mouth went slack, as did his other muscles. His eyes glazed. Arthur closed them with the tenderness of a father and bowed his head.

The sad flood swelled into an ocean of anguish. I thought I might drown in it too.

I—was—England.

You still are, I reminded him.

Arthur disengaged, retrieved Sir Meliagraunce's sword, and rose to resume checking for survivors when of a sudden he whirled and bolted for the cave.

Hank, his torso bandaged, lay on the ground just inside the cave's mouth, head and limbs thrashing. Clarence and Ælferd were rubbing their

---

† In *A Connecticut Yankee in King Arthur's Court*, the Yankee referred to the nobility as catfish: all big-mouthed bluster and scum-sucking action. *—kib*

heads; other cadets lay unconscious. How they had gotten into such a state I could not begin to guess.

Arthur angled the ring so I could watch Merlin—clean-shaven and garbed like a peasant woman—twirl about, laughing and flailing his arms like a lunatic.[†]

"I am Merlin! You shall die of the poisonous air bred by the good knights you have slaughtered with your evil devices—except him. He sleeps now and shall sleep thirteen centuries."

The wizard's victory dance spun him close to the fence. From the lights on the tell-tale board, I saw that the fence was live. Arthur must have noticed too. He lunged at Merlin and grasped the blouse's sleeve. It tore.

"Merlin!" Arthur said. "Watch—"

Momentum crashed Merlin into the fence, which electrocuted him in a huge shower of sparks. Convulsing, Merlin fixed his gaze upon Arthur. His mouth dropped open. Sheer astonishment cascaded over his face as he must have recognized his king.

Careful not to touch the smoking body, Clarence made an umpire's signal. "Out!"

I felt Arthur's wince through our link.

Clarence turned. "Wart, help me move Sir Boss deeper into the cave. Ælferd, we need lights, inside and out. And have someone bring the Boss's chronicle to us."

"Sure thing…Boss," said Ælferd with a hint of a grin.

The Yankee's successor did not share it.

As Arthur and Clarence stooped to lift Hank, Ælferd flipped several switches. Countless lights winked on, brightening my view through the ring and illuminating several tunnels. Arthur and Clarence entered the leftmost tunnel with Hank.

---

† Merlin's final appearance—disguise, dancing, dialogue, and death—is exactly as described in *A Connecticut Yankee in King Arthur's Court.* The primary difference, of course, is that Twain had killed off Arthur already.—*kih*

Floodlights rigged to trees dotting the hillside blazed on all round us. Clarice, Alisande, and I had remained hidden, so we felt no immediate need to move. Such was not the case for two figures, also on foot, further up the hillside from our position. My raven friends interrupted their meal to grant me the favor of a closer look. The images they transmitted were not comforting in the slightest degree.

Alisande was the first to express a wish to break cover.

"Have a care. Ratcliffe and Gildas are also here." I pointed a nod at the spot where I had watched them dive into a thicket.

"OUT!"

The Yankee's wife pursed her lips and blew a riff. "My Hank needs me," was all the justification she cared to supply. She resumed her grim climb.

The Yankee needing that dear lady was no news flash.

The fact that Arthur and Clarice needed me—though both were too proud to admit it—was no news flash either.

I asked Clarice to stay with me, and, to my surprise, she did not balk at the request.

We kept cautious tabs upon our enemies as we ascended. Ratcliffe surged further ahead every time Gildas stopped to intone last-rite prayers over a dying knight. At length, even we women, led by Alisande, overtook the archbishop, but we took especial care to give Gildas an extra-wide berth. If he chanced to observe three "Camelot guards" investigating the massacre, he did not seem to care.

Ratcliffe had reached the cave's mouth when he stooped to grab something. I stood yet too far down the hillside that not even a vision-enhancing spell could afford me a clear view. Before I could contact either of my raven friends, he pocketed the object and scurried into the cave.

CHAPTER XXX.
EVER AND ALWAYS.

ARTHUR EMERGED from the leftmost tunnel's shadows. I had not seen his ring glow so brightly, even during his most grueling Holy Rollers Fight Club match, a sign that its protection spell was laboring overtime. As Merlin had predicted, the poisoned air had begun working its lethal magic.

My brother watched Alisande ascend to the cave's mouth, now strewn with the bodies of fallen cadets. I saw no sign of Ratcliffe, but I sent Arthur an updated warning. Two warnings, in fact; the second in regard to being careful not to overtax the ring's healing function. Even forces of nature are bound by limits.

Alisande bent down to speak with Harold, who was still moving a little.

I could not read her lips, and I doubted that the dying youth possessed the capacity to speak. He waved his uninjured arm to identify the tunnel where Arthur was standing. Alisande grasped Harold's hand, kissed it, and rose on wobbly legs. She pressed a hand to her temple. Color had leeched from her face.

"You shall perish if you tarry here," Arthur said.

"Everyone perishes, Wart." Her thin smile gave no hint regarding whether she realized that "Wart" had abandoned his old-man persona in speech as well as posture. "But not everyone has the good fortune to choose the time or place."

The view shifted as if Arthur had bowed, and he led her into the tunnel.

By this time, Clarice and I had achieved the summit. We peered into the cave in time to see Ratcliffe enter the gallery from the rightmost (and wrong) tunnel, notice Arthur and Alisande, and begin sneaking after them. Clarice closed her eyes and raised her hands, palms up.

"Rù-rà!"

Confusion was the spell she chose, and an excellent choice it proved to be. Ratcliffe's stride faltered. He stopped, eyed each of the remaining tunnel openings in turn, and chose another wrong one. I gave my apprentice an approving nod. We waited till Ratcliffe's footsteps faded into silence before raising wards to protect us from the lethal air. With luck, the toad would succumb and end our mission.

I held that thought uppermost in my mind, false though I knew it to be, to obscure the truth of what I had foreseen. Ignorance of one's fated demise is a gift everyone, highborn and low, deserves to receive.

As Clarice entered the correct tunnel, with myself a few steps behind her, I resumed monitoring Arthur.

In the tunnel's deepest reaches, he and Alisande came upon the bodies of Hank, Clarence, Ælferd, and two other cadets. Clarence had collapsed with a hand on the Yankee's bloody torso bandage, as though he had intended to change it. Hank's chronicle lay tucked where Clarence must have placed it, close to its author's hip. Whilst Alisande knelt beside her husband, Arthur tried to rouse the cadets. None of them responded. After making the sign of the Cross over each and finishing with one final, sorrow-laden sigh, Arthur knelt near Alisande and Hank, though not close, as if feeling reluctant to intrude.

His voice in my head looped on thoughts of guilt, regret, and grief, sustained by an undercurrent of anguish that broke my heart anew. The most comforting thought I could craft was:

Hush, Arthur. I am here. For them; for you. Always, my beloved brother and liege, for you. The past is past...

I could not bear to telegraph the concluding phrase. To do so would have been a lie.

For sooth, beloved sister. This battle is no game, and it shan't wage for much longer.

I closed my eyes against the welling tears, and to shutter my thoughts till I could reassert control. His assessment had hit far closer to the mark than I could risk affirming to him.

Whilst I wrestled my emotions into submission, Arthur shifted to give me a better view of the Yankee and his wife.

Alisande was chafing Hank's hand. He stirred but did not wake. Alisande pressed that hand to her lips and held it there.

"Sandy? You are so dim, so vague, you are but a mist, a cloud..."[†] The Yankee's eyes remained shut.

"Hank!" she cried. "Thank God! Hank?"

His head thrashed. "Oh, Sandy, you are come at last—how I have longed for you!"

"Wake up, Hank! I beseech you!"

The ring's view swung to show me Clarence, whose coughing fit had disrupted his efforts to push himself upright. Arthur shifted to assist him.

"Wart? My lady! I'm so sorry. I couldn't stop Mer..."

A spasm gripped Clarence's body. After it released its hold, he toppled and did not move again. Arthur laid him flat and formed the sign of the Cross.

"Go with God, Amyas le Poulet. You would have made a fine knight... in some era, if mayhap not this one." He regarded Alisande. "My lady, we must go."

---

† Hank's dialogue in chapters 30 and 33 comes straight out of his death scene at the end of *A Connecticut Yankee in King Arthur's Court. —kih*

Though tears streaked her cheeks, her smile revealed steely determination. "Ever and always. I shall never break that vow to him." Alisande withdrew Hank's pipe from her pouch, laid it upon his palm, and curled his fingers round the bowl. She kissed his unresponsive lips and laid down beside him, his chest her pillow. "Ever and always…my Hank…" She uttered a long sigh, and her limbs relaxed.

Clarice and I entered the gallery to find my brother still kneeling, head bowed and shoulders trembling, amidst the bodies. The Yankee was asleep, as Merlin had claimed. I found no pulses on the necks of any of the cadets. Alisande's was weak, her breathing was shallow, and her pallor had worsened.

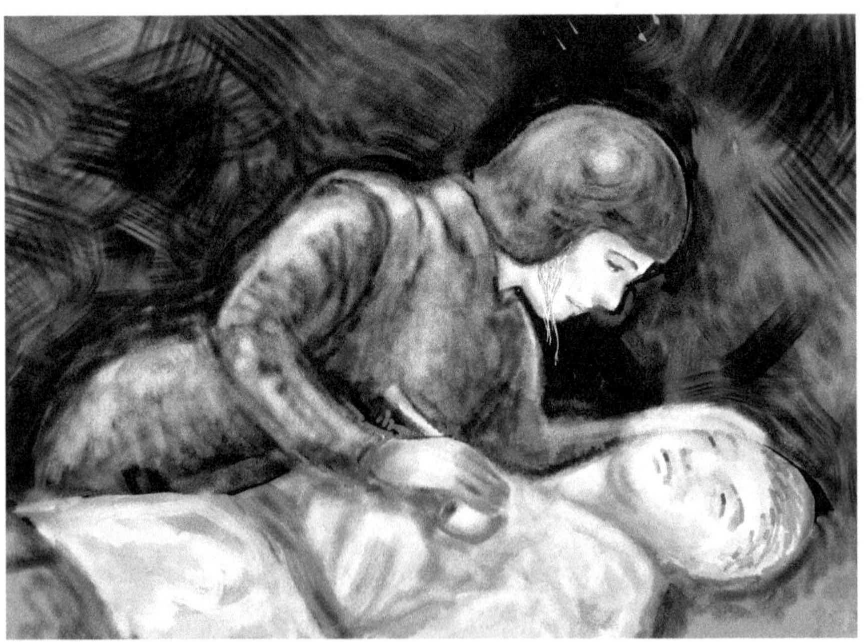

"EVER AND ALWAYS…MY HANK."

"Is she—?" Arthur began.

"There is yet a little time," I said.

"Can you wake Sir Boss?" Clarice asked.

"No more than Merlin could have broken one of my sleep spells. But I can do the next best thing for her." I laid my palm upon her cheek. "For both of them."

Within the first few bars of my hummed healing spell, Alisande's color started to improve, if too slowly for my satisfaction. On the verge of asking Clarice to assist, a sharp crack rang out, followed close on by pain that ripped through my right shoulder.

Astonishment killed my scream.

CHAPTER XXXI.
SETTING THE FUTURE INTO MOTION.

HE BULLET'S impact knocked me off balance. I jammed the heel of my left hand to the wound as I fell. Pain a hundred times worse than childbirth wracked my body. My disguise spells dissolved, leaving Alisande dressed in her traveling clothes and the rest of us in what we had been wearing upon arrival to this century: Arthur clad in his Vatican plate armor, and Clarice and me dressed in black skirt suits. As my healing spell faded, I sensed—moreso than saw—the return of Alisande's pallor.

Arthur and Clarice whirled to face the attack, and I labored to sit up. Ratcliffe was standing in the tunnel, Archbishop Gildas a pace behind him. The toad was wearing armor but no helmet. The chain holding his time-folding device was visible round his neck, but the object itself lay concealed beneath the breastplate, which explained why its view had been useless to me during our climb. Gildas's plain white vestments were muddy and streaked with the blood of at least one knight whose dying act had been to grasp it.

Ratcliffe was holding a revolver trained on us. Sword in fist, Arthur stepped in front of Clarice, who had stooped over me. She replaced my hand covering the wound with both of hers; through them, I could feel the vibrations of her healing hum. Sparks began to shimmer, and my pain lessened by the twinkle, allowing my gasping lungs and racing heart to ease.

"What did I tell you, Your Grace?" Ratcliffe said.

"King Arthur—impossible! I watched Sir Mordred deliver your mortal wound!"

"I got better," Arthur deadpanned.

My choked-off laugh came out as a sputtered cough. I used the motion of pressing fist to lips to disguise the fact that I had initiated my own healing spell to augment Clarice's.

"I never dreamt that the rancor you harbored for the executions of your traitorous father and brothers would have festered into destroying all record of my existence," said Arthur.

Upon shifting my fist to my shoulder, I withdrew the bloody bullet. It took my last mote of will to bridle the outcry. That my face scrunched into a grimace I could not control. The bullet grew hot in my fist.

"But we haven't—ah." The toad had the audacity to croak a laugh. "You've been to the future. What did you think?"

My wound's bleeding stopped. The pain subsided. Since our adversaries' attentions stayed focused upon Arthur, I cast a spell to dress Clarice in her favorite shrimp-colored gown and conjured a black gown and circlet for myself, reasoning that once the shock of seeing his resurrected king wore off, Gildas would be easier to deal with if our clothing did not present him with a fresh shock.

"A grim and evil place it is," Arthur said.

Ratcliffe grinned.

The wound closed.

The archbishop advanced into the gallery. He said—

"That, of course, is a matter of perspective."

No sign of my wound remained.

"Enough of this. Time to set our future into motion," Ratcliffe declared.

He squinted, holding his weapon higher. I presumed that he had targeted Arthur. Before he could shoot, I flung my bullet at him, magically emulating a gun's force. My aim, in retrospect, I also should have enhanced with magic. I had intended to kill the toad, but the bullet grazed his hand, and he dropped the gun. It bounced on the cave's rocky floor and skittered toward Gildas. Growling, Arthur charged at Ratcliffe.

Gildas snatched the revolver. My spine's tingle warned me that the toad must have shown him how to use it.

With Gildas watching the combatants, his gun hand trembling, and myself concentrating upon all three men, I failed to notice when Clarice rose and edged closer to Gildas's position until it was too late.

Ratcliffe raised both hands. "I'm unarmed! What of your precious honor? Your chivalry?"

"You forfeited courtesy when you attacked my sister." His tone made my blood run cold; the same applied to his opponent, to judge by the panicked widening of the toad's eyes. "Say your prayers."

Arthur readied his sword. Gildas's finger tightened upon the trigger. Clarice lunged at Gildas. The sword arced for Ratcliffe's neck. The gun fired.

Clarice's body passed between the bullet and Arthur.

The sword connected with Ratcliffe, beheading him. Ratcliffe's body fell. His head rolled a fair distance away from the body.

The bullet hit Clarice in the gut, driving her backward into Arthur. He stumbled, dropping the sword to flail his arms.

I leapt to my feet.

"Arthur! Clarice! No!"

Yes.

They crashed into the cave wall. Arthur's head struck hard, and his blood gushed onto the rock. He and Clarice slumped to the ground.

Gildas was shaking so much that I feared he would drop the weapon and kill us both.

"Seas bìth!" I cried, invoking a more emphatic time-freezing spell than the one I had employed in the parlay tent.

Gildas had released the revolver. Obedient to my spell, the weapon stayed suspended in midair.

NO GREATER LOVE

I fell onto my knees beside Clarice and Arthur. Heaven alone knew how I could find them through the blur of tears. Clarice would resume bleeding out the instant I touched her, but I had no other choice. Heedless of the gore, I bore down onto her gut wound. Desperation drove my healing song. I poured my soul into it as never before.

Please, dear God, please, please, please! Let her live!

Clarice gripped my hands and gazed at me. "Get Ratcliffe's…time-folding device. And…David's…"

"Of course," I said whilst continuing to beg God for her life. "Wait. *Who?*" I felt confusion knit my eyebrows.

"The monk…outside the parlay tent."

Ah. The adder's first victim, I dredged from my memory's depths.

"Ambrose sent David to fetch Arthur years ago…years from…ye…" Clarice sucked in a breath. "That t–tech…"

"I know. Please conserve your strength and let me heal you." I tried to sound calm but feared that I had not succeeded.

"I wish…I'd d–dated…Da…" The *v* rode the puff of her final, rattling breath.

Her grip loosened, and her eyes glazed.

"My dear child, I am so, so sorry!"

I gathered her into my arms. Mindful that loud sound could shatter the time-freezing spell, I hugged her in silence for a long, long time.

"I AM SO, SO SORRY!"

CHAPTER XXXII.
A Word of Interjection.

Y DREAM! My very dream, down to the last grunt and groan. How had that crazy witch of a queen known?

The book shuddered in my hands. I slammed it shut and dropped it onto the table, stood, and pivoted to scan the weird not-a-gym room stuffed with every curiosity from aardvark skulls to zombie toenails, searching for the exit.

Don't give me that look. You've thrown down a book or two yourself, admit it. And if by chance you haven't, give it a go. You'll love how satisfying it feels.

Writing popped and sizzled across the book's cover, demanding my attention.

Crazy? Witch? Excuse me?

With a gasp, and willing—and failing—to slow my racing heart, I stepped back a pace.

"I'm sorry, okay?" To be extra safe, I added, "Your…Majesty?"

I scrubbed my face with my hands. What on earth could I be thinking? Remote viewing across time? Could that really be a thing?

And not just viewing, but somehow she could read my thoughts too? *Oy.*

And I had called her crazy.

You are not crazy, the book—Queen Morgan?—declared. *And your supposition is quite correct. I am Queen Morgan.*

Double oy.

The writing on the book's cover cleared. My head did not.

I understand this may seem a bit much, my dear.

I snorted.

Do not do that. It is not ladylike.

"Ha; fine lot you know. I am no lady."

On the contrary, you are far more than you ever could have imagined.

"Indeed! Prove it," I said.

The book did nothing for God alone knew how long. At length, the cover went blank again. One letter appeared, a capital *k*. A couple of seconds passed before the *k* was joined by an *e*. This rhythm repeated through the addition of another *e*, followed by a *p*. Nothing else appeared.

"Keep? Keep—what?"

If she wished for me to keep calm, her tactics were having the opposite effect.

READING.

I gave another, louder snort, whirled, and stomped to the door. The book could go twaddle its pages for all I cared. I clamped onto the doorknob, twisted it, and yanked for all I was worth.

Nothing happened.

Damned sticky door.

I gave the knob a harder pull. Kicking and pounding the door didn't work either.

"What? You're going to hold me prisoner in this asylum of yours till I do your bidding like a good little minion, is that it?" I plopped onto the floor in front of the recalcitrant collection of planks, cross-legged and cross-armed; cross all over, in point of fact. "Fine. I'll wait."

The door flew open and crashed into the wall with the force and noise of a gunshot.

Go, then, if you must. Oh, dear God, she was speaking in my head now. *But remember this: in my book your answers lie.*

"Why can you not just skip all the folderol and tell me, for God's sake?"

I do not repeat myself.

Of course not; it probably was forbidden by some Royal Rule or another.

A shiver rippled across my mind, as if Her Majesty had chuckled.

I stood and peered through the doorway. Night had fallen; in so doing, it had dragged so much fog down with it that the streetlights struggled to make a dent. The orbs put out a brave glow but couldn't penetrate more than a yard or two.

Damn.

I hated walking in the bloody fog, especially in the dark.

The mist swirled and parted as if a celestial hand had drawn the drapes.

"Thanks, Your Majesty." I took a few steps.

What she said next halted me in my tracks:

That was none of my doing.

"What? How—?"

That spell was cast by you.

In contrast with Her Royal Irksomeness, no rules forbid me to repeat myself.

"What???"

You understood me.

Remote viewing, telepathy, and now magic too? "What the hell is going on with me?"

The queen did not reply. Instead, I heard a soft thump and rustling behind my back. I turned and approached the book. It had opened to the page where I had left off.

Of course it had.

CHAPTER XXXII.

I expelled my frustration in a long, noisy sigh. In spite of all my instincts screaming to the contrary, I picked up the book, dropped back into the chair, and resumed reading *Queen Morgan's Further History*.

"I HATED WALKING IN THE BLOODY FOG."

CHAPTER XXXIII.
FOR THE BILLIONS.

ITH THE tenderness of a new mother, I kissed Clarice's brow and lowered her to the cave floor a little to one side so I could reach Arthur. Not ready to break the time freeze, I gave his head a cursory examination without touching him.

This head wound seemed every inch as severe as the damage inflicted by Mordred's sword. However, since far less time had elapsed, I felt confident of my chances to heal him here, rather than having to haul him to Avalon. I closed my eyes, flexed my fingers, pressed them to the wound, and began to hum.

Warm healing energy coursed through my body and into his in a flood of Biblical proportions, as if we had indeed relocated to Avalon. A quick peek affirmed that we remained inside Merlin's Cave. I resumed concentration upon my spell.

I know not how long I had knelt thus engaged when I became aware of a faint but persistent tapping upon the back of my right hand, as though the most stubborn butterfly in all Creation had decided that its only path forward was through me. I opened my eyes.

Arthur had regained consciousness and was trying to swat me away.

"Stop…Morgan…"

Icy terror invaded my focus.

"I can save you, Arthur."

His head twitched in the barest of shakes. He tried moving his mouth, but no sound emerged.

Let me die so my legend may live. So that the billions born after me might live better lives.

It was the first time he had ever initiated a mental conversation with me. A sick pit formed in my gut. I drew a deep breath, banishing the terror from my voice. "I care not one fig for the billions. I must save you."

Then as your liege lord, Morgan, I command you not to heal me.

Oh, dear God Almighty.

"No, Arthur. Please don't…"

Even through what had to be excruciating pain, his stare ordered me to desist. My oath to him forbade disobedience. With a breaking heart I stopped the healing spell. Its energy dissipated into nothingness. Tears spilled down my cheeks. Affection softened his gaze for a few moments. He drew a gasping breath. His throat rattled as he sighed it out; his chest did not rise again.

My anguished scream echoed throughout the cave.

The time-freezing spell shattered.

Ratcliffe's revolver clattered to the cave floor behind me. I twisted to find Gildas staring at me as I knelt amidst the bodies, his mouth opening and closing like an air-starved fish.

"Wh—what have you done?" he had the gall to ask.

Wrath exploded within me like a match in an oil barrel. I rose and stalked to him. His eyes rounded, and he shrank away.

"This is none of my doing, Archbishop. You killed an innocent young woman and your God-ordained king. A mad dog is more fit to wear those holy robes than you are." I clutched his cassock, bloodying it much as the dying knight had done, but higher. I wanted so very much to choke him, but as satisfying as that might have felt, it would have proven me to be no better than he. I released the fabric with a downward jerk.

Horror cascaded over his face. A spasm wracked his body, and he blinked several times, gasping and chafing his arms like a man waking from the worst nightmare Morpheus[†] had ever fashioned. He said:

"Merciful God, I have taken a life. Two lives! What in heaven's name could have possessed me to commit such evil?" That last bit came out more as a moan.

Heaven had naught to do with the theory spawned by his fascinating word choices, but rather than asking where the archbishop stood regarding interactions between demonic beings and mortals, I chose a humanistic approach: "The lust to avenge your father and brothers fueled your wrath. No doubt Ratcliffe tempted you with promises of growing your power base, which played to your envy and pride and must have goaded your greed." After ticking the points on my fingers, I said, "Five of the seven deadly sins,[‡] Your Grace, am I right?"

"I cannot deny your assessment, Queen Morgan." Gildas's posture sagged, as if his frame had become inadequate for bearing the weight of his conscience. He stripped off the bloody cassock but retained the plain

---

[†] Morpheus, whose name in Greek means "shape" or "form," is the best known of the myriad ancient Greek gods of dreaming, popularized in the Latin narrative poem *Metamorphoses,* written in A.D. 8 by the Roman poet Ovid.

[‡] The seven deadly sins (a.k.a. capital vices and cardinal sins) represent major classifications within the teachings of the Roman Catholic Church. At a time when the vast majority of parishioners were illiterate, it became common for artists to represent these sins with animals. Queen Morgan accused Archbishop Gildas of engaging in the sins of lust (goat), wrath (lion), envy (snake), pride (peacock), and greed (frog). The illustration on the next page shows the sins of gluttony (boar) and sloth as bystanders. I selected the sloth to represent its namesake sin, rather than the traditional snail, because it was my late daughter's favorite land mammal. *—kih*

tunic and breeches he was wearing underneath. Dried blood from dead knights transferred onto the breeches as he rubbed his palms on his thighs. "I am so very sorry, Your Majesty. What should I do now?" His hands kept rubbing and rubbing and rubbing as if his brain had lost control of them.

Whether his apology had been directed at me or my brother, I could not ascertain.

I touched one of his forearms, and the rubbing stopped. "You have made your confession. Now live out the remainder of your days as a hermit. In complete anonymity. That is your penance for being blinded by temptation."

If he noticed that I had omitted the most important component of the formula, he made no comment. Dispensing God's forgiveness never has been part of my job description.

Gildas gave a slow nod. "Aye…a just penance. Thank you, Your Majesty."

Faint groans drew my attention. Alisande was convulsing. She did not have long.

"Now begone, *Hermit* Gildas," I said to the contrite cleric. "I have one life yet to save, God willing."

He bobbed a bow and turned to wander back into the tunnel.

In the rightful timeline, Gildas the hermit had styled himself "The Wise" for the authorship of a quaint little epistle written as if Arthur had never existed, and he had owned the stones to refer to me as naught but "the Lioness of Damnonia"—that being a pun on the Romans' name for the region encompassing Cornwall, Dumnonia, where Arthur and I were born. The ancient me had viewed Gildas Sapiens's *De Excidio et Conquestu Britanniae—On the Ruin and Conquest of Britain*—as a grand jest; the me I had been fated to become could not have given a bullet-riddled fig whether this Gildas would scribe naught but his shopping lists for posterity.

I knelt and laid a hand on Alisande's brow. My rekindled healing energy coursed into her. After a few minutes, the moans and convulsions stopped and her color improved. I kept the spell active until her countenance appeared peaceful.

"Sleep, Lady Alisande," I said in Gaelic. "Wake when your husband and soulmate wakes."

In my copy of Hank Morgan's chronicle, he died in a bed at a nearby inn some unknown number of days after his waking in 1879, and Alisande had remained in France with their daughter.

Yes, I mucked with the timeline. Deliberately, thoroughly, and willfully. Sue me.

Smiling, Alisande nestled against her husband's chest.

"Ah, watch by me, Sandy," he murmured. "Stay by me every moment…"

"For ever and always…my Hank…"

Neither of them opened their eyes.

Though I held the Yankee in no particular regard, his dear lady wife deserved happiness if anyone associated with this entire wretched business did, and I was smitten by the desire to learn how their altered story would play out. However, she was not wearing any adornments suitable for my remote-viewing spell. I was about to abandon the idea when I spied Hank's pipe. Such an odious and harmful practice, smoking, and yet Alisande had never seemed to mind when he lit up. I grasped the stem, since his fingers were curled about its bowl, and added a filtration spell for good measure, not so much for his benefit as for hers. I wanted her ever after to be the longest and happiest on record.

After removing the enchanted ring from Arthur's hand, the final services I needed to perform for him and Clarice involved preserving their dignity in death. With magic I caused their bodies to lie flat, hands pressed together as if in prayer, and I set a warding spell to keep the higher-order creatures at bay whilst allowing the bacteria and fungi to perform their vital roles. I did not rearrange Ratcliffe's body into the prayer position, since I presumed that would have been contrary to how he had conducted his life, but I did shift his head into proximity with his neck once I recovered his time-folding device. Whether I granted him the favor of a warding spell, thoughtful reader, I shall leave you to ponder.

After cleansing my flesh and clothing of all blood and filth, I looped the chain holding the time-folding device over my head and tucked it inside my gown. Next, I summoned the same black cloak I had worn the first time I had ridden to the Salisbury Plain battlefield to augment the gown and shoes I was already wearing. My circlet felt cold and alien upon my brow, and I would have yanked it off had it not been crucial to duplicate my appearance to the last detail. An energy ball whirled upon each of my palms. Muffled thunder rumbled outside the cave.

"To Arthur's last battlefield," I said in Gaelic.

I clapped my hands.

Merlin's Cave disappeared in a brilliant white flash.

CHAPTER XXXIV.
WARNINGS.

Y AIM with time travel proved more accurate than I had been with a bullet. This was not saying a great deal, I warrant, but I had intended to arrive outside the parlay tent on the Salisbury Plain moments after my younger self had cast her time-freezing spell, and that was where I found myself when my vision cleared. Movement had ceased amidst men, creatures, and vegetation. Banners had stopped midflutter. Pipers, drummers, and trumpeters stood poised to play. No waves lapped the river's banks. The silence was eerie and absolute.

An adder, on its way into the parlay tent, had coiled to strike an unsuspecting monk suspended in the act of pacing.

A memory surfaced, and I scrutinized the monk. The cut and color of his robe appeared authentic, but the smoothness of its weave suggested commercial rather than native rough-spun linen. The stubble of his tonsure indicated that its maintenance was not habitual. The typical monk was a pasty, squinty academic, not the ruddy, athletic, and altogether handsome male specimen gladdening my eyes.

He had to be the Ambrose minion Clarice had mentioned, and I could well understand her attraction. This David was no Sandy, nor even Sir

Launcelot, but the youngest and most vain version of myself would have seduced him in a trice. I hoped that repairing the timeline would facilitate a happier fate for the younger Clarice, and for David too.

I unfroze the not-a-monk.

Giving me an open-mouthed double take, he checked his stride. As he shook his head, he must have noticed that no one else was moving.

"What the hell—?" He covered the gaffe with a deep bow. "I crave your pardon, my lady. Might I inquire as to what is happening here?"

I smiled at his adorable earnestness. "No need to pretend with me, David. You must abort your mission and return to the twenty-first century without delay."

His eyes widened. "Who are you? How do you know my name—and that I'm from the future?" The flaring of his caution caused his eyebrows to lower. "What do you know about my mission?"

I hooked a finger on the chain and pulled out Ratcliffe's time-folding device. David's eyes went wider yet, and his eyebrows nigh disappeared into his tonsure. "I have business here, but if you tarry, you shall be killed," I said. "And Clarice Centralia shall be keenly disappointed."

"Killed?" He swallowed hard. "Wait. What? Clarice?" A slow grin banished his fear. "Really?"

"She has what might be called 'a thing' for you. And only you. It shall remain unfulfilled should you die here."

I pointed at the bush by David's foot and the time-frozen adder beneath it. David swallowed again and took a giant sidestep clear of the snake's path.

"Wow. Okay. I believe you. And thanks for the save…Queen Morgan?" My nod confirmed his supposition. "But what about the king? He'll die in this battle." He lowered his eyebrows. "Or are you here to kill him before his other enemies do?"

I resisted the urge to sigh. "If that were my intent, would I have bothered to save your life?" The old me would have qualified "life" with "pathetic."

Strike that. The old me would have left the adder to bite him.

The squirrels in his head seemed to trample upon that claim awhile. "I suppose not," he conceded at length, "but—"

"Helping the king is the nature of my mission," was all he needed to know. "Go now; your time grows short."

David pushed up his robe's sleeve to access his time-folding device, which had bonded to his inner arm above the elbow. He touched the button, and its green light began blinking to indicate that it was marshaling its power.

I said, "When next you see me, do not be surprised if I behave as if we have never met. And, David, be good to Clarice. She deserves it a hundredfold."

The "Yes, ma'am" formed on his lips a moment before he vanished. Its sound vanished with him.

I parted the parlay tent's flaps and hurried inside.

The huge canvas field tent appeared every cubic inch as I remembered it, furnished with a large, crude table surrounded by three camp stools, one of which was occupied by Bishop Gildas—or, rather, it had been; he had frozen in the process of diving under the table, and the angle of his stool was far closer to the horizontal than the vertical. The table was tilted, the treaty document sliding groundward, the ink and candles toppling over. The quills, forming a skewed *X*, had not yet hit the ground. The other two stools stood vacant and upright as if the factions' leaders had eschewed their use.

All the tent sides had been lowered, and no one had thought to lay a carpet over the grass and dirt. Small wonder the adder had gotten a notion to creep inside.

Arthur, Mordred, and their knights had frozen midcharge, faces contorted in rage and weapons drawn. Whilst most of the other men's swords were canted forward, Arthur's pose brought to mind a batter in the box, cocked and ready for the pitch.

The sword-gored body of Ambrose Hinton lay to one side.

My slightly younger self, attired in our favorite black business skirt and jacket, red blouse, red-soled heels, circlet, and solid gold London Knights logo lapel pin, stood facing Arthur, reaching for him. Her back was to me, and she seemed unaware of my presence.

"Stop," I said.

She whirled to face me. Astonishment dominated her countenance. "What in the name of—? You are—me!"

I forgave her multiple violations of the Royal Rules. If I could not forgive myself, who on this side of heaven would?

"I deliver a warning," I said. "And a request."

The younger me crossed her arms. "I am listening."

"The future did not—will not unfold as I—we would wish."

When she asked me to explain, I glanced at our surroundings. The people and objects had shifted a bit further along their trajectories, but not so much so that I felt cause for alarm. Yet.

I began with the plaster that had to be yanked off:

"Sandy is gone. Dead. Without ever having met me—you. Us."

"No! No, no, no, no, NO!" I folded my weeping younger self into an embrace. "Oh, Sandy…"

"I have mourned his loss and have reconciled myself to it," I said when I judged that her tears had run their course. "Our relationship would never be the same, his and mine. You can prevent that calamity if you return to him without delay."

She pulled back, swiping at her cheeks. With a flick of the hand, her makeup returned to its typical perfection. She glanced at our brother. I noticed the angle of Excalibur was different; whether she did too, I cannot say.

"What about Arthur? The future needs him. I need him!" She flashed me an apologetic look. "And…I need to know that he forgives me." With her right hand, the younger me rubbed a spot above her heart. The Cross pattern glowed, piercing the layers of brassiere, camisole, blouse, and jacket. The lapel pin above it reflected a flash, the younger me winced, and then the pattern dimmed to its normal state of invisibility.

The sigil was her—my—our penance for our part, ever so many years ago, in King Uriens's rebellion against Arthur at the dawn of our brother's reign. The magical brand, applied by Merlin upon Arthur's command, glows whenever my hand hovers too close as a reminder that I remain powerless to remove it. Touching it inflicts an electric twinge that delivers increasing heat through prolonged contact. On rare occasions, when the need to remember and repent feels the most acute, I choose to activate the sigil, though I had not felt that need in God knows how long. Perhaps not since the day I was the woman standing inside the parlay tent wearing the black business suit, red blouse, red-soled heels, circlet, and gold London Knights logo lapel pin.

I grasped her hand, pulled it away from her chest, and pressed it between mine, willing that hand and her heart to cool.

"He does forgive you—us—with all his heart. But your future world does not need him," I assured her. "I fear what may happen if you try to return with him."

She extricated her hand from mine. "Surely the changes cannot be that bad. Other than Sandy," she hastened to add.

I pursed my lips, casting about for something to say that would not taint her knowledge of a future that could not, under any circumstances, be allowed to develop. A memory came to my rescue. "I—we—once confessed to Sandy that our youngest self was too blinded by rage to heed a warning from the future. Will you heed me?" It felt silly, but I had to ask: "Do you trust that I have our best interests at heart? Not just yours and mine, but Arthur's, Sandy's, and the entire world's interests too?"

She glanced round, no doubt trying to decide whether she could in fact trust her older self. Excalibur had descended lower. The treaty and quills had settled onto the ground. One candle lay moments (in real time) from igniting the parchment. The other objects and people had shifted more too.

"What of our youngest self?" she asked. "Her actions shall start this cycle all over again."

A WARNING AND
A REQUEST

That was mayhap the easiest component of the mission. "I shall deal with her," I said. "You must prevent the future Brad Ratcliffe from time-folding back to this era."

She barked a laugh. "That odious toad bollixed the timeline? Lord God Almighty, I should have known."

I gave her a brief smile. "You—we—cannot know everything."

I removed Ratcliffe's time-folding device from my neck whilst the younger me hastened to pull Ambrose's unit from her skirt's pocket. She stowed his laser pistol in her jacket, and then conjured torso padding and a full suit of armor to replace his twenty-first-century clothing and shoes. A looter might think it odd that this "knight" had been skewered with no damage to the breastplate or quilted undertunic, but he would be obliged to live with that little mystery.

"Take this." I offered her Ratcliffe's unit. "But use Ambrose's to return to the day you and he left our London Knights office."

"You intend to strand yourself here." The words came out more as an observation than a question.

"The world shall one day need its once and future king," I replied, "but it will be overwhelmed by two of us."

"A fair point," she said as she activated Ambrose's device. I heard its warmup hum. Its light began emitting a slow green oscillation. "Are you certain this will work? My magic cannot—"

"Your magic is more than equal to this task. Trust me," I said. "Better still, trust yourself. Concentrate upon Sandy and our office, and let the technology do the rest."

I wished her Godspeed and gave her hands a swift press, mindful to let go and step well clear before the blinking light transitioned to solid green.

Too late, I realized that I had neglected to inform her that when we had embraced following my announcement of Sandy's fate, I imbued her lapel pin with a remote-viewing spell, presuming that she would lock Ratcliffe's unit in a vault. If she instead elected to put it on display, so much the better.

Hasten not to a judgment, sweet reader. It cannot be considered stalking if the target is oneself.

Her mouth opened wide and rigid in a scream, but no sound reached my ears before she disappeared.

The movements of men and objects were gaining speed. I had mere moments to touch Excalibur's scabbard, bathing it in a shimmery aura that dissipated as fast as it formed. I prayed that I had made the spell strong enough.

I dashed behind the fallen parlay table as the temporal dam shattered. The treaty burst into flames, and Arthur's last battle began.

CHAPTER XXXV.
NEW AFTERMATH.

EVENING HAD progressed well along its transformation to night when silence returned to the battlefield, though of course not as absolute as when time had stopped. The background noise consisted of small rustlings and clankings punctuated by the occasional groan or cry. The ravens, hundreds upon hundreds of them, were the only scavengers in attendance; those of mammalian—including human—classification remained too timid to begin their grim work. Sounds pertaining to the purposeful movement produced by soldiers ministering to their fallen brethren-in-arms were far enough away that I could not have heard their conversations without magical assistance, and I lacked the desire to try.

With my every nerve primed at high alert, I emerged from the parlay tent. My companion at the commencement of the ordeal, Bishop Gildas, had rushed out upon the heels of the fighting knights, begging them to stop. I could have warned him that he would have had better success begging the sun to rise in the west, but I knew he would not have heeded me. Where he went after disappearing through the tent flaps, I had no idea and no compunction to learn. Dead on the blade of some war-blinded knight's sword, if the laws of karma were operating here.

The battlefield was strewn with thousands of corpses; horses and hounds as well as knights and soldiers. As I scanned the carnage, I began to make out little eddies of movement as survivors wandered about, stooping now and again, sometimes kneeling for a time, and sometimes delivering a fatal blow. It mattered naught who had smitten whom. My heartache deepened with each stab.

I flattened my hand upon my chest till the magic brand heated to the point of being unbearable. And then I kept my hand in place and bore the pain anyway.

The Battle on the Salisbury Plain never was a situation of "us" versus "them." It was "us" versus "us," and I had played as big a role in starting that sorry business as Arthur, Mordred, Guenever, Launcelot, Gawaine, or anyone else.

Punishing myself nonstop for a year and a day would not propel me a single step closer to atoning for my selfish, vengeful, contemptible actions.

Movement in the near distance attracted my attention, and I lowered the hand. I did not bother to invoke a cooling spell. A knight was hastening to another who lay propped against an oak growing on the riverbank where the water had carved a sharp curve. That curve would cause folk to name the site of Arthur's final battle Camlann,† a word already ancient on the day of my birth. It meant "bent sword," though some reality-rooted monk during the parade of centuries would one day mistranslate it as "crooked bank," causing later scholars to accept the new phrase as Gospel.

---

† As a proponent of the northern English borderlands-based King Arthur, I prefer "bent sword" for the meaning of "Camlann," a mashup of the Scottish Gaelic *cam* ("bent") + *lann* ("sword"). —*kih*

By the fanciful tree heraldry on the moving knight's surcoat, I recognized him as Sir Bedivere. I needed no clues to discern the identity of the recumbent man.

I chose a route that kept me hidden and crept close enough, with the aid of a spell that muffled my noises whilst boosting everyone else's, to improve my view.

Bedivere was bleeding from multiple untended wounds, to which he seemed to pay no mind as he knelt beside Arthur. He ripped a strip from the hemline of his surcoat and used it to bind Arthur's bloody head. An occasional moan told me Arthur was still clinging to life.

"Excalibur lies with the Lady of the Lake, my liege," Bedivere said. "This I swear upon peril of my eternal soul." I had failed to notice that Arthur's scabbard was empty.

The twitch of my brother's head was more spasm than nod. He had lost the ability to speak. Instinct warned me to act fast.

"Sleep, Arthur," I whispered in Gaelic, "like unto death." This sleeping spell, unlike the one I had laid upon the aged Cardinal Ratcliffe, carried a stasis component to prevent the worsening of Arthur's medical condition. I had done the same for Alisande.

My brother closed his eyes with a sigh, and his head lolled.

"Alas, in my accursed unbelief I tarried overlong!" Bedivere's words, uttered to no one in particular, came out more as a ragged moan. He bowed his head, then threw it back and uttered a long, loud howl that wrenched a prayer from my soul.

The rumble of hoofbeats shattered my reverie. My youngest self and her entourage—nine knights and three ladies-in-waiting—had careened into view. It felt far weirder to see her, wearing the identical garb I had conjured for myself down to the last stitch and button loop, than it had been to confront the me wearing the twenty-first-century power suit. As her knights secured the party's horses and formed a perimeter, and the ladies kept close to their mistress, I watched her examine Arthur and touch his bloody bandage, recalling her intent and the keenness of her disappointment upon realizing that he was already dead (although this time, in truth, he was not).

Of a sudden, the reason for the weirdness occurred to me. The business-suited Morgan stood far closer to me in sentiment and shared experiences. This woman could have been a stranger paid to portray the worst version of me in the history of scenery-chewing casting choices.

"The king is dead," she announced with the emotion of a Vulcan Kolinahr candidate.

Nininane, Vivien, and Galfrieda burst into wails. To a man, the knights saluted with their swords. Most removed helmets to swipe at moist eyes. The face of my youngest self adopted a contemptuous cast.

Pray that you, sweet reader, never come face to face with your shortcomings in such a literal fashion. I had quite forgotten just how very frozen my heart had been. Shame branded my soul and galvanized my resolve.

The youngest me turned that contemptuous look upon Arthur's knight companion. "Named he a successor, Sir Bedivere?"

The most loyal and selfless man ever to sit at the Round Table shook his head. "Methinks the man upon whom rests the future of England is Sir Boss."

Her response was too quiet to overhear, but I needed no spell to boost the volume. The words rose unbidden from my memory's depths: "Not if I hold any sway." To her knights, much louder, she said, "Make a fire; we are cold."

The men hacked apart a ruined battle wagon and formed a pile with the planks. The ladies lugged the smallest pieces as they struggled with their tears. The youngest me ordered Vivien to fetch her herbs, strewed a heaping handful onto the wood, wove a pattern in the air with her hands, and ignited a blazing bonfire. As the flames leapt higher and brighter, goaded by her boosting spell, storm clouds gathered. Lightning flashed.

Concealed from everyone's view, I turned my palms upward and summoned twin balls of whirling energy. The lightning would help me too.

My timing had to be perfect; I had no desire to chase my amok-running youngest self from era to era for eternity.

I clapped my hands in conjunction with a lightning strike. The blast rendered Sir Bedivere, the ladies, and the Castle Gore knights unconscious. The youngest me disappeared in a pillar of black smoke. Her horrified scream echoed into silence. I shall never forget the sound…or the guilt.

BREAKING THE CYCLE

There had been no smoke the first time I had attempted to travel to 1879 for to waylay Sir Boss, when my magic collided with the future time-folding device's activation to pull me into 2079.

Panic pretzel-twisted my gut. If my youngest self had perished, I too might cease to exist. A few calmer breaths later, I realized that God in His mercy had spared me that fate.

The cycle was broken.

CHAPTER XXXVI.
The Barge.

I STRODE to the riverbank, whilst the ladies and knights yet lay in their swoons, and conjured a small barge moored at a dock. A finger-snap gave the barge a black sail, a black-swathed platform amidships, and a black-cushioned bench spanning the platform's length. The vessel carried neither oars nor poles, since I could freshen the wind as the need arose. The night mists had begun gathering upon the water's surface as if wishing to investigate my work.

I roused my ladies and asked them to wake Bedivere and the other knights.

"Men, carry the king onto the boat. Make haste!" I clapped my hands—with no spell primed—to punctuate my point. "Lady Galfrieda, Lady Niniane, Lady Vivien: you three shall accompany me."

Bedivere stood and glared at me, the knuckles of his right hand whitening upon his sword's pommel, an understandable reaction considering what he knew of the history up to that point betwixt Arthur and the ancient me. The Gore knights alternated confused glances at each other and at me, and the ladies backed away ever so slowly, as if to move any faster might invite me to pounce upon them.

Right. I was not the "me" they had expected. That me would have rather died than do anything for Arthur's benefit,—or for anyone else's, in sooth. If that me had conjured the barge for some nefarious scheme, she would have fried the lot, Bedivere included, and started over with a fresh, malleable minion set.

"I forbid it, sorceress," Bedivere said, his sword hand flexing. "Thou shalt not wreak evil upon the king."

A denial would be worse than useless, of course; this situation required an unexpected tack. I glided to him, hands raised in supplication. "Good Sir Bedivere, may I treat your wounds?" I imbued my tone with every last drop of kindness and compassion that I possessed.

He relaxed his stance a little and nodded—thanks in no small measure to my reputation as "The Wise" in regard to my healing skills,—but his countenance continued to radiate wariness through the pain and fatigue. I hummed a cradle song as I touched each cut, abrasion, and bruise. His joints, bones, and organs seemed sound, but I added that component to my spell in case I had missed a strained ligament, a slight fracture, or something more life threatening.

In due course, the bleeding stopped and the wounds closed. I retreated a pace whilst he examined himself. His astonishment grew with each wound site he touched until it blossomed into wonderment and gratitude.

"A thousand thanks, Queen Morgan, but…why?"

"My days of enmity with the king are done." Further explanation would have confused him, which might have hindered my mission.

"Wilt thou permit me to perform one last service for my liege?" Bedivere asked.

"Of course."

I had a fair idea of what that service might be. I ordered my knights to steady the barge and stand ready to assist whilst Bedivere gathered Arthur into his arms. The royal armor proved too heavy for the battle-fatigued man, and all of us were loath to strip it off. Three of my knights rushed in to help Bedivere get my brother settled on the platform. Others assisted my ladies to board. One hastened to the oak to retrieve Arthur's riven helmet and crown. When he offered it to me, I almost smiled; instead, I told him to give it to Bedivere, who had knelt beside Arthur, one hand on Arthur's forearm, tears trickling down his cheeks.

The knight bearing the helmet cleared his throat. Bedivere glanced at him, saw the man's royal burden, and stood without bothering to dash the tears. He accepted the helmet and nestled it with utmost care into the crook of Arthur's near elbow. With his right hand he made a fist and laid it against his heart, head bowed.

Bedivere might have held that pose for the rest of his days, but I needed to get him ashore.

I touched his elbow, delivering a cooperation spell. "Come, fair Sir Bedivere. 'Tis time for this vessel to depart." To preserve the illusion that this was a death barge, I did not reveal its destination.

Bedivere did not ask to accompany me. I thanked God for that mercy; being obliged to deny Arthur's best friend would have been leagues beyond awkward.

As two of my knights helped Bedivere disembark and two others cast off the moorings, I delivered a final request to the men: "Pray for thy rightful liege lord, King Arthur, and for his humble servant and sister, that I might with the aid of the Lord God help Arthur to become the Once and Future King."[†]

The wind stirred, the sail filled, and the barge drifted free of the dock. I did not need to hear the knights' assent to know I possessed it.

The knights, led by Bedivere, drew their swords and held them aloft. They had rendered their salutes for Arthur, as was proper, but I had not shed

---

† The dialogue that begins "Pray for thy rightful liege lord, King Arthur…" appears in this book's prequel, *King Arthur's Sister in Washington's Court*, where the sentence was recorded by Queen Morgan's scribe in the context of a witness having recalled her words. —*kih*

"BEDIVERE MIGHT HAVE HELD THAT POSE FOR THE REST OF HIS DAYS."

enough of my vanity to stymie the hope that my men might be honoring me too. I raised my open hand to return the salutes on our king's behalf.

The mist thickened, obscuring the dock and its occupants. When Vivien would have yielded her seat to me, I asked the ladies to shift closer. I settled onto the bench between Galfrieda and Niniane, and off we sailed.

CHAPTER XXXVII.
A Puzzling Predicament.

HE WAY to Avalon cannot be plotted on a map. Compasses and globes and computers are useless, as are even the very stars themselves.

Avalon is not a place in the geographic sense. It is a state of being.

I did not write about my first journey because there was little to tell. We had drifted for what seemed like a matter of minutes before the mists parted, and Avalon's blessed shores appeared. The experience caused me to assume that entry was a function of one's sincerity of intent.

You know, savvy reader, what is said to happen when one assumes.

This time the barge hung suspended in the misty limbo for so long, I began feeling like a right jolly old ass.

No manner of spells, incantations, lamentations, or prayers dissipated that infernal mist. My dear little goldfish Niniane even tried shouting. The brief elevation of our spirits was the only notable accomplishment of that particular experiment.

As the exposure dragged on, and sensing that making progress might have to become a team effort, I began indoctrinating the ladies as my apprentices. I solicited their permission first, of course; an unwilling practitioner carries the potential to wreak all manner of harm. Vivien decided to activate a drying spell to keep all of us from becoming soaked to the skin. Niniane augmented her friend's effort by creating a canvas canopy. Galfrieda conjured food and drinks as the need arose. The drying spell did double duty.

My stasis spell upon Arthur remained steady, and I gave it periodic boosts as a precaution. He had lain moments from death when I cast it, and I feared that I would lose him should the spell fail before we reached Avalon's restorative environment.

To take our minds off our puzzling predicament, I started regaling the ladies with stories of my adventures in the late twenty-first century, not the second sojourn but the first: about Sandy, of course, and Clarice, and the baseball games, and helping President Malory, and the smallpox victims that Malory had resolved—against everyone's better judgment—to assist. When I described the flying steel dragons (limousines), hovering crystal castles (airborne office buildings), and the suboceanic speeding worm (the Transatlantic Bullet Train), I am certain they thought the mist had driven me mad, but they kept listening, and I kept talking. We had naught else to do.

I relayed the tale of how I had killed a man and was jailed for it, how Sandy came to my rescue, and how our fortunes soared after that sorry incident. By the time I reached the part about Ambrose dragging me back to the commencement of Arthur's final battle, we all noticed that the mists had thinned; dim, lumpy shadows appeared, suggesting a land mass. And I noticed that Galfrieda, Niniane, and Vivien no longer regarded me as if I were a raving lunatic. Mayhap they decided that stories stuffed to bursting with specific details, the bad as well as the good, must have actually transpired. I had not intended to mention the schemes of Ratcliffe and the original Gildas that led to my tribulations in an altered future world, but I felt confident that the mists were disappearing in direct proportion to the exercising of my wind bag. So I drew a deep breath and nattered on.

I would have had better luck shouting.

After I finished, those shadows remained every mote as dim and lumpy as before, nor did they appear one micron closer.

At least my ladies now sat in full possession of the facts. Whether they believed those facts to be true was a matter of debate, but no one suggested that I check myself into the nearest sanitarium should we ever find the exit to our misty prison.

I solicited questions from the ladies as a further way to pass the time.

"THEY KEPT LISTENING, AND I KEPT TALKING."

"What about your remote-viewing spells, my lady?" Vivien asked. "Do you think you can see what those other people are doing from here—wherever 'here' is?"

"Aye!" squealed Niniane, clapping her hands. "Please have a go at the pipe first. I wish to know if Lady Alisande did indeed wake with her Hank." Her cheeks colored, and she dipped her head. "If it pleases Your Majesty."

"It pleases me very much, Lady Niniane, and I thank you for the request," I said with a smile.

Galfrieda glanced, frowning, at the stubborn mists. "Are you certain your spell can penetrate this stew, Your Majesty?"

Not in the least; however, "We shall never know if I do not make the attempt."

I squared my shoulders, closed my eyes, reminded myself that I am indeed a force with which Fortuna must reckon, and entered a meditative trance.

CHAPTER XXXVIII.
A Fish-eye View.

ARKNESS GREETED me. I was not surprised. Disappointed, indeed, for it proved that the remote viewing attempt had failed, and no small part of me had hoped for success in this endeavor. However, the darkness possessed the virtue of being devoid of that infernal mist. My ladies, each with their hands touching my shoulders and back, could see what I was seeing, and the darkness provided a most welcome break for all of us. I elected to linger in its monotony a while longer.

Soon I became aware of a bouncing light. At birth, 'twas the size of a pinprick. My mind's eye had to be playing a prank. I abandoned that notion when the light grew to a dot like the paper waste from a hole punch, thence to bilberry. The light swelled through the spectrum of cherry tomato, golf ball, peach, and grapefruit before it steadied at cabbage size.

A male face floated into view, its craggy features distorted in a globular fashion. I thought it odd till I realized the curvature of the pipe's bowl was functioning like a fish-eye lens. Behind the first man, who was holding a lantern, I could discern the silhouette of a second figure who seemed to be standing, limned in a second light source, likely another lantern.

The first man said: "I say, sir! Madame! Odd place for a nap, what?"

The second man stepped closer, and his face's details sharpened,—if in fact such a word may be applied to a fish-eye view. "And why, pray tell, are ye dressed so strangely?" he asked.

He must have been referring to their medieval garb, which had lain preserved as part of my spell upon Alisande to keep their modesty intact.

The angle of the pipe suffered an abrupt shift; Hank must have pushed himself up.

Fortuna had deigned to be kind, for once. Unlike the flat images produced by Ratcliffe's time-folding device, the pipe offered a three-dimensional view, though obscured in places where it came in contact with solid matter, such as the Yankee's fingers or the ground. The latter seemed to be the case at present; I presumed that Hank had set down the pipe, and I watched him twist and look at Alisande, who also was sitting up. Both of them appeared quite groggy yet.

"What—? Sandy, you're here!" Love banished the grogginess in his gaze.

AN ODD PLACE FOR A NAP

"Does 'ever and always' mean something different to you, my beloved Hank?" Alisande returned his loving look in full measure.

I caught a glimpse of lips meeting lips before the pipe was knocked aside in the couple's haste to embrace.

I could sense my ladies' disappointment over being deprived of the romantic details, and I sympathized, but the pipe's new position afforded me a better look at the two men. From their builds, demeanors, and the supplies they were lugging, the tell-tale tools being the notebooks and whisk brushes, I judged them to be archaeologists. This theory bore out as they traversed the gallery in a methodical pattern, the first man recording an inventory of the unburied skeletons and artifacts as the second dictated details of each finding. They left the human remains undisturbed, but the first man did pick up Ratcliffe's revolver, which had belonged to one of the cadets, a weapon Hank himself must have fashioned. In any event, the archaeologist seemed less interested in the piece itself than its function, and he correctly deduced how it had been discharged. He directed his companion to investigate Clarice's skeleton. I winced as the second man knelt and rummaged about a bit before locating the spent bullet. But rather than rising right away, he doffed his cap and bowed his head, still kneeling beside Clarice.

A tidal wave of grief threatened to sever my concentration. I willed myself to maintain focus.

At length the man donned his cap and stood, displaying the bullet between thumb and forefinger. "This woman appears to have been killed by gunfire, daft as that may sound given these remnants of the medieval-era textiles she was wearing." He pointed at the exposed lower thoracic region of Clarice's spine. "But the groove on this vertebra has nae other explanation."

"You don't think that sword could have done the job?" asked the first man.

The sword Arthur had taken from the dead Sir Meliagraunce had landed midway between Clarence's skeleton and Arthur's, making it difficult to ascertain which man had wielded it.

CHAPTER XXXVIII.

The second archaeologist pushed his spectacles onto his nose's bridge. "Perhaps, but judging by its breadth, I expect it would have nicked at least one of the ribs too. These are all intact." He shrugged. "We may ne'er know what occurred here."

Hank shuffled into view, with Alisande half a pace behind him, one hand upon his shoulder.

"I reckon mysteries are your stock in trade," he said. "I sure as shootin' don't want to spoil your fun."

The Yankee's features enlarged to grotesque, fishy proportions as he stooped to pick up the pipe and his chronicle. The pipe's view swung about, again showing me the archaeologists.

Hank must have asked them for tobacco and a light; the bespectacled man patted his pockets and shrugged, and his colleague shook his head. "I never could tolerate all that nasty smoke," he said.

Hank looked down into the pipe's bowl. "Quite all right. I can wait. Now if you'll pardon us, good sirs, my wife and I will mosey on out of your way. I don't suppose the White Horse Inn is open for business?"

"I say! That ancient establishment has housed a museum for decades," said the nonsmoker.

"Just how long have ye been asleep, friend?" asked the other archaeologist.

"Have you heard of Rip Van Winkle[†]?" Hank asked.

Both men grinned and tipped their caps.

Alisande's brow furrowed. "Rip—who?"

"I'll fill you in, love," her husband assured her. "We have all the time in the world."

Darkness descended as Hank stowed the pipe in his pocket.

[†] "Rip Van Winkle" is the title of a short story by American author Washington Irving, first published in Irving's anthology *The Sketch Book of Geoffrey Crayon, Gent.* in 1819. The story's title character is a Dutch-American villager in living in the Catskill Mountains of colonial New York who, while squirrel hunting one day, encounters a group of mysterious Dutchmen. Rip helps them carry a keg, and in return they invite him to imbibe their potent liquor. His drunken slumber lasts twenty years, and he awakens to a very changed world, having missed the American Revolution in its entirety. *—kih*

CHAPTER XXXIX.
Fish in the Pond.

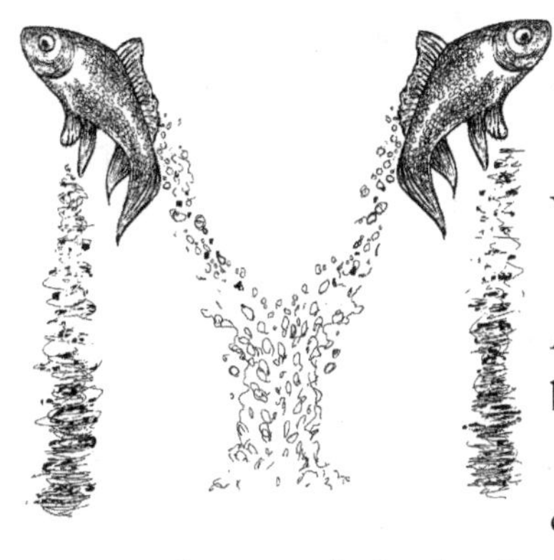

M Y LADIES and I spent quite some time chatting amongst ourselves about what Lady Alisande and Hank might be doing, buoyed by the certainty that the mists had thinned more. At least, the ladies were certain; I clamped a lid upon my elation lest it jinx our chances of winning free.

During the course of our conversation, I had to refuse their pleas to access the pipe again.

"My dear ladies, Mr. and Mrs. Morgan deserve their privacy. I intend to afford them that courtesy." Niniane puffed her cheeks as if to protest; I raised a finger. "No exceptions."

And that, of course, ended the matter.

The moment Alisande realized that her sweet baby girl had been dead for more than a thousand years was an experience I wished to avoid, though I kept that reason to myself. It is difficult enough to live with the fact that my own son is centuries gone. Having to watch another woman endure that torture would trigger the anguish ever simmering within myself.

When we ran out of happy, sultry speculations regarding Alisande and Hank, we retreated into our own thoughts. I cannot speak for the others, but I tried once again to will the mists to part for us. If anything, it made them thicken a tad.

Weary of the endless damp grayness, I accessed the London Knights lapel pin belonging to the younger, luckier me. My ladies caught on to what I was doing and hastened to crowd closer, with my leave, for to make themselves part of the connection.

I found myself looking at the inside of a WC. And not just any dank old WC. This lavatory was bright, clean, roomy, and the walls surrounding the banks of sinks, soap dispensers, and hand dryers were decorated with framed, plexiglass-shielded London Knights posters and pennants. As my other self stood washing her hands, I studied the face reflected in the mirror. Though her gaze was tilted down to attend to business, I recognized that look of intense concentration, for I had formed it often myself.

She was mulling the best course of action in a serious situation.

What that situation was—and, more to the point, when it was—did not become clear until she approached the reception area of her office suite.

I do mean that it was *her* office, not mine or ours. In my version of events, Sandy's sister, Amanda, was my private secretary. She had helped her brother keep the other politicians from barging into my sanctum upon the heels of their crony Ambrose the day he had intended to banish me to Arthur's era.

Sandy was still present, and I drank in the glorious sight of his beloved face as a desert-parched man gulps the water that he knows will save his life. All of the politicians I remembered from before—the corpulent Dan Dowley, the athletic and handsome but treacherous Douglas Blacklance, and the rest—were waving fists and shouting to be permitted entry. I looked at the woman helping Sandy and performed the mental equivalent of a double take.

The woman was Clarice.

In my timeline, Clarice had signed on as President Malory's aide and resided in Washington, DC. How this Clarice had come to be employed as the secretary of the other me, I could not begin to fathom.

It brought to mind a time-travel episode of the classic television series *Stargate SG-1* that ended with Colonel O'Neill being astonished to discover the addition of fish to his deliberately fishless pond. Time travel is far messier than the monotone minions of *Star Trek*'s Bureau of Temporal Investigations ever let on. (Yea, I had turned to fictional sources during my days of researching time-travel methods; guilty as charged. I feel no guilt over how much enjoyment those shows gifted me.)

Perhaps this meant that the magical spark empowering my Clarice would manifest in another corporeal body. The speculation spawned the hope that I could craft an enchantment for sensing the spark's presence, and I set the idea to simmer in the back of my mind.

As grateful as I was to see this version of my dear departed apprentice, however, her presence raised the concern that something had happened to Amanda. Had the Sanctuary Districts never been abolished? Had Amanda and Sandy never reconciled this time round? Had some evil befallen her? Did she even exist in this timeline? I pondered the possibilities whilst my younger self observed the proceedings unnoticed by everyone else, probably due to an invisibility spell. She turned, and the lapel pin's view shifted to the office door. In flew Amanda, followed by, of all people, the not-a-monk David, who had grown his hair to a pleasing length and had traded his robe and cowl for a business suit.

The look he exchanged with Clarice told me they were indeed working on their happily-ever-after. Then he and Amanda waded into the fray.

I could not hear the commotion, but it seemed to have ratcheted up many notches, to judge by the increased tension on everyone's faces, and the emphatical gestures.

Sandy shoved several politicians aside and rushed through the door leading into the private office.

All movement stopped.

The younger me must have cast a time-freezing spell. As I wondered why, she threaded past Amanda, David, Clarice, and the politicians without touching any of them before reaching a corner of the reception area heretofore hidden from my sight. In it stood the one man present who was neither shouting nor gesturing. His arms were folded, the top arm twisted as if he were studying his wristwatch.

It mattered naught that his face was canted downward. I would have recognized the odious toad anywhere.

She flicked her fingers, and a time-folding device appeared on her palm, presumably lifted from somewhere upon Ratcliffe's person. He unfroze the moment her dirk sliced his throat, but his body had no chance to either spurt blood or fall before she cast another spell to send it to God alone knew where.

It was as if I were watching the ancient me, the hate-brimming, revenge-thirsting, wrath-lusting me: judge, jury, and executioner all rolled up into one. The acuteness of my discomfort,—in spite of the unquestionable necessity of this particular execution,—served to remind me how much I had changed.

Mayhap this occurred to the younger me as well; she hesitated awhile before stepping into her domain.

The time-freezing spell had captured Ambrose and a fourth version of ourselves in the process of dematerializing. Her attempts to touch either of them proved as futile as touching the afterimage produced by the discharge of a flashbulb.

I had no idea what this would portend for the timeline. Without Ratcliffe to interfere, however, it seemed logical that Arthur would kill Ambrose, as he had done to save my life, and then…

A thought smote me. What if I and my party were being denied entry into Avalon because another version of Arthur and me already existed there? The more I tried to dismiss the idea, the more the misty limbo entrapping us felt like an airport's holding pattern, the primary exception being that this weather would not clear with the next gust.

How many times were we fated to repeat this sorry cycle of events? What could we do to break it…and have it stay broken?

When was the last time I mentioned how much I despise time travel?

My brain swirling with these questions and a thousand more, I realized that the final vestiges of Ambrose and our other self had faded from existence. There was no flash of light, no mouths contorted into silent screams, or any other indication of their fates, save one clue.

When time's normal flow resumed, the view through the lapel pin became obscured by Sandy's chest. How, you might wonder, did I know it was Sandy's? Because I had never clung to anyone else that long in my entire sixteen-century existence. During that embrace, she could have made a full confession of her actions against Ratcliffe, and perhaps against Ambrose and our fourth self too.

JUDGE, JURY, AND EXECUTIONER

Sandy was—is—forever shall be—such a daisy.

Almighty God, how I yearned to be the woman sheltering in his arms.

I shall never know what she said to him, but confessing everything to my soulmate before we could enjoy another moment together is what I would have done. I wished for her and Sandy, to the very core of my being, all the happiness their world could offer them.

CHAPTER XL.
LAMENTATIONS.

HEN I exited my trance, I expected the way to Avalon to be clear.

Through the stubborn mists wafted the razz of a divine snort.

It proved too much for my ladies. Niniane and Vivien uttered keening howls that carried on for so long, I had no idea how they were managing to breathe. No magic spells or words could calm them. The best I could do was to lay a hand upon each heaving shoulder and hum a healing melody. The stalwart Galfrieda helped me for a while, but the battle to curb the tremor of her chin ended in a burst of sobs. That proved too much for me.

"Arthur needs to be in Avalon to survive! I cannot heal him on this barge! I have disclosed everything! My motivations are pure!" I knotted my fists and shook them. "My ladies cannot bear any more of this lunacy! Neither can I! Why must we continue to suffer so?" The next bit I delivered with the volume of a veteran brigadier:

"What more do you want from me?"

Why, yes, I did yell at a supernatural fogbank, Royal Rules be damned straight to hell and back. Thank you for noticing.

The ladies noticed too, but they were too astounded—or, likelier still, too fearful—to comment.

At least my outburst had helped them to rein in their bolting emotions.

Hoping that the third time might indeed prove to be the charm, I relaxed my hands and submerged my anger for to enter another remote-viewing trance when my gaze lit upon Arthur's unconscious form.

This was not the same Arthur I had brought to Avalon the first time, but I loved him not one jot less.

A realization crystallized.

"Now see here," I said to the swirling grayness in as reasonable a tone as I could muster, "if we are being barred entry on account of the unfinished business betwixt me and this version of my brother, I cannot address that lack whilst he languishes in this state."

Or could I?

During my first sojourn in the late twenty-first century, I had heard tell of patients recalling in precise detail statements that loved ones had made whilst the patients had lain comatose. Niniane, Vivien, and Galfrieda might think my behavior odd; then again, speaking to an almost-dead man might seem no odder than the other behavior they had witnessed since waking from the concussive blast unleashed by my youngest self's aborted time-travel spell.

'Twas the last idea my brain could conjure.

I eased onto my knees and grasped Arthur's hand. Its coldness gave my heart a panicked lurch. After feeling faint puffs from his nostrils upon the backs of my fingers, I boosted the stasis spell. In the process of giving him the healing ring, I recalled that it was still imbued with the remote-viewing spell too. Absent his consent, the risk of him mistrusting my motives outweighed the restorative benefits. I disabled the remote-viewing function and slipped the ring onto his pinkie. If, upon waking, he chose to mistrust the motives behind a spell yielding naught but positive results, our relationship stood on far worse footing than I had believed.

I inhaled a deep breath and hoped—nay, prayed—for the best.

"Arthur Pendragon, High King of England," I began, head bowed and my right hand pressed to my heart. The magical Cross sigil glowed and burned, precisely as I needed it to. "I, Morgan, Queen of Gore, do humbly acknowledge you as my rightful lord, liege, and master. I swear fealty to you and henceforth pledge my life and my lands unto your good will, upon pain of death in the forswearing thereof."

I held the pose, hoping for some sign, however small, that he had heard me.

Sensing not even the smallest eyelash-twitch from him, I pressed harder with my right hand, tightened my chest muscles against the self-imposed pain, and forged on:

"I am sorry for the years of malice-laden strife betwixt us, Arthur. I am sorry that I turned Uriens and Mordred against you. I am sorry for attacking you, and Guenever, and Camelot, not once but many times. I am sorry that I stole Excalibur's scabbard with the intent to jeopardize your life. I am sorry for failing to forgive you for Accolon's death…but I do forgive you now, with all my heart. I pray to God, Jesu, and all the saints that you can hear me and set your heart at rest." My hand lifted of its own volition, gifting me a respite from the pain. "I am beyond thankful that you never held my actions against Uwaine. You were the best uncle and commander a promising young knight could ever want, and I am sorry that I could not appreciate that till now."

I balled my fist and jammed it back against my heart. The arcing surge from the reactivated magical brand left me gasping and wheezing.

After I regained control of my breathing, I said, "Arthur, my beloved brother and liege, I am so very sorry for every evil I have ever wrought upon you. Including the evil of being trapped in this eternal limbo, unable to live…or die."

I might have added "Godforsaken" to my description of the limbo had I not recalled, just then, words spoken by the kindliest priest I had ever had the privilege of knowing:

If I take the wings of the morning and remain in the uttermost parts of the sea; even there also shall Thy hand lead me and Thy right hand shall hold me.

More tears welled than my blinking could purge.

At some point, I became aware of my ladies' hands upon my shoulders and back. Vivien pried my fist from my chest. My muscles went limp at the abrupt cessation of pain and I sagged into her arms. The voices' blended humming, tuneful but feeble beginners' emulations of my healing spell, enveloped me. If they had intended to impart comfort, their actions engendered the opposite effect. I pulled away from Vivien and returned to Arthur, bowing over his chest till I felt the unyielding chill of his breastplate on my forehead. I embraced him as hard as I dared.

UNVARNISHINIG THE TRUTH

"I am sorry," I forced myself to whisper, "that I disobeyed a direct command from the other you. The fact that I know England will one day need its once and future king is no excuse. The fact that I did not disobey *you* is no excuse either. The unvarnished truth is that I cannot let you go, and for that selfish evil, I am so, so sorry."

The dam of my emotions shattered, and I sobbed my guilt-ridden grief onto that great, metal-clad heart.

CHAPTER XLI.
AVALON AT LAST.

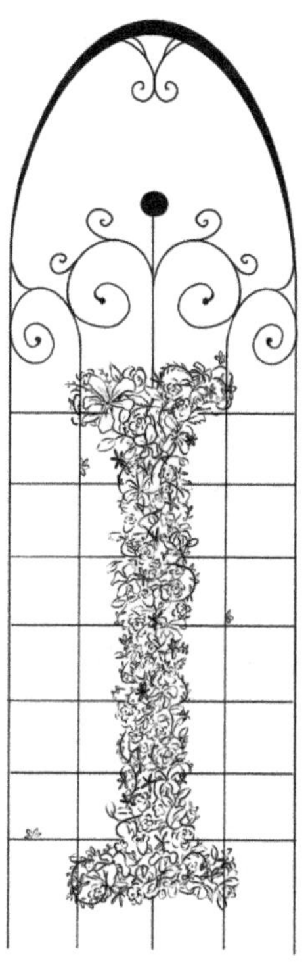

KNOW not which of my ladies uttered a gasp, but
I recognized Vivien when she said, "Your Majesty!
Praise God, Jesu, and all the saints, you did it!"

I raised my head.

The mists were gone.

Whether that had been any of my doing, unto
the smallest fraction, I chose not to debate.

Avalon's eternal sunshine bathed our faces in its hopeful glow. Our
nostrils were blessed with the scents of roses, lavender, and honeysuckle.

The barge glided to a stop at a dock where several robed, hooded monks
and nuns stood waiting. The women chanted prayers whilst some of the
men secured the barge, some carried Arthur ashore, and the rest helped
me and my ladies disembark. Everyone stepped into a box formation with
my brother and his bearers at its centre.

Everyone except me.

Standing on the dock, as the procession made its slow, prayerful way
to a compound of stone buildings in the near distance, I yanked off my
crown and flung it into the water. I stared at its ripples till they flattened,
and longer. Much, much longer.

CHAPTER XLI.

I am the daughter of Duchess Igraine and Duke Gorlois. My mother named me in honor of the Mór Rigan, the Great Queen, speaker to ravens and goddess of war. I wonder what she would have named me had she foreseen how much strife and war and death I would cause. I thank God she never lived to see those dolorous days.

My brain conjured images of the Salisbury Plain battlefield: the maimed, dying, and dead amidst heaps of splintered wagons, sputtering fires, trampled tents, broken trumpets, punctured drums, and shattered weapons; the Scarlet Dragon and Gold Double-headed Eagle banners at the parlay tent's entrance fluttering in the fitful breeze; flocks of ravens circling overhead and spiraling downward in ever-increasing numbers. Their cackling conveyed gleeful anticipation.

Once again, I saw Sir Bedivere and the other knights standing in the crook of the riverbank, saluting their beloved liege.

Perhaps Igraine had indeed foreseen her daughter as the terrible Mór Rigan incarnate, come to claim the greatest sacrifice a nation can make.

I stepped off the dock but did not hasten to catch the procession.

Some call me Queen. In truth, I married into the title and wielded it to run roughshod over my subjects, my lovers, and my first husband, King Uriens, all in the name of my Divine Right. The lowliest peasant woman holds more claim to the Crown than I.

The procession halted at the arched iron gateway in the complex's outer wall. I stepped up to Arthur's side and laid a hand upon his shoulder.

Some call me "The Wise." I am in truth the greatest of fools. I wasted three decades of my life blinded by hatred of my half brother, Arthur, my God-ordained liege and lord. My rage forced him to make choices that hurt us both. All England suffered with us.

Together with my ladies and Avalon's resident religieux, we progressed down an ivy-covered colonnade till we reached the building that housed the sleeping chambers. One of those chambers, if the layout had not changed since my first visit, would have been converted into a workroom for mixing herbs, blending salves, crafting plasters, and distilling potions.

Tendrils of mist accompanied us as if they were honoring Arthur too.

Some call me a prophet. I foresaw countless events that I leveraged for my benefit. Sometimes that knowledge benefited other people, but most often that was not my intention. Never once, to my eternal shame, did I exercise God's gift for the benefit of His Church.

The monks entered a small, candle-lit chamber and laid Arthur on the narrow bed. I unwrapped the bloody strips of Sir Bedivere's surcoat to reveal Arthur's wound. It looked horrific against the pallor of his face. The sight shocked everyone else into the semblance of statues. Two sharp claps of my hands broke that spell, and most of the people departed upon various errands to bring bandages, hot water, towels, chairs, food, drink, medicines, more candles, and other supplies. Two monks removed Arthur's boots and armor. He was wearing a torn, grimy, sweaty, padded tunic and leggings underneath. Another monk placed the hewn helmet and crown upon a side table with reverential care.

Some call me a peerless healer. I can heal a broken body, God willing, but I never once employed His gift to heal a broken soul. Should God in His mercy choose to grant me more time with the living, I vow to remedy this grievous lack.

As Galfrieda applied clean bandages and the nuns continued praying aloud, I hovered my hand over Arthur's head wound. Sparks flashed from my palm and fingertips to arc round his head. Blood soaked the bandages within moments. Whilst Galfrieda changed the dressing, I redoubled the force of my healing spell. I hummed so much, I had scant time to breathe. Clarice could have given me a break, but of course that was not to be. When that heartache subsided to a manageable level, I resolved to train my ladies in the magical healing arts at our earliest opportunity.

All call me "le Fay"—sorceress and seductress. I have heard it whispered from the shadows lest I vent my wrath upon those who dare utter it in my presence. In sooth, "le Fay" is the one title I deserve and the only title I shall never deny.

Minutes, days, eternities passed for us. I repaired Arthur's helmet, crown, scabbard, and armor, and the monks polished the pieces till they gleamed like new. I drilled my ladies to perfect the healing spell and other magic, advanced as well as simple. The four of us served in rotation to minister to the king. We maintained the healing spell, spooned liquids into his mouth and rubbed his throat to make him swallow, bathed him with damp towels, changed the plasters, read to him, and dozed at his side. Now and then, monks lifted Arthur to change his clothing and bed linens. Nuns in a constant stream brought food, drink, hot water, bandages, and medicines, emptied the privy pot, gathered the soiled items, and removed the discarded ones. I could have performed all of those chores using magic, but those dear, blessed people insisted upon helping in any way they could.

Everyone prayed over him from time to time.

One man called me mother. Uwaine stood honored amongst men at the Table Round. But he died upon his uncle's last battlefield, and twice—nay, thrice his mother failed to succor his final moments. The fact that the second and third times I was consumed by the need to ensure the greater good is no excuse. I bear the harshest indictment that can be levied against a parent, and I pray that my son has forgiven me.

I grieve that I shall never hear it from his lips.

The day that Arthur's bandage stayed clean throughout all four of our shifts was the day I knew he was out of danger. I canceled the schedule of constant monitoring and sent Vivien to bring four monks. Whilst she remained occupied by that errand, I conjured for Arthur a fine embroidered tunic and leather leggings. The men used the bed linens to carry him outside to the brightly colored, open-air pavilion I had created for to increase his exposure to the restorative properties inherent in Avalon's atmosphere. Niniane and Galfrieda were waiting for us there.

One man called me his soulmate. I ache for Sandy with each passing hour, and I hope with all sincerity that my other self enjoys as much happiness in his arms as I did. They deserve nothing less.

Together we got Arthur settled upon the pavilion's bed. I sent the monks to bring Arthur's armor and its stand outside, so he would see familiar objects in the off chance that he woke alone. Then I dismissed everyone to their well-deserved rest whilst I retired to my workroom to resume my writing.

At no time had I exchanged my long black cloak and gown for any other mode of dress.

My crown remained drowned in the waters into which I had cast it on the day Avalon deigned to let me enter.

"I YANKED OFF MY CROWN AND FLUNG IT INTO THE WATER."

CHAPTER XLI.

The world deserves nothing less than Arthur's promised return. Here in mist-shrouded Avalon, where time exists in the eyeblink of a dream, it is my honor to tend the king and await the hour God has appointed for him to resume his destiny. Whether it be Arthur's wish that I accompany him or remain here, I shall accept his command as his obedient servant and loving sister.

Nininane burst into the workroom, breathless and disheveled but beaming. I cocked an eyebrow at her.

"Queen Morgan!" It came out more as a gasp. "Please forgive the intrusion, my lady, but Galfrieda believes the king's time is nigh!"

'Twas not the first time my little golden-haired fish had delivered such a message, but of course I had to see for myself. Again.

"Very well. You go on ahead whilst I make the final preparations to this tome. If I am to leave Avalon, please stow it where we discussed."

My "final preparations" included binding the pages, applying the hologram and spark-sensing spells, stowing the chronicle inside its box, activating the magical lock, and enchanting it to unlock upon sensing Clarice's spark. "Final" was a hopeful term; I had lost count of the number of times I had executed this checklist, even to resetting the enchantments. Nininane had yet to participate in her portion, which was to carry the boxed book to the barge. I did not hold a great deal of confidence that Arthur would want me to accompany him, but I resolved to be prepared.

"Yes, Your Majesty." Niniane dropped a curtsy, rose, and swished back out the way she had come.

I signed the last page with a flourish.

I, Morgan, have written this chronicle with mine own hand. May God have mercy upon my lord King Arthur and upon us all now and forever.

Soli Deo gloria.

Amen.

CHAPTER XLII.
A Postscript by the Queen.

AVALONIAN DAWNS are glorious affairs wherein everything, from the tallest building to the smallest grass shoot, becomes bathed in a golden glow. I am not certain by what mechanism this effect is achieved, since Avalon, to the best of my understanding, lies outside of time and is therefore exempt from the physics of the earth's rotation. Regardless, all of us—the conscious ones, anyway—appreciated the daily dollop of gilt beauty.

'Twas a dollop of consolation to counteract the daily disappointment we suffered upon realizing that our exalted charge, glowing just as golden as everything else, remained comatose.

This morning, Arthur was not only awake, he was laboring to push himself up. I gathered my skirts into both fists and hastened closer.

The severity of his expression halted me dead in my tracks.

"Morgan! What deviltry is this? Where are my knights? My men?" I raised my hands in a gesture of surrender, but before I could form an answer, he plunged on: "The battlefield…my sword…*you!* You got your revenge at long last. I am dead because of you!"

He stood and pressed a hand to his head, swaying. My ladies rushed in to assist him, but he waved them off and sat. They looked to me, confusion wrinkling their brows. I dismissed them with words of praise and thanks. They curtsied and departed. When I regarded Arthur, confusion was wrinkling his brow too; perhaps he was attempting to recall any time he had heard me utter praise to a servant. Even without having survived the worst concussion since the invention of the cudgel, he would have come up short on that score.

I knelt in place, hands clenched and head bowed, chin to chest. "My most excellent liege, I am responsible for bringing you here for to heal you, not to murther you."

The creak of the bed's ropes and the rustling of fabric told me that Arthur had stood. I dared not look up. I could have cast a cooperation spell upon him, but I craved true responses, not magic-induced ones. He said:

"This is not heaven? Or a perverse version of hell? A demon in the semblance of my sister sent to torment me in a pleasant garden for all eternity?" A light rustling punctuated his pause, suggesting that he had stepped closer. "Or are you dead too, making this place hell for me, mayhap, but heaven for you?"

Something in his tone prompted me to raise my head. He had extended his right hand, his lips bent ever so slightly into his patented almost-smile.

I grasped his hand and rose. The effort of bearing my weight made him sway again, and he did not veto my suggestion to sit back down.

A thought made me chuckle. "It would have been easier for you if this were heaven...or hell."

"Easier? Easier than what?"

"Than reclaiming your throne," I said. "England needs you again—though when, I have no idea. My foresight cannot penetrate Avalon's veil. All I know is that you are awake now because the need is now." Unlike the first time, when I took the matter of his waking into my own hands rather than leaving it to God. The damning revelation would require an entire book—this book—to explain, so for the moment I kept it to myself.

I pointed a nod at the riverbank, and Arthur turned his head to follow the line of my gaze. The barge sat moored at the dock, but a Scarlet Dragon sail had replaced the solid black one. The platform was swathed in red and supported the box containing my chronicle. Niniane, Galfrieda, and Vivien were helping the nuns bedeck every exposed square inch of oak with floral garlands, loose petals, and bouquets. Their joyous hymns continued non-stop. The flowers' blended scents created an altogether new and delightful fragrance to gladden the nose and lift the spirit.

Arthur looked down at his hands, clenching them and grimacing.

"England does not need a king whose final act caused the wholesale slaughter of his people." His whisper sounded raw with anguish.

"England survived, Arthur." I punctuated the assurance with a brief embrace. "There were some bleak times through the centuries, I warrant, but your people overcame them, and they thrived." Mayhap they were no longer thriving, as evidenced by Arthur's awakening, but I chose to keep that worm-can shut.

"You know this…how? You said—"

"I can no longer see the future. But by God's grace, I have lived it."

Arthur's countenance displayed a war between his skeptical self and the fact that he had never heard a false claim proceed from my mouth. (The adulteress-detecting cloak counted as an innuendo at most; I had never put forth the verbal assertion that Guenever would fail the test.)

When I asked him whether he could recall anything I had said to him whilst he had lain unconscious on the barge, he shook his head. I felt a needle of disappointment but not surprise. His spirit had crept far closer to death's portal than the first time I had assayed his healing here. I shifted to kneel before him.

"Then there remains ancient unfinished business yet betwixt us. I pray that you might forgive my arrogant and altogether inexcusable delay." I used the pause forged by his astonishment to continue. "Arthur Pendragon, High King of England: I, Morgan, Queen of Gore, do humbly and forevermore acknowledge you as my rightful lord, liege, and master…"

CHAPTER XLII.

He matched my kneeling pose but would not look at me. "Morgan, stop. I am not worthy."

I reached for his shoulders and pulled him closer. With his leave, I removed the bandage. His head was whole, with naught but a faint scar from Mordred's nigh-fatal blow. I kissed the spot as a mother would kiss her child.

"WHO WOULD RECOGNIZE ME OTHERWISE?"

"Hush, Arthur. I swear fealty to you and henceforth pledge my life unto your good will."

"Not your lands too?"

The tone was a tease, but the question required a truthful reply: "I no longer rule Gore. Avalon—this place where we are now—never was mine to pledge."

Arthur nodded, stood, and placed both hands upon my head. "Queen Morgan of Gore, I accept your fealty, freely offered and fairly sworn, and I pledge to protect you from all your enemies. Rise, my good and faithful servant." He extended his hand. "And my beloved sister."

I accepted his invitation and rose into his embrace. In that moment I realized that I possessed something that the younger me never would: proof of our brother's forgiveness. I prayed that Sandy's love would ease her torment.

As we parted, monks trooped into the pavilion and removed Arthur's armor and padding from its stand. Arming the king began with swapping the fancy embroidered tunic for the plain—though no longer grimy, sweat-stained, or torn—padded one. Whilst the men attached the shiny metal plates, Arthur kept his attention fixed upon me. "You ask for no fealty gift, Morgan?"

"Your life is my gift," I said. "I ask naught but that you live it well."

That last bit was for the sake of formality; I knew beyond all doubt that my brother would make the absolute most of this second opportunity God in His mercy had seen fit to grant him.

By this time, Arthur stood encased neck-down in armor. The monks withdrew to a respectful distance. I hefted his crown-encircled helmet and presented it to him. Being a realmless sovereign had occluded my right to place it on his head, and a sad twinge lanced my heart. "Godspeed to you, my liege. And my beloved brother." I entertained the thought to imbue the helmet with a remote-viewing spell but dared not do so without his leave.

After returning the helmet to the stand, he gifted me his most unroyal grin. "Black is a trifle severe for my triumphant return, dear sister, is it not?"

CHAPTER XLII.

It took me a moment to realize that he was referring to my attire, and another moment to realize why. I beamed and snapped my fingers. My gown changed to the hue of the dragon on the sail, a warm, vibrant scarlet. "May my ladies join us?"

"Of course," he said, and I sent them the mental news. "But you are missing one crucial detail. I would be honored to present it to you, of course, but…" Arthur glanced down, patting his dawn-gilt metal power suit, and shrugged.

I laughed. "Indeed. Who would recognize me otherwise?"

With a flick of my wrist, I conjured a gold circlet into his hand. Whether 'twas the same circlet I had flung into the river, I shall leave you, faithful reader, to ponder.

Arthur crowned me. I rose. He kissed me on both cheeks and retrieved his helmet, but did not don it. Instead, he offered me his free arm, and I settled mine on top. That he had not crowned himself—as he must have done countless times before charging into battle—was a decision I elected not to debate.

Chorused by the monks, we marched to the barge. The addition of the nuns' voices swelled the chorus to divine proportions as Arthur and I climbed aboard to join my ladies. Monks untied the mooring lines and cast us off. The Scarlet Dragon sail billowed, and the barge drifted free of the dock.

Mist rising from the water engulfed Avalon's blessed shore. I gazed into the mist, at the place I appreciated to the very core of my soul but wished never to see again, till I could no longer hear the singing above the rhythmic slap of waves upon the barge's hull.

END OF THE MANUSCRIPT

Final P.S. by A.A.

ΛTHER THAN setting the book aside, I hugged it to my chest, eyes closed. Its metallic cover grew warm, almost fleshlike, as if it were hugging me back. The sensation made my thoughts whirl faster.

What had the queen meant by Clarice's "spark?" Reincarnation?

If my body housed the soul of Clarice Centralia, it might explain why this world had never felt quite right. My mother had insisted that I was an "old soul," but the best explanation I ever got out of her while growing up was that I possessed maturity beyond my years. She had been psychic: foretelling friends' pregnancies, welcome if unexpected callers, natural and manmade disasters, and the like. Now I wondered if she had believed that I was the reincarnation of someone else's daughter but kept it to herself so that I might develop into my own person.

Am I still…me?

"You are one hundred per cent still you, Amidala Anderson."

Screaming, I shot out of my chair as if from a cannon. It rocked from the force of my exit. The book slipped from my grasp. My balance faltered past the tipping point, and I windmilled my arms.

The dreaded commotion of myself, the chair, and the book hitting the floor did not happen.

The chair righted itself and scooted to catch me. I landed on its plump seat with an *oof* of expelled breath. The book remained suspended in midair for a moment before floating over to settle upon the table.

My panic seemed to float away with it.

"You!" I squeaked to the attractive, auburn-haired woman standing before me, proving that not all of my panic had succumbed to her calming spell.

Then my brain registered the presence of a figure beside her. Though his hair shaded more golden-brown on the spectrum than auburn, their faces' shapes and complexions displayed an indisputable familial connection. Both were dressed in high-end business attire. She wore a gold circlet; he did not.

I stood. My legs felt too wobbly to trust to a curtsy, so I bowed at the waist and held the pose. "Your Majesties."

"Please rise," he said, and I did. "My sister deserves such formalities. The prime minister does not."

"The prime…" I shook my head in a vain attempt to clear it. "What?"

She said, "Allow me to introduce you to The Right Honourable Arthur Richards."

"You can't be prime minister, sir." The soul/spark/whatever that I possessed apparently came equipped with the stones to argue toe-to-toe with royalty. Huh. Since neither of them had summoned an executioner's axe, I forged on with: "The incumbent is an old chap; Howard…Harry…Harold Whitechurch. Labor Party. Yeah, that's it."

The queen smiled. "My dear, how long have you been inside this shop?"

It sounded like a trick question, but no more clever answer occurred to me than the truth. "Overnight, at least. I arrived after lunch. It was nighttime when I got to the part about…" Unsure how someone with a proven track record of executing people might react to the mention of an agonizing event in their past, I adopted a different tack. "That is, when I recognized my dream. Now I presume it's the next day. But if your brother is the prime minister…"

I felt like spouting an ancient *Lost in Space* line from the original series, not its reboot: "That does not compute!"

Her Majesty rescued me, sort of. "Harold Whitechurch has been retired for five years."

Thank God my jaw was hinged to my head. "Five years!"

What. The. ACTUAL. Hell?

"I SHOT OUT OF THE CHAIR AS IF FROM A CANNON."

"Not counting the years it took for me—with Morgan's help, of course—to build my power base in preparation for the post." As if that was going to help.

I opened my mouth and closed it, again and again, as question after question popped into my head just to be shoved aside when the next, more important question formed. There were so many, I couldn't decide where to start. Testing where my newfound stones came down upon the subject of proprieties, I plopped onto the chair, closed my eyes, and pressed my fingers to my throbbing temples, willing myself to wake from this bloody nightmare.

Thumping and clattering reclaimed my attention. I looked up to see that the queen had conjured chairs for herself and her brother, along with a table laden with tea and biscuits. The king—prime minister?—whatever was already falling to. Her Majesty saluted me with her teacup and invited me to partake. "Please, my dear," she said. "It will help you feel better."

Before I could refuse, my traitor stomach rumbled. I complied with its demands and had to admit that both it and the queen were right. A swig of milky tea and a few bites of biscuit smeared with clotted cream fortified me to ask: "Is this some sort of pocket dimension?"

"I daresay that would be a scientific explanation." The queen's smile broadened. "I prefer to call it an Avalon satellite region—hence the thicker than usual fog. Brilliant job parting it, by the by."

Courtesy dictated that I thank her, but the legion of questions demanded satisfaction. I began with, "Aren't you concerned that time is passing at lightning speed outside this—whatever this place is—as we speak?"

She gave a graceful, dismissive wave. "I disabled the time-suspension spell before Arthur and I entered."

"Of course. But why go to all this trouble? Why not just talk to me face to face"—on the cusp of saying "like a normal human being," I realized that might give offense and substituted—"in my flat? And why, forgodsake, did you suspend me out of time for however many *years?*"

"For God's sake, indeed." Queen Morgan finished a biscuit and dabbed her lips with a cloth napkin. "Or rather, at His bidding."

I gave her a double-take. "What—?" After having suffered from the machinations of a hundred corrupt popes, nobody believed in divine intervention anymore. Did they?

Do I?

"We do apologize for the upheaval in your life, Mistress Anderson," said the king/prime minister. "Be assured that we have settled affairs with your landlord, employer, creditors, and friends. Not having a spouse or any close relations spared us those spots of awkwardness. Everyone believes you are living in America now. You need not fear any reprisals once you leave this place."

"Okay…thanks, sir. I take that to mean that you didn't fake my death." Talk about a spot of awkward. They confirmed my supposition. "But, with all due respect"—I cast a glance heavenward, in case a smiting was on the way—"it still doesn't explain why."

The queen arranged her napkin upon the empty plate, flicked her fingers, and the ensemble disappeared to the last crumb. The king's place setting and mine, her teacup, the biscuit stand, and the tea set remained. It didn't occur to me to flinch at her open display of magic, and her nod seemed to carry approval. She said:

"This experience has been a test, in the main to gauge how strong of a spark you possess. Had you departed at any time prior to our arrival, or if you had bolted when you first saw us, I would have returned you to your original timeline with you being none the wiser. The fact that you have stayed—"

I raised my hand, and the queen invited me to speak. I might have gotten away with arguing but felt unsure about interrupting. "This may be a dumb question, ma'am, but I must ask: we're in a different timeline now?"

"Not different so much as improved," said His Right Honourable Majesty. "It's the reason I chose to become prime minister…and chose affiliation with the Conservative Party. In this capacity I wield tremendous influence over legislation, and since the sovereign knows my true identity, she and I enjoy a particularly close working relationship."

"Once you assured her that you had no interest in assuming the throne," his sister said, and he confirmed the statement with a sharp nod.

"She—King Edward's firstborn, who was called Charlotte, Princess of Wales the day before I set foot inside this…Avalon bubble?"

"The very same," he said. "She kept Charlotte as her regnal name, in honor of two of her ancestors."

"God save the queen." I surprised myself by how much I meant it. But, "Her Majesty is well and truly okay with…" I caught myself before making another gaffe and resorted to circling an upraised finger. "…all of this?"

"Queen Charlotte is an intelligent, forward-thinking monarch," King/ Prime Minister Arthur said. "One of her first acts, in her role as Head of the Church, was to implement my suggestion to abolish the fees for sacraments and prayers. Church membership and revenues from voluntary contributions soared off the charts at once and continue at a good clip to this day." His expression shaded from proud to determined. "With the economy and unemployment and international relations and terrorist threats and everything else that still needs fixing, however, she knows she needs all the help she can get."

"Which brings us back to the subject of yourself, Mistress Anderson," his sister added. "My spell on the book was able to sense in you a similar level of innate magical ability as Clarice had been privileged to possess. That is what I meant by 'spark.' Your subconscious parting of the fog demonstrated that to me beyond all doubt."

"So…my soul remains my own?" Yesterday—whenever that was—I had not believed in the existence of souls; now, it felt like the most precious treasure I could ever possess. And of a sudden this whole bizarre experience lent credence to my mother's belief that I had been born with an "old" one.

"Indeed. And I have cause to believe it is every inch as virtuous as Clarice's was—as mine was not, in the earliest decades of my life. Because I had lacked ethical guidance, I wrought ever so much evil, to my eternal shame. By God's grace, that wretched behavior did not manifest in Clarice whilst she served as my apprentice." The queen gave a long blink and the faintest of sighs. "With your permission, Mistress Anderson, I would like to train you to achieve your full potential."

"Or I could live the truth you invented for me and move to America?" Morgan le Fay wasn't the only person in the room who could devise tests. "No harm, no foul?"

She inclined her head. "You may indeed, if you so choose, and with our blessings." After taking a sip of tea, she lowered the cup and turned her frank gaze upon me. "But be advised that I would be obliged, for security reasons, to cleanse your memory of this encounter."

Naturally.

Queen Morgan's proposal to turn me into a bona fide magic-wielder sounded leagues beyond intriguing, but instinct warned me against appearing too eager. "What would I be doing, ma'am, as your apprentice?"

"That shall depend upon where your magical aptitudes lie and how well they complement your other talents." She must have seen an expression on my face that prompted her to raise a finger, and I left my protest unvoiced. "A more complete answer I cannot supply at this time, but I do foresee that with my guidance, you shall accomplish any task to which you set your mind."

"And I promise you shall want for nothing," said His Right Honourable Majesty, "for as long as you remain in our service."

I stroked my chin. Fantastic recruitment package aside, what sort of people would I be committing my talents, my life, perhaps my very soul to, really? I could think of one way to find out.

After bracing myself with a hot swig of tea, I set down the cup, nailed Queen Morgan with my gaze, and asked her leave to pose a personal question. She lifted an eyebrow but assented. I sucked in a deep breath and said:

"If we're in an 'improved' timeline, as you claim, where is Sandy now?"

Her response came damned close to toppling me out of my chair again: the Queen of Serene, the Countess of Keep Calm and Carry On, the Duchess of Don't Let Them See You Sweat…blushed.

And not just any quick, mill-run of a blush, either. This one went to her roots and stayed there as her lips formed the sweetest smile I had seen adorning the face of any woman.

The pause spun longer, and my curiosity climbed higher as I awaited her reply. Rather than speaking, however, she looked at her lap, where her hands lay folded. I searched for a wedding ring, but the fingers of her right hand covered the traditional spot on her left. Her smile deepened.

"May I, dear sister?" Her brother's tone was as tender as it was soft. She nodded. He regarded me and said:

"Her Majesty is expecting her second child…and the first with her present husband, Sanford 'Sandy' Leroy Carter. A better man I have never known, in this era or any other, and I possess every confidence that he shall make a fine father." The royal siblings shared an affectionate look.

"Sanford?" I felt my eyebrows bunch. "I thought his Christian name was Alex—oh. That Sandy was born into the other timeline." My cheeks heated to the scorching point, but the sensation receded upon the realization that I had not been fried for the impudence. "Please forgive me, Queen Morgan. I didn't mean to—that is, I—" God, how I hated to sound like such a dithering fool. "Please accept my humble and heartfelt congratulations. I am so very happy for you. For both—for *all* of you." I hoped they could discern that I meant the sentiment to include the right honourable royal uncle as well as the wee prince or princess. For the queen's sake, given all that I'd read about her, I was rooting for the latter.

"Thank you, dearest child. But you have done nothing to require forgiveness. Not one little thing." The queen took my hands into her warm ones, imparting a depth of love I had not felt in the decades since my mother's passing. "Now, what say you to our offer?"

A new job and lifestyle, facilitated by new abilities and assisted by powerful new friends, to help them turn England, the United Kingdom—and, by extension, perhaps the entire world—into a better place for everybody? It was a prospect nobody in their right mind could refuse.

"It is my greatest honor to accept the position as apprentice to Your Majesty. Here's to the future." I lifted my teacup. "May I prove worthy of the faith you both have placed in me."

"Of course you shall, my dear Amidala," said Queen Morgan as the three of us clicked our teacups together. Her lips bent into a playful grin. "I have seen it."

THE END
…of the beginning.

Art Credits.

HE ART contained herein is copyright ©2025 by Sophia Kelly Shultz, except as noted below.

Jessica Headlee's signature is used with permission.

The font Danger on the Motorway, used to letter the Holy Rollers Fight Club arena marquee in Chapter 16, is licensed for commercial use from Chequered Ink Ltd. of Bath, UK.

The decorative line in A Word of Explanation was first licensed for commercial use in *King Arthur's Sister in Washington's Court*.

Cover art stock photos:

• Medieval woman ©2015 by Hotdamnstock.com, ID MED0061

• Antique pocket watch ©2009 by Juri Semjonow, Depositphotos.com ID 4656979

• Gold necklaces ©2015 by Depositphotos.com, ID 70198767

• Big Ben and Houses of Parliament © by sborisov, Depositphotos.com ID 11708316

Public Domain art and fonts:

• Mark Twain's signature

• Text font: Adobe Caslon Pro; based on Caslon, designed 1734–1770 by William Caslon

• Title font: Bodoni MT; based on Bodoni, designed 1790s by Giambattista Bodoni

• Drop cap font: EmporiumCapitals; chapters 19, 25, 35, and About the Ghost's Minion

• Advertising font: Kelmscott; chapter 4, Persimmon's Soap logo

• Headline font: Iglesia; chapters 20 and 40

• Headline font: Caliope Victorian; chapter 21 text and art

• Dingbat font: IntellectaHeraldics; scene separators in chapters 25 and 27, and at the end of chapter 41

• **Art adapted by Kim Iverson Headlee** from Daniel Carter Beard art created for the 1889 edition of *A Connecticut Yankee in King Arthur's Court*: chapter 26 drop cap, based upon the Chapter XLIII illustration "One of the 52;" chapter 28 drop cap, which was the Chapter III drop cap (unmodified); chapter 35 drop cap, based upon the Chapter IX drop cap; Art Credits drop cap, based upon the Chapter IV illustration "Queen Guenever was as naïvely interested as the rest."

The Persimmon's Soap logo in chapter 4 was adapted by Sophia Shultz from original art copyright ©2014 by Jennifer Doneske, created for *King Arthur's Sister in Washington's Court*.

The dragon's head, copyright ©2014 by Jessica Headlee, created for Kim Iverson Headlee's novel *Snow in July*, was adapted for the illustrations in chapters 36 and 42, and the drop cap for About the Ghost's Minion.

The raven atop Arthur's helmet, the drop cap for chapter 36, is copyright ©2014 by Tom Doneske and is the drop cap for A Word of Explanation in *King Arthur's Sister in Washington's Court*.

Art copyright ©2023 by Anna Winebarger: Drop caps for A Word of Explanation and chapters 1–14, 17–25, 27, 30, 31, 33, 34, 37, 38, and 41; spot illustration for chapter 1; "In Libro Veritas" plate of Pope Gildas XIII in chapter 11.

Art adapted by Sophia Shultz from original art created by Anna Winebarger: Drop caps for the Preface and chapter 16; spot illustrations for chapters 3, 4, 5, and 8.

About the Ghost's Minion.

K IM IVERSON Headlee lives on a farm in the mountains of southwestern Virginia with her family, cats, fish, goats, someone else's cattle, half a million honey bees, and assorted wildlife. People and creatures come and go, but the cave and the 250-year-old house ruins—the latter having been occupied as recently as the midtwentieth century—seem to be sticking around for a while yet.

She has been a critically acclaimed author since 1999, channeling Mark Twain since 2007, and a student of Arthurian lore for more than half a century.

Follow Kim on *BookBub*:
    https://www.bookbub.com/authors/kim-iverson-headlee

Other published works by Kim Iverson Headlee:

Lost Son, a Dragon's Dove Chronicles novella, e-book, audiobook, and paperback, Pendragon Cove Press, 2026.

Raging Sea, The Dragon's Dove Chronicles, book 3, e-book, audiobook, hardcover, and paperback, Pendragon Cove Press, 2019.

The Challenge comic book, illustrated by DC and Marvel Comics artist Tim Shinn, e-book and print, Pendragon Cove Press, 2019.

Twins, the novella genesis of book 6 of The Dragon's Dove Chronicles, e-book and paperback, Pendragon Cove Press, 2017.

The Business of Writing: Practical Insights for Independent, Hybrid, and Traditionally Published Authors, e-book and paperback, Pendragon Cove Press, 2016; latest edition updated for Seattle Worldcon 2025.

Kings, a sword-and-sorcery crossover novella by Kim Iverson Headlee and Patricia Duffy Novak, e-book, audiobook, and paperback, Pendragon Cove Press, 2016.

The Challenge, a Dragon's Dove Chronicles novella, e-book, audiobook, and paperback, Pendragon Cove Press, 2015.

King Arthur's Sister in Washington's Court by Mark Twain as channeled by Kim Iverson Headlee, illustrated by Jennifer Doneske and Tom Doneske, e-book, audiobook, hardcover, and paperback, Pendragon Cove Press, 2019; the 2015 paperback and hardcover editions published by Lucky Bat Books..

Liberty, second edition, e-book, audiobook, hardcover, and paperback, Pendragon Cove Press, 2014.

Snow in July, illustrated by Jessica Headlee, e-book, audiobook, hardcover, and paperback, Pendragon Cove Press, 2014.

Morning's Journey, The Dragon's Dove Chronicles, book 2, e-book, audiobook, hardcover, and paperback, Pendragon Cove Press, 2014; the 2013 paperback edition published by Lucky Bat Books.

"The Color of Vengeance," a short story excerpted from Morning's Journey, e-book, audiobook, and paperback, Pendragon Cove Press, 2013.

Dawnflight, The Dragon's Dove Chronicles, book 1, e-book, audiobook, hardcover, and paperback, Pendragon Cove Press, 2014; the 2013 paperback edition published by Lucky Bat Books.

Liberty, writing as Kimberly Iverson, paperback, HQN Books, Harlequin, 2006.

Dawnflight, first edition, paperback, Sonnet Books, Simon & Schuster, 1999.

Forthcoming:

Zenith Glory, The Dragon's Dove Chronicles, book 4, Pendragon Cove Press.

Prophecy, the sequel to *Liberty*, Pendragon Cove Press.

www.ingramcontent.com/pod-product-compliance
Lightning Source LLC
Chambersburg PA
CBHW060850210726
48293CB00006B/1739